ACCLAIM FOR KING ROBIN

"A sexy retelling of the Robin Hood legend."
Rebecca Coffey—Author and journalist (Forbes, NPR)

"Thought-provoking. A real page-turner."
Bob White — Chairman Worldwide Robin Hood Society

"Gusto. Humor. Eros."
Ralph Keyes — Author of The Post-Truth Era

"Smart, brisk. A parable for our dystopian times."
Thelma T. Reyna, Ph.D.—Award-winning author and editor

"A timeless dilemma in a fascinating book."
John Thorndike—Award-winning author

"Deep characters. Surprising plot twists."
Daniel Holland—Director/writer/producer

"Crackerjack. Truly cinematic, yet realistic."
Jennifer Silva Redmond—Editor and screenwriter

*"On the same plane as Rise of Empires, Knightfall,
The Last Kingdom and even Game of Thrones"*
James Chatterton—Story analyst (HBO, Anonymous Content)

Copyright © 2019 TXu002183279
ISBN 978-0-9994457-0-9

Beck and Branch Publishers
New York, NY

A NOVEL

KING ROBIN

R. A. MOSS

BECK AND BRANCH PUBLISHERS

Ides of May 1215

The candle quivered in the draft from the chancery's only window. Under its feeble light, King Robert pored over the tax scrolls spread across the table, oblivious to the late hour. A monarch's need for silver never ended.

A distant voice beyond the door broke Robert's trance. "Stand back!" one of his Royal Guards yelled angrily. A roar of voices filled the hallway as the guard screamed in pain.

The king rose from the table, kissed the amulet around his neck, and strode across the room rubbing his temples. He'd had too much wine at supper again – and now this. From pegs on the wall, Robert slipped a chain maille tunic over his nightshirt, strapped on his sword belt and opened the door.

About twenty paces down the narrow hallway, a group of armed peasants rushed toward Robert in the torchlight, their faces flushed with rage. "There's the king!" one of them screamed.

Drawing his sword, Robert charged toward the intruders. Closing quickly on them was his best chance to stay alive. He'd have more room to retreat and buy time until help arrived. There was no other way out of his chancery.

Although outnumbered, Robert knew the narrow hallway reduced the peasants' advantage. They'd have to come at him one at a time.

The first man he faced jabbed at him viciously with a pitchfork. Robert parried the prongs with his sword then grabbed the wooden staff and pulled. As the peasant stumbled forward, Robert slashed his blade across the man's neck. His opponent slumped to the floor, jugular vein spurting.

Another intruder quickly followed, a huge peasant brandishing a sword. Robert noticed the man's clumsy grip on the captured weapon. This one would be easy.

The big man slowly raised the sword, hoping to strike a crushing blow. Before his blade reached its zenith, Robert crouched and thrust his weapon into the man's groin. As the peasant screamed in agony, Robert stabbed him again, this time in the chest. The giant collapsed backward, falling into his comrades.

Robert stepped forward, gaining valuable ground.

The next man was armed with a meat hook and moved with menacing grace. He was probably a butcher, Robert realized. The weapon he wielded was a familiar friend. This was not an enemy to take lightly.

Robert feinted a thrust at the butcher's chest. The man quickly parried with the meat hook, ready to slash with a counter stroke. The move was quick and clever. But Robert knew the butcher was no warrior.

Robert feinted again. This time when the butcher parried, Robert swivelled his sword, slicing deeply into the man's flesh between wrist and elbow. As the butcher instinctively grabbed his wound, Robert finished him with a thrust to the heart.

The peasants attacking the palace were no match for Robert's martial skills. But at sixty-one, Robert wondered how long he could keep up the fight. The answer came with a searing flash of pain. Someone behind the fallen butcher had slashed Robert's thigh with a pike.

Giving ground now, Robert fought defensively, warding off a rain of blows. Sensing victory, the voices of the intruders grew to a roar again.

As his attackers closed in, Robert's hopes suddenly rose. Behind the peasants he saw the glint of metal helmets under the torches lighting the hallway. His Household Knights had finally arrived.

Then everything went black.

* * *

Robert opened his eyes as his senses slowly returned. His cheek was pressed against the cold stone floor.

Far away there was a murmur. Voices? Footsteps? He could not tell.

Robert sat up, his temple throbbing and swollen. Probing at the pain with his hand, he found his cheek and neck wet with blood. Robert blinked, straining to focus his eyes. As his vision cleared, his memory became sharper as well.

The hallway leading to his chambers was a tangle of bleeding bodies in the macabre poses of death. The faces of the peasants and guards were frozen in an absurd mix of expressions… rage… sadness… terror… shock… peace.

The peasants' revolt had failed. But the price in lives had been high.

Robert rose and limped toward his chancery. A rip in his calf-length nightshirt revealed a wine-coloured wound on his right thigh. Passing through the open door, he entered the room and sank into a chair behind the table. The peasants had nearly reached the heart of the palace, the deepest push of any previous attack. Robert knew there would be more.

But not tonight.

These revolts were spasms of rage, spontaneous and leaderless. Robert had long ago ferreted out anyone in England who might lead a real uprising against him. His political enemies were now dead or in a dungeon. No, the brushfires breaking out against his rule were not conspiracies. They were usually provoked by one of his soldiers.

His Royal Guards had become difficult to discipline. In earlier times, a man under his command found guilty of abusing a citizen would have been flogged or executed. Robert could no longer afford the luxury of a lofty conscience. His men-at-arms were the only base of power whose loyalty he could count on.

The lack of support among his subjects had once troubled him. But not anymore. After 23 years on the throne, suppressing discontent had become a reflex – a far cry from the days he'd roamed Sherwood Forest in Lincoln green.

Hurried footsteps from the hallway drew Robert's gaze. The captain of the Household Knights bowed quickly and entered the room.

"You're hurt, Sire," the captain said, eyes widening in alarm. "I'll fetch your physician."

"Wait," Robert said, rising to his feet. "Before you bring the doctor, have your men walk through the city in squads. I want a show of strength. But make sure your men don't provoke anyone else. Is that clear?"

"Yes, Sire."

"And tell the steward to have the bodies in the palace cleaned up before morning. The princess returns tomorrow."

The captain bowed in response, then backed out of the room.

Sitting down again, Robert tore away a strip of tablecloth and fashioned a bandage for his bleeding forehead.

He then paused, staring at his red-stained palms. His skin was thin and deeply creased, the joints bent and gnarly. It seemed like only yesterday his hands had been smooth and supple. Slowly, Robert's mind drifted to the past, a time before the years had withered his soul as well.

Nones of September 1164

Robert dreaded the walk into town. The farm north of Nottingham where he lived with his mother and grandfather was less than two miles away. But it wasn't the distance that bothered the ten-year-old. It was the young hooligans he'd find not long after entering the town.

They caught up to Robert as he reached King Street.

Robert stared straight ahead, ignoring the jeering chant from the half-dozen boys gathered behind him.

"Big bear sniffing 'round the fair young maid. Nine months later, a cub was made," the boys called out, their voices tinged with laughter. "Big bear sniffing 'round the fair young maid. Nine months later, a cub was made."

Robert knew the chant all too well. He'd heard it every time he entered the village alone for as long as he could remember. Yet the meaning of the verse was still a mystery to him.

He knew it was somehow connected to his father. But all Robert had been told about his father was that he'd gone to London looking for work and died there long ago, whilst Robert was still a babe-in-arms.

Robert had once asked his mother why the village boys taunted him. Her answer did little to dispel the mystery. "The words of fools and the droppings of horses litter the streets of every village," Anna Webber told him. "We'll not speak of this again, Robert."

Those thoughts dissolved as the bell at Lenton Abbey began to toll.

Robert broke into a run toward the church. Friar Tuck had threatened to twist off his ears if he ever arrived late for his Latin lesson. As Robert entered the rectory of the stone church, the pack continued to taunt him.

"I'm not late, Friar! The bell is still ringing!" Robert said bursting into the room, gasping.

The portly young priest smiled. "Catch your breath, Robert. You'll keep your ears today," he said, laughing softly.

Mustering the courage, Robert finally asked the priest a lingering question. "Friar, why do the boys in town say those things? Does it mean something about my father?"

The friar's smile faded. "Ask your mother."

"I did. She wouldn't tell me."

"Then that will have to be your answer – for now. When the time is right, you'll know."

Robert sighed. "What do I do about those boys?"

"The Lord says, 'the hand of the diligent will rule,' my son. Follow His guidance," the friar answered, handing the boy a wax tablet and stylus. "Now stop whining and start your lesson."

***

After his lesson, Robert slipped warily out of the rectory, on the lookout for his tormentors. He was relieved to find the pack with their backs to him, walking away.

Then he noticed their attention had turned to a new victim. Although Robert could not see the girl's face, he knew straight away who they were taunting – his neighbour, Faye Rolfe.

"Hey, harelip! Taking home some carrots, are you?" one of them yelled as he tried to grab the basket she carried. Faye clutched the basket tighter and hurried on, her head bowed in shame.

"Me mum's making rabbit stew! You best watch out, harelip!" another taunted.

Robert had known Faye since he'd toddled. She lived on a farm near his and was a bright and gentle girl of twelve, made shy by her disfigurement. Not surprisingly, she rarely came into town alone. By the basket Faye held, Robert guessed she'd been sent shopping.

His fists clenching, Robert began to tremble with rage. He'd tried to ignore the taunting of these bullies. But he could not ignore their cruelty toward Faye.

Breaking into a sprint, he raced down a side street, intent on getting ahead of the pack. Near the town gate, he found the site for his revenge – a deserted alley off King Street between a stable and a potter's shop. Now he needed a weapon.

The solution came from the potter's firewood pile. Finding a yard-long length of elm, Robert took cover behind the edge of the building and waited.

Faye appeared first, turning onto King Street, tears streaming down her cheeks. A few paces behind came the pack, calling out and gesturing, revelling in their torment.

Robert waited until Faye had passed, then stepped out of the alley and swung at the nearest bully. His blow found home near the boy's ear and sent him to the ground, howling in pain.

The other boys stopped, shocked by the sudden attack. Robert seized the advantage and struck another one. After his second victim went down, the rest of the bullies scattered.

"You're mad!" the last boy he'd struck yelled at Robert before he rose and ran away, bleeding from a gash on his forehead. "I'm telling the constable."

After the boys had fled, Robert turned to face Faye.

"You did a brave thing, Robert Webber. May the Lord bless you," she said, wiping the tears from her face. "Now, run before they bring the constable."

* * *

Sir Ralph Talbot had chosen a wide meadow in the south of Sherwood Forest near Angel Creek as the site for his hunting camp. Although the king owned all the forests in England, as the Baron of Nottingham, Sir Ralph had inherited the right to hunt at his leisure in Sherwood Forest.

The morning's hunt completed, Sir Ralph had a canopy tent erected and a noonday meal served from their hunt. Soon, the smell of spit-roasted venison filled the meadow. The shields of the hunting party, adorned with the baron's crest of a black bear on a field of gold, were stacked in a circle near the men.

Beneath the tent, Sir Ralph sat at a long table with the hunting party: his constable and three men-at-arms along with the Sheriff of Nottingham. A bevy of servants stood nearby as the baron and his guests tucked into their plates of fresh-killed venison and turnips.

"You chose a fine day for a hunt, Sir Ralph," the sheriff said. "The wind was calm and the game never once caught our scent."

"Pure luck, Sheriff," Sir Ralph replied.

"All the same, you've been a good caretaker of the king's land," the sheriff said. "The forest has not been overhunted."

Sir Ralph weighed his words before answering.

The sheriff was the king's representative in the shire. He not only oversaw the king's properties like Sherwood Forest, the sheriff was also a royal tax collector. Although a commoner appointed at the pleasure of the king, a sheriff's power could rival that of a lord. That made Sir Ralph's accord with the sheriff an uneasy dance.

"I would never abuse the hunting privileges my family has inherited," the baron finally said to the sheriff.

The constable lifted his cup in a toast. "You may not hunt often, m'lord. But I'd say the morning's hunt was one of your best," he said. "You brought down a bounty of meat today. You'll have plenty of venison left for the baroness and your daughter."

"Aye," the men-at-arms said in unison, raising their cups.

Sir Ralph smiled coyly. "I'd say my huntsman and his crew did a masterful job of steering the game before my bow."

"You're too modest, m'lord," the constable replied. "Your skill with the bow rivals that of a royal marksman." Unlike the sheriff, the constable was Sir Ralph's vassal and eager to praise his liege.

Sir Ralph signalled to the servants for the dishes to be cleared. "Enough flattery," the baron said to his constable. "You said there was news I needed to hear."

"Shall we take a walk and stretch our legs, m'lord?"

The baron nodded and the two men left the table. They walked in silence past the party's horses, grazing in the meadow. When they reached the bank of Angel Creek, the constable finally spoke. "Charges were brought against a lad in Nottingham, m'lord. Someone you might be interested in… Robert Webber."

Sir Ralph's eyebrows rose. "What kind of charges?"

"He beat a couple of boys bloody with a club. Their parents say it was unprovoked."

"Has anyone come forward in his defence?"

"A serf named Rolfe said Robert was defending his daughter from a half-dozen boys."

"Was the girl harmed?"

"No, m'lord. Just insulted. She's a harelip."

"Seems the boy has courage, taking on six hooligans," Sir Ralph said, holding back a smile. "Drop the charges against him."

The constable grimaced. "Considering the boy's… well… special status," he said, "your decision is a delicate one, m'lord. Some might raise a cry of favouritism."

"I see what you mean," Sir Ralph answered. "What do you suggest?"

"Send the boy away for a while, m'lord. It needn't be a real punishment."

"His mother won't like it."

"She'll like it better than a flogging in the town square."

The baron rubbed his chin, mulling over his verdict. "The boy shows a flair for boldness. We might have a warrior on our hands. Have him sent to the monastery in West Bridgford. The monks there will teach him more than Latin. He'll learn the sword and the bow."

Kalends of June 1172

The old man entered the doorway of the thatch-roofed cottage. "The steward is here," Simon Webber called out to his grandson. "Best say goodbye to your mother now, Robert. I'll put your belongings on the horse," he said, then shuffled outside with Robert's saddlebags.

Robert rose from the chair where he'd been sharpening his sword and walked to his mother who was waiting by the door. At eighteen, he now stood a head taller than Anna Webber.

Flouting the aristocratic fashion of the day, Robert was clean shaven with close-cropped locks. Like his mother, he had raven hair, a celestial nose and full lips – finely-wrought features that had already won the favour of more than a few lasses across the shire.

Anna Webber's sober manner revealed barely a glimmer of the comely maid who'd once turned heads in all of Nottinghamshire. Save the pendant set with a purple stone she'd worn as long as Robert could remember, her attire was modest as well.

She took her son's face in her hands. "You're going to meet new people in London, Robert. Most of them will be above your station. They'll have wealth and own land. They'll wear finer clothes and be better schooled. But so long as you keep your honour and your word, they will never be better people. Deeds make a man, Robert, not a title. I want you to promise you'll remember that."

"I will, mother. I will," Robert said, fidgeting.

"No matter how high you have the good fortune to rise, never forget you come from humble folk. You must always respect the poor and treat them fairly, son."

Robert sighed. "Mother, please. These are the same things you've said a thousand times."

"And are they any less true now?" Anna said, hands on her hips.

"No, but–"

"Then you'll do well to respect your elders, Robert Webber. You may wear fine clothes, know how to read Latin, and carry a sword. But that still does not make you an equal to your mother," she said firmly.

"Of course, m'lady," Robert said, with an exaggerated bow.

Anna's eyes narrowed. "Impudence will not serve you well in London, Robert. Sir Ralph has granted you a rare privilege by taking you to the capital. I expect you to show your patron the proper respect and obedience at all times."

"Mother, we can stop pretending. I know Sir Ralph is my–"

"No. Stop right there," she said, shaking her head. "You know nothing at all."

"Everyone knows he's–"

"I will not hear of this, Robert."

Robert shrugged. "Very well. We'll continue the puppet show."

"Listen to me," she said, locking her son in a hard gaze. "I gave my word to your patron that his privacy would always be respected – and when someone breaks their word, everyone in their family can suffer. We live well for common folk, but that can all go away. Do you under-stand?"

Robert was stunned – then ashamed. Until that moment, he'd never realized that the gifts and privileges his father had showered on their household all these years had come with a price: his mother's silence.

Thanks to her, the Webbers lived more like merchants than serfs. They had Sunday clothes, a four-room stone cottage with a kitchen, even a barn for their animals. Their candles were made of beeswax instead of tallow. The Webbers could afford to celebrate the feasts of Ëostre in spring and Christmastide in winter.

Meanwhile, their neighbours wore the same ragged clothes year-round, lived with dirt floors, drafty walls made of sticks and daub, and shared their one-room homes with chickens, sheep and pigs at night. Hunger was a constant companion.

Robert kneeled and kissed her hand. "Please forgive me, mother. I'll keep my word on all you've asked."

Touching his chin, Anna urged him to stand again. "I want you to have this," she said, removing her amulet and placing it around Robert's neck. "Let it be a reminder of the promise you've made."

Robert gently stroked the pendant, then tucked it into his tunic. He knew the amulet was a legacy from his mother's family. "This stone will always be with me," he said, then strapped on his sword, and walked outside.

Astride a brown palfrey, Sir Ralph's steward waited to lead Robert to London. After mounting the white gelding brought by the steward, Robert waved farewell.

"You carry our honour and our pride, son," his mother called out from the door of the cottage.

Nones of June 1172

R obert looked around, slack-jawed, as they entered Westminster Hall. "Close your mouth, boy," Sir Ralph whispered.

Robert could not help himself. The largest royal hall in Europe dazzled the eye. The vaulted ceiling rose to ten times a man's height and ran at least seventy paces, with twelve windows along each side. The room ended in an immense arched window that spanned the entire wall. Elaborate carvings and decorations covered the casements and arcades. "This is magnificent, Sire," he said in awe.

"The hall is grand, without a doubt. But what's inside is even grander," the baron said, leading Robert inside. "Look at the people around you, Robert. This is where the power of the kingdom lives and breathes."

Robert scanned the swirling eddies of finely dressed men and women moving through the hall. "Where's the king?"

"Probably watching you through a peep hole," Sir Ralph answered with a grin. "It's said he has them all over the hall to spy on the courtiers when he's not holding court."

"Is that true, m'lord?"

"Well, you might ask the king's son, Richard," the baron replied. "The prince is that strapping young fellow with the ginger hair and beard," he said, gesturing with his chin. "He's most likely in London begging money from his father for another crusade. Richard was leading armies before he could grow that beard."

Robert was impressed. But looming larger in his mind was Sir Ralph's reason for coming to London – something he'd learned about only yesterday.

Arriving in the city with the steward, Robert was taken to Sir Ralph at Chatham Manor, the home of the baron's cousins in London. After dinner, Sir Ralph had revealed his reason for coming to the capital.

A month earlier, the Sheriff of Nottinghamshire had delivered a royal writ. The king had revoked the baron's hunting privileges in Sherwood Forest. Now, Sir Ralph was here to arrange an audience with King Henry and persuade His Highness to change the decision.

"Has the time been set for your audience with the king?" Robert asked.

Before answering, the baron led them to an isolated spot where they could watch the crowd but remain unheard. "That depends on the portly gentleman with the long grey beard by the pillar. He's the Lord Justiciar, Robert de Beaumont. He decides who'll see the king and when."

"So, you'll speak to the justiciar today?" Robert asked.

"That would be pointless," the baron explained. "The justiciar has hundreds of petitioners for the king's time and I'm a backwoods baron with no influence in court."

"Then why are we here?"

Sir Ralph smiled. "A fair question," he said, then placed his hand on Robert's shoulder. "I've not been completely selfless in bringing you to London, Robert. You're here for a mission."

Robert was surprised – but pleased. "I'll gladly serve you however I can, m'lord."

"I don't believe you'll find the mission very burdensome," Sir Ralph said slyly. "You see the young lady near the justiciar, the one in the white gown?"

Robert followed Sir Ralph's gaze and felt his pulse rise as he spotted her. Framed by honey-gold tresses bound by a circlet was an angelic face of creamy-smooth skin with features finer than any of the milkmaids he'd cavorted with in Nottingham. "Yes, m'lord. I see her," he finally said.

"Her name is Marian. She's the justiciar's daughter. I'm counting on you to win her favour and bring me into the justiciar's inner circle."

"I'm not sure I understand, m'lord."

"You're the talk of the young maids back home, Robert. And I know you've wooed more than a few," the baron said smiling slyly. "If you could charm Lady Marian, she might be inclined to recommend my petition to her father."

Robert lowered his eyes, troubled by the request. This seemed a violation of the honour his mother had asked him to uphold. Yet, she'd also made him promise to obey Sir Ralph.

Sensing Robert's reluctance, the baron added, "From what I've heard about the justiciar's daughter, this mission should not be difficult. They say Marian's quite fond of handsome young swains."

Before he'd decided, Robert heard himself say, "Yes, m'lord. I'll do as you wish."

* * *

The feast was in full swing when Lady Marian arrived at the great hall of Chatham Manor. Robert watched the butler take her blue velvet cloak, revealing a satin gown with a gathered waist that defined her sensuous figure. The butler then presented Marian to Sir Ralph, the host of the feast.

After an exchange of formal greetings, the butler led her to the tables where Robert and nearly a dozen other guests watched jugglers perform whilst a quartet of troubadours played harps and flutes.

Robert rose when Marian was brought to the vacant chair beside him. "Welcome, Lady Marian. I'm Robert Webber," he said with a slight bow.

She nodded in return and sat down. "For a baron from a far province, Sir Ralph seems to have spared no expense tonight," Marian said, looking over the generous platters of squab, haddock, shellfish and fruit on the table.

"I know Sir Ralph considers it an honour to have you here, m'lady."

Marian smirked. "Yes, I'm sure he expects I'll find this evening amusing."

As Robert was aware, Sir Ralph had arranged the feast carefully. Marian had been seated next to him at a small table near the troubadours. With the music playing nearby, their conversation would remain private.

Robert raised his goblet and smiled. "To a lovely dining companion."

Marian sighed and listlessly lifted her cup. She then speared a fillet of haddock, placed it on her plate, and began to eat.

Robert followed her lead and, for a time, they ate in an awkward silence.

"I'm reading volume three of Historia Regum Britanniae," Robert said abruptly.

"I find history boring," she answered and continued eating.

Robert squirmed in his seat for a moment, then said, "Do you hunt? I won the top prize with the bow at the Nottinghamshire fair."

"How thrilling," Marian said dryly.

"I was also Champion of the Sword at my school in West Bridgford."

Marian rolled her eyes and said, "Did this puerile bragging help you bed the scullery maids back home?"

Confused by her pique, Robert tried another approach. "What I admire most about my patron Sir Ralph is that he–"

"You can drop the act. I know Sir Ralph is your father."

Robert's face froze.

"What?" Marian scoffed. "Do you think you're the only bastard here? London is thick with them."

"Say what you will, m'lady. I'm bound by an oath to my patron."

"An oath? We're not in Camelot, yokel. What kind of a fool takes an oath?"

"I did," Robert said, his anger rising.

"And I suppose you'll stand by your word to the death and all that nonsense?"

"I will," he said firmly.

"That's as ridiculously provincial as the cut of your hair."

Robert put down his goblet and rose from the chair. "I'll not be insulted," he said curtly. "Please excuse me, Lady Marian."

Marian stared in amazement for a moment, then reached for his hand. "I apologize. Please sit down."

Back in his chair, Robert sat stiffly, staring straight ahead.

Marian stroked the tablecloth for a moment, then said, "Perhaps I've been less than polite. In any case, leaving me will not reflect well on Sir Ralph."

Robert looked toward the baron. Sir Ralph had noticed the incident, his face showing concern. "I agree," Robert said, his voice losing its edge.

Marian leaned close to him. "Look, I think it's time we spoke frankly," she whispered. "I know Sir Ralph wants an audience with the king to recover his hunting privileges. I suspect he's asked you to court me so he can curry favour with my father. Am I right?"

Robert hesitated. "Yes," he confessed. "I've been doing Sir Ralph's bidding, it's true. But my attentions are not a farce. I find you very pleasing."

"Well," she said smiling, "you're finally being honest with me – and I think it's charming," she said, looking into his eyes invitingly. "Can you charm me some more? Because in truth, I find you pleasing as well."

"I think your father looks like a walrus."

Marian laughed, resting a hand on his leg. "Oh, I think we're going to get on quite well."

* * *

The torches on the outer walls of Chatham Manor cast circles of light into the darkness as Robert and Marian wandered outside to the garden. A crescent moon was rising, plating the treetops in silver.

During the last two hours, they'd talked, laughed and danced over uncounted cups of wine. Now, as they strolled into the darkness, their vibrant mood turned intimate.

"You seem more learned than most nobles I know," she said as they strolled outside. "I find that surprising."

"Sir Ralph had a Franciscan priest teach me Latin in Nottingham before I was ten. Friar Tuck helped me prepare for school at West Bridgford," he answered. "I read a lot of history… but I favoured archery and swordsmanship."

"I've heard Sir Ralph has a daughter but no male heirs."

"Yes, that's true."

"That explains why he dotes on you," Marian said. "He misses the company of a son."

"Marian, I'd prefer not to speak of–"

"I'm sorry," she said quickly.

Robert nodded. "Thank you."

Marian stopped walking and touched his arm. "Before we go any further, there's something I need to say."

"What is it?" Robert said, taken aback.

"My father's name is Robert. May I call you something else?"

"Certainly," Robert said, relieved.

Marian rubbed her lips as she looked him over. "I think I'll call you Robin," she said after a moment. "You're certainly cocky like one," she said laughing softly.

"Then Robin it is."

After leading them deeper into the garden, Marian said, "I've only known two kinds of men, Robin. Some have courted me to gain favour with my father and others have courted me for their own pleasure. But none of them has ever been bold enough to spurn me – for any reason."

He laughed softly. "As you said, I'm just a simple yokel."

"No, I sense you're not simple at all." Marian chewed her lip, then said, "My father sent me here tonight against my wishes. He insisted that I spy on Sir Ralph. What I found instead was a young man unlike any I've met. You were born a peasant and seem to shun fashion. Yet, you carry yourself like a lord. People in court think honour is something quaint and pointless. But not you."

Robert gazed at the sky. "For as long as I can remember, my mother has told me I'm the equal of any man so long as I remain true to my honour."

"Your mother must have been very beautiful to catch Sir Ralph's eye. But tell me, where did a peasant girl get such noble thoughts?"

"Not from books. My mother cannot read Latin. These things come from her heart. I think fate made her wise."

"I wish my father were that wise."

"How could the Lord Justiciar to the king not be wise?"

"Oh, he's cunning, make no mistake. But he thinks of people as pawns in his games of power. Even his only child."

"What do you mean?"

Marian stopped and faced him. "I'm betrothed. My father wants an alliance with the Earl of Kent, so I was promised to his son. My feelings didn't matter."

"What's he like, your betrothed?" Robert asked, suddenly jealous.

Marian smiled. "He's not likely to see you as a rival," she said. "He prefers men."

"Does your father know?"

"Of course. My father knows everything. But it made no difference," she said. "There's a bright side to it, I suppose. I can take as many lovers as I please. My romantic life will always be full and free."

"I don't believe it will. Not for someone who loves deeply – and I sense you do," he said, looking into her eyes. "I think you'll keep searching until you find someone worthy of your love. Then, I think you'll be faithful – forever."

"I'd rather not think about that tonight," she said, lifting her face toward him invitingly.

Robert kissed her, brushing his lips against hers, gently at first, then passionately as she pressed against him. He caressed her slender body through her gown and felt her nipples harden under his fingers. She responded by stroking his thigh, and then under his tunic.

Breathing heavily, Marian broke their embrace. She took his hand and led him deeper into the garden. There, in a dark spot where the walls met, Marian kneeled before him and parted his tunic. Robert gasped as she took him into her mouth. Not long thereafter, he moaned, rocked by an ecstasy more intense than any he'd known.

When Marian rose to face him, he was panting for breath. "I've never been pleasured this way," he whispered. "Marian, you astound me."

"A taste for fine wine isn't the only custom England's nobles have learned from France," Marian said with a smile. She then kissed him, cradling his face. Slowly, her hands guided him downward along her body until he was kneeling before her. Lifting the hem of her gown, she led him to the damp centre of her passion. Robert was surprised to find his way unfettered by other garments.

Relishing the smoothness of her thighs against his cheeks, Robert pleasured her with his lips. Marian's fingers tightly into his hair. Finally, with a soft groan, she arched her back in the final throes of desire.

When it was over, he stood and they held each other tightly, neither wanting to part. Finally, Marian said, "I don't want to leave you. But we should go back inside before we become another topic of gossip at court."

Later that night, as he lay in bed alone, Robert's thoughts kept returning to Marian.

She was comely and witty – and the memory of their exotic lovemaking still thrilled him. But there was more to Marian than that.

For the first time, he'd met someone with the boldness to accept him without judgment, someone who gave him liberty to be himself without shame.

Marian's checkered reputation did not trouble him. His mother's example had taught him that a woman scorned by prigs could still live with honour. Marian was only seeking love – and perhaps she'd found it.

Only as he drifted off to sleep did he wonder whether Marian would ask her father to approve Sir Ralph's request.

Ides of June 1172

The courtyard outside Westminster Hall was crowded with petitioners, luminous in their finery and redolent with perfume, all awaiting an audience with the king. Robert overheard fragments of conversations in English, French and German. They spoke of judgments on wills, scutage, and boundary disputes. Their talk sounded important and made Robert anxious – especially since Sir Ralph's entourage seemed much smaller than the rest. The baron had brought only his constable, his steward and Robert.

When the bailiff sent word that their party was next in line, Robert began to sweat.

Sir Ralph, however, seemed at ease. "Are you prepared to meet the king, young Robert?" he asked, smiling confidently. "It's you who made this possible."

"I've been thinking, m'lord. Now that you have an audience with the king, are you sure he'll change his mind?"

"You ask a shrewd question, boy," Sir Ralph replied, then leaned close and whispered, "I have a secret alliance that will bring the king around."

The large doors into the hall swung open. "Sir Ralph Talbot, Baron of Nottingham!" the bailiff called out.

"We're on," Sir Ralph whispered to Robert, then strode into the hall, followed by his entourage, three paces behind.

They walked through a corridor in the hall formed by two rows of Royal Guards. Behind the soldiers, the gaze of hundreds of courtiers followed their progress. Robert spotted Marian among them as they neared the royal dais.

Ahead of them sat King Henry, his ornate throne raised six steps above the floor. He was flanked by a coterie of ministers and clergy, the Lord Justiciar nearby on his right.

About ten paces from the throne, the three men in the entourage stopped. As was customary, Sir Ralph would approach the king alone.

Reaching the foot of the dais, Sir Ralph kneeled and bowed his head.

"We welcome you, Baron," the king said solemnly.

"Thank you, Your Highness," Sir Ralph replied, rising to his feet.

"What business brings you here?"

"Sire, my barony's hunting privileges in Sherwood Forrest were recently revoked. I'm here beseeching you to reconsider. These privileges have been in my family for three generations."

"Is that the entire basis for your petition?" the king said, looking bored.

"Custom dictates that a monarch should respect hereditary traditions, Sire."

"Please tell me, Baron," the king said, arching an eyebrow. "Where is this custom written?"

"As I believe Your Highness knows, customs are not written laws."

"De Beaumont," the king said to his justiciar. "You are the realm's highest legal authority. Is it within my rights as king to take back the hunting privileges of Sherwood Forest or any other forest in the kingdom?"

The justiciar nodded. "That is your right under the law, Sire."

"Well, there you have it," the king said to Sir Ralph.

"Your Highness," Sir Ralph replied, "Isn't it true that you want to revoke my hunting privileges in Sherwood Forest, not so you can hunt there yourself, but to sell the privilege to some other noble and raise money?"

The king smirked, "Well, Sir Ralph. Perhaps you can pay me directly and spare me the trouble of finding a tenant."

A burst of laughter filled the hall.

Sir Ralph's face reddened. "It pains me to take this step, Sire," he said, producing a scroll from his tunic. "But I have here a declaration signed by three other barons whose hunting privileges you've revoked. We have united to protest your decree. Your Highness is betraying loyal nobles of the realm to pay for wars of vanity in France. And that, Sire, makes a mockery of the customs and traditions you swore to uphold."

Gasps of shock rose from the courtiers.

King Henry's eyes narrowed. "Your petition is denied," he said seething. "You may leave this court."

Instead of withdrawing with his face toward the king as custom decreed, Sir Ralph turned his back on Henry and walked away.

Hissing and insults from the courtiers followed Sir Ralph as he left Westminster Hall.

* * *

When Robert entered the drawing room at Chatham Manor, he found Sir Ralph beside a tall window, a goblet of wine in his hand. The baron was flushed, his hair matted with sweat.

Robert bowed. "You asked to see me, m'lord?"

"Come in Robert. Sit down," the baron said. "Would you like some wine?"

"No, thank you, m'lord," Robert said, taking a chair.

"I have bad news, Robert. My petition at court has not turned out as

I expected," he said, a slight slur in his voice. "The king has charged me with contempt. As punishment, he's doubled the taxes on my demesne this year."

"Can he do that, m'lord?"

"He's the king," he said with a shrug. "My alliance with the other barons has dissolved. They fear a similar punishment."

"Then they're without courage or honour."

"Don't be too quick to judge them, Robert," the baron said. "These lords have peasants who would suffer as well. If Henry raises their taxes, these lords would be forced to increase their share of crops from the serfs who work their land. Sadly, the peasants often starve." Sir Ralph took a swallow of wine and shook his head in disgust. "It's this king. He's a tyrant. Henry is not only revoking hunting privileges to grub money from the gentry. The scutage he demands has gone up as well."

Robert mulled his father's words, wondering why the lords pressed the full burden of Henry's taxes on the peasants. Too abashed to pursue this, he asked a different question. "What is scutage, m'lord? The monks at West Bridgford never mentioned this."

Sir Ralph nodded, tenting his fingers. "Scutage was used by kings long ago as a separate royal levy to pay for soldiers during times of war. Henry has revived scutage and made it another permanent tax." The baron wiped his lips with the back of his hand and scowled. "This king is bleeding us all to pay for his wars of glory in France. He cares more about his precious legacy than the well-being of his subjects. Worst of all, he puts the burden of collecting his greedy loot from commoners on the lowest nobles like me."

"We should resist this injustice, m'lord."

"I don't intend to give up," the baron said, taking another draught of wine. "But I can't have you here. You'll return with the steward to Nottingham – today."

"Why can't I stay?"

"There's danger brewing here."

"Then I must stay and protect you, m'lord," Robert said, rising to his feet, hand on his sword.

"Your mother would never forgive me if any harm came to you."

"But–"

"I won't hear any more. You'll go. Do you understand?"

Remembering his vow to his mother, Robert bowed his head. "Yes, m'lord," he said.

As Robert started toward the door, Sir Ralph extended his palm. "Farewell, Robert. You show the makings of a fine man."

As Robert shook his father's hand, he could not help wondering if this would be their last moment together. The look in Sir Ralph's eyes betrayed the same thought.

***

"Heeeah!" Robert yelled at the gelding, flicking the reins, urging the horse to a gallop.

From his own horse behind Robert, the steward called out, "Where are you going, Master Robert? This is not the way out of London!"

Ignoring the steward, Robert steered his mount at a breakneck pace through a series of narrow streets, swerving between people on foot and other riders. Sir Ralph had ordered him to return to Nottingham – but the baron had not dictated the route.

After several near misses, he arrived at his destination… the Lord Justiciar's manor near Westminster Hall. Surprisingly, the steward had managed to keep up.

"Please wait for me," he told the steward before approaching the door. It was nearly suppertime and Robert hoped he'd find Marian at home.

The butler seemed aghast when Robert asked to see her, but he still led Robert into the parlour, then disappeared up the stairs. Not long thereafter, Marian entered the parlour.

"I had to see you," Robert said. "I'm returning to Nottingham."

Marian looked around to make sure they were alone. "I heard about the king's fine on Sir Ralph," she said, keeping her voice low. "I can see now that your patron doesn't know Henry very well. If I'd known Sir Ralph had planned to challenge the king in open court, I would have cautioned against it. The king does not tolerate dissent of any kind," she said, then touched his cheek and added, "I'm glad you're leaving London."

Robert's eyes widened in surprise. "You don't want me to stay?"

"I do," she answered. "But you're in danger here."

"Do you think the king would dare send his warriors against us?"

Marian lowered her voice to a whisper. "This king's enemies have died mysteriously before. Not long ago, an archbishop who defied him was killed during an argument with four off-duty soldiers. The soldiers were never charged with a crime."

"I'm willing to fight, but Sir Ralph ordered me away."

"One sword wouldn't make a difference against the power of a king, Robin," she said. "Sir Ralph acted wisely. You must go – quickly," she said, guiding him toward the door.

Robert took her hand. "When will I see you again?"

"Whenever God decides," she said. "I pray it won't be long."

Kalends of July 1172

The church bell tolled sombrely as the funeral procession left Lenton Abbey.

Behind a priest bearing a large cross, six monks carried the body of Sir Ralph Talbot under a pall embroidered with gold and jewels. Following the pallbearers along Abbey Street were the baron's widow and daughter, trailed by a host of visiting nobles including Prince Richard, sent by King Henry to honour Sir Ralph. Next came Robert, his mother and grandfather, along with Sir Ralph's steward. The rest of the procession was the largest group of all, the common folk of Nottingham.

Keening and wailing rose from the long column, coming loudest from those hindmost in the march: the village's poor, sick, and lame. According to custom, they would receive a free meal as a reward for their displays of grief.

Robert walked in silence, burning with anger. Three days earlier, Sir Ralph's body had been brought to Nottingham by a detachment of Royal Guards. The men-at-arms claimed to have found the baron's corpse on a road near London, stripped of all possessions, the apparent victim of highwaymen. The bodies of his constable and others in his party were also found nearby.

Robert had no doubt their tale was false. In one cowardly deed, the king had killed his father whilst exonerating himself.

As the procession turned onto King Street, Robert locked his eyes on Prince Richard. Sending his son to the funeral was a masterstroke of guile by the king.

The loss of his father had wounded Robert far more than he'd imagined. Their time in London had brought them closer, leaving a chasm of loss. But the pain of Sir Ralph's death cut even deeper.

The Webbers had lost the stipend Sir Ralph regularly provided – and no mention of Robert or his household was made in the baron's will. The king had not just killed Robert's father. He'd snuffed out his family's prosperity as well.

The funeral procession arrived at Talbot Hall and passed through a side gate that led to the family's private chapel. There, the baron's remains would be placed in a tomb alongside his ancestors. This was the closest Robert had ever been to his father's home.

Looking toward the baroness and his half-sister walking ahead of him, Robert pondered the gulf of rank between them. Robert was grateful Sir

Ralph's wife had given the Webbers a place near the head of the procession. But unlike his sister, Robert knew he would never be interred here.

No matter what glory he might attain, he would always carry the taint of low-born blood.

Nones of July 1172

Robert chopped hard into the elm, his axe driven by desperation. There was no time to lose. To plant more rye before harvesttime, his family would need to clear additional land. Without Sir Ralph's stipend, they might starve before the end of winter.

Whilst felling the third tree of the day, the distant clopping of hooves drew Robert's gaze. Nearly a half-mile away, four warriors were approaching their cottage. By the three lions on their shields, Robert recognized them as Prince Richard's men.

Axe in hand, Robert ran toward the cottage. If they'd come to kill him, he would not die without a fight. Nearing the house, Robert saw his mother feeding chickens and his grandfather gathering wood. "Go inside!" he called out to them.

Robert met the men-at-arms near the front door, chest heaving, axe in hand.

"Are you Robert Webber?" their leader asked from his horse.

"I am," he said defiantly.

"Prince Richard invites you to join him for a hunt tomorrow at noon. His Highness asks you meet him at the meadow near Angel Creek in Sherwood Forest. Do you know the place?"

Robert's eyes narrowed and his body stiffened as a surge of rage rose in his chest.

His father had been laid to rest just two days before. Yet this arrogant prince was already insulting his father's memory, flaunting the king's withdrawal of Sir Ralph's hunting privileges.

His mother, who had been watching from the door, walked to Robert's side and whispered, "Anger is not a friend in times of peril, son. See what the prince wants."

After staring at the warrior for a moment, Robert exhaled slowly and spoke. "Tell the prince I'll be there," he said, already planning his revenge.

* * *

The white gelding snorted and shook his head in protest.

Wary of an ambush on the woodland trails, Robert had taken a torturous route to Richard's hunting camp in Sherwood Forest, leading his steed over steep hillocks and deep ravines.

Emerging into a wide meadow, Robert saw Richard's camp a quarter mile away.

All seemed quiet. A dozen men-at-arms loitered on foot near the royal tent, their horses grazing nearby.

Robert adjusted the quiver on his shoulder, making sure the arrows were in easy reach. He might be this hunting party's prey.

Along with the bow that hung from his saddle, he carried his sword and a dagger hidden in the folds of his tunic. He'd considered selling his weapons to help his family. Now he was glad to have kept them.

Approaching the camp, he sought to steel his will.

He was prepared to become an assassin. But one thought still troubled him. His only chance to kill Richard might be from behind. Would slaying a man without the chance to defend himself be honourable?

King Henry had shown no honour at all. He'd used henchmen and lied to avoid blame for his father's murder. But Robert knew his act of vengeance would likely be his last – his only legacy. In the end, he'd concluded the king's foul deeds merited Richard's death, no matter the form. The pain of losing a son was the justice due the king. Still, the thought gave him no pleasure.

Within a hundred paces from the camp, the same warrior who'd led the others to his farm rode out to meet him.

"Prince Richard has been waiting for you. Please follow me," he said before wheeling his horse back toward the camp.

Riding behind the soldier, Robert noticed the crossbow slung across the man's back. The weapon made him wary. A crossbow was usually used for war, not hunting.

Arriving at the tent, they both dismounted and the soldier opened the tent flap. "Your Highness, Robert Webber is here," he said, then stepped aside to let him pass, leaving Robert and Richard alone.

Robert kneeled and bowed his head. "Your Majesty," he said.

"Please rise, Robert," the prince said. "Save the pomp for court. The field of the hunt is like the field of battle. We're less formal here."

Robert stood. "Thank you, Sire."

The prince's tent was surprisingly spare – a pair of camp chairs flanking a small table, with a larger table behind bearing trays of food.

"Take a seat Robert. Have you eaten?" Richard asked, extending a plate of fruit.

Robert sat down. "I'm not hungry, Sire," he answered.

"That's a shame. The apricots are delicious, just picked this morning," the prince said then turned to put away the food. "I'm sorry about the loss of your... patron," he said with his back to Robert.

The moment had come. Robert reached for his dagger, ready to stand

and strike. But Richard's next words saved his life.

"Marian tells me that's how you refer to Sir Ralph."

Robert released his dagger and remained seated. "You know Lady Marian?" he said, taken aback.

The prince turned to face Robert again. "We were practically raised together in court," he answered. "She says you're a man of honour and skilled with weapons."

"I'm pleased by her kind words, Sire. But Marian never mentioned she'd met you."

"Marian was being wise. Discretion is a rare virtue at court," Richard said, taking a seat. "But here and now, it's time we spoke bluntly, Robert," he said, pushing back a lock of ginger hair. "We both know Sir Ralph and his party were killed on my father's orders."

Robert stared in shock. After a moment, he said, "Why are you telling me this?"

"My father is a tyrant who does not deserve the throne – and I intend to replace him," Richard said calmly. "You hate my father for killing Sir Ralph. We have a common enemy."

"If you know the king ordered the death of my patron, why haven't you exposed him?" Robert asked, frowning warily.

"I wish it were that simple," Richard said with a dry grin. "The warriors who killed Sir Ralph would never betray their king. Without evidence, my father would have my head for treason."

Robert's eyes widened as he grasped the prince's motives. "Your father sent you here as a ruse to cover a murder – and you're using this against the king to recruit me for your cause."

"Marian was right. You keep sharp wits about you," Richard said, stroking his beard. "Yes, I need officers like you in my army, Robert – men who hate my father more than they love money. Mercenaries will change banners to serve the highest bidder."

"I would be honoured to serve you, Sire. But I cannot," Robert said. "My family needs me on our farm. They lost the stipend from Sir Ralph that kept me at liberty."

"Whatever Sir Ralph provided, your family will have again, plus another pound per year for you… after you join my army. My troops are forming in Norwich under the Earl of Norfolk. Our campaign against my father begins within the month."

"Sire, I have no troops to bring to your cause. Aside from a horse and a few weapons, I have nothing to offer."

"You value yourself too lightly, Robert," the prince said. "I'll arrange for your provisions and a proper suit of maille. There are units in my army I can assign to your command."

Robert was dazed. He'd entered this tent as an assassin. Now he was being offered a chance to avenge his father's death – and provide for his family. "I need time to think on this, Sire."

"Time is one thing I cannot give you, Robert. I leave tomorrow to secure more allies," the prince said, then rose to his feet. "Do we have a bargain?" he said, holding out his palm.

Robert stood and took his hand. "I came here to kill you, Sire. I'm pleased that I did not," he said, smiling.

Richard smiled back. "My captain has had his crossbow trained on you all this time," he said, pointing to a slit in the tent behind Robert. "If you'd stood whilst my back was turned and made a move against me, it would have been your last."

Nones of August 1173

Astride his horse on a wooded knoll and flanked by his lieutenants, Robert scanned the landscape around the village of Thetford, savouring his first command.

Fields of summer barley, tawny and ready for harvest, surrounded the village. Overlooking Thetford on a nearby bluff was the local lord's manor.

Within a few days' time, Richard's army would arrive to attack the manor, burn the crops, and seize the village. Robert's orders were to reconnoitre Thetford until they arrived and set up a camp for the assault.

As the only officer without his own men or a noble title, Robert had been given the dregs of Richard's army. The bulk of his troops was a detachment of pioneers – about a hundred workmen with little military training who built shelters and dug latrines. Their tools doubled as weapons. As a protective force, Robert was assigned two companies of light archers, mostly yeomen hunters armed with a motley collection of homemade bows.

But instead of laying the groundwork for an assault, during the last two days Robert had put his men to work on a different mission. He had deployed his rag-tag force to capture the town.

Now, he was ready to launch his operation.

Robert pulled out the amulet hanging below his chain maille, kissed it, and put it back. He then spoke to the brawny man on the horse to his left. "Give your men the order to proceed," he said to John Little, the leader of the pioneer detachment. Little only in name, John's hulking physique and brutish features belied a quick and resourceful mind.

Little rode off down the hill and disappeared into the woods. Moments later, a handful of pioneers on foot emerged from the trees below and fanned out through the rye fields. Robert had chosen a Sunday for his operation, knowing most of Thetford's townsfolk would be in church or at home instead of the fields.

When the pioneers were halfway to the town, they stopped and began setting fire to the rye. Before long, flames and smoke were rising from the tinder-dry fields.

As Robert expected, the people of the town ran toward their crops carrying buckets of water. Around the same time, two dozen warriors on horseback charged out of the lord's manor toward his men. Seeing the approaching men-at-arms, the pioneers began a retreat to the woods at a hard run.

Robert turned to the officer on his right. "Alert your troops. The horsemen are on their way," he said to the leader of his archers, Gilbert Whitehand.

As Whitehand rode away, Robert watched the enemy riders close on his men. Some of his troops would not reach safety he realized with regret. But he could also see that, in their haste, most of the enemy warriors were lightly armoured, carrying only swords and shields. His plan was working.

The first of the pioneers reached the woods and entered a narrow road through the dense cluster of trees. The enemy riders spurred their horses harder, eager to reach the arsons before they melted into the woods. But instead of dispersing, his men stayed on the trail. The riders charged after them, drawing closer. Robert heard a scream as a straggler in the pack was cut down by a horseman's sword.

The riders were over two-hundred yards into the woods and nearly atop his men when a tree fell across their path. Another tree fell, and then a third. The horsemen reined in their mounts as the pioneers melted into the woods. Without warning, a volley of arrows from the trees rained down on the riders. Several fell before they could raise their shields. Another volley brought down more, the arrows easily piercing the bodies of those without chain maille.

"It's a trap!" Robert heard the enemy leader call out. "Back to the manor!"

Wheeling their mounts, the riders began a full gallop in retreat, arrows falling around them like hail.

From the trees, a rope dropped across the trail ahead of the riders. As the leader's horse approached, the rope was pulled taut. His horse stumbled and fell, sending its rider to the ground. In the narrow path, the horses galloping behind fell over the first, spilling in a heap. Whilst the horsemen milled about in chaos, nearly one hundred pioneers swarmed out of the woods and fell on them with axes, picks and shovels.

Robert spurred his horse toward the fight. His raw troops would need every able man to win against these seasoned warriors. Dismounting near the head of the column, he drew his sword and stepped into the melee of men and horses.

A warrior on horseback swung at his head with a mace, the ball making an evil whoosh as it missed. Robert kneeled and grabbed the rider's stirrup, then thrust his sword into the man's leg. The man screamed and bent to strike at Robert again. As he did, one of Robert's men behind the rider, drove a pick into the horseman's back. The man fell and was swarmed by the pioneers.

By now, Robert's archers had moved in, shooting point blank into the mounted targets. The riders fought bravely, offering no quarter, but their fate was sealed. Within minutes, the slaughter was over.

Robert held his sword aloft. "You showed great valour today," he called out. "God save Prince Richard!"

The troops cheered and laughed, hoisting their tools and weapons with pride.

Robert sheathed his sword and signalled his lieutenants to join him. "There's more to be done before this town is ours," he said to Little and Whitehand. "You know the next steps. Prepare your men."

* * *

The villagers of Thetford were putting out the last of the fires in their fields when a startling sight halted their labours. Approaching on horseback under a flag of truce, Robert and Whitehand led a slow-moving column of the local warriors' steeds. Laid across their saddles were the dead bodies of the men-at-arms.

Moving past the fields, Robert brought the silent procession of nearly two dozen horses to the edge of Thetford and stopped.

Most of the townsfolk slowly gathered near his column, staring warily, uncertain why he was there. Robert waited patiently.

Before long, the Baron of Thetford, Sir Edward Blake, rode out to meet him with a trio of warriors under his own flag of truce.

"State your business," Blake said from his horse.

Robert nodded respectfully to the lord, then spoke loudly so that the townsfolk could hear. "Sir Edward, as a show of goodwill from my liege, Prince Richard, I've come to return your dead for proper burial along with their horses and weapons."

On cue, Whitehand dismounted and handed the reins of the long train of horses to the village lord.

"Tell Prince Richard that his gesture is admirable," Blake said after taking the reins.

"My lord, Prince Richard is fighting a tyrant. He has no quarrel with you or the people of this village," Robert said loudly. "Although Richard has the power of a great army under his command, the prince does not want bloodshed or destruction. He asks only to live together in peace and prosperity under an England without a despot as her ruler." Robert paused, then spoke again, his voice growing in passion. "Under Richard's rule, you and the villagers will no longer be punished with high taxes on your land and abusive scutage. Your people will no longer be forced to take food from the mouths of their children to pay for wars of glory in France!" he said, his fervour reaching a crescendo. "For the good of your people and for the cause of justice, I beseech you, m'lord… join the righteous cause of Prince Richard!"

A cheer rose from the townsfolk.

Blake looked around, shocked by the villagers' reaction. After a moment, he said, "You may tell Prince Richard that if he comes here to state his case, he'll be received in peace."

Robert bowed. "You're a wise and honourable leader, m'lord," he said before slowly riding away.

Ides of August 1173

Sir Hugh Bigod, the Earl of Norfolk, scowled as he arrived at Prince Richard's camp. The soldiers gathered near the regimental campfires were rowdy and drunk, their weapons scattered carelessly.

The earl's misgivings about Richard had grown since he'd formed an alliance with the prince. Sir Hugh had already committed three regiments of his men-at-arms and poured a good deal of his wealth into their confederacy. But Richard's character worried him. Although he was brave in battle and a popular leader, the prince was high-handed, impulsive and lacked discipline. The condition of this camp made that all too clear.

Entering Richard's tent, the earl found the prince and a young officer whose name he couldn't recall lounging in camp chairs, holding goblets of wine.

"Your Highness, I'm shocked by the readiness of our troops," the earl said frowning. "This is not how an army prepares for a battle."

"Pull up a chair and have some wine, Hugh," the prince said smiling. "There won't be a battle tomorrow."

The earl remained standing. "I thought we agreed to assault Blake's manor and destroy his crops."

"I met with Blake yesterday," the prince said, beaming. "He's agreed to join our alliance."

The earl looked surprised. "Blake has been one of Henry's strongest allies. What changed his mind?"

"The audacity of this brilliant young officer," the prince said, waving his cup toward Robert. "He opened the door for me to meet with Blake and persuade him to join us."

"You didn't burn Blake's crops?" the earl asked, still frowning.

"No. There wasn't any need."

The earl shook his head. "Your Highness, this goes against our strategy to defeat Henry. We agreed to put pressure on the king by destroying the resources of his allies. As you've just proved, Sire, alliances can change. But crops can't be replaced as quickly."

Robert spoke for the first time. "M'lord, what good would it serve His Highness to become king over a realm of starving subjects?"

The earl stiffened. "Pardon me, Sire," he said, addressing Richard. "But the name of your brilliant young officer escapes me."

"Well then, Hugh," Richard said amiably. "Let me present once again,

Robert Webber. You met him in Norwich not long ago."

Robert stood and bowed. "At your service, m'lord."

The earl's eyes narrowed. "Yes, now I recall meeting this… officer," he said, lips curled with disdain. He then turned his back on Robert and addressed the prince. "Your Highness, if we win this war, you'll be forming a new court in London. The gentry will not be pleased to know their new king consorts with persons so far below his station."

"It's unfortunate you feel that way, Hugh," the prince said with a shrug. "I've made Robert Webber my new adjutant."

Nones of May 1175

Perched in the steeple of a two-storey church, Robert scanned the town below him.

Braintree was nearly deserted – with good reason. When the townsfolk learned Prince Richard's army was marching toward their Essex county city, most had fled with their possessions or taken shelter behind heavily bolted doors. But taking the crossroads town would not be easy. It was guarded by a garrison with two regiments of the king's troops.

Robert turned his gaze toward his archers hiding in the treetops nearby. The crossbows of the six men were trained on two targets less than fifty paces away: a pair of guards in the turret of the enemy garrison at the edge of town. Robert had tested all of Richard's bowmen and chosen six with the keenest aim and strength of nerve. The outcome of the battle for Braintree rested on their skill.

From the steeple, Robert could see the back of the garrison and the wide meadows beyond. Barely visible in the distance, most of the garrison's troops were facing Richard's army moving into position for an attack. Robert knew the sides were roughly even in number, with the advantage to the garrison's troops who held higher ground.

The sign to proceed with his own assault would begin at any moment.

As he waited, Robert's thoughts turned to Marian. She had become their rebellion's eyes and ears at Henry's court. Through a trusted servant, Richard had asked Marian for details about Braintree's garrison. The letter she'd sent in reply had shaped their battle plans. Robert was grateful for Marian's help toward their cause. But her relationship with Richard left him unsettled.

Thoughts of Marian vanished as the sign Robert had been waiting for arrived: Richard's infantry was slowly advancing toward the centre of the garrison's line.

After kissing his amulet, Robert rushed down the narrow staircase toward the floor of the church, holding his scabbard tightly against his side. His sword, along with the crossbow and quiver slung across his back, would be all he'd carry into battle. He'd wear no helmet or chain maille today. Speed and agility would be more important.

Leaving the church, Robert sprinted from cover to cover, out of sight from the guards in the turret, until he reached a granary at the edge of town. There, hiding behind the large building, two dozen of his men led by Gilbert Whitehand waited with a tall ladder. Less than forty paces away stood the northwest corner of Braintree's garrison.

Although it had no moat, the garrison was still imposing. With walls twice a man's height and a square turret in each corner, a direct assault would have been long and bloody. But Robert had spotted a weakness in the fortress during his reconnoitring – a blind spot at the corner of each turret.

Inside the garrison's thick stone walls were only two wooden structures: the constable's home and a barracks for the troops. But most of the men from the barracks were now facing Richard's army in the meadow south of Braintree.

The lightly defended garrison also had another weakness they'd learned about thanks to Marian. Both the constable in command and his troops were green and poorly trained.

Viscount Phillip de Mantes had been appointed Constable of the Garrison by the king as a favour to his father. The young viscount had brought a contingent of ceremonial troops to Braintree, bright and shiny in their regalia but with no combat experience. Known to have little stomach for battle, the young viscount rarely left the garrison. These facts were also part of Robert's strategy.

Now, the time to execute his plan had arrived.

Meeting the eyes of his archers in the treetops, Robert unsheathed his sword and pointed toward the turret. A half-dozen arrows flew. Four head-shots found their mark. Both guards fell silently, dead before they hit the turret's floor.

In single file, Robert and his men scurried toward the corner of the turret and set the ladder along the building's edge. Speed was everything now.

Robert led the way, stopping at the top of the turret to look around. So far, they'd not been seen. As Robert had hoped, the inexperienced troops guarding the walls had clustered near the opposite side of the garrison to watch the battle in the meadows, leaving his entry point unguarded.

Robert turned left, moving low along the parapet at the top of the wall. On the ladder behind him, Gilbert went right. Every man who followed them dispersed in alternate directions, their crossbows cocked. Robert's men were nearly all on the parapet when a guard near the gatehouse raised the alarm.

"Intruders!" he yelled, pointing to Robert's column advancing toward him along the ramparts. Robert took aim, dropped him, and reloaded as he charged forward.

As the defenders responded, the inside of the garrison was filled with a hail of bolts and the roar of battle. The screams of men merged with the clink and thud of bolts striking stone and flesh. Robert's men were outnumbered. But their marksmanship and training more than evened the odds.

Robert's crossbow teams moved forward along opposite parapets of the garrison like a killing machine. The men on Robert's side would launch their bolts, keeping the garrison's defenders pinned down whilst those on Gilbert's side moved forward, reloading on the run. In alternating bounds, they advanced relentlessly along the walls toward the gatehouse at the front of the garrison. The long days of drills Robert had put his men through were paying off in the heat of battle.

Robert stepped over the bleeding bodies of the garrison's men strewn along the parapet as he neared the gatehouse above the entrance to the fortress. In the arched entryway ahead, he saw one of the Constable's personal guards – a large, imposing man in heavy chain maille, his sword and shield ready. "Target!" he called out to his men, pointing toward the warrior. Struck by a swarm of close-range missiles, the armoured soldier staggered back a step, then fell, bolts piercing his shield, legs and helmet.

Moving past the guard's body, Robert drew his sword and entered the darkness of the corridor. A large room with shafts of lights lay about ten paces ahead. Cautiously, he stepped inside.

Sunlight streamed through a row of windows facing the battle in the meadow. Robert did not have to look to know what was happening. Richard's forces would be feinting and retreating, creating a stalemate that would pin down the garrison's main force.

Around a row of murder holes in the stone floor were stores of arrows and bubbling caldrons of tar to pour on any attackers to the garrison's gate below. In a corner of the room, a lone man in full-length maille without a helmet stood trembling.

Robert approached the soldier and placed his sword under the man's chin. "Sir Phillip?" Robert asked calmly.

"Y-y-yes," the viscount stuttered, closing his eyes, expecting to die.

"M'lord, you're my prisoner. You'll order your men to surrender and open the gate."

Kalends of July 1175

Astride a finely groomed white charger, Prince Richard waved to the cheering crowd as his victory procession neared the drawbridge of Norwich Castle.

Standing more than six deep along each side of the road, they called out to Richard: "Long live the prince! Welcome, Your Highness! God save Richard!"

Behind the prince rode Robert, at the head of Richard's officers. Wearing his finest clothes, Robert basked in the cheers of the crowd – not for glory but revenge. Each victory brought him closer to the day Henry would face justice for the murder of his father. He had reason to believe it might be soon.

Over the last three years, Richard had gained control of four key towns on the path to London: Thetford, Woolpit, Sudbury, and now Braintree. Richard's promise to end his father's harsh taxes was winning the prince more support each day. Already, most nobles in the north-east shires were in Richard's camp. The rest were neutral, allowing the prince's army to move at will in the countryside.

The dull thumping of the horses' hooves became a clatter as the procession crossed the wooden drawbridge and entered Norwich Castle. At the entrance to the great hall, Sir Hugh awaited them, accompanied by his wife and a platoon of servants. "Welcome, Your Highness," the earl called out. "We're eager to celebrate this victory."

Following the prince inside, Robert saw a large table in the centre of the cavernous two-storey hall. After the prince was led to the head of the table, the earl took a seat on Richard's right whilst his wife, Lady Farah, sat down on his left. Robert was escorted to a chair next to the countess, a sign of his newfound status. Gilbert Whitehand, John Little and the other officers were given places at the table in descending order of rank.

After a tedious toast by the earl, the banquet was served. Conversations were formal at first, but as the wine flowed, the banter among the officers did as well. Soon, laughter echoed through the great hall.

Seated beside the countess, Robert tried not to stare at her. Much younger than her husband, her alluring face had an aquiline nose and exotic amber eyes. Her attention, however, had been riveted on the prince during the meal.

The countess finished her wine and signalled for more. As the footman filled her goblet, the countess addressed Richard, batting her eyes.

"They speak of your courage in battle, Your Highness. Tell me, were you in danger taking the garrison at Braintree?"

"My part in the battle was a farce, Lady Farah. I was never in danger," Richard answered. "My role was to lure the constable's troops out of the garrison. No, it was Robert Webber who risked his skin," he said clapping his adjutant on the shoulder. "He took the garrison with a handful of archers," the prince said, then reached into a fruit platter and held up two apples. "…along with some rather large fruit."

Lady Farah blushed as she joined in the laughter round the table.

Sir Hugh glared at Robert, his thick brows furrowed. "This all sounds eccentric and risky," he said. "What do you call this kind of combat?"

Robert shrugged and smiled slyly. "Effective, perhaps?"

The young countess joined the laughter again, brushing Robert's sleeve with a slim-fingered hand. She took another sip of wine and turned to her husband. "And where were you during all this, m'lord?" she said jokingly. "Having a piddle? I know how much trouble you've had with your bladder."

The table fell silent.

Sir Hugh gripped the arms of his chair, his face suddenly red.

After an uneasy silence, Richard spoke. "I think it's time we three retired to your chamber, Sir Hugh," he said calmly to the earl and Robert. "We have matters to attend."

"I agree," said the earl, glaring at the young countess. "My wife has had enough amusement for one evening."

Wordlessly, the trio adjourned to the earl's private chamber, then settled into padded chairs. A footman brought a tray with wine and left them alone.

The prince took a sip from the goblet and cleared his throat, trying to break the tension. "You're a good host, Hugh. This is a fine wine. A pity some of us enjoyed it more than the rest."

The earl nodded, grateful for Richard's tact. "Any word from our spy in London?" he asked.

Robert leaned forward, eager for news of Marian. Despite his many conversations with Richard, he'd never summoned the nerve to ask the prince about her.

"I'm afraid we'll lose Marian's help in two months," Richard answered. "The date for her wedding is finally set. She'll marry in September and move to Canterbury."

Robert's stomach churned at the news.

"That's a loss to our cause," said the earl, then smirked and added, "and a loss for many young men in London – although London's loss will, no doubt, be Canterbury's gain."

A twitch in Robert's hand betrayed an urge to strike the earl.

Richard seemed to share Robert's scorn as well. "I'm not amused, Hugh," the prince said, his face drawn tightly. "Lady Marian has risked her life for our cause."

"That was crude of me, Sire," the earl said quickly. "But the important thing now is deciding where to strike next whilst we still have Marian's help," he said. "The Earl of Bedford's woollen mills are an obvious target. But Henry may already be reinforcing Bedford's castle. We might consider–"

Richard lifted his palm, cutting him off. "I'm tired of trying to bleed Henry to death, Hugh. We're strong enough now to meet the Royal Guards in the field."

"I think it's best to stay with our strategy, Sire," the earl argued. "Remember Vegetius… 'famine is more terrible than the sword.'"

"No," Richard said, his face placid. "I want to defeat my father – once and for all."

"With respect, Sire. That would be foolish," the earl said, his voice rising. "So much can go wrong in a set-piece battle. If it fails, we risk losing our heads."

Robert sneered and said, "With respect, Sir Hugh. Some of us risk our heads each time we capture a town."

The earl's eyebrows furrowed. "Remember your station, peasant," he said bitterly. "Curs are expendable."

Robert rose to his feet, shaking with anger.

"Sit down, Robert," the prince commanded. "I'm sure Hugh will apologize."

"What?" the earl said, eyes bulging.

"Robert Webber has proven himself the equal of any man I've met, Hugh. When you insult him, you insult me as well."

The earl slowly lowered his head. "I apologize, Your Majesty," he said, biting off the words.

"Very well, then," the prince said. "Let's begin the plans for our final battle with the king."

Nones of August 1176

Two miles from the village of Brentwood, Richard signalled his advance party to stop on a small rise. Below them, the London Road snaked west toward the capital, some fifteen miles away. "This is where we'll fight the king's army," the prince said to his officers, dismounting from his horse. "Have the men make camp."

Robert and the other fifty-three men of the prince's scouting entourage got off their steeds and stretched. They'd been in the saddle for seven hours since leaving Richard's army at its campsite near Chelmsford.

The officers and soldiers in the advance party dispersed to set up a defensive perimeter whilst the servants began working on a meal. Night would be falling soon and there was no time to waste.

Richard summoned Robert with a wave of his hand. "Walk with me, Rob," he said leading him away from the others. "When our army gets here, I want you and Whitehand to lead the raids that lure Henry's Royal Guards to us," he said when they were out of earshot.

"I'll do my best, Sire," Robert answered flatly, staring into the distance.

Richard stroked his beard. "I'm also uneasy about morale."

"The men seem fit and eager, Sire."

"It's not them that worries me," the prince said calmly. "It's you."

"Me, Sire?"

"You've lost your fire, Rob. Instead of giving me clever ideas, you seem distant and distracted. You once told me that the priest who taught you Latin in Nottingham said, 'the hand of the diligent will rule.' I need you to be diligent for this battle."

"Sire, I'm sorry to disappoint you – and Friar Tuck," Robert said, eyes downcast.

The prince sighed. "I don't like to meddle in the private matters of my officers. But may I speak frankly?"

Robert nodded. "Of course, Sire."

"This change began when you learned of Marian's wedding. It's clear you have a strong attraction to her and this marriage troubles you."

Staring at the ground, Robert said, "There's nothing I can do about her marriage."

"You can go see her in London. Tell her how you feel."

"You're joking, Sire," Robert scoffed.

"No," the prince said, shaking his head. "The plans for her wedding could change. Her father may not be so keen on an alliance with the Earl of Kent if we win this battle and I become king. And if we lose… well, at least you'll be together one last time."

"You'd grant me this privilege near the eve of a battle?"

"Take the best horse you can find. Just be back in two days. It will take at least three days for Sir Hugh and our army to get here," he said, then lowered his voice. "Whilst we're speaking of personal matters, there's one other thing you should know, Rob," he said. "Marian and I are like brother and sister. I'm not your rival," he said, then clapped him on the shoulder. "Now go – and come back the man I need to defeat my father."

* * *

The afternoon shadows were spreading across the courtyard of Westminster Hall when Robert saw Marian leave the tall building. He'd been waiting for her near the abbey west of the hall, a spot Robert knew she would cross on her way home.

Wearing a monk's hooded robe and carrying a handful of scrolls, Robert had lingered on the busy street for over an hour, relieved no one had noticed him. To complete his disguise, he moved with a slouching limp.

Marian walked toward him, her eyes turned down. When she was within a few paces, Robert dropped a scroll.

"I'm so sorry, m'lady," he said bending down, blocking her way. Whilst fumbling awkwardly to retrieve the document, Robert lifted his head, revealing his face. Seeing Marian's startled look, he winked. Quickly grasping the ruse, she regained her composure.

As Robert rose unsteadily, he reached out to her.

"Let me help you, friar," she said, taking his hand.

"You're very kind, m'lady," he answered, passing the note hidden in his palm. "May the Lord bless you," he said, then hobbled away.

Hours later at Chatham Manor, Robert walked to the window of his room and looked outside again. The torch-lit portico was still empty. The note he'd passed to Marian asked her to come here tonight. As the night grew longer, so did his worries.

He'd travelled over fifteen miles from Richard's camp to see her, his mind in turmoil the entire way. There were so many things he wanted to say – but the thought of holding her again overwhelmed everything else.

Then Robert saw a carriage enter the lane to the manor. The lamp hanging from its roof swayed back and forth, creating an undulating cone of light as it approached the portico. He rushed downstairs to the garden.

As Robert had instructed, the footman ushered Marian to the entrance into the garden and left them alone. She walked toward him slowly, backlit by the glow from the door. A sheer gown clung to her, revealing a lissom frame.

Robert opened his arms and they embraced.

For a long time, they held each other in silence, relishing the closeness of their bodies. With her face against his chest, Marian finally spoke.

"I'm sorry about your… patron," she said softly. "But I'm glad you left London. You could have been killed along with Sir Ralph."

"Avenging his death led me to Prince Richard and I'm proud to serve him. He'll be a just and honourable king."

Marian raised her face to meet his eyes. "You took a great risk coming to London. Why are you here?"

"I came to see you. We're camped nearby."

"Does Richard know you're here?"

"My coming here was his idea."

Marian smiled faintly. "Seems Richard knows us both quite well."

"I've missed you," Robert said, inhaling the scent of her hair.

"I've missed you, too."

Robert broke their embrace and took her hands. "You can't marry him, Marian," he said, voice breaking with emotion. "You deserve a husband you can love."

"What I deserve doesn't matter. My father is too powerful."

"Your father may be a powerful man today. But what if Richard–"

Marian gently placed a finger over his lips. "All we have is tonight, Robin," she murmured, pressing against him. "Let's make the most of it."

Beckoned by her half-closed eyes he kissed her. His lips moved sensuously from her mouth to her slender neck as his hands caressed her body until they were both breathing heavily. Gently breaking their embrace, Robert took her hand and led them upstairs.

"The place is ours," he said opening the bedchamber door. "The baron and his family are at their country home."

Marian removed her veil, letting her golden hair fall free. She then walked to him and unbuttoned his tunic.

Robert felt his loins stir as Marian removed his shirt. "What's this?" she said, discovering his amulet. "A gift from another lover?"

Robert blushed. "It's from my mother," he said sheepishly.

"Well, we can't have her come between us tonight, can we?" she said with a smile, then removed the pendant and let it drop to the floor alongside his shirt.

Robert cradled Marian's face and kissed her. His hands then moved slowly lower to take off her gown, revealing her smooth shoulders and the taut nipples of her breasts. After the gown was on the floor, Robert lifted her in his arms and carried Marian to the bed.

As he lowered Marian onto her back, she placed a hand on his chest. "Not this way," she said, looking into his eyes. "A child would do neither of us any good." She then deftly guided him until they could pleasure each other with their lips. Robert eagerly complied, thrilled by this new form of passion.

In the heat of their lovemaking, they lost all sense of time.

When their ardour was finally spent, they clung to each other, wordless and blissful.

As the fire in his loins cooled, Robert recalled all he'd meant to say to Marian before their passion had swept all words away.

She knew he was a low-born bastard – yet she loved him all the same. He knew Marian's wanton ways had been a search for love – and she'd found that love in him. They loved each other with eyes wide open, without any shame. And if Richard became king, the time would come when they could be together.

But as the first light of dawn glowed through the window, Robert found himself unable to say the words aloud. Another urge had returned. To win her love, he needed to defeat Henry.

He kissed Marian gently until she awoke. "I need to return to our camp," he said softly.

* * *

The monk's robe was hot and itchy. Astride his horse, Robert's face was beaded with sweat as he baked under the robe's woollen hood in the bright August sun.

At a bend in the road ahead, the shade of a hamlet laden with trees beckoned him. He tapped his horse's ribs with his heels, bringing him to a trot.

Taking the London Road back to their camp was the fastest route – but also the most dangerous. His compromise had been to wear this infernal monk's robe with the hood up to maintain his anonymity. Still, the memory of his night with Marian made the heat seem trivial. As Richard had hoped, the edge that drove him was back.

Reaching the hamlet, Robert pulled back on the reins, stunned by the sight ahead. Approaching the bend in the road was a slow-moving column of soldiers bearing the Earl of Norfolk's red and blue coat of arms on their shields.

This didn't make sense. He was less than five miles outside of London and the earl's troops were moving toward an enemy city, not in a battle formation, but in a vulnerable road march column.

Something was wrong.

Robert got down from his horse and walked the mare to a patch of grass between two cottages about a dozen paces from the road. Whilst the horse grazed, he pulled his hood low and watched the slow-moving column pass by.

Leading the formation was a small security detail of mounted warriors. Then he saw the earl.

Riding a stout brown charger, Sir Hugh was chatting with one of his captains, looking pleased and relaxed. Behind the earl was another company of mounted warriors, followed by a detachment of infantry – at least five hundred men. Then a prison cart came into view between the cottages.

Robert pressed his fist against his mouth when he saw its occupant. Squatting in the back of the cart, bound in chains, was Prince Richard.

The purpose of Sir Hugh's column was now clear. The Earl of Norfolk had betrayed Richard and was delivering him to the king.

As the cart moved out of sight, Robert was seized by a vast emptiness, like his chest had been hollowed. Vengeance for his father… Marian's love… his family's stipend… they were all gone.

It was worse than death.

It was defeat.

The sweat on Robert's face blended with tears.

Nones of June 1177

The sun was nestling into the trees as Robert unharnessed his horse from the harrow and led the gelding toward the barn. He'd been at work since dawn, something he'd done almost daily since returning to Nottingham. The work helped dull the pain.

Nearly a year had passed since their rebellion had been crushed. But Robert's memories were still fresh. The only bright moment of that day had been finding several of his men who had survived Hugh Bigod's betrayal.

He'd come upon the weary soldiers on the road to London, trailing the earl's column, hoping for a chance to rescue the prince. The men then told him how Richard had been captured.

Near dark on the previous night, Bigod had arrived at their advance camp with almost half his army. Although three days earlier than expected, the earl's presence raised no alarms. But during the night, Bigod's men fell on Richard's troops whilst they slept.

Outnumbered ten-to-one, most of Richard's men were slaughtered and the prince was captured. A few managed to escape, Gilbert White-hand and John Little among them. Uncertain what to do, they'd dogged the earl's troops until they happened upon Robert.

The last of Richard's men still alive gathered around their second-in-command, shoulders slumped and grim-faced. "Any ideas, Rob? Do we try for a rescue?" Gilbert asked, not sounding very hopeful.

Robert shook his head. "I've seen their numbers. We'd be throwing our lives away." Despite his own despair, Robert wanted to give the men hope. "You've fought bravely, but our families need us now. We should go home and care for them," he said, his voice faltering. "It's been an honour fighting alongside you."

The men nodded and slowly walked away, leaving only Whitehand and Little.

"I've got nothing back home, Rob… no family… no prospects," John said, staring at the ground.

"Aye, same for me," Gilbert said, nodding.

Little raised his eyes. "What do you plan to do, Rob?"

"I have family in Nottingham. Without my pay, they'll need help on the farm."

"Would you be needing an extra hand, then?" Little asked.

Whitehand smiled faintly. "Seems I'm available, as well."

Nones of July 1177

A year later, Robert still swelled with pride that Whitehand and Little had chosen to share their fate with him. As Robert expected, his mother and grandfather had welcomed the pair.

Approaching the barn, Robert saw Anna and Simon shelling peas on a bench. Beside them, Gilbert was fletching arrows.

On a ladder close by, John was thatching the roof of the rooms he'd added to the barn. After months of sleeping in the hayloft, the new rooms were now quarters for the men. Despite the loss of Richard's stipend, the farm had prospered.

John had put the power of Robert's horse to work by building a harness and harrow from scraps of leather and wood he'd found around the farm. Gilbert was more than earning his keep as well. Whitehand's skill with the bow put game on their table almost every day. The men showed signs of taking root in Nottingham.

John was courting their neighbour Faye Rolfe and often returned from his visits to her home with a smile that lasted days. Meantime, Gilbert's poaching of game in Sherwood Forest had made him an expert on the terrain – and avoiding the new sheriff who guarded it.

Being wary had become routine for Robert and his men. Although the Earl of Norfolk likely thought they were dead, they kept up with the news his grandfather brought from his visits into town. The word from London was that Richard's execution was imminent. Developments in Nottingham were sobering as well.

Sir Ralph's widow had died, leaving Talbot Hall to Robert's half-sister, Juliet. She'd married the Earl of Devon who took over the title of Baron of Nottingham – a title that should have been Robert's. With Juliet now living in Devonshire, Talbot Hall had become the home of the Sheriff of Nottingham.

Despite the unsettling news, Robert and his comrades stayed busy on the farm whilst keeping an eye on the horizon.

"We'll be having supper soon," Anna Webber called out to the men on her way to the cottage. "Get yourselves cleaned up."

At the large water basin in the barn, the three men stripped to the waist and began to wash.

"Your new harness and harrow worked well today, John," Robert said, removing his amulet before beginning to scrub. "What you've done with odds and ends is a wonder."

John slapped his broad, hairy chest. "I was raised in Manchester. We get very little there – and learn to make do with it."

"Get very little is right," Gilbert said, smiling slyly. "I hear the men in Manchester are such an ugly lot, they raise a cheer whenever a farmer brings his sheep into town."

"Well, if the likes of you ever owned a farm, Gilbert Whitehand, you'd never raise chickens, 'cause you'd need a fair-sized cock for that," John said with a laugh.

Gilbert grinned and splashed water at John. "Look out! The big man is showing us his tiny wit."

All three men joined in the laughter.

"You two go on to the house," Robert said to his comrades. "I still need to shave."

"That's a wasteful habit, Rob," Gilbert said. "Why not let your beard grow like a man?"

"Come on, Gil," John said, pulling him through the door. "If Rob wants to look like the prettiest maid in the shire, that's his affair."

John and Gilbert's laughter continued as they walked toward the cottage whilst Robert stropped the razor and looked at his reflection in a pan of water by the window.

The rough banter of his friends had lifted his spirits. After a year, Robert still felt the sting of their defeat. But a part of him was easing into his life in Nottingham.

Was it his fate to be a farmer? He still longed for Marian, there was no denying that. But maybe he was destined to marry a country girl who'd give him sturdy children to work their farm in his dotage. Would that be so bad?

Robert said little through supper and the rest of the evening as he weighed these thoughts.

The next day, as the five of them were finishing breakfast in the cottage, the sharp-eyed Gilbert noticed something through the open door. "Looks like a very fat priest on a very small mule is paying a visit," he said, pointing to a figure in the distance.

Although he'd not seen him in years, Robert recognized the priest. "It's Friar Tuck. I think it's best if you and grandfather see what he wants, mother," Robert said. He then nodded to Gilbert and John. "The three of us should stay inside." Robert did not want to take any chances. The friar might be spying for the earl.

Anna walked outside. "Good morning, Friar," she called out, intercepting the priest a good way from the door. "What brings you here?"

"I have a letter for Robert," the friar said from his mule. "Do you know where I might find him?"

Anna cocked her head. "Who is this letter from?"

"I think you'll recognize the seal," the friar said, producing the letter from his robe and handing it to her.

Anna drew a sharp breath as she took the folded sheet. Pressed into the red wax sealing the letter was Prince Richard's royal stamp.

"Should I happen to see Robert, I'll make sure he gets the letter," she said, gathering herself.

The priest smiled knowingly. "I'm sure the sender will be glad to hear that," he said before riding away.

Ides of July 1177

Holding his hat tight against the wind, Robert followed a sergeant of Dover's Royal Guards toward the edge of the cliff. Ahead of them, the English Channel glimmered in the sun, the coast of France a faint strip on the horizon.

About a hundred paces away, two men stood at a table under a canopy tent near the cliff's edge. As he walked closer, Robert recognized Prince Richard, his long ginger hair fluttering in the breeze. Reaching the tent, the sergeant waved Robert forward and remained a discreet distance away.

"Rob!" the prince said. "I'm glad to see you're alive!"

Removing his hat, Robert knelt and bowed his head. "Your Highness," he said. "I'm happy to see you're well… and free."

"Please rise, Rob. Let me look at you." Robert stood and the prince clasped his shoulders. "You seem fit and tanned. Country life agrees with you," he said, then playfully rubbed Robert's close-shorn hair, "although you still seem determined to look like a bumpkin."

"How did you know where to find me, Sire?"

"You once spoke of the friar who taught you Latin in Nottingham. If you were alive, I thought Friar Tuck might get a message to you," Richard explained. "But I'm being rude," he said, tapping his forehead. "Robert Webber, I'd like to present Maurice, the finest engineer in Europe. He's going to build our realm's largest castle on this spot."

"Honoured to meet you," Robert said with a courteous nod.

"Likewise," Maurice replied. "It seems you two have much to talk about. With your permission, Sire, I'll take my leave."

"Before you go, Maurice," the prince said. "Would you be kind enough to show Robert your plans?"

"Certainly, Sire," Maurice answered. He then pointed to the stone walls fifty paces on either side of them that ran to the edge of the cliff. "As you can see, we've started the castle's bailey. When they're finished, the walls will enclose the castle like this," he said, pointing to a "U" shaped perimeter on a large drawing pinned to the table. "The cliff in front of us is over three hundred feet high and, of course, requires no wall."

"And this is the keep, I presume," Robert said, pointing to the square near the centre of the drawing.

Maurice nodded. "Yes, we're preparing the foundation for the keep. It's just over that rise," he said, pointing to the bluff before them.

"The castle in Dover will be an impregnable fortress… and a grand palace," Richard said proudly. "Thank you, Maurice."

"Gladly, Your Highness," the engineer said before he bowed and walked away.

After Maurice was out of earshot, Robert said, "Sire, I'm confused. I thought you were to be tried and executed."

Robert smiled. "I discovered my father is far too vain to kill any of his children. That would be admitting there's a flaw in his blood. No, he thinks removing me from succession to the throne is punishment enough. For good measure, my father made a pair of my cousins in the Anjou line heirs to the throne behind my brother John. That way, the old fox can keep both of his sons on a short leash," he said. "Sir Hugh wasn't happy that I kept my head – until my father appeased him with more land."

"But you're free, Sire. That's surprising."

"Oh, I spent a few months in a dungeon," Richard said evenly. "But my mother convinced the king to send me into exile in Wales. It was there I got the idea that earned me my freedom – and that's why I sent for you, Rob." The prince put his hand on Robert's shoulder. "I'm taking command of an army in France and I want you to join my staff."

"I'm still confused, Sire. What's the mission of this army?"

"I intend to defeat my father's enemies in France, once and for all."

Robert stepped away from Richard's hand, his eyes wide in shock. "But what of our rebellion? The king's wars in France were the main reason we rose against him. We all agreed these wars are what drove the king to raise taxes and scutage to the point of cruelty."

"Victory will solve that problem, Rob," the prince said, turning up his palms. "If we end these wars quickly, their drain on the realm's treasury will end as well."

Robert shook his head. "Forgive me, Sire. But this seems like sophistry. There's no honour in abandoning one's principles."

"So, you'd have me be a martyr?" Richard said, suddenly stern. "Grow up, Rob. A martyr will never bring justice – or avenge your patron's death."

Robert's face hardened. Then he bowed. "Your Highness, I beg to be excused. Clearly, I'm not the man for your army."

"Hear me out, Robert," the prince said, his voice once again calm. "How is your mother?"

"She's well, Sire," Robert said stiffly.

"I'm sure spending a year with her was something you cherished. But be candid with me, Rob. Is that the life you want?"

Robert stared at the expanse of water for a moment. Then he said, "I've asked myself the same question."

"What I offer you is not perfection. But it is a means to an end," the prince said. "Yes, our rebellion failed. But if you're patient, you can help revive it again. Living out your days as a farmer will do nothing to help our people. But joining me will give you access to power. Which would your mother prefer? That you live as a peasant or as a man of consequence with the ability to help others?"

"I think she'd want me to live with honour."

"Honour means serving justice, does it not?"

Robert nodded. "Yes, it does."

"Think years into the future, Rob. Joining me will give you the power to change things for the better. Have you considered that your pride is preventing you from serving the cause of justice?"

"It's possible. But—"

The prince raised his palm. "Before you answer, let me remind you there are rewards for serving honour as well," he said. "I have a king's resources now. Your stipend would increase ten-fold. That means your mother could live in luxury, Rob," he said. "And there's the possibility of a peerage for you as well. How would your mother feel about that?"

Robert pictured his mother's face as she learned her son had become a member of the gentry. "I think she would be pleased," he admitted.

"Then make your mother proud and serve honour as well… join me, Rob."

"It's not my choice alone, Sire," Robert said. "I travelled here with two of my men and I can't abandon them,"

"Who are these men?"

"Gilbert Whitehand and John Little."

"I remember them well," the prince said, smiling broadly. "They'd be fine additions to our army. I'll have the captain arrange pay and billets for them in the garrison. You, of course, would join my personal staff again – as field marshal of the army." The prince paused, letting the weight of that sink in. Then he extended his palm and said, "I need you. Rob. Can I count on your service?"

Robert took his hand. "Once again, you've changed my life, Sire."

"I'm not finished yet," the prince said smiling. "Marian is not far from here in Canterbury. You might want to pay her a visit before we sail for France."

* * *

The target range in the garden of the Earl of Kent's estate was deserted, save for one archer.

Marian placed her foot in the crossbow's stirrup and drew the bowstring back onto the weapon's nut. Most women who hunted lacked the muscle to cock a crossbow. But through years of practice beginning in her teens, Marian had developed the strength.

After placing a bolt in the flight groove, Marian levelled the weapon. Aiming the head of the missile just above the centre of the target some twenty paces away, she squeezed the trigger.

The bolt struck the bullseye – the third one in a row.

Marian lowered the weapon and exhaled slowly. Target practice with a crossbow might have appeared unseemly for a young bride to some in her social circles. This bothered Marian none at all. The regimen cleared her mind, creating a retreat from anguish and worry.

The butler appeared at the entrance to the hedge-lined range and bowed his head. "Ma'am, a gentleman from Prince Richard's court is calling for you."

Marian put down the bow, removed the quiver and donned her wimple. The custom that a married woman cover her hair in public was annoying. But today she was unbothered. Visitors to the earl's manor in Canterbury were rare and she was eager for company.

The sound of footsteps on the gravel path to the enclosure grew louder until a figure appeared at the entrance.

"Seems we're forever destined to meet in gardens," Robert said smiling.

Marian stood silently for a moment, stunned. "Robin," she finally said, her eyes welling. "I thought you were dead."

He walked to her and they embraced, holding each other tightly, eyes closed.

After a moment, Marian gently broke away. "Where have you been?" she said, looking into his eyes.

"I was in Nottingham with my family until a fortnight ago. Then Richard sent for me in Dover."

Marian nodded knowingly. "It's no surprise Richard would send for you now that he's taking command of the king's forces in France."

"As usual, your knowledge of the court is keen."

"Not anymore. By the time news reaches me here, it's third-hand gossip. Everyone knows about Richard's campaign to France."

Robert smiled. "Apparently Nottingham is still the home of ignorant yokels."

"You don't forget insults, do you?" she said, smiling in return.

"Not when they come from someone I love," Robert said, taking her hand and bringing it to his lips.

Marian slowly withdrew her hand. "Robin," she said, eyes downcast. "We can't."

Robert lifted her chin. "Has something changed between us?"

"It seems you've been a prophet," she said, turning her face away. "You told me that once I found the man I love, my days of searching for love with others would be over. You were right about that."

"That man is your husband?" he said, eyes wide with surprise.

Marian sighed softly. "No, Robin. It's you."

"Yet you tell me this without any joy. What's wrong?"

"I'm no longer the woman who enjoyed toying with men at court," she said, clasping her hands. "I'm married – and the woman I am now honours her vows of fidelity."

"The man you married is not a real husband," Robert said. "Those vows are a sham."

"I made them, all the same," Marian said, looking into his eyes. "I'm sorry, Robin. I love you. But we can't be lovers. Not anymore."

Robert shook his head. "This makes no sense, Marian."

"Honour is not about sense. It's about duty. You more than anyone should understand that."

"But I love you, Marian. Your husband doesn't."

"A woman worthy of your love would not break her marriage vows. If I did, someday you'd come to doubt my faithfulness to you."

Robert stared at the ground, considering her words. Perhaps Marian was right. The price of honour was always pain. Before he could answer, Marian spoke again.

"There's something else," she said, closing her eyes. "Richard doesn't know it yet, but my husband Clement plans to join his campaign in France. His protégé wants to go to war and Clement insists on joining him."

"That's absurd. Richard won't allow a pair of inexperienced officers on his staff."

"Clement is bringing three regiments of his father's troops to the campaign. You know Richard. He will not refuse the troops – and even if he did, the king will insist Richard accept them."

"Why?"

"The Earl of Kent is second only to the king in wealth and land. If his son wants to play at being a soldier, Henry will grant his wish."

Robert exhaled slowly. "This can't end well," he said, looking away. Then he turned and met her eyes again. "All the same, there's something I want you to know, Marian. Your sacrifice to virtue will not be yours alone. No one will share my bed until we're together again."

Kalends of May 1178

Dressed in full battle gear, Richard and Robert sat side-by-side astride their horses, watching their troops file past in a ragged column. The slouching gait and glazed expressions of the men betrayed an army in retreat.

"I've failed you, Sire," Robert said, removing his helmet. "We had more men but still lost today. I don't deserve this command."

"I'll be the one to decide that," the prince said. "You may command the troops, but this is still my army. I'm not going to sack my field marshal for losing his first battle."

"You're far more generous than I deserve, Sire."

"It's a setback. But this is a problem we can fix," Richard replied, shedding his own helmet. "Fortunately, our casualties were low."

"That's no surprise," Robert scoffed. "Our foot soldiers ran like rabbits when the enemy cavalry charged from the flank. After that, our entire line collapsed."

"Your tactics were sound, Rob. But even though we outnumbered them, I thought a victory today was unlikely," the prince said.

Robert's eyes widened. "I don't understand, Sire. Why didn't you say so?"

"You were eager for this battle, Rob, and I didn't want to clip my new field marshal's wings. But these men weren't ready."

"I trained these men myself, Sire," Robert said, his head sagging. "I deserve the blame."

"These men did not lack training, Rob. They lacked purpose," the prince said, stroking the neck of his horse. "The men under your command in the past were Englishmen who fought for pride and duty." Richard pointed with his chin toward the soldiers walking by. "Except for Clement's parade-ground soldiers, our men are foreign mercenaries hired by my father. They fight for pay and want to live to collect it. When things look dire, they'll cut and run."

"Then how can we win a war with this army, Sire?"

"We need to make them fear our discipline more than they fear the enemy," the prince said. "That's why I propose that from this point forward, any man who deserts the ranks be hanged for cowardice."

"That seems too harsh, Sire. The men will desert us when discipline is that severe."

"Along with discipline, we need to give these men rewards for victory that are worth risking their lives," Richard said. "I know you've opposed it in the past, Rob. But we should let these men take their share of plunder."

Robert shook his head. "Letting men loot is not honourable, Sire."

"Isn't justice a part of honour? Taking from the rich to give to the poor is a form of justice," the prince said. "There would need to be rules, of course. No ravaging of women or theft from the clergy. But whatever booty our soldiers can find among the homes of the wealthy after we take a city would be a just reward."

"I'll admit, this defeat today argues that you're right, Sire. But I still have my doubts about these measures. I may not be the best man to lead your troops."

"I know of no better leader, Rob. At Thetford, you took a rabble and turned them into fighters. At Braintree, your cleverness and courage took a fortress. But now it's time you learned another kind of courage – the courage to be stern. I know you can do that, Rob."

"This is not an easy choice for me, Sire."

"Rob, we can turn today's defeat into a lesson that transforms this army," the prince said. "If these men had been fighting for the spoils of war and feared punishment for breaking ranks, they would have mustered the courage to repel that cavalry charge. Then we'd be celebrating a victory. Winning this war quickly for my father will give us power – power we can use to achieve a greater good. But we need to be resolute to achieve our goals."

Robert considered Richard's counsel. He'd given his word to lead the prince's soldiers – and Richard was right. He'd never get the chance to avenge his father or help the poor of England without leading these troops to victory. After a moment, he looked at the prince and said, "I'll announce the new rules for discipline and spoils to our officers tomorrow."

"I'm proud of you, Rob. Your strength as a leader is growing equal to your courage in battle," Richard said. He then wheeled his horse. "I'll see you at supper. But first I face the sour task of writing the king. My father expects victories, not excuses."

Robert bowed his head as the prince galloped away.

Later, as Rob rode alone toward their camp, an officer on horseback approached him at a trot. Robert grimaced when he recognized Marian's husband, Sir Clement.

"I'd like a word, Marshal," Clement said, guiding his horse alongside Robert's.

Since encountering Clement at their first staff meeting, Robert had been unimpressed with him. Clement had little interest in military matters and was fond of haughty barbs. But his face now seemed to have lost its usual conceit.

"Please be brief, Sir Clement," Robert said. "There are matters that need my attention in camp."

"It's about my protégé, Will Scarlett. I trust you remember him."

Robert nodded. "I do," he said. Robert recalled the young man as serious and quiet, with a nimble and athletic mien.

"Will is infatuated with glory. I'd hate to see that foolishness lead him to harm."

"That 'foolishness' is how armies win wars."

"I meant no offense, Marshal," Clement said with a slight nod. "Will has just volunteered for your personal cavalry detachment. I only ask that you assign him to less dangerous duty. Will is from a very old and noble family who would be crushed by his loss."

"All the men under my command have families who would mourn them."

"Surely, you see the difference, Marshal. His uncle is an earl. These are people of the finest breeding."

Robert turned to face Clement, his face hard. "I cannot afford the luxury of giving special treatment to anyone under my command. Will Scarlett will be tested in training. If he earns a place in my cavalry, then he'll keep that privilege."

Clement sniffed. "I see," he said. "I can't say I'm surprised by your reaction."

"Would you care to explain that?" Robert said, struggling to remain calm.

"It seems clear you harbour personal resentment toward me," Clement said. "Marian has made no secret of her relationship with you. I think you dislike me for whom I choose as a bed partner – and whom I choose not to sleep with at all."

Robert clenched the pommel of his saddle. In an icy voice, he said, "Sir Clement, I suggest you ride away quickly – or it may not be Will Scarlett's family mourning a loss."

* * *

A day later, Robert was still unsettled about allowing their army to plunder. Once given free rein, savagery could be hard to contain. Still, he'd given the prince his word. Now, with Richard and their officers gathered under the shade of a maple near their camp, Robert needed to put his qualms aside.

"We're going to change our rules of engagement," he told the roughly two-dozen men. Robert then laid out the army's new methods for discipline and rewards. As he spoke, Robert noted the faces of Gilbert Whitehand

and John Little. His long-time comrades took the news soberly, without enthusiasm. After he was done, Robert said, "Any questions?"

The circle of men was silent for a moment. Then Sir Clement spoke. "My men are not mercenaries, Marshal. They should be exempt from this punishment."

Robert exhaled slowly. "Your men may not be mercenaries, Sir Clement. But they're hardly seasoned troops. They ran away like all the rest yesterday. In any case, an army can't have two kinds of discipline."

Clement shrugged with disdain. "I find that unacceptable."

"Well then, Sir Clement," Robert said with a smirk. "Perhaps you can set an example of courage and start leading your men from the front lines. It must get very dull guarding the baggage carts at the rear of our army."

Clement's face reddened as the other officers broke into laughter. "I will not suffer insults from the likes of you, Robert Webber," he said bitterly. "You were part of a rebellion against our king and I'll make sure His Highness knows where to find you."

His eyes on fire, Robert gripped his sword. "If you think –"

Richard raised his palm. "Enough," the prince said sternly. Every officer lowered his eyes. "The new rules of engagement will be obeyed by all our troops. Now go and inform your detachments."

As the gathering dispersed, Robert saw Will Scarlett approach.

"May I speak with you, Marshal?" the young man said.

Robert nodded in reply.

"I hope you won't hold my sponsor's opinion against me," Scarlett said. "I agree with your decision to increase discipline. The behaviour of our troops yesterday was a disgrace."

"I'm glad to know you agree. But let me be clear. The skills and instincts you show in your training will determine your fitness for my cavalry. Nothing else."

"That kind of honour is why I want to serve with you, sir," Will said, then gave a courteous nod and left.

Robert watched the young officer walk away, envying the simplicity of Will's world.

* * *

For the third time that morning, the soldiers repeated the drill.

With Robert and John Little watching from a distance, three platoons of warriors ran under the cover of their shields carrying the pieces of a siege tower toward an escarpment that simulated a castle wall. At the foot of the cliff, the teams began assembling their platforms. Once their towers were complete, the men raised them upright with pulleys and poles.

After the last tower was erected, Robert looked at the sand clock on his field table. "Still not fast enough!" he yelled toward the troops. "Again!"

"Maybe I can make the plank mechanism simpler," John said to Robert. "That seems to be taking the most time." John's siege towers included an ingenious device to breach a castle's walls. Once erected, a hinged oak plank powered by a coiled rope would flip from the top of the tower onto the castle's parapet, giving their men a foot path over the wall.

Robert shook his head. "No. They need to learn how to assemble the towers faster. Without storming the castle at Amiens, our campaign in France is finished."

The next objective for Richard's army was Amiens, a town whose castle dominated a key crossing on the Somme River. Controlling the city would protect Richard's supply line from England as his army drove deeper into France. Laying siege to Amiens' castle would have stalled their campaign.

To capture the castle, Robert had worked with John to exploit a weakness of the fortress: the lack of a moat. Their plan called for Richard to draw the castle's defenders to the entrance of the fortress with a diversionary attack using conventional, slow-moving siege towers on wheels and a battering ram against the castle's gate. Once the defenders were massed near the entrance, Robert and his men would breach the castle's lightly defended rear wall with John's portable siege towers.

Watching the troops take down the platforms to begin their next drill, John scratched his beard and said, "So tell me, Rob. Will you be taking Sir Clement's boy into your cavalry?"

"Will Scarlett rides well – and his sword is even better. On martial skills alone, he's the match of any man we've got. But like any novice, how his nerve will hold up in battle remains to be seen."

"Word around camp is that Scarlett and Sir Clement had a row and they're no longer sharing a tent."

Holding back a smile, Robert said, "John, if I didn't know you better, I'd say that sounds like gossip."

* * *

The following day, whilst Robert and John were putting the troops through their fourth tower drill, Robert spotted the camp constable approaching at a gallop.

"His Highness asks that both of you come to his tent immediately," the constable announced without dismounting.

"Is there a problem?" Robert asked.

"Sir Clement has been found dead in the woods outside camp – killed with a blade."

"Tell His Highness we're on our way," Robert said.

Moments later, Robert and John mounted their horses. "Who do you think killed him?" John asked as the two set out toward Richard's tent.

"Hard to say," Robert answered. "Clement didn't have many friends. But he did have some well-known enemies."

"Aye – and you're at the top of the list."

The two rode on in silence until they reached Richard's tent.

From his camp chair, the prince looked up and waved them inside. "The constable is already investigating the murder. But we can't let Clement's death delay our attack on Amiens," Richard said. "Rob, you'll return with the body to Canterbury for burial. John will supervise the training on the siege towers until you return."

Robert's eyes widened. "Me, Sire?"

"We don't have much time. So, I'll be blunt, Rob," the prince said. "Everyone knows you're a suspect in this murder. However, the constable has determined Clement was killed early yesterday evening – that's when you were having supper with me. So that rules you out as a suspect," he said. "However, Clement's family has probably heard about the quarrels between you two. I can't think of a better way to remove you from suspicion than to send you to Clement's funeral in my stead."

Robert nodded. "Yes, I can see the sense of that, Sire. Someone innocent has nothing to hide," he said. "But is it wise for me to leave so close to our assault on Amiens?"

"Right now, it's more important to clear the air about this murder. My field marshal cannot lead an army under a cloud of suspicion."

"What of Will Scarlett, Sire?" Robert asked. "Shouldn't he go to the funeral?"

The prince shook his head. "You'll have to go without him. Will's out of camp on cavalry patrol and the constable has not yet confirmed his whereabouts at the time of Clement's death."

"I see," Robert said, rubbing his chin. If the gossip about their breakup was true, the suspicion was reasonable.

"We don't have much time and you've a long way to travel, Rob," the prince said. "John knows your plan and he'll continue to drill the men. You'll leave for Canterbury right away. Be back in less than a fortnight."

Nones of June 1178

Waiting in the mourners' line behind a dowager from Exeter, Robert stifled a yawn.

Sir Clement's lying in state filled the great hall at his father's manor with gentry from all corners of England. Standing by the coffin, the Earl of Kent and his family greeted each visitor as they filed past.

Representing the prince, Robert was near the front of the line – and he was grateful. His hurried trip to Canterbury had kept him awake for nearly five days. All he could think of was getting some sleep – and seeing Marian.

Since arriving at dawn with his detail of troops, he'd delivered the body to the monastery in preparation for the viewing, then made sure his men and their horses had proper billets. After a bath and a shave, he'd been hurriedly dressed in formal attire by a squad of valets, then rushed to the great hall for the funeral reception.

When his turn before the earl arrived, Robert bowed and said, "On behalf of His Highness, Prince Richard, I extend his deepest sympathies."

The Earl of Kent responded with an icy stare. Finally, he spoke. "You may tell Richard that I accept his condolences in the spirit in which they were given."

Moving down the reception line, Robert came to Marian. Dressed in black, her expression was hidden behind a veil.

"I'm sorry for the loss of your husband, Lady Marian," Robert said gently.

"Thank you," she said, gazing toward the floor.

Robert waited, hoping she'd say more. During the long journey to Canterbury, Robert had thought only of Marian. How would she react to the death of her husband? Could they become lovers again? Marian kept her face down, offering no clue.

Robert sighed and walked away.

Entering the apartment he'd been given at the earl's manor, Robert found a valet waiting in the parlour. Lavishly decorated, the room had enough chairs for a dozen visitors and a large window with a view of the estate's manicured gardens.

"Would you care for something to eat, sir?" the valet asked.

"No, thank you," Robert said, walking through a tall door into the bedchamber. "Please leave word that I don't wish to be disturbed," he said, then closed the door.

Taking off his hat and tunic, Robert collapsed onto the bed still partly dressed. In a moment, he was asleep.

A knock on the door awoke him some time later.

"I asked not to be disturbed," Robert said groggily.

"I have a message from Lady Marian," the valet called out from the parlour.

Scrambling out of bed, Robert opened the door. "What's the message?"

"Lady Marian asks that you meet her at the target range for breakfast tomorrow."

"Thank you," Robert said. "Please, tell her I'll be there."

Despite his weariness, Robert did not sleep much after that.

When morning finally came, Robert walked to the parlour window and peered into the garden. After locating the entrance to the target range through the tall hedges, he hurriedly changed clothes and walked outside.

Entering the practice area, Robert saw her. Still wearing black, Marian sat behind a small table with trays of bread and fruit. A footman holding a pitcher hovered nearby. She gestured to the chair across from her. "Good morning, Robert. Please sit down."

The footman filled two goblets on the table with ale.

"Thank you, Frye," she said to the servant. "You may retire."

After the footman was gone, Robert said, "I'm confused by this cold reception, Marian. I thought you would be happy to see me."

"My in-laws know about us, Robin. Just talking to you will be a scandal to some of them," she said evenly. Then she managed a faint smile. "But I'm glad you're here. Richard was wise to send you. It clears you of suspicion. The earl's family knew about your quarrels with Clement."

"How did they hear about that?"

"People talk, Robin. Word travels fast."

Robert rubbed his chin. "From the earl's reaction yesterday, I'd say he still suspects me."

"I wouldn't worry about that. My father-in-law knows everything he does is under scrutiny. He's expected to be grieving. But the truth is, he's probably relieved. Clement was always an embarrassment."

Robert was stunned. "Seems I have a lot to learn about noble families," he said. "Do you think he cares who killed his son?"

"I think the earl knows who killed Clement – but he'll never press charges."

"Will Scarlett?" Robert asked. "They'd quarrelled before Clement's death. Richard kept Will in camp until his whereabouts at the time of the murder could be confirmed."

"No, it wasn't Will," Marian said. "I think Clement was killed on Richard's orders."

"The prince?" Robert said, startled by the thought.

"Richard is the one with the most to gain – and the one least likely to be prosecuted," she explained. "Richard needs your help to win his war in France. When Clement threatened to betray you to the king, it put Richard's victory in jeopardy," she said. "I know Richard. He'll do anything to win."

Robert chewed his lip. "What you've said about Richard makes sense. He invited me to dine with him the night Clement was killed. That accounted for my whereabouts and established my innocence. Keeping Will Scarlett under suspicion also helped Richard cover his tracks," Robert sighed. "This is troubling, Marian. I must take it up with Richard."

"That would not be wise, Robin," she said, reaching for his hand across the table. "There's a shred of happiness in this tragedy. We can be together again – but not if you shun Richard."

"I love you, Marian. But I cannot serve a man without honour," Robert said soberly, pulling back his hand. "In any case, I must leave immediately. We're on the verge of a battle and my men need me."

Kalends of July 1178

Arriving with his escorts at their army's campsite, Robert found only the cold ashes of regimental campfires and patches of dead grass where their tents had been pitched. Exhausted from their long journey, some of the men groaned. Robert did not reprimand them. He was bone-weary himself.

"Field Marshal!" a young officer called out from the distance, galloping toward Robert's men. Once he'd reached them, the lieutenant breathlessly said, "His Highness ordered me to wait here for you. Our spies discovered the castle is expecting reinforcements. Prince Richard has launched the attack and asks that you take command of the assault on the rear wall."

Robert turned to face his escorts. "Let's move!" he called out, urging his horse into a gallop.

After a hard ride of several miles, they reached their command post in the woods near the rear of Amiens Castle. Astride their horses, John Little, Gilbert Whitehand, Will Scarlett and several other officers turned to face Robert as he rode into their group.

John Little wasted no words of greetings. "Our men are being slaughtered, Rob," John said, pointing toward the three teams assembling the siege towers at the back wall of the castle.

Robert scanned the wall that rose three times a man's height. More archers were arriving along the battlements, raining a murderous shower of arrows down on his men. Clearly, Richard's diversionary attack on the front gate had not fooled the castle's commander. Although Richard's army outnumbered the castle's defenders by more than three-to-one, that advantage would soon be gone if he continued losing men.

Robert now faced a choice. Call off the attack and avoid a bloodbath – or move ahead with an assault on two fronts against the castle. Either way, there was no time to consult Richard. The decision would be his own.

Robert pulled the amulet from his tunic and kissed it. After replacing the pendant, he called out to one of his aides. "Ride to His Highness and tell him to press his attack. His assault is no longer a diversion. He needs to break down the gate and breach the front wall. We're putting our bollocks on the line today."

After the aide rode away, Robert turned to Gilbert Whitehand. "On my signal, take your mounted archers within range of the wall. Your men need to pin down the castle's bowmen so we can finish the siege towers."

Whitehand nodded. "We'll be ready, Rob," he said and rode toward his men.

Robert's head swivelled. "Where's my cavalry commander?"

"He was killed on a patrol this morning, sir," Will Scarlett said.

Robert studied the young officer. Scarlett seemed calm – and this was a day to gamble. "Congratulations, Will. You're now in command of my cavalry," he said. "Assemble your troops behind me," he said riding forward into the meadow.

"Yes, sir," Will replied.

Moments later, Robert was at the head of over three hundred mounted men. "On my command, we'll ride to the wall and dismount," he called out to his troops. "You're going to help the infantry build those towers and then go over the wall and take that castle. Kiss your ponies goodbye, lads. You'll fight on your feet today! Are you ready?" he said, raising his sword.

The men let out a hoarse roar.

Robert looked toward Gilbert Whitehand at the head of his archers. Drawing his sword, he pointed it toward the wall. Two hundred mounted bowmen broke into a gallop toward the castle.

He then turned to face the cavalry men behind him. "Let's move!" he yelled, waving his sword.

The thunder of over a thousand hooves shook the ground as they charged forward.

Riding closer to the wall, Robert could see the extent of the carnage. Scores of arrow-pierced bodies lay bleeding on the ground around the three unfinished siege towers. Huddling behind their shields, the men still alive were struggling to assemble the platforms under the merciless volleys of arrows and bolts from above.

Even with the new men Robert was bringing to the fray, their chance of breaching the wall seemed hopeless. They were losing men too quickly.

Robert slowed his breathing, trying to calm his mind. The solution came in a flash of clarity.

They would need to abandon one of the siege towers.

As he dismounted, Robert was buoyed by the sight of Gilbert's archers launching arrows upward toward the defenders. Moments later, the rain of arrows coming toward his troops slackened.

Moving among the men, Robert reorganized them into two teams. The experienced builders of the infantry would concentrate on assembling the siege towers. His cavalry men would protect the infantry with their shields. Robert noticed Scarlett's steadiness as he kept the cavalry troops in order under the hail of arrows.

Their progress assembling the towers was marked by shrieks of agony as men fell, pierced by missiles. Despite the savage losses, they continued doggedly until both siege towers were complete and then erected. The time had come to breach the wall.

"I'll lead the troops in the left tower," he said to Will Scarlett. "You'll lead in the other. We'll launch our ramps at the same time. Wait for my signal."

Will nodded and dashed toward the structure.

With arrows flying past him, Robert scrambled up the tower followed by his troops. At the top of the platform, the arrows were like a blizzard. Taking cover behind his shield, Robert looked toward Will's tower. The young officer met his eyes and nodded. He was ready.

Robert pulled the release lever on the plank. The hinged platform flipped out of the siege tower and onto the top of the wall.

"Follow me!" Robert called to his men. He then ran across the plank behind the cover of his shield and hurled himself at the defenders on the wall's rampart. The collision sent their bodies sprawling into a tangled pile. The soldiers on the plank behind Robert charged into the melee as well.

In the clash of bodies, some men fell off the rampart whilst the others wrestled on the narrow ledge. Locked in a fight at close quarters, the men stabbed, slashed, clawed, punched, bit and kicked each other in a brutal frenzy.

Amid the chaos, the viciousness was intimate. A defender bit Robert's forearm before Robert gouged the man's eye. Another clutched Robert's throat before Robert kicked him in the groin. The blood and entrails from the torn bodies covered friend and foe alike with a shared patina of violence.

As his men overwhelmed the defenders on that section of the wall, Robert untangled himself from the bloody brawl and recovered his sword.

"This way!" he yelled, leading his troops along the rampart toward the front of the castle. Whilst charging toward the defenders, an arrow ripped through his calf. Robert stumbled and went down, barely avoiding a fall from a rampart slick with blood. "Keep going!" he said waving the men on, unable to stand. The men flowed past him like a river as he crouched against the wall.

Breathing heavily, Robert watched his troops clash with the defenders along the rampart, slowly driving them back. Despite the pain, he managed a smile.

They'd breached the wall and would soon outnumber the defenders inside the castle. Before long, Richard's assault against the front gate would break through the castle's weakened defences. Although much bloodshed was still to follow, he knew the battle was over.

Robert cut a strip of fabric from the bottom of his tunic and wrapped his leg to stanch the bleeding. Then he leaned his head against the wall, giving in to exhaustion.

When the surgeons arrived, he accepted their aid. His work for the day was done.

At dusk, with his wounds being treated at their field hospital, the news finally reached Robert.

Amiens Castle was theirs.

* * *

A long parade of soldiers marched past Robert, raising their swords in salute.

Robert reached for his sword to acknowledge their tribute but found his scabbard empty. Looking up in confusion, he saw the faces of the soldiers no longer had features, just empty globes of flesh turned toward him.

Then a voice called out to him softly. "Field Marshal… Field Marshal…"

Robert opened his eyes, slowly waking from the dream.

Will Scarlett knelt before his hospital pallet. "I'm sorry to wake you, sir," he said, bowing his head. "His Highness has been looking for you. Are you well enough to ride?"

Though he longed for more sleep, Robert nodded. "Yes, I think so," he said, sitting up. He'd wanted to speak with Richard about Clement's death and there was no point in wasting time. Robert rose to his feet and took a few tentative steps. The pain from his heavily bandaged leg was tolerable.

After mounting their horses and riding for a while, Robert said, "I'm sorry for your loss, Will. It's a shame you couldn't attend Sir Clement's funeral."

"Thank you, sir," Will said, staring straight ahead. "But I shared no grief with anyone there."

After that, Robert rode in silence with the young officer. Will led him from the hospital through the torchlit gate of the vanquished castle. The scene inside was everything Robert had dreaded.

Under the moonlight, soldiers roamed among the houses inside the bailey, breaking down doors, hauling out plundered goods, arguing with each other over the spoils. Then Robert saw an infantryman pin a woman against a wall, tugging at her skirt.

"You, there!" he yelled at the soldier. "Release that woman!"

The soldier fled into the darkness as the woman retreated into a doorway.

"Do you know that man?" Robert asked Will.

"No, sir," Scarlett answered.

Robert sighed, knowing it was impossible to pursue him. "Will, you know our rules about women. If you see any other men assaulting women, stop them."

"Yes, sir," Scarlett nodded.

This lack of discipline only added to Robert's doubts about Richard. No matter the cause – or the rewards – he would not follow a leader who lacked integrity. Richard would need to explain himself about Clement's death.

Will dismounted at the castle's keep and gestured toward the large double doors. "His Highness and the officers are celebrating inside."

Robert carefully dismounted from his horse and walked gingerly toward the doors. A din of voices and the clatter of crockery drifted into the night. Pushing open the doors, he saw a large room with over a hundred men at a series of tables savouring a feast. Servants moved among them with trays of food, ale and wine.

As he walked slowly inside, every face turned toward him. The hall fell into silence.

Then a chant began, almost a murmur at first. "Webber. Webber. Webber." The volume rose. Men pounded the tables with their goblets as they yelled. "Webber! Webber! Webber!" As the chant grew louder, they stood and stomped their feet. "WEBBER! WEBBER! WEBBER!"

Hearing the field marshal's name, soldiers outside the hall in the bailey took up the chant. Soon, Robert's name reverberated throughout the castle. "WEBBER! WEBBER! WEBBER!"

The hair on Robert's neck rose with excitement. The sound was like a force he could lean against. His eyes watered from the power of the moment.

Finally, Richard stood and raised his palms. After the chant abated, the prince pointed to his field marshal and said, "My fellow warriors, let's raise our cups in tribute to Robert Webber, the hero of Amiens!"

The roar that followed was heard over a mile away where the now-homeless villagers of Amiens were camped for the night.

* * *

Robert awoke blinking at the midday sun streaming through the row of windows in the bedchamber.

The throbbing in his head matched the pain in his leg as he sat up in the bed.

Last night, almost every officer in the hall had wanted to share a drink with him – and Robert had obliged. At first, he'd told himself it was his duty to honour the men. But after several rounds of wine, he had to admit the hero worship was exhilarating. The price for that indulgence was now coming due in a skull-splitting headache and a tongue that felt like fur.

He barely remembered being led to this large bedchamber in the keep. From its size and rich furnishings, it must have been home to one of the handful of French nobles they now held as hostages. Their ransoms, John Little had explained last night, would help fund Richard's campaign in France. But…

Did he want to remain a part of that campaign? Last night's celebration had made it impossible to speak to Richard about his misgivings.

Robert rose to relieve his bladder. He'd need to make time today.

One of his aides appeared in the doorway. "Good to see you're finally awake, Field Marshal," he said with a bow. "I have your gear packed. His Highness ordered the army on the march as soon as possible."

"Where is the prince now?"

"His Highness and his entourage left this morning. Our orders are to march south on the road to Laval."

Robert rubbed his face. His confrontation with Richard would have to wait.

Later in the day, as their army moved toward Laval in a long column, Robert found himself riding alongside John Little and Gilbert Whitehand.

Traveling with his comrades was a comforting routine for Robert, born of many years together. During a break in their march, the three dismounted and stretched their legs under the shade of an oak, away from the others.

"Looks like the celebration last night took its toll on you, Rob," John said with a grin. "You look paler than a Scotsman's arse."

Gilbert wagged his finger at John with theatrical scorn. "Show some respect for your field marshal, you fecking ingrate."

"It's a fair bit of a hangover, no doubt about it," Rob said, rubbing his temples.

"If you don't mind my saying so, Rob," Gilbert said grinning. "You're good at abstaining with the ladies but not so much with the wine. Might do you better to flip those around, eh? A bit more time in the Happy Valley will take the edge off – without the hangover."

"Don't listen to him, Rob," John said. "Gil's idea of a female companion has four legs and bleats when she's satisfied – which isn't very often."

Robert laughed softly. Their joking about his chaste habits didn't bother him. In fact, he was proud of it. His vow to Marian was the only principle he'd not somehow compromised.

John pointed with his chin toward his new horse, a stout charger taken from a noble of Amiens. "Who would have thought the likes of us would wind up being grandees in the prince's army, eh Gil?"

"Belt up, John," Gilbert said smirking. "Don't go getting all full of yourself just 'cause you finally got a horse that won't wheeze under your oversized arse."

"Oh?" the big man said to Gilbert. "Like you'd be doing anything but poaching flea-bitten squirrels if we hadn't thrown our lot in with Rob and joined this army."

For a moment, Robert smiled – then his smile faded. "You two have done well in Richard's army," he said to his comrades. "It's a good life for both of you," he said, then looked away and added, "But I may be leaving the army and I want you to stay."

John's eyebrows rose. "With respect… Have you gone daft, Rob?"

Robert stared at his boots. He did not want to air his doubts about Richard's connection with Clement's death. Instead, he said, "The looting I saw last night troubles me."

"You can't get all dainty about what happens in a war, Rob," John said. "Those men followed you over the plank yesterday, didn't they? I doubt they would have done it without knowing there was something in it for them."

"Besides," Gilbert added. "If you leave, the looting will only get worse. You're the only command officer who gives a rat's arse about that."

John laid a large hand on Robert's shoulder. "After what you did yesterday, there's talk His Highness will make you a lord, Rob. You could do a lot more good for common folk like us if you was a noble than if you quit this army out of pride."

"I'll consider what you've said," Robert answered, relieved to see their column was moving again.

Whilst riding in silence with his companions, Robert mulled their words. What Gilbert said was true. He was the only senior officer who would try to curb the wantonness of their troops. Was justice for the death of one contemptible man worth putting countless innocent civilians at risk? When weighed against these consequences, indulging his honour began to feel like vanity.

And then there was Marian. They would have no future together without Richard's blessings.

That evening, after their army made camp, Richard called a meeting of his commanders. When the briefing was over, the prince asked Robert to stay.

"With all the celebrations last night, I never had a chance to ask, Rob. How were you treated by the Earl of Kent in Canterbury?"

Robert stared at the ground for a moment. The time had come to confront Richard about Clement's death. Instead, he met Richard's eyes and said, "The earl said your condolences were received in the same spirit they were given."

Richard laughed and shook his head. "The old coot hasn't changed. That's the slyest way I've ever been told to fuck myself."

Nones of September 1181

A gust of wind whipping off the sea brought the taste of salt to Robert's lips.

From the ship's swaying deck, he studied Dover's white cliffs. Richard's castle on the heights was nearly complete. The walls of the bailey and the three-storey keep jutted above the green meadows capping the steep chalk escarpments.

The channel crossing had been uneventful, the weather mostly fair. But for Robert, the journey back to England was a mix of relief and regret.

His three years in France had passed quickly. After their first victory at Amiens, the battles and sieges blurred into hazy memories of gore and glory. Their army had surged south into France, gaining mercenary recruits from the cities they conquered... Laval, Alençon, Angers, Seuil du Poitou and, finally, Taillebourg.

Their victorious siege of Taillebourg had earned Richard the name Lionheart – and brought an end to their campaign. King Philip of France had sued for peace. All the territory Richard had conquered would remain under English control.

Jubilant about Richard's string of victories, King Henry had put Richard back into the line of succession to the crown. Now, Robert would be joining Richard in London to serve as his military adviser in court.

The courier bearing the king's message that day had arrived with other news from London – a wedding announcement. The Lord Justiciar had promised his widowed daughter as a wife to the new Earl of Berkshire, a young man who'd just inherited the title after his father's death. For Robert, the news of Marian had been devastating.

Throughout their campaign in France, Marian had never been far from Robert's thoughts. His desire to avenge his father... his dreams of justice for common folk... even his honour... all these had faded in the meat grinder of war. The only hope he'd clung to had been returning to Marian.

Had she willingly accepted the betrothal? The thought haunted him. After years of keeping his vow of loyalty to her, the end of the war had brought him no peace.

The ship's timbers creaked as a large swell rose. Robert steadied himself against the rail.

He was tired of fighting. The thrill of battle was gone. Yet the life ahead of him in London seemed empty and flat. The thought of becoming a farmer, however, inspired him even less.

Robert heard footsteps behind him on the deck. Gilbert and John were joining him at the rail.

Whitehand shaded his eyes, looking toward a pair of fishermen in a small boat plying the waters. "That'll be John and me soon… working for a living again," he said with a sigh. "Those poor sods think they have it hard. They just don't know, do they?"

"Aye," John said nodding. "Spilling blood's a shite way to make a living. But it gave us a purse full of silver to buy a new life."

After making landfall, the pair planned to buy land in the only place they'd ever felt welcomed – Nottingham. Their decision consoled Robert about his move to London. Despite the considerable increase in his family's stipend from Richard, his mother would be fortunate to have John and Gil as neighbours. Time was taking its toll on his family. His mother's last letter, dictated to Friar Tuck, told of treating his grandfather's aching bones with a nine-herb charm.

For over six years, Robert, John and Gilbert had worked and fought together. Miraculously, all of them had survived. They'd sweated, bled and laughed as one. Yet, each man understood the hard truth of the life they'd chosen. Any moment together could be their last.

As the ship sailed into the harbour, they stood by each other in silence. Brothers could not have been closer. But there was nothing more to say except goodbye.

Ides of November 1181

"**M**ister Robert Webber!" the butler announced as Robert entered the anteroom to the dining hall at the Palace of Westminster. Scarcely a head turned in his direction – and that pleased Robert. He wanted to avoid attention at this banquet to celebrate Prince Richard's engagement. Robert had spent nearly a month's pay on a new black velvet tunic, leggings and curled-toe shoes that he hoped would blend in with the fashion of the other guests.

Over a hundred courtiers and nobles were milling in the large anteroom outside the dining hall where the noonday banquet would be served. Robert would have preferred storming a parapet than entering the room.

Near the centre of the vestibule was Richard. As Robert walked toward the prince, a familiar face intercepted him.

"Marshal," Will Scarlett said with a slight bow. "It's good to see you. I've heard you're now Prince Richard's military adviser in court. Congratulations."

"Thank you," Robert said with a smile. "But we're no longer on campaign, Will. Please call me Robert."

"Forgive me, ...Robert. Habits die hard after three years in the field."

"You'll get used to it soon enough. You didn't stay a green officer for long."

"I have you to thank for that. You gave me my first command when a lesser man would have resented me… for a number of reasons."

Robert cleared his throat, uncomfortable with the praise. "What brings you to London?"

"I've been managing the court affairs of my uncle, the Earl of Dorset," Will replied. "Sir Arnold is a great admirer of yours and asked to meet you. Could you spare a moment?"

Robert inclined his head politely. "Of course."

Will led him to a tall man of middle years with a mane of flowing grey hair. The earl was speaking to a pair of ladies, his gestures smooth and studied.

Will touched the earl's sleeve. "Uncle, I'd like to present Marshal Robert Webber."

"Ah, the hero of Amiens," the earl said, smiling broadly. "A pleasure to meet you, sir. I want to thank you for the kindness you showed my nephew."

"Rewarding good leadership is not a kindness, Sir Arnold," Robert answered. "Your nephew earned my confidence in him."

With a flourish of his wrist, the earl said, "How very gracious of you. Look here, Marshal. I know your time is in demand, but I want you to know that I am in your debt. If there is ever anything I can do for you, all you need do is ask."

Robert placed a palm over his chest. "Thank you, m'lord. It's been an honour to meet you," he said before walking toward the prince.

As Robert approached Richard, he noticed the prince was in an animated conversation with a younger man, shorter and stouter than the prince, but with the same colour hair. Robert waited for a lull in their conversation, then approached the prince. "Your Highness," he said with a bow.

"Welcome, Rob, I'm glad you're here," the prince replied with a smile. Richard then turned to his short companion. "Brother, I'd like to present my adviser, Robert Webber," he said, turning a palm toward Robert.

Robert bowed. "Your Highness," he said, realizing the stout fellow was Prince John, Richard's younger sibling.

His nose in the air, John inspected Robert like a newly bought stallion. "So, this is the genius behind your military conquests," he sniped to his brother.

"I'm happy to take credit for discovering Rob's many talents," Richard answered.

"Sire, you honour me beyond my merits," Robert said to the prince.

"Not at all, Rob," Richard said. "I'm also proud to call you a friend."

John sniffed. "Richard, you sound like a farm boy who's gotten too fond of the livestock," he said. "They serve a purpose, brother. But we needn't get too attached."

"That's very regal of you, John," Richard answered smiling. "Never let it be said you stooped to showing fondness for a subject."

Stymied by his brother, John spoke to Robert. "Tell me, Webber," he said. "Are you the one Richard paid to start calling him Lionheart? If so, congratulations. The name seems to have caught on with England's unwashed hordes."

Before Robert could answer, Richard said, "Save your wit for our chess game tonight, brother. You'll need it. Right now, Rob and I have matters to discuss. Please excuse us," he said and ushered Robert away.

When they'd reached a quiet corner of the vestibule, Richard said, "Don't let my brother trouble you. For a while, he expected to be king. Now that I'm first in line for the crown again, he's taken to bullying common folk to make himself feel powerful."

"That's unseemly for a prince, Sire," Robert said, surprised by Richard's restraint toward his brother's insults.

"I agree with you – and my father does as well. But John is being brazen because the king isn't here to scold him. Our father's taken ill." Richard then stepped closer to Robert and spoke in a low voice. "Look, Rob. I have several other people to meet right now. But I'd like to speak with you in my apartment after the banquet. Will you stay?"

"Of course, Sire."

"One other thing… say nothing about this visit to anyone. Understood?" Robert nodded in assent.

"Good. I'll send my valet to fetch you. In the meantime, there's some-one here I think you'll want to see," Richard said, gesturing toward a small alcove behind Robert.

Turning in that direction, Robert saw Marian seated alone on a bench.

Their eyes met and Robert left the prince without bowing. Walking toward Marian, a swirl of emotions coursed through him. By the time he reached her, the only thing he could manage to say seemed inane. "How long will you be in London?"

"I'm staying in the city with my father… until the wedding next month," Marian said, a catch in her voice. "Then I'll move to Berkshire."

Robert stared at his curled-toe shoes. "Berkshire's not far from London," he blurted, desperate for something to say.

"No, it's not far at all," she said, fingers fluttering at the sleeve of her gown. "How long have you been in London?"

"Not quite a fortnight," he answered. Robert then drew a deep breath and took her hands. "Look, Marian. I need to know… Is there any chance for us?"

Marian sighed. "I want us to be together, Robin – more than anything," she said, raising her eyes to meet his. "But I have no choice. The king be-lieves a marriage between the new Earl of Berkshire and the daughter of his justiciar will ensure the earl's loyalty. My father complied, of course."

Robert gently brought her hands to his chest. "You're the only woman I'll ever love, Marian."

"I love you too, Robin. But our lives aren't our own."

Robert released her hands. For a long moment, they faced each other in silence. Then the bells of the abbey pealed noon. Robert looked toward the entrance to the royal hall. The crowd in the vestibule was moving into the dining hall.

"Your father will be waiting," he said. "You should go."

Marian lowered her eyes and followed the crowd. At the door, she stopped and looked back at him, then went inside.

Like someone sleepwalking, Robert entered the large room and was led to his assigned place at a table separate from Marian.

The dining hall was draped with colourful banners – red cloth with England's royal crest and blue cloth with the crest of Navarre, the kingdom of Richard's bride-to-be. Robert barely noticed them.

Rows of tables with benches were laid out for the guests. Facing these rows at the end of the hall was the table of the royal family on a dais. Richard and his fiancé, Berengaria of Navarre, sat at the centre of the table. On either side were Prince John and Queen Elanor.

The banquet began with a series of toasts in honour of the couple – and the alliance their marriage would create. Robert raised his goblet along with the other guests and vacantly repeated the words.

The men at his table were aides to other nobles. Most knew each other and gossiped in low voices, ignoring Robert. He was happy to stay silent.

When the food was finally served, he ate very little. Nothing had any appeal – except for the wine. The servants kept his goblet full and Robert diligently emptied it. The musicians, jugglers, dancers and acrobats who performed throughout the meal failed to cheer Robert.

After a final round of toasts, the banquet ended. As Robert rose from his chair, a servant appeared at his side. "Please follow me, Mister Webber," he said demurely.

After the short walk to Richard's apartment in the palace, the valet led Robert into a spacious parlour. "Please make yourself comfortable. His Highness will join you as soon as he can," the valet said before leaving the room.

* * *

Robert stared at the violet glow of dusk through the arched windows of Richard's parlour as the bells of the abbey sounded vespers. For the last few hours he'd waited for the prince, listlessly perusing Richard's collection of scrolls, mostly histories on military campaigns to the Holy Land. The writings had failed to interest him. His thoughts kept returning to Marian.

The door hinge squealed. Robert turned and saw Richard's valet enter the room with a tray of fruit, meat, cheese and wine. The valet placed the supper on a small table, lit several candles and said, "His Highness will be here soon," before leaving.

Moments later, Richard entered the room and closed the door behind him.

"Please eat something, Robert," the prince said, waving toward the food. "You've been here for hours."

"You're very gracious, Sire. But I'm not hungry."

"Well, at least join me in a drink," Richard said, pouring wine into a pair of goblets and handing one to Robert.

"Thank you, Sire," Robert said, accepting the cup.

Richard took a draught of wine and dropped into a padded chair. "Sit down, Rob. We need to talk." After Robert took a seat beside him, the prince asked, "Has anyone seen you here besides my valet?"

"No, Sire."

"Good," Richard said. He then leaned close to Robert and lowered his voice. "Rob, from the day we met, I've known of your hunger to avenge Sir Ralph's murder," the prince said, swirling the wine in his cup. "The chance to end that famine has finally arrived."

"Sire, I'm not sure what you mean."

"You and I have an opportunity to fulfil our dreams, Rob. For a long time, you've wanted to see the king dead – and I've wanted to be king. Tonight, the time has come for both."

Robert stared into his cup. After nine years, the fervour to avenge his father had waned. "Even if I still wanted to see the king dead, how would that be possible? He's always heavily guarded."

"Come with me," Richard said, rising from the chair. The prince opened an interior door in the cabinet and led Robert into his bedchamber. In a soft voice, the prince said, "Behind this bookcase is a secret passageway into the king's bedchamber. My father had these passages built in all the royal apartments as an escape route from danger when I was a child. The only ones who know about them besides the king and me are my brother and my mother. My father had the workmen killed," Richard said, then led Robert back into the parlour.

"The king is ill and very weak," Richard continued. "His doctors examine him every hour on the hour as the abbey bell tolls. Otherwise, he's alone. If he was found dead between those visits without any outward signs of violence…"

"…the doctors would assume the illness caused his death," Robert said, completing Richard's thoughts. "But why do you need me, Sire?"

Richard stroked his beard. "Frankly, I'm not sure I can take my own father's life, Rob. But even so, my brother and mother would suspect me because I know about the secret passageway. But I plan to play chess with my brother tonight. If the king died whilst that happened, there would be little cause for suspicion. Once the deed is done, you'll leave the palace without seeing me again."

"I'm sorry, Sire. I can't do this," Robert said, shaking his head. Smothering a helpless old man was not an honourable act of vengeance.

The prince sighed and swallowed another draught of wine. "How many lives have you taken, Rob?"

"I've never kept count."

"Let me ask you something else," Richard said calmly. "Which is better… to take a life or to save one?"

"To save one. But why is this question important?"

"Because I can assure you that by taking one life, you'll be saving countless others," Richard said. "My father is a tyrant. We both know that. So long as he rules, innocent women and children will starve because of his cruel taxes. Men will die in pointless wars, leaving widows and orphans. But if you have the strength of will to act, you can stop that, Rob," he said. "Your desire for revenge nine years ago put you on the path to this moment," he said. "Yes, we'll both gain something by his death. But that does not make it wrong."

Robert found it hard to dismiss Richard's words. But there was a hole in his reasoning. "Why not just wait for the king to die?" he asked.

"He may recover. A chance like this may never come again, Rob. The circumstances are perfect. We must act tonight."

Robert looked out the window. Night had fallen and the city was dotted by candlelight. "What you say makes sense, Sire. There's more at stake here than my pride. But I'm not sure I can do this. My hunger for revenge is gone."

"There's more in the bargain for you than revenge, Rob," the prince said. "Remember that as king, I can make you a noble with a touch of my sword. Think of how much justice for common folk you could create with that kind of power."

"Sire, I've fought and bled to bring justice to others. Can't I be spared this burden? Haven't I sacrificed enough?"

"You're right, Rob. You've made many sacrifices – and those sacrifices should be rewarded. That's why I'll make you this promise… When I'm king, I'll make sure Marian is not forced to marry the Earl of Berkshire. She'll be free to marry whomever she pleases…. and I'm certain that will be you, my friend."

Robert closed his eyes and sighed, searching within for an answer.

Richard put a palm on Robert's shoulder. "You're my right hand, Robert Webber. I trust you with my life," the prince said after Robert's eyes opened. "Will you do this for your liege, for justice, and for yourself?"

Kalends of December 1181

The choir of monks began a sonorous chant as King Henry's coffin centered St. Peter's Abbey, borne by a half-dozen friars. Following the remains of the monarch in slow, measured steps were Queen Elanor and her sons, Richard and John.

The royal family passed through a corridor between hundreds of courtiers and high officials lining both sides of the church. Standing among them near the front of the abbey, Robert studied Richard's face as he walked by. His expression of stoic grief befitting a new king was convincing.

Robert had not spoken to Richard since the night of Henry's death, four days ago. As the new king, Richard had been immediately drawn into an eddy of state affairs with high officials of the court and delegates of other kingdoms.

The voices of the monks stopped as the coffin reached the altar, leaving a cavernous silence. After a moment, the archbishop spread his arms and began the funeral Mass.

As the familiar ceremony continued, Robert again reflected on a troubling question. Should he tell Richard the king had not died by his hand?

As he'd huddled in the dark passageway that night waiting for the church bell to toll, finding the will to act had been hard. In battle, taking a life was impulsive, a matter of survival. But this had been different.

The idea of killing the old man to be with Marian repulsed him. He pushed that callous thought aside.

He then plumbed his memories for an outrage that would stoke the fury to act. The sight of his father's mutilated body… women and children starving under Henry's unjust taxes… the king's petulance and cruelty… the things that had once driven him toward revenge, now failed to spur him on.

His mother's amulet – and the promises of honour he'd made to her – weighed like a millstone around his neck. Then, as the bell began to toll, a distant memory arose and the fire in his chest began to burn.

He remembered the bullies in Nottingham taunting Faye Rolfe.

Her look of anguish, their cruel mocking of her misfortune, these had been the thoughts that filled Robert's mind as he entered the king's bedchamber, prepared to kill Henry.

Instead, he found the lifeless body of a shrivelled old man on the bed.

Despite the risk of being discovered, Robert laughed.

God had taken the king's life – and spared him the dishonour.

The choir began to sing again as the archbishop raised the chalice to consecrate the bread and wine. After the congregation rose, the new king led the way to receive communion, his mother and brother behind him.

Robert looked above the altar to the statue of the crucified Jesus. Then he bowed his head in thanks, still astonished by God's perverse mercy.

Ides of March 1182

Windsor Castle's gatehouse came into view as Robert and his warrior escorts emerged from the forest. The day-long ride from London had been favoured with clear spring skies. Robert's future, however, remained cloudy.

For several agonizing days following Henry's funeral, Robert had waited at Chatham Manor to hear from the new king. To a man accustomed to swift action, the delay had been torture. Sensing Robert's brooding mood, his father's kin at the manor had avoided him.

Yesterday, a courier finally arrived with a letter from Richard. The tersely written document ordered Robert to leave for Windsor Castle the next morning and wait there for further instructions.

Riding nearer to the fortress, Robert saw the top of the keep peering above the walls, still catching the last rays of the afternoon sun. The rest of the castle was already in shadows.

At the gatehouse, Robert's party dismounted and he presented the king's letter to the Captain of the Guards.

"We've been expecting you, Mister Webber," the captain said. "Your men will be shown to their billets in the garrison by my sergeant. I'll take you to your apartment myself," he said leading Robert into the castle. "You'll be staying in the Upper Ward along with our other royal guest."

"Another guest? Who else is here?"

"I've been asked not to say, sir," the captain explained. "You'll see presently."

The answer came as Robert and the captain crested a slight rise, giving them a view of the Upper Ward's plaza. There, on a bench between two blossoming saplings, Marian sat waxing the string on her crossbow.

"The steward will serve supper in the drawing room shortly, sir," the captain said before walking away.

Marian looked up from her work and smiled.

Hurrying his steps at first, Robert finally broke into a run. As he reached the bench, she stood and they embraced.

Breathing heavily, he looked into her eyes and said, "What are you doing here?"

"Like you, I'm here on the orders of our sovereign," she answered, laughing softly. "Richard wanted this to be a surprise."

"I don't understand."

"Our new king struck a bargain. Richard agreed to keep my father as his Lord Justiciar if he annulled my betrothal to the Earl of Berkshire." Marian paused and met his gaze, her eyes welling. "I'm free, Robin."

A breeze surged, fluttering the sleeve of Robert's shirt. In that moment, he felt as if a fog over his senses had lifted. The evening sky glowed with a new splendour. The wind murmured through the young trees, carrying the scent of blossoms. He touched her face. "I've waited for you, Marian," he said, then kissed her tenderly.

The kiss grew more ardent and soon their hearts were pounding. Marian put her hand on his chest. "We're expected for supper," she said, her eyelids heavy with desire.

"I've no craving for food," Robert said softly. "Do you?"

She shook her head and smiled. "I'll let the steward know we'll be retiring early."

Kalends of June 1182

The blossoms of spring were now the full leaves of summer.

On a blanket spread over a grassy bank of the Thames, Marian and Robert lay across from each other, playing chess. As he waited for Marian to make her move, Robert gazed at the keep of Windsor Castle rising above the trees to the south.

The last three months had been the best days of his life.

Beside him, Marian was dressed in a simple tunic and leggings, a change from the elegant gowns she wore in London. In his eyes, the plain garb underscored her beauty.

For the first time, Robert had found a true companion. He'd discovered his attraction to Marian went beyond the sensual – although they'd explored many avenues of pleasure. Marian's ingenuity at avoiding conception had inspired them both.

The bond sparked by their lust had deepened as they strolled the castle grounds, boated on the river and spent evenings in their parlour, often playing chess. A surprise for Robert had been Marian's talent with the crossbow during their hunts in the countryside.

These times together had flourished with ideas. They shared their knowledge – and opinions – on court politics, history, authors, music, even the breeding of horses and dogs.

Yet, both steered clear of their private lives. Each had a history they were reluctant to divulge.

Robert's memories of his life before joining Marian at Windsor Castle now seemed like the tales of a stranger. Honour, vengeance, even justice – these ideas felt abstract and distant. After their time together, Robert wanted nothing more than to remain at Marian's side as her husband. Only one barrier now stood in that path. He needed the king to make him a lord.

Marrying a commoner would demean Marian and her family. And without an income from a baron's land, he would be forever dependent on his wife. Worse still, their children would be tainted with the same shame Robert had known all his life. Robert had faith Richard would keep his word about a barony. Only a loyal friend would have bargained for Marian's freedom – and arranged their time together here.

"Look," Robert said, pointing toward a pair of swans appearing around a bend in the river.

The stately birds were taking turns dipping their heads into the water and grooming themselves. Gradually, their bobbing became synchronized until they were facing each other, chest to chest. Staring into each other's eyes, the swans slowly raised and lowered their heads in unison, their necks forming the shape of a heart. The graceful ritual continued until the cob gently mounted the pen and completed their mating. The pair then resumed their grooming, swimming close to each other.

"They say swans mate for life," Marian said, putting down her chess piece and turning to face him.

"Then a pair of swans would make a fine crest for the Webber coat of arms."

"Do we really need to wait until you're a lord before we're married? The king has been generous in giving us this time together. But his promise of a barony may never happen."

Robert touched her cheek. "We need to be patient, my love," he said. "When I become your husband, it will be as an equal, not a commoner hoping to –"

Robert stopped as he noticed the castle's steward approaching on horseback.

"Pardon my interruption," the steward said, nodding to the couple in respect. "A courier from the king just arrived with messages for each of you," he said, holding out a pair of neatly folded parchment sheets bound with red wax bearing the royal seal.

Robert stood and took the documents. "Thank you, Mister Miller."

"You're welcome, sir," the steward said before riding away.

Robert held out the message addressed to Marian.

Marian shook her head. "I don't need to open it. I recognize the style," she said, lowering her eyes. "My father's scribes prepare all royal documents. We're being invited to Richard's coronation." Raising her gaze, she sighed and said, "Our time here is over."

"We both knew this day would come," Robert said gently, taking her hand. "But there's a bright side, my love. Being called back to London brings me one step closer to a lordship – and the day we can marry."

Nones of July 1182

As an official guest of the coronation, Robert was expected to arrive at St. Peter's Abbey at least an hour before the king made his entrance.

Walking into the church through a side door, Robert glanced toward the front of the abbey where the king would enter. Outside, men-at-arms in gleaming helmets lined both sides of the procession route, their pikes adorned with red banners bearing Richard's three golden lions. Behind the guards' stern countenances were thousands of eager faces, common folk anxious for a glimpse of the new king whose reign promised to bring peace, justice – and most of all – relief from King Henry's cruel taxes.

Robert had yet to meet with Richard in private since he'd become king. But it was clear the new monarch had not forgotten his former field marshal. Indeed, the king's attention had given Robert cause for embarrassment.

Ten days earlier, the butler at Chatham Manor had brought a visitor to the parlour of Robert's apartment. "This man is here on the king's orders, sir," the butler said, handing Robert a royal missive before leaving.

Robert read the brief message then studied the visitor. He was small and close to middle age with a neatly trimmed beard and simple but well-cut clothes.

"My name is Arthur Bland, sir," he said with a courteous bow. "As you've seen in the king's letter, His Highness has appointed me as your valet."

"I didn't ask for a valet, Mr. Bland," Robert answered, extending the document to Bland. "Please thank the king but tell him I respectfully decline."

Bland did not budge. "His Highness said you'd be reluctant to accept my services, sir," he said in a dry voice. "That's why he commanded me to be insistent – and make it clear His Highness is paying for my retainer."

"I see," Robert said, putting the letter on a table. "Apparently, the king feels I need to lose some rough edges before I appear at his coronation."

"That would not be my place to say, sir."

"That's a very diplomatic answer, Mr. Bland," Robert said, rubbing his chin. "Let me put this another way... Did the king say which of your services I needed most?"

"Your choice of attire was mentioned by His Highness."

Robert sighed. He knew better than to resist Richard's impulses. Besides, Robert was not confident in matters of fashion. "Well, then," he said. "Let's look through my wardrobe."

With Bland trailing him, Robert walked into his bedchamber and opened the armoire. "I suppose we should start with my hat," he said taking it down from a high shelf and handing it to the valet.

Bland examined the hat at arms' length, then handed it back to Robert. "This style of hat has adorned the heads of many a gentleman in court, sir," Bland said evenly. "To regretful effect, I'm afraid."

Robert tossed the hat onto the bed and retrieved the tunic he'd worn to Richard's engagement feast. "Is this suitable for the coronation, Mr. Bland? It came at a dear price."

Bland cleared his throat. "Court styles are like pears, sir. Once they've been plucked, they become overripe quite quickly."

"I presume my choice of footwear doesn't meet with your approval either," Robert said, showing Bland the curled-toed shoes in the bottom of the armoire.

"The work of that shoemaker is spoken of in terms of awe, sir," Bland said. "Then again, so is the plague."

Robert laughed and raised his hands in surrender. "Mister Bland, I am clay in your hands. Please mold me into a gentleman."

A week later, after visits to a chapelier, tailor and cordwainer recommended by Bland, Robert was pronounced ready for the coronation by his new valet. Robert had to admit, the plumed hat, embroidered tunic and knee-length boots he wore today gave him a confident air.

Entering the abbey, Robert walked to his assigned spot near the front of the nave. He'd been given a middle-status position along the ornate red carpet the king's procession would take through the church. To his surprise, Marian was among the courtiers gathering for the ceremony.

"You're not standing with the justiciar?" Robert asked, walking up to her. According to protocols, Marian should be near her father and other high dignitaries in the church's transept near the altar.

"I needed an excuse to see you," she said in a low voice after he was close to her. Marian drew him away from the others where they could speak privately.

Robert fought the urge to embrace her. They'd seen each other only once since their return from Windsor Castle – a Lammas Eve celebration at the justiciar's home with no chance for privacy. After spending several months together, he felt incomplete without her company.

"I'm glad you came. I've missed you," he said.

"I've missed you as well, my love," she said. "But there's news from court you need to know. The king plans a crusade to the Holy Land."

Robert's eyes widened with surprise. "Richard never mentioned a crusade."

"The crusade surprised my father as well."

Robert's voice turned bitter. "To raise an army, Richard will increase taxes and conscript men away from their families. Nothing will have changed from his father's reign," he said. "Who put this idea in the king's head?"

"The Archbishop of York. He's got his eye on becoming a cardinal. The pope would look favourably on any clergyman who'd deliver an army to fight under the banner of the Holy See."

Robert slowly shook his head. "If Richard asks me to lead his troops, I'll refuse," he said sternly. "I won't leave you again, Marian."

"I don't think the king will ask."

"Why not?" Robert asked, his pride wounded.

"The Archbishop of York is a bigot."

"I don't understand."

"When His Highness proposed you lead the army, the archbishop said some ugly things," Marian said lowering her eyes.

"What did he say?"

"What he said is not important, Robin."

"Marian, please tell me what he said."

Marian sighed. "The archbishop said the bastard sons of nobles sired with Saxon women invariably betray the highborn and should be set out at birth."

Robert's stomach tightened with anger. "I've been patient long enough," he said tersely. "I need to see—"

Marian touched his arm, cutting him short. "Listen…"

A roar of voices rose in the distance outside the church. The king's procession was approaching St. Peter's Abbey.

Like an ocean wave, the courtiers around Robert and Marian surged toward the edge of the red carpet. Every face in the church now turned toward the entrance.

The clamour of the crowd continued to rise as the king drew closer. Robert felt his pulse quicken as the noise became deafening. Soaring above the roar, the flourish of a dozen trumpets sounded as the procession entered the building.

The trumpets gave way to a hundred-voice choir as the monk at the head of the column bearing a large gold cross stepped onto the red carpet. Behind him followed a score of clergymen and an equal number of earls and great barons. Several of the nobles carried the regalia of the monarchy – the royal sceptres, ceremonial swords, ornate spurs and the crown itself.

The voices of the choir swelled to a crescendo when King Richard finally appeared. Flanked by six guards on each side, the bareheaded king was clad in a long red cape clasped by a chain of jewels and topped with ermine fur.

The entire procession moved at a slow, deliberate pace that allowed the courtiers to bask in the pageantry.

Robert felt his chest swell. The majestic music and ceremonial pomp touched a part of him he could not control. At that moment, Richard seemed more than an ordinary man. He was someone superior and worthy of veneration.

Robert's awe persisted during Richard's walk to the altar and the high mass that followed.

But the illusion was shattered during Richard's public oaths after the mass. Standing before the ornate golden throne, the new king swore to bring peace and honour to the kingdom, to show reverence towards God and the holy church, and administer fair justice to the people.

Robert knew full well Richard had already violated most of these promises.

The rest of the coronation seemed a haughty farce.

With a fanfare of trumpets, Richard ceremoniously sat on the throne for the first time. He was then given a sceptre tipped with a cross for his right hand and another with a dove for his left. The archbishop anointed his head with oil.

Finally, in a moment of absolute silence, the priest placed the crown on Richard's head.

When the king stood, the choir broke into song and a cheer erupted from the courtiers, reverberating from the stone walls of the church.

Robert watched in silence as Richard left St. Peter's Abbey amid a deafening ovation that followed him out of the building and was picked up by the crowds outside, eventually fading in the distance.

Marian leaned close to him. "Wasn't that a stirring ceremony?"

Robert took a deep breath, deciding how to answer her. He knew the coronation had been a glorious sham. But what was there to gain by speaking the truth? His happiness with Marian still depended on Richard's good will. "The pageantry was well performed," he finally said.

Nones of September 1182

Their footsteps echoing in the domed hallway, Robert followed Richard's valet toward the king's chancery. Robert noticed the entrance was at the end of a long, narrow passageway – an approach created for defence, he imagined.

The valet knocked on the arched door. Hearing the king's permission to enter, the valet opened the door and led Robert inside.

Both men bowed after entering the room. "Mister Webber, Your Highness," the valet announced.

Seated behind a heavy ornate table, Richard rose and dismissed the valet with a wave.

"I regret not having the time to see you sooner, Rob," the king said. "There's a reason my ministers are called the Privy Council. They hover around me from morning until night like flies around a dung pile."

"Evidently, being monarch is not as glamorous as I'd imagined, Your Highness," Robert said, smiling. Still, Robert was sure the king was lying about seeing him.

Before entering the hallway to the chancery, Richard's valet had escorted him through a large room filled with nobles and clergymen waiting to see the king. Why hadn't he been moved ahead of the other petitioners before today?

The king's lie made a difficult decision simple, however. He would not tell Richard his father was already dead on the night the prince had asked him to become an assassin.

Their score on withholding the truth was even.

"Please sit down, Rob," the king said, nodding to one of the chairs before him. From a pitcher on the table, Richard filled two goblets with ale. "It's good to see you again, my friend," he said, handing Robert a goblet.

"Thank you, Sire," Robert said, accepting the cup and taking a seat. "And thank you for freeing Marian from her betrothal – and our time at Windsor Castle."

"You deserved it. So did she," the king said, settling into his chair. "I hope you're finding Arthur Bland helpful."

"I like him. Bland doesn't fear speaking his mind."

"You both have that in common."

"Then you won't be surprised when I ask why you summoned me today."

"Never one to waste time, are you?" Richard said before taking a sip of ale. "I want to make you Marshal of the Royal Guards, Rob. You'll have command of the garrisons in my palaces across the realm. The justiciar tells me that's over four thousand men. You'll be paid handsomely, too. Your family's current stipend will double."

Robert bowed his head. "I'm honoured, Sire. As usual, you are exceedingly generous," he said. "Would the commission include a title?"

"Marian told me that's what you want most – and why," he said. "Now that I'm king, I can give you a knighthood. You'll earn the right to be called Sir Robert."

"Your Highness, I gratefully accept this honour. But with all respect, I want more than an empty title. I can't ask a woman like Marian to wed a man without land."

"Rob, there are no vacant baronies in the realm at the moment."

"What of Nottingham, Sire? I've been told the Earl of Devon who married my half-sister seldom visits the shire. He's an absentee lord who doesn't need the land."

"My support among the nobles is too unsteady to risk taking away any land – especially from an earl. My cousins in the Anjou line, Guy and Bernard Curtmantle, would pounce on that and gain another ally to strengthen their claim as heirs to the throne. The Curtmantles now have the Earl of Norfolk in league with them as well. Apparently, Sir Hugh hasn't forgiven either of us," Richard said. "But you have my word. You'll have your barony when the time is right. In the meantime, your commission with the Royal Guards will provide you with quarters at all my palaces. Marian can join you as a guest at any time."

"Your Highness," Robert said, staring into the bottom of his cup. "I want Marian to be my wife, not a camp follower."

"I'll be blunt, Rob. I need you to accept this commission," Richard said, then took another draught of ale. "As I'm sure you've heard from Marian, I'll be leading a crusade to the Holy Land. Whilst I'm gone, my brother John will rule as regent." Richard wiped his lips with the back of his hand. "You've met John. He's harsh and petty by nature. That's why I need you. As Marshal of the Royal Guards you can keep my brother's worst instincts in check. I'll make sure your command of those troops will be outside John's jurisdiction. He'll be a toothless wolf without direct control of the Royal Guards."

"There's another way to prevent John from becoming a poor regent, Sire."

"By all means. Please tell me."

"Don't go on this crusade."

Richard shook his head. "That's out of the question. Word has already been sent to His Holiness in Rome. It would be a humiliation to all of England if I changed my decision."

Robert swirled the ale in his cup, studying the golden liquid. He knew Richard was using half-truths to justify breaking his word. Would he dare call the king a hypocrite to his face? Before he could answer, Richard spoke again.

"I know what you're thinking, Rob," Richard said. "You helped me become king. Yet I'm committing the same sins as my father – fighting a war that will raise taxes and risk people's lives. But things aren't so simple when your own arse is on the throne. My cousins would like nothing better than an excuse to resurrect their claim to the crown. Not defending the faith with enough vigour would give them that excuse," he said. "The Archbishop of York has wide support for this crusade among the gentry. His Grace tells me I need a grand act of faith toward the church to keep the kingdom together."

Robert was not convinced. Richard had lusted after the glory of crusades his entire life. But what good would it serve to refuse the commission? The king would still launch the crusade, leaving the people of England under the regency of a despot. He could still serve the cause of honour – and keep his hopes for a barony alive. "I had to speak my mind, Sire," he said after a moment. "I didn't expect to change your decision."

"Your conscience is why I want you for this post, Rob. I need your integrity to keep my brother in line. There's no one else I trust to do this," Richard said, then drained the last of his ale. "At my first public proclamation, I'll announce the new crusade and name John as regent. I want to publicly appoint you Marshal of the Royal Guards as well." Richard rose to his feet. "Will you serve your king and country?" he asked.

As custom dictated, Robert stood and bowed. "I will, Your Highness," he said softly, eyes turned toward the floor.

Ides of December 1182

A light snow was falling, carried on a biting breeze. The cold, however, had not kept away the crowd gathered within the bailey of Westminster Palace.

Standing on the upper balcony of the palace's three-storey keep, Robert saw thousands of upturned faces waiting for the king to appear. They'd come on this feast of Candlemas to hear King Richard's first royal proclamation. Alongside Robert on the left side of the balcony were the ten men of the king's Privy Council. On the right were Prince John and the Archbishops of Canterbury and York along with another half-dozen clergymen. Both groups on the balcony cast sidelong glances toward each other across the gap between them where the king would appear.

Whilst they waited, Robert scanned the grandstand below, where the king's courtiers were gathered. Near the front, he spotted Marian's familiar blue velvet cloak. She met his gaze and smiled.

With a fanfare of trumpets, Richard finally emerged onto the balcony and the crowd broke into a cheer. Chin held high, the king calmly accepted the ovation, his gold crown glinting under the overcast sky. Clad in a flowing white robe topped with ermine, Richard stood in contrast to the men dressed in black around him. After a long moment, he raised a palm to silence the crowd.

"My loyal subjects," the king called out. "Above all other pursuits, our role on earth is to praise God's glory. As your king ordained by God, it is my duty to uphold our faith," he said. Richard then pointed toward the east with a stately flourish. "To our great shame, heathens control the Holy Land where our saviour gave his life to forgive our sins," he said. Richard unsheathed his sword and placed the hilt over his heart. "It is God's test of our devotion to drive the heathens out. As men of England, there can be no higher calling than to take back the Holy Land!" he said with growing ardour. "And as your king, I will lead a new crusade that will preserve a place in heaven for the faithful of England!" he shouted, thrusting his sword into the air.

The fanfare of trumpets rose again along with a full-throated roar from the crowd.

From the courtiers' grandstand, a chant began. "Long live the king! Long live the king! Long live the king!" The rest of the crowd joined in as Richard thrust his sword into the air in time with the chant. Soon, more than a thousand voices carried the incantation. "Long live the king!

Long live the king! Long live the king!"

Awed by the spectacle, Robert felt his breath quicken. Despite his knowledge of Richard's duplicity, Robert still found the moment stirring.

Before the chant could fade, Richard sheathed his sword and raised his hands to calm the crowd. "This benevolent crusade has the blessings of our archbishops and the clergy," Richard said, gesturing to his right. The archbishops made the sign of the cross towards the crowd who joined in the ritual.

Richard then extended his arm toward Prince John. "In my absence, my brother John will act as regent here in England."

As cheers arose, Prince John grandly twirled his palm to the crowd, accepting their ovation with a gratified smirk.

As the cheers faded, Richard spoke again. "And to keep order and protect our kingdom, I appoint as Marshal of the Royal Guards the hero of Amiens… Sir Robert Webber."

As Richard gestured toward him, Robert was surprised to hear the volume of the cheers eclipse those heard for John. Glancing toward the king's brother, Robert saw John's face redden with anger.

Robert sighed. His new commission was only moments old. But the acrimony with John had already begun.

* * *

"Are you sure I'm expected to wear different clothes, Mister Bland?" Robert asked his valet. "I'd prefer to set an example of reason and thrift."

"Ostentation is the coin of the realm in court, sir," Bland answered, picking specs of lint from the shoulder of Robert's lavish new robe. "As a high officer, you're expected to be extravagant."

Robert scowled. Just two hours ago, at the proclamation of Richard's crusade, he'd worn an expensive black tunic with matching cape, hat and trousers. Now, for the farewell feast in the palace's dining hall, Bland had chosen a diagonally stitched scarlet robe with a matching hat and striped leggings. "All this waste over pomp seems absurd," he said.

"Rest assured, sir. Prince John will notice your attire. If he sees you wearing the same clothes at the proclamation and the feast, he'll mock you as a churl – especially after his humiliation today."

Robert shook his head. "I still don't understand the crowd's reaction. Outside of my comrades, I'm not well known – and I'm pleased with that."

"The reaction did not surprise me, sir," Bland replied. "Your name is known far wider than you think. Nonetheless, someone has taken measures of late to burnish your public reputation."

"I don't understand, Mister Bland. What measures?"

"Your deeds at the battles of Thetford, Braintree and Amiens have been a source of court gossip for weeks, sir."

"Where did these stories come from?"

Bland smiled slyly. "His Highness does not leave much to chance, sir."

"Mister Bland," Robert said, turning to face his valet. "I'm starting to believe the king may have sent you to do more than advise me on fashion."

"I would never presume to counsel you on such important matters, sir," Bland said with a courteous bow. "But if you were to ask me about any members of the court, I think His Highness would be pleased if I share what I know."

Robert rubbed his chin, considering this opportunity. "What can you tell me about Prince John?" he said after a moment.

"Prince John is very shrewd, sir. But he's also predictable. The prince assumes everyone is as ruthless as he is. That can be a weakness."

"And the Archbishop of York?"

"His Grace is of the Benedictine order, which means he's quite learned. But the archbishop is also fond of luxury and wealth. His well-known disdain for common folk comes from a bloodline His Grace considers equal to that of a king."

"Anything I should know about Queen Elanor?"

"The queen mother is a devoted parent who never fails to extol the virtues of her sons," Bland said. "In John's case, she's forced to work much harder to find them."

Robert laughed. "Thank you, Mister Bland. I trust your counsel will serve me well tonight," he said, then looked out the window toward the setting sun. "I should leave now."

"I would advise waiting, sir. As a high official, you're expected to make an entrance after most of the courtiers have arrived."

Robert sighed. "This posturing is tedious."

"Perhaps a brief tour of your new accommodations would make good use of the time?"

As dictated by custom, Robert had not moved into the marshal's quarters at the palace before his official appointment earlier in the day. "An excellent idea, Mister Bland. Please lead the way."

For the next half-hour, Bland led Robert through the rest of the marshal's suite at the Palace of Westminster. Located in the circular keep at the centre of the fortress, his quarters included a half-dozen richly decorated rooms with large windows. From these casements, the commandant could see every corner of the palace and respond quickly to its defence. Despite his qualms about extravagance, Robert could not help feeling a surge of pride.

The bells of St. Peter's sounded a quarter past the hour as they completed the tour.

"Most of the courtiers will be in the dining hall by now, sir," Bland said. "This would be a good time for you to leave for the feast."

Exiting his quarters in the keep, Robert passed through the palace gate where a squad of Royal Guards in red tunics bowed to their commander. Crossing a large courtyard, he paused at the anteroom to the dining hall. The footmen bowed and opened the tall double doors. Taking a deep breath to compose himself, Robert stepped inside.

"Sir Robert Webber, Marshal of the Royal Guards!" the bailiff announced as he entered the hall.

Every face in the cavernous room turned in his direction. Several courtiers bowed as he passed. Suddenly warm, Robert tugged at the collar of his robe.

A servant carrying a tray appeared. "Would you care for some wine, Marshal?"

"Thank you," Robert said, taking a goblet from the tray. Whilst sipping the wine, he saw Marian approaching.

"Congratulations, Marshal," she said smiling. "Your new commission is well deserved – and your entrance most well timed."

"I beg your pardon?" Robert said, eyebrows arched.

Marian leaned close and whispered in his ear. "Look behind me. John is furious that you upstaged him again by arriving later than he did."

Robert glanced toward the prince. John's face was furrowed in a scowl. "Marian, I didn't mean to embarrass him," he answered softly. "I thought that—"

"His Majesty, The King!" the bailiff suddenly bellowed.

Along with everyone in the hall, Robert bowed as Richard strode through the doors.

With all eyes glued on him, the king moved through the crowd. He nodded graciously to a few of the courtiers, granting them a prize that would elevate their standing in court. When he reached Robert, the king stopped.

"Are the quarters at the palace to your liking, Marshal?" Richard asked.

"The accommodations are as gracious as their benefactor, Your Highness," Robert answered.

Richard laughed and every courtier within earshot joined in. "Your tongue is growing gilded, Marshal," he said smiling. "You're taking to court like a fledgling hawk to hunting." Richard then put his hand on Robert's shoulder. "Come, we have a few matters to discuss before we sit down to eat," he said, leading Robert toward an alcove. "Have you seen John?" Richard asked as they walked.

"He's over there, Sire," Robert said, pointing with his chin.

Richard met his brother's gaze and signalled for John to join them with a quick curling of his fingers.

His scowl unchanged, John walked toward them. "To what do I owe this honour, Your Highness?" the prince said with exaggerated deference after reaching them.

Richard waved both men into the alcove where they could speak alone. "The preparations for my crusade are nearly complete. I'm ready to leave except for one thing… I need to make it clear how the two of you will govern in my absence," he said calmly. "John, this is no time to mince words. The regency is yours by dint of blood, but by temperament, you're unfit to rule. I've made Robert nearly your equal because his integrity will keep your impulses under control. You may not agree, brother. But I'm doing you a favour."

John stared sullenly at Richard. "And if you die in battle?"

"Pray that never happens, John," Richard said. "But if it does, I hope you'll have the sense to make Robert your Justiciar. Because without him, your reign as king will be very short."

Kalends of September 1183

From the ramparts of the gatehouse at Duffield Castle, the Earl of Derby studied the enemy troops setting up camp in the stubble of freshly reaped wheat fields. Beyond the range of his archers, over three-hundred Royal Guards were preparing for a siege. The red-clad soldiers swarmed over the campground, raising tents, erecting barricades, and building animal pens, supply sheds and latrines.

Despite the ominous preparations, the earl was calm. He was certain the Guards' siege would fail.

Anticipating the arrival of the king's troops, the earl had made preparations of his own. He'd commandeered most of his peasants' fall harvest and livestock. With these provisions now inside Duffield Castle, the earl's troops had enough food for the winter. The Royal Guards, more than 100 miles from their garrison at the king's palace at Oxford, did not.

Although his troops were outnumbered, the Earl of Derby did not fear a direct assault. With high, stout walls built on a rocky bluff, Duffield Castle could repel a force three times the size of the Royal Guard contingent deploying outside the fortress.

Besides, the earl knew the commander of the Royal Guards preparing for the siege. Constable Percival Nash was rigid and cautious, with little stomach for bold action.

Satisfied conditions were well in hand, the earl descended from the ramparts and walked toward his chambers for a noonday meal. Near the door of his keep, a priest approached the nobleman.

"M'lord, I beg you reconsider this battle with the Regent," the town's abbot said, "Word is spreading across the realm of your letter to Prince John refusing to pay his scutage. When other noblemen learn of your righteous protest, they'll raise their voices as well. It's not too late to negotiate, m'lord. Don't let this come to bloodshed."

The earl shook his head. "I'm sorry, father. But before Richard left on his crusade, the king assured us the royal shield money would not be raised," he said sternly. "Prince John has reneged on his brother's promise and doubled the scutage on every earl and baron. This shameless treachery insults my honour and I will not abide it," he said before entering his keep.

* * *

Guiding their mounts through the harvested fields surrounding Duffield Castle, a pair of horsemen approached the rear of the Royal

Guard camp, speaking as they rode.

"The Regent wasted no time throwing you into a snake pit, Marshal," said Will Scarlett.

Robert smiled wryly. "I expected nothing less from John," he answered. "But the prince is right. The Earl of Derby's act of rebellion could spread to other nobles if he isn't brought back into line."

Will nodded in agreement. "The anger among earls and barons runs deep. My uncle says the doubling of the scutage is a pain no other monarch has ever inflicted on his nobles."

"Leave it to John to set a watermark for greed."

Approaching the camp, Will's horse caught the scent of feed and surged forward. Will tugged on the reins. "How will you bring the earl back into line, Marshal?"

Robert shrugged. "That remains to be seen. Constable Nash knows the Earl of Derby. His knowledge could be useful."

After entering the Royal Guard camp, the pair dismounted at the constable's tent. The commander's sentries bowed to the two men and waved them inside.

"Marshal!" Constable Nash called out as Robert and Will entered the tent. "I was not expecting you. I'll arrange for your quarters immediately."

"That can wait, Mister Nash," Robert said. "We have more urgent matters to attend."

Over the next hour, Robert questioned Nash about the Earl of Derby. Their adversary, Robert learned, was impulsive and vain. The earl's brash letter to Prince John refusing to pay the scutage confirmed this. The earl was also ruthless. To feed his troops inside the castle, the earl had commandeered his peasants' harvest. Many of Derby's peasants would be left to starve outside the fortress during the coming winter.

"We don't have enough men to storm the castle," Nash concluded. "We'll need to ask the regent for more provisions to support our siege."

Robert placed a hand on the constable's shoulder and said, "A siege over the winter here will fail, Mister Nash. The earl holds the advantage."

"We could come back again in the spring," the constable offered.

"That would give the earl more time to increase his stores. No, this matter must be resolved now," Robert said. "Mister Nash, have your men ready for an assault at dawn."

Nash stiffened. "We'll lose many good men against those walls, Marshal."

"A man willing to sacrifice innocent lives to appease his pride rarely has the nerve to risk his own," Robert said.

* * *

The next morning, as the sun broke over the barren fields, two regiments of Royal Guards stood in battle order before Duffield Castle, their steel helmets reflecting the orange dawn. Behind them waited hundreds of archers and pioneers with ladders.

A military adjutant roused the Earl of Derby from his bed. "The Royal Guards are deploying for an assault, m'lord," he said nervously.

"Order all our men-at-arms to the ramparts immediately," the earl said. He then dressed hastily and rushed to his command post above the gatehouse. Looking at the troops arrayed before his castle, the earl's confidence began to waver. Had Percival Nash lost his mind, he wondered?

As the earl pondered his chances of repelling an assault, two riders emerged from the ranks of the king's soldiers under a flag of truce. Wearing helmets and chain maille, the pair rode slowly until they were just outside the castle gate, then stopped.

"Let them enter," the earl ordered before descending the rampart stairs to meet them.

The pair had dismounted and removed their helmets by the time the earl reached the emissaries.

"Good day, m'lord," the older soldier said, nodding politely. "I'm Robert Webber, Marshal of the Royal Guards."

The earl swallowed hard, his throat suddenly dry. Percival Nash no longer led the troops outside his castle. Before him now was the hero of Amiens, a warrior who had taken fortresses more formidable than his own. The earl's confidence vanished like a fog in a breeze.

"Marshal…" the earl said haltingly. "I didn't know you were in command here."

"The Regent has sent me to resolve this matter – by reason or force," Robert said plainly. "It's a fine day for a battle, m'lord. But I'm hoping we can come to a sensible resolution."

By evening, the Earl of Derby had signed an agreement to pay his scutage in instalments.

Ides of September 1183

Answering Prince John's summons, Robert found the regent alone in his chancery at Westminster Palace.

"You had no right to negotiate payments of the scutage," John said angrily, tossing the Earl of Derby's agreement on the floor. "You've set a terrible example for the other nobles."

Robert made no move to pick up the document. "Negotiating to pay the scutage is a better example for the lords than open defiance through force, Sire," he said. "You'll still get the earl's silver… without any loss of life."

"You've made me look weak, Webber," the regent said. "Next time, I'll send my own proxy."

"That is your prerogative, Sire. But keep in mind. Whoever you send will not be in command of the Royal Guards."

"Get out!" John screamed, spittle flying. "I've seen enough of you."

Robert bowed and left for his own quarters at the palace.

After six months as Marshal of the Royal Guards, Robert had no illusions about his role. He was not protecting the homeland. English soil had not been threatened by a foreign power in living memory. No, the Royal Guards were a blunt tool used by kings to suppress usurpers and enforce the collection of taxes and scutage on the realm's nobility.

But with John as regent, the marshal's role had changed. Robert's primary mission was to control the prince's greed, decadence and cruelty.

The task was dispiriting. The only consolation was knowing this post was a path to a barony and his marriage to Marian.

Arriving at his quarters, Robert found Will Scarlett waiting in the parlour. "Marshal, I have troubling news from a friend at the Exchequer," he said, rising to his feet.

Robert exhaled slowly. Troubling news was the last thing he wanted to hear, Still, Will's connections in court were among the many assets that made him a valuable adjutant. "What have you heard?"

"Prince John plans to increase the taxes on the families of the men conscripted for Richard's crusade."

"Are you sure?" Robert said in shock.

"My source tells me the prince sees this as an opportunity to confiscate new land from the families who can't pay."

Rubbing his face, Robert dropped into a chair. John's greed was disgraceful. He was exploiting the weakest of his subjects – the families of men who bled and died to serve the throne his fat arse sat upon. John would throw them off their land without any qualms, leaving them to starve. This injustice could not stand. But resisting the prince would be perilous.

Robert had no authority to overrule the regent's taxes. Whatever he did to stop John would be outside the law. Would he jeopardize his family's new life of comfort? Would he risk a barony – and the chance to wed Marian?

His fingers touched the amulet beneath his tunic. A fire in his belly that had nearly been extinguished began to smoulder again. Robert stood and said, "I can't allow this to happen."

"Will you send a message to King Richard?"

"Getting a message to him in the Holy Land could take months. Winter is almost here. The families of these men may be dead of hunger before we hear from the king."

"What's our plan then, Marshal?"

Robert put a hand on his adjutant's shoulder. "Will, you cannot be involved. I don't have the authority to stop John within the law."

"Prince John is a craven thief, Marshal. Whatever you do to stop him will be a just cause," Will said, then smiled. "And respectfully, sir. You do not have the authority to keep me from serving that cause."

"Thank you, Will. Your insubordination honours me."

His adjutant nodded. "What are your orders, Marshal?"

"We need men who can be trusted," Robert said, then walked to the table and picked up pen and parchment. "Arrange for a courier to Nottingham. I'll draft a letter inviting John Little and Gilbert Whitehand to join us in London."

Ides of October 1183

On a narrow trail through the New Forest, the High Sheriff of Hampshire was half-dozing in the saddle. Riding with him was his six-man security detachment – the lot of them slouching and jaded.

The night before, the sheriff and his men had binged with ale and wenches well past the witching hour in Portsmouth. They'd had good reason to celebrate.

Each man's share of their haul in taxes had been the best ever. Their pack mule's saddlebags were swollen with silver from the port city's shipping merchants.

Riding ahead of the sheriff on the forest trail, the security detail's sergeant was schooling a young recruit. "Let me tell you, boy. Old King Henry wrung the merchants hard for taxes in his day," the sergeant said to the young warrior on the horse alongside him. "But Prince John, God bless him… he puts the old man to shame."

"God save the Regent!" the sheriff called out, prompting a burst of laughter from the detail.

Rounding a bend in the narrow path, the sheriff's cheer was dampened by the sight ahead. A hay-laden cart with a broken wheel was blocking their path. The peasant who owned the cart must have unhitched his draft animal and gone for help, the sheriff reasoned.

"This looks suspicious, sheriff," the sergeant said over his shoulder. "There's no way around that cart," he said, pointing to the rocky bluffs on either side of the road.

The sheriff scoffed. "You sound like an old woman, sergeant. Do you think anyone would dare threaten a high sheriff on official business?" he said with disdain. "Have your men dismount and move the cart – and be quick about it. I want to be in Winchester before dark and sleep in my own bed."

Grumbling, the men got off their horses. As they approached the cart, a sharp whistle sounded from the woods. Suddenly, two men in black hoods emerged from under the straw of the cart, crossbows ready to launch. From the woods around them, two more masked men stepped out from behind trees, their crossbows trained on the tax collector.

"Tell your men to unbuckle their swords, sheriff," one of the bandits called out.

The sheriff swallowed hard. "Do as he says," he ordered his men.

Instead of removing his sword belt, the young recruit unsheathed his blade. A bolt through the neck sent him to the ground, gurgling in pain.

"Does anyone else care to be as foolish?" the bowman said, reloading his weapon.

A few minutes later, the sheriff and his men were blindfolded and bound firmly to the cart.

After the masked men mounted the sheriff's horses, one of them said, "We spared your lives so that you can tell Prince John his tyranny will be resisted."

Then, they galloped away with the party's horses and the pack mule laden with silver.

* * *

Once they were a fair distance from the sheriff and his men, Robert stopped and removed his hood.

John Little, Gilbert Whitehand and Will Scarlett did the same. The masks would create suspicion from anyone they might encounter.

"It's unfortunate we had to take a life," Robert said to his comrades. "But it was a clean kill, Gil."

"Aye," Gilbert answered. "I took no pleasure in it."

Astride the sheriff's horses, they rode to the spot in the forest where they'd left their own mounts. After switching steeds, they scattered the sheriff's horses and set off with the pack mule.

Whilst they rode deeper into the forest, Robert assessed the success of their mission.

The raid would have been impossible without Will's friend at the Exchequer. Knowing the sources and amounts due to every tax collector in the realm had led them to Hampshire's sheriff. His take from the export taxes on Portsmouth's merchants was substantial but not enough to merit a large escort. Recruiting John and Gilbert had been essential. In the future, however, they would need fatter targets – and more men to seize them.

As the sun began to set, the four men dismounted near a stream to make camp for the night.

John Little walked to the pack mule and hefted its saddlebags. "Should we count how much silver we got, Rob?" he asked smiling.

"Don't go getting greedy, you lug," Gilbert said. "That money's not for us."

"I'm not wanting any of the money," John protested. "It's a matter of pride. I want to know how much we took from that scoundrel of a regent."

Will Scarlett nodded toward the saddlebags. "According to the ledgers, there should be enough silver here to pay the taxes for at least two dozen families who would have forfeited their land."

"I'm still not sure how you plan to give the families the money," John said.

"We won't give the money to the families directly," Will explained. "My source at the Exchequer will mark their taxes as paid on the regent's tax scrolls."

"Why doesn't your source just mark their taxes as paid?" John asked. "We wouldn't need to risk our hides taking the silver from a sheriff."

"John's auditors at the Exchequer would notice a shortfall," Will replied.

John's eyes widened. "You're saying the silver we took today will still end up in John's coffers?"

Will nodded. "Yes. But it will be credited to the families of soldiers serving in Richard's army. That's the only way we can keep John from seizing their land."

"So, the families will never know what we've done for them?" Gilbert asked.

Robert shook his head. "No, they won't."

"That's mighty big of you, Rob," Gilbert said.

"All of us are doing something honourable here," Robert said. "But what we did today is just the start. Thousands of women and children will starve if we let Prince John have his way. We need to recruit more men and continue our raids in every shire in England."

Gilbert whistled softly. "That's a tall order, Rob."

"I know," Robert replied. "And it won't get any easier. The sheriff today was complacent. Once the prince hears about our raid, he'll send out more guards with his tax collectors – and they'll be more wary."

"We have an uphill fight, that's for sure," John said, then broke into a smile. "But when has that ever stopped the likes of us, eh?"

Nones of May 1184

The Regent's butler led Robert through a courtyard blooming in marigolds and phlox before entering Prince John's private dining hall at the palace.

"Sir Robert is here as you ordered, Your Highness," the butler said with a bow, then left the room.

Seated alone at a long table, the prince was devouring his noonday meal. Spread before the regent was a broad array of fare… a suckling pig, slices of venison, filets of salmon, an assortment of pastries, several wedges of cheese and a tall mound of fruit.

Robert stood silently before the table, waiting for the prince to speak.

Instead, John continued his assault on the food without looking up. After a long drink from a goblet of wine, he belched. "Do you have any idea how many of my tax collectors have been robbed in the last six months?" John finally said.

"According to the Constable of the Exchequer, over two dozen sheriffs have been accosted, Sire."

The regent picked at his teeth with a fingernail. "And how many of the robbers have been arrested?" he asked casually.

"None yet, Sire."

Suddenly, John slammed his fist against the table, sending food to the floor. "That is unacceptable!" he screamed. "You have over four thousand men under your command and the treasury has lost nearly that many pounds! You've failed to protect the wealth of the kingdom!"

"Providing security for tax collectors is not the responsibility of the Royal Guards, Sire. My men are—"

The regent cut him off. "Enough excuses, Webber!" he screamed. "I've written to my brother demanding you be dismissed. Once he learns how much your negligence has cost the treasury, I'm certain he'll agree. I suggest you enjoy your quarters in the palace… whilst you can," he said, waving him away with a leg from the piglet.

Robert left the prince's dining hall holding back a smile. The prince's tantrum was a tribute to the success of their raids.

Since the first raid in Hampshire six months ago, they'd recruited over a dozen loyal men and found more sheriffs ripe for the picking through Will's source at the Exchequer. Their operation had also spawned a surprising dividend. Emboldened by their raids, imitators in other shires had begun robbing local sheriffs as well.

Prince John's complaints to Richard did not trouble Robert. Infatuated with his war, Richard would ignore his brother. But Robert knew John was clever.

Before long, the regent would conclude only someone with inside knowledge of his tax ledgers was behind the raids. If their operation was exposed, they could no longer protect the families of the men serving in Richard's army. They'd need to rein in their efforts – for a while at least. In the long run, more lives would be saved, he concluded.

His mind made up, Robert walked to the palace's garrison and entered Will Scarlett's duty station. His adjutant was seated at a small table, quill in hand, drafting orders.

"Will, can you join me for a walk?" Robert asked.

"Of course, Marshal," Will replied, putting away his writing tools.

The pair walked in silence until Robert led them to a private spot on the rampart of the palace. "Your work on the raids has been excellent, Will," Robert said. "But we need to stop for a while. John has noticed how much our raids have cost him. If we keep this up, he'll figure out someone inside the Exchequer is involved."

"I'm disappointed to hear that, but I understand, Marshal," Will said soberly. "I'll inform my source."

* * *

The trio of young ladies playing cards smiled invitingly at Will Scarlett as he entered the parlour. "Won't you join us in a game, Will?" the eldest of the Fanning sisters asked.

"Regretfully, Margaret. I cannot," Will said, placing a hand on his chest. "I'm here to see your brother."

Margaret rolled her eyes. "You've become such a bore since you met Adam. Whatever do you two talk about so much?"

"Just as you said, Margaret. It's all very boring," Will answered with a smile.

"You're a hopeless tease, Will," she said. "Adam is in the library – with his nose stuck in a book, I'm sure," she said, then gestured toward the stairway at the rear of the parlour. "You know the way."

"Thank you," Will said with a courtly bow.

Climbing the stairs, Will recalled the first time he'd come to visit Adam Fanning. Will had met his sisters at court after his return from France. Only later did he learn they had a brother his own age who was a scribe at the Exchequer. After being introduced to Adam at their home, Will understood their reticence.

Beyond an angelic face, Adam Fanning was a troubling presence. He was small, frail and walked with a limp from a club foot. Adam spoke in fits and starts, averted his eyes, and rocked back and forth anxiously. Will's first conversation with Adam began awkwardly.

But when Will mentioned his personal interest in history, Adam surprised him by naming every Roman emperor and the number of years they'd reigned. As they continued to talk, Will discovered Adam's astounding knowledge on a wide range of topics. Near midnight, when Will finally took his leave, Adam invited him back – something his sisters later said Adam had never done before.

Will understood what it meant to be an outcast. In Adam, he'd found a companion who most others would have shunned. Along with Adam's intelligence, Will came to admire his unflinching frankness and compassion. Their transition to lovers happened effortlessly.

The door was open when Will reached the library. He entered the room and closed the door.

Sitting behind a stack of books, Adam looked up and said, "I have the latest list of sheriffs, Will. Do you want it now or would you rather have sex first?"

"Adam, you have a magnificent memory," Will answered with a smile. "But you never remember anything I've said about the art of conversation."

Adam covered his cheeks with his palms. "I'm sorry," he replied, then stood and bowed. "How are you today, Will?"

Will bowed in return. "I'm well, my friend, and you?"

"I'm pleased to see you," Adam said before producing a folded sheet from his tunic. "Here's the new list."

"Thank you," Will said, tucking the document into his vest. "This will be the last batch of sheriffs we'll need for a while."

"Why? There are nine hundred twenty-seven families of soldiers still left with taxes due."

"I know, Adam. But the prince is furious about the amount of money he's losing – and he's holding the Royal Guards responsible. If we continue to sack his sheriffs without finding a culprit, John will become suspicious and may uncover our arrangement. We need to stop our activities for a time."

Adam shook his head. "It would be wrong for us to abandon those families."

"That's true. But for now, we have no other choice."

Adam stared at the table for a moment. "There is a way I can clear the Royal Guards of suspicions from Prince John."

"How?" Will asked, taken aback.

"I can find sheriffs who are stealing from the prince. If the cheats are caught by the Royal Guards, John will not suspect you are also sacking his other sheriffs."

"How could you tell which sheriffs are stealing?"

"That is not hard, Will. Based on past prosecutions, I have seen a pattern. The sheriffs who have been caught stealing have three things in common. They have higher than average expenses. Their tax assessments are lower than average. And they reported an increase in partnerships within their shire."

Will's eyes widened. "Why haven't you told anyone at the Exchequer about this?"

"No one asked."

After rubbing his chin for a moment, Will said, "Do you remember which sheriff is our most likely suspect?"

"I remember everything I read, Will," Adam said flatly. "There are thirty-nine counties in the kingdom, each with its own sheriff. Nine sheriffs fit the profile of a tax cheat. The new Sheriff of Yorkshire fits the pattern more than any other tax collector this year. His name is Desmond Benning."

"Can you make a copy of Benning's tax collection report for me?"

"That should not be difficult," Adam answered. "I can have it for you tomorrow evening."

"Adam, I think you may have saved a lot of innocent people from starving," Will said, then cupped Adam's face and kissed him.

Kalends of July 1184

At an hour past midnight, Will Scarlett arrived at the deserted water-front of Scarborough harbour. A crescent moon shimmered on the bay's ink-black water.

After scanning the area to make sure he was alone, Will moved quickly toward his destination: the two-storey harbourmaster's station at the end of a long pier jutting into the bay.

Walking onto the dock, Will stepped gingerly on the creaky planks, staying close to the railing. Within twenty paces of the harbourmaster's station, he froze, eyes wide with alarm.

Two men near the end of the pier were walking toward him.

From the way the men moved, Will sensed he had not been spotted. But any sudden moves might give him away.

With no chance of retreat, Will slowly lowered his body over the edge of the pier until he was hanging by his fingertips above the water more than a man's height below. Falling into the harbour would be a death sentence. He could not swim.

As the men's footsteps on the planks grew louder, Will tried to silence his ragged breathing.

Would the men notice his fingers on the deck? Will could only pray for luck.

"Who's on duty after our shift?" a man's voice said from above.

"Simms and Proctor," the other man answered.

"You can bet your arse they'll be late," the first man said with a dry laugh.

Finally, the footsteps and voices faded. Will held still for a count of ten, then hoisted himself back onto the pier. The waterfront guards likely covered a lot of ground and would not return for a while. Shaken but determined to complete his mission, Will sprinted to the harbourmaster's station.

As he expected, the doors of the darkened building were locked. But after trying the windows, he found an unlatched shutter and scrambled inside. Lighting a candle with his fire-starter, Will walked through the empty station house until he discovered a cache of documents on the second floor.

His excitement growing, he riffled through the rolled parchments and then smiled as he found his prize.

Their search for evidence of corruption by the Sheriff of Yorkshire had struck gold.

* * *

"Good evening, sir," the marshal's valet said to Will Scarlett as he arrived at the commander's quarters in Scarborough Castle. "The marshal and his guests have been expecting you," Arthur Bland said, then led Will into the parlour.

Entering the room, Will saw the marshal, John Little and Gilbert Whitehand lounging in padded chairs.

"Welcome, Will," his commander said, rising to his feet. The marshal then addressed his valet. "That will be all for today, Mister Bland."

The valet nodded and left the room, closing the door behind him.

The marshal walked to a table with pitchers of wine and ale. "Help yourself, Will," he said, refilling his own goblet with wine. "We're eager to learn what you discovered last night."

Will smiled broadly as he reached into his tunic and handed his commander a scroll. "We've caught The Sheriff of York cheating the crown, sir," he said proudly. "There were more sacks of wool shipped by merchants from Scarborough harbour than Desmond Benning reported to the Exchequer last year. This document proves it."

The marshal studied the scroll. After a moment, he said, "Good work, Will."

"Thank you, sir," Will answered. "When do we arrest Benning?"

"We're not ready to detain him yet."

"Why not, sir?" Will asked. "We have documented proof the Sheriff of York is a cheat."

"The evidence we have isn't enough, Will," the marshal said, shaking his head. "Desmond Benning has powerful connections. Before the Archbishop of York nominated him for sheriff, Benning was steward of the archbishop's estate. The sheriff might claim the harbourmaster's ledger is a clerical error and the archbishop may exonerate him."

"For all we know, the archbishop may be crooked too," Gilbert said.

"All the more reason we're not ready to arrest Benning," the marshal said. "We need proof that the merchants on this document are bribing the sheriff before we can expose him."

John leaned forward and pointed toward the scroll. "Which of the merchants shipped the most wool last year?"

The marshal scanned the harbourmaster's ledger. "Rufus Grey," he answered.

"Let's find out more about Mister Rufus Grey," John said, stroking his beard. "I might have a way for us to lure a rat out of the barn."

In the hall outside the parlour, Arthur Bland pressed his ear against the door. He did not want to miss a word of what John had to say.

Nones of July 1184

John Little nodded toward the stately, two-storey home beside the large warehouse with a sign that read GREY GOODS. "I'm guessing Mister Rufus Grey lives close to the merchandise," he said to Gilbert Whitehand.

"A safe bet, that," Gilbert agreed. "But we best put on our play at the warehouse. Two dock workers looking to unload pinched goods wouldn't come calling at the big house, would they?"

John's face soured. "I never said we should go to the house," he answered as they walked toward the warehouse. "Stop trying to make me out as a dolt."

"Quit your whining," Gilbert said. "I'll be the one playing the fool today – although you look the part far more than I."

The pair ended their bickering as they passed through the wide double doors of the warehouse open to the street. Inside were sacks of wool and grain, barrels of wine and spices, tin ingots and other trade goods stacked on pallets in long rows. The mix of odours was both enticing and repulsive.

After asking a worker to see Rufus Grey, they were led to a loft overlooking the warehouse. Seated behind a large table covered in ledgers, Grey looked up, annoyed at being disturbed. "What's your business here?" the merchant asked.

John took off his hat. "My mate and I have a dozen sacks of wool for sale, sir."

"What's your price?" Grey asked.

"Six shillings for the lot, sir," John said.

Grey studied the pair. "Do you have a writ of possession?" he asked.

"Is that necessary?" John said.

Grey shook his head. "I suppose not."

"That's a relief!" Gilbert said, smiling broadly.

John elbowed Gilbert in the ribs. "Shut up, you clod," he muttered.

Grey smiled slyly. "I suspected this was the business of thieves," he said. "My price is three shillings for the lot. Take it or leave it."

John glared at Gilbert and exhaled slowly. "We'll take it," he said.

"You can bring the goods here tomorrow – after dark," Grey said, his gaze returning to the ledgers and waving them away with a flick of his fingers.

* * *

At the reins of a mule-drawn cart, John guided the heavily loaded vehicle slowly along the moonlit street toward the warehouse. "Do you see Grey?" he asked Gilbert, seated on the bench beside him.

"Only an oaf would think Grey's going to stand outside all night waiting for us," Gilbert said tartly as the cart reached the warehouse doors.

"Then get down and knock, you worthless bag o' bones."

A few moments later, one of the large warehouse doors opened slightly and Rufus Grey emerged. After glancing up and down the street, Grey opened the doors all the way and waved them into the dimly lit warehouse.

Once John had guided the cart inside, he stepped down and stood next to Gilbert whilst Grey closed the doors behind them. Moments later, three husky men wielding cargo hooks stepped out of the shadows.

"Get rid of these two," Grey said to his men.

As the men walked toward them, John little raised a palm. "Before you go doing anything rash, Mister Grey, you might want to count the sacks in the cart," he said calmly, pointing toward the tall load covered with a tarp. "Did you think we'd be simple enough to bring all the merchandise here?"

Grey signalled for his men to stop. "You're more clever than you look," he said, walking toward the back of the cart. "But what's to keep me from killing you both and taking what you've brought?"

"I'm betting you're shrewd enough not to leave any money on the table," John answered.

Reaching the rear of the cart, Grey lifted the tarp.

The merchant's mouth gaped as Robert and Will stepped out of the cart in Royal Guard uniform, swords drawn.

"Rufus Grey, you're under arrest for receiving stolen goods!" Robert announced, placing his blade under the merchant's chin.

Seeing their boss in the custody of Royal Guards, Grey's henchmen scattered.

"Let them go," Robert said to his men. "We need to take Mister Grey upstairs and review his ledgers."

* * *

In the loft above his warehouse, Rufus Grey sat with his shoulders slumped, staring at the accounting documents spread on the table before him.

Waving his hand over the scrolls, Robert said, "Mister Grey, you not only traffic in stolen goods, these documents prove you also bribed the Sheriff of Yorkshire to reduce your taxes."

"I didn't do that willingly," Grey said, eyes shifting from side to side. "The sheriff forced me."

"How?" Robert asked.

"He threatened to raise my taxes if I didn't go along with his scheme."

"Will you testify against the sheriff before the regent?"

Grey squirmed in his chair. "I can't do that. Desmond Benning has powerful friends."

Robert sat on the edge of the table. "Your business is making deals, Mister Grey. Here's a deal I'll offer you," he said, leaning toward the merchant. "If you testify before the regent that the sheriff coerced you into a bribe, I'll see that the charges against you are dropped for dealing in stolen goods – and attempted murder."

John laughed. "I'm hoping you won't testify, Grey," he said from the doorway. "Seeing you thrown into a dungeon will be a fine sight."

"Aye, you greedy crook," Gilbert added.

"How do I know you'll keep your word if I testify?" Grey asked.

"We're after bigger fish than you, Mister Grey. And a good fisherman doesn't eat his bait," Robert said. "We want to expose the sheriff's corruption. Without charging you with theft and murder, your testimony against Desmond Benning will be more credible. But if you refuse to testify, then we'll bring all the charges against you." Robert shrugged and then said, "The choice is yours. We'll win either way."

Grey rubbed at the sweat forming on his brow. "What do you need me to do?" he said.

"We'll start with a signed statement," Robert said, sliding a pen and parchment toward the merchant. "Then you'll tell us everything you know about Desmond Benning."

* * *

The Sheriff of Yorkshire rose from the bed and hastily began to dress.

Throwing off the bed covers, his mistress sat up and tugged at his shirt. "I'm sick of this, Desmond," she said angrily. "Since you became sheriff, you just dip your wick and then scurry off like a cur."

"I've got matters that need my attention, Alice," Desmond Benning answered, pulling on one of his boots.

"In the middle of the night? That's bound to be something crooked."

"You need to mind your place and show some respect, woman."

"You best show me some respect, Desmond. Otherwise, I'll let the Archbishop know you're not the choirboy he thinks you are – and maybe your wife as well." The pair had become lovers a half-dozen years earlier when both were employed by the Archbishop of York, Desmond as his steward and Alice as his housekeeper.

Desmond dropped his boot and gave her a hard look. "You wouldn't dare."

"Try me," she said, lifting her chin insolently.

Sitting down on the bed, Desmond softened his voice. "I'm sorry, Alice. You're right. I've been churlish. You've always been very dear to me."

"You'll need to prove it," Alice said, sensing she'd gained the upper hand. "You've been sheriff for over a year. It's about time you bought me some fine presents."

"Alice, being sheriff is an honorary position. The pay is not much more than I earned as the archbishop's steward." Like most sheriffs, Desmond had been nominated by a local lord – in Benning's case, the Archbishop of York.

"Don't play the fool with me, Desmond Benning," she scoffed. "Merchants all over Yorkshire have been slipping you purses full of silver to shave their taxes."

"That's a malicious rumour," he said indignantly, rising to his feet.

"Rumour, eh?" Alice said standing to face him, flaunting her nakedness in defiance. "Rufus Grey's housekeeper tells me she's seen you come calling in the dead of night. What sort of business between a sheriff and a merchant takes place at such an hour?"

Desmond took her hands and kissed them. "My dear, Alice," he purred. "I take your affection for granted sometimes. Please forgive me. I'll stay a while longer."

Alice smiled slyly. "You can go, Desmond," she said, guiding him toward the door. "But the next time you're here, I expect a pearl necklace as penance."

Outside the room, whilst walking along the inn's dimly lit hallway, the sheriff was startled by four men who emerged from the stairwell, blocking his path. They were dressed in the red uniforms of the Royal Guards.

"Desmond Benning, you'll come with us," the leader of the Guards said.

* * *

The dim light of dawn crept into the stone cell through a small barred window.

Desmond Benning rose and began pacing. For hours, he'd huddled in the dark, brooding on his fate in the brig of the Royal Guards' garrison. Despite the arrival of morning, the sheriff saw no cause for hope.

The Royal Guards had not explained why he'd been detained last night. But Desmond was sure someone close had betrayed him. Not many people knew about his trysts with Alice, a time when he'd be without his usual security escort. Most worrisome of all, anyone that close could implicate him in deeds that would send him to prison – or even the gallows.

Desmond had never imagined being caught. The merchants whose bribes he'd taken had just as much to lose. Now, he cursed himself for his greed – and his carelessness.

The rattling of a key unlocking the heavy wooden door interrupted Desmond's anxious thoughts.

The youngest of the Royal Guards who'd detained him entered the cell. "Here's your breakfast," he said sternly as another Guard handed him a mug of water and a torn loaf of bread.

Taking the food and drink, Desmond addressed the younger Guard who seemed to be in charge. "I'm a representative of the crown! Why am I being held here?" he demanded, hoping to intimidate the junior officer.

The young guard glared at him for a moment. Then slapped the mug from his hands, sending it clattering to the floor. "I've told you several times, Benning," he said through gritted teeth. "You'll know soon enough."

Fearing a beating, Desmond backed away from the angry soldier.

Whilst Desmond cowered in the corner, the oldest of the Guards entered the cell. "I want to speak to the prisoner alone," he said. By his tone and manner, Desmond guessed he was in command.

After the two were alone, the commander said, "Please forgive my adjutant, Sheriff. Like a lot of young officers, he can be overzealous."

Desmond nodded, but said nothing, afraid of angering the Guard leader.

"Sheriff, my name is Robert Webber."

Desmond's eyes widened. "The hero of Amiens?"

"I've been called that, yes."

Desmond bowed in deference to his captor. "Sir Robert, I regret we meet under these circumstances," he said meekly. From what Desmond knew of Webber's reputation, this was not a man to trifle with.

"Mister Benning, you're in very deep trouble," Webber said sombrely. He then handed Desmond a sheet of parchment. "Read this," he said.

Looking at the signature, Desmond saw Rufus Grey's name. His anger rose as he read the merchant's testimony. "This isn't true," he said. "I never forced Grey to pay me."

"That doesn't matter, Sheriff. The shipping logs of the harbourmaster in Scarborough prove you lied about the number of wool sacks shipped by Rufus Grey. You've betrayed the trust of your office and cheated the crown. That's a very serious offense."

Desmond's head slumped. He was cornered. Then a gleam of hope rose in his mind. "Is there any kind of arrangement I can make with you as atonement?" he asked the soldier.

"As a matter of fact, there is."

Desmond's face brightened. "If we can dispense with these accusations, I'd be willing to compensate you handsomely – on a regular basis."

"You misunderstand me, Mister Benning," Webber said. "I don't want to be paid. I want you to sign a confession stating you bribed Rufus Grey, then return the money due the crown on Grey's taxes. In exchange, I'll see that all other charges against you are dropped."

"What other charges?"

A half-smile crossed Webber's face. "To begin with, you just attempted to bribe a member of the Royal Guards," he said. "But that isn't all. We know from comparing your reports to the Exchequer with the harbourmaster's logs that you've cheated on the taxes of other merchants in Yorkshire." Webber then looked Desmond in the eye. "However, if you confess to bribing Grey, we won't investigate your bribes to these other merchants – or seek to recover any additional money due the crown."

Desmond's eyebrows rose. Webber's offer would allow him to keep the bribes from the other merchants. He'd need that money to pay for lawyers and perhaps to grease some palms in court. Under the circumstances, he was getting off lightly, Desmond realized. "Sir Robert," he said softly. "I think we have a bargain."

Ides of August 1184

"His Royal Highness, the Regent!" the Sergeant-At-Arms called out as Prince John entered Westminster Hall.

The murmur of voices ceased throughout the cavernous room. Several hundred heads bowed in reverent silence.

His chin held high, John walked slowly to the centre of the dais. After a dramatic pause, he sat down upon the throne.

Arrayed to his right were the members of the Privy Council. On his left were various members of the clergy with the Archbishop of York standing closest to the regent.

John cast his gaze across the courtiers, savouring their deference. All eyes were lowered, even that of his nemesis Robert Webber. In the gilded dress uniform of the Royal Guards, Webber stood in the front row, flanked by three of his soldiers.

In his early days as regent, John had enjoyed holding court. But the pomp and ceremony had quickly grown tedious. Worse still, the lack of any real power to enforce his will made the grand spectacle especially galling.

But that was about to change. Today, he would end the stalemate his brother had imposed on him with Robert Webber.

"Before I hear from the court's petitioners," John said solemnly to those gathered in the great hall, "I have a royal proclamation.

"On this day, the crown of England bestows its blessing on the founding of a new order of the Holy Church… the Order of the Cross. The mission of this order will be to purge the heresy and paganism that is infecting our realm. Already, over one thousand men-at-arms have taken the vows of the order. These men of faith will bring piety along with law and order to the kingdom… where others have fallen short," he said, turning his gaze toward Webber. Then with a theatrical flourish, John made the sign of the cross. "May God bless their mission!" he called out.

A cheer rose from the courtiers, sparked by the shills John had planted among them. The regent smiled contentedly, his eyes once again returning to Webber. Surprisingly, the Marshal of the Royal Guards seemed calm. The insolent fool would soon enough grasp the weight of this proclamation, John told himself.

The Order of The Cross had been conceived by the Archbishop of York – but John had quickly seen the order's potential – a brilliant stroke that served two masters.

The archbishop could sate his appetite for rooting out heretics. Most importantly to John, the Order of The Cross gave him an armed force that would do his bidding. Robert Webber would no longer be the sole commander of troops in every shire of the realm. Real power was finally within John's grasp.

Whilst relishing his imminent triumph, John was startled when Webber spoke out.

"If it pleases Your Highness, I have good news regarding law and order in the kingdom," Webber said with a courteous bow.

John was leery. Still, he had no choice but to respond. "What news is so opportune as to disrupt the protocols of my court?"

"My men have recovered over six hundred pounds stolen from the treasury and have the culprit in custody, Sire."

Rubbing his beefy jowls, the regent said, "Recovering the crown's money is always welcome news. Thank you, Sir Robert," he said, nodding. "Now, let's begin the petitions."

Despite John's attempt to dismiss him, Webber spoke again. "Your Highness, this may not be the last of the thieves who remain at large. We believe there are others like him."

The regent glared at Robert. "Who is this culprit your men stumbled upon?"

"Desmond Benning, the Sheriff of Yorkshire, Your Highness."

A collective gasp filled the hall.

The regent stared slack jawed for a moment, then composed himself. "That's a bold accusation. Do you have proof?"

From the folds of his tunic, Webber produced several documents. "I have a signed confession from Benning for accepting a bribe to reduce the taxes of a merchant in Scarborough," he said, holding aloft one of the documents. Webber then raised another sheet of parchment into the air. "I also have that merchant's signed testimony stating he was coerced by the sheriff into this crime. In addition," he said, showing the men on the dais a third document, "I have a copy of the shipping ledger of the harbourmaster of Scarborough which confirms Benning falsified his tax reports to the Exchequer." Webber returned the documents to his tunic and said, "The sheriff and the money he's stolen are being held by my men in the palace garrison."

The regent's eyes darted to the Archbishop of York. The prelate's face was pale with fear. In a flash of cunning, John realized that Webber had given him the opportunity to remove a rival for control of the Order of The Cross – and a way to deflect any blame toward himself. "Your Grace," the regent said to the archbishop, "didn't you nominate this man as Sheriff of Yorkshire?"

"Well, yes… but I had no idea… he didn't seem…," the archbishop stammered.

The regent tilted his head and said, "Wasn't this man your steward before you nominated him as sheriff? Surely you should have known something about his character."

"Your Highness," the clergyman said, voice tinged with panic. "You have to believe me. I would have never knowingly nominated a thief to serve as your sheriff."

"Well, you must admit that, at the very least, this shows a gross error of judgment, Your Grace," the regent said.

The archbishop lowered his head. "I throw myself at your mercy, Sire," he said weakly.

Waving him away with a flip of the wrist, the regent said, "I suggest you excuse yourself until I've decided what to do about this matter," he said. As the archbishop retreated from the dais, the regent turned to Webber. "It's a shame you haven't been as diligent at stopping the brigands who have been robbing honest tax collectors."

"If I may remind Your Highness, in bringing one dishonest sheriff to justice the crown gained ten-fold in silver what it loses to a band of robbers accosting a single tax collector," Webber said without rancour. "It's a wise use of my men – especially as it's likely there are more dishonest sheriffs like Desmond Benning across the realm."

Frustrated by Webber's argument, the regent exhaled slowly and said, "Bring Desmond Benning and the money to my chambers after court. Now, step aside. There are petitioners here with permission to see their regent."

* * *

Robert raised a goblet of ale. "Let's eat, drink and be merry, men," he said to his comrades. "We won a battle today."

Will, John and Gilbert hoisted their cups. "Hear, hear!" they replied.

Gathered in the marshal's quarters at Westminster Palace, the four men were still in the dress uniforms they'd worn to court earlier in the day.

"You gave it to him good, Rob," Gilbert said, laughing. "John's mouth was gaping like a mackerel out of water when he heard the crook was the Sheriff of Yorkshire."

The others joined the laughter. Then, John Little stuck a sombre note. "Why couldn't we keep Benning's money, Rob?" he asked. "We could have saved more families from losing their land."

Gilbert nodded. "I agree with John."

"We need to think ahead," Robert answered. "Putting crooked sheriffs behind bars keeps John's suspicions away from us. We won't help many families if we all end up in jail."

Will drained the last of his ale and said, "My source at the Exchequer will soon give us the names of other sheriffs who are cheating. Benning won't be the last."

"Which is more important, Rob?" John asked. "Catching crooked sheriffs or sacking them in the countryside?"

"We now have a war on two fronts," Robert said to his men, "and we must win both."

Kalends of February 1185

Kneeling beside Robin under the covers, Marian increased the vigour of her strokes, moistening him with her lips. But despite the hoarseness of his breath, she could feel Robin's interest waning.

Emerging from the sheets, she stretched out by his side. "Do you need to rest for a moment, my love?" she said softly.

"I'm sorry, Marian," he said, looking into her eyes. "I'm not sure what's wrong."

"I think your idea of meeting again here at Windsor is lovely," Marian said, touching his cheek. "But you've seemed distracted since I arrived."

Robert turned to face the ceiling. "Our time here in Windsor before Richard's coronation were the best days of my life. I wanted that again for us. But it's useless. I've been a fool to think I could bring those moments back."

"The love between us hasn't changed, Robin," she said tenderly. "Something else is troubling you. What is it?"

Robert slowly shook his head. "I'd rather not speak of it."

She gently moved aside Robert's amulet and stroked his chest. "The more you try to ignore this burden, the bigger it will become."

"There's nothing you can do, Marian."

"You belittle me by hiding whatever is troubling you, my love. You need to air these worries. I'm strong enough to bear them. Talk to me, Robin."

Robert exhaled slowly and rubbed his temples. "When we exposed the Sheriff of York, I thought we might deter John's greed. But that was six months ago. Since then, we've failed to capture another corrupt tax collector," he said quietly. "John is still gaining power, Marian. He's throwing more families off their land than ever. I'm not sure if we can stop him."

"That surprises me. The talk at court is how often John's sheriffs are being robbed."

"That's true – but our impact on John's wealth is weakening. We've recruited men across the realm to sack John's tax collectors. But riders from the Order of The Cross are now escorting the richest targets. Our men are left with raids against the small fry who carry less silver."

"I thought the Order of The Cross was created to stamp out heresy?"

"The Order of The Cross still persecutes heretics," Robert said, his voice growing tight. "But since John took over their leadership from the archbishop, he's seizing the property of anyone arrested for heresy. It's increasing John's wealth every day."

"I didn't know," Marian said. "That's appalling."

Robert shrugged. "John is shameless, crass and greedy. But he's getting away with it by spreading money to his cronies."

"You were able to expose the Sheriff of Yorkshire. Why haven't you captured any other crooked tax collectors?"

"The source we've used to find the corrupt ones has failed us since then. We've wasted time following dead ends. My men are getting frustrated."

Marian propped herself on an elbow. "I may have a way to find tax collectors with corruption in mind," she said. "My father has records of everyone who has petitioned to buy land from the crown. That's usually a sign of someone who has come into money. I can give you the names of any sheriffs on that list."

Robert nodded, his mood brightening. "A list like that could be helpful."

"Take heart, my love. You'll prevail over John," she said. "When Richard returns, you'll have proof of his abuses of the throne. Eventually, you'll bring John to justice."

"I want more than justice. I want to marry you – and that will take a barony from Richard," he said. "I won't give up on that, Marian. I promise you."

"I'll hold you to that promise," she said, languidly stroking his loins.

Before long, his enthusiasm rose again.

Ides of April 1185

Riding into the treeless valley, Will Scarlett saw the Carlisle silver mine for the first time.

Ahead were nearly two-dozen cone-shaped buildings scattered like dunce caps across the landscape. He'd been told that inside each of the odd structures was the opening to a mineshaft.

Near the centre of the mineshafts was Will's destination: the fortified headquarters of the Carlisle silver mine. Protected by stout walls, the headquarters compound held the crushing house, smelter and the monastery of the religious order that owned the mine.

He'd travelled over 300 miles from London to expose what Will believed was a corrupt sheriff – and this silver mine held a key piece of evidence in the tax collector's prosecution.

According to a document he carried from Adam Fanning, the High Sheriff of Cumberland had collected taxes on nearly two-thousand pounds of silver smelted here in the last year. If the monastery's ledgers showed more silver had been mined, they would expose another swindler.

A great deal was at stake for Will in Carlisle. Since their initial success with the Sheriff of Yorkshire, they'd failed to find enough evidence to convict two other sheriffs identified by Adam. Those failures had been costly. Countless hours of surveillance and travel expenses had gone for naught. Not surprisingly, enthusiasm was waning for Adam's venture among his comrades.

Thanks to Lady Marian, however, the outlook of nabbing a crooked sheriff here seemed promising. The list she'd copied from her father showed the Sheriff of Cumberland had petitioned the justiciar to buy land from the crown. The same sheriff had also been among the nine originally identified by Adam's calculations.

Will hoped this formula would be vindicated as he approached the silver mine's headquarters. Buttoning the collar of his Royal Guards uniform, he rode up to the gate.

"Tell the abbot the Adjutant to the Marshal of the Royal Guards is here to inspect the security of the mine," he said to the pike-wielding workers acting as sentries at the entrance to the compound.

Will was quickly led to a vestibule of the monastery and asked to wait.

Settling into a plush chair, he reflected on the differences between this operation and the one in Yorkshire. To his relief, this mission lacked any subterfuge. The Royal Guards were tasked with protecting the crown's lands – which included all the mineral wealth of the kingdom. So Will's visit to the mine would be unquestioned. However, his relationship with the abbot who managed the mine was somewhat complicated.

Several decades before, one of Europe's richest veins of silver had been discovered on church land in Carlisle. Since then, the crown had shared half the profits of the silver mine with the local monastery and taxed them like ordinary merchants for managing the operation.

The sound of shuffling steps and laboured breathing from a corridor brought Will to his feet. A moment later, the abbot appeared in the vestibule.

"Good day, sir," the abbot said, a wide grin hoisting his pudgy cheeks. "I'm Father Gerome. And you are?"

"Will Scarlett, Father," he said with a nod. "I'm sure you're busy. My inspection of your facility won't take long."

"We're delighted you've come all the way from London to oversee our protection, Mister Scarlett," the priest said, leading them outside through a side door of the monastery. "We can't be too careful with so many brigands about these days."

Over the next hour, the portly priest led Will around the facility, huffing with exertion but remaining cheerful. Beginning with the vault where the smelted silver was stored, they inspected the assayers' stations, the crushing house, and the smelter. The inspection concluded with the compound's defensive posts and the men assigned to each one.

"As you can see," the priest said as they returned to the monastery, "we take the protection of the king's silver very seriously."

"Thank you, Father," Will said. "I'd like to inspect your chancery as well."

"That's highly unusual," the priest said, raising an eyebrow.

"It's a new policy, Father. I'm only following orders."

"Very well, then," the priest said pleasantly, leading him into the monastery.

Crossing a large courtyard, the pair entered the chancery where a bevy of monks were hunched over tables preparing documents.

"I'd like to see your records on the total weight of silver smelted here, Father," Will said.

For a moment, the abbot appeared startled. Then his smile returned. "I'm happy to show you that document, Mister Scarlett."

Unlocking a door within the chancery, the abbot led Will into a room whose walls were lined with niches containing rolled scrolls. "This is where we keep our records," he said. "But I'm surprised you want to see them."

"As you may have heard, Father, not all theft of the royal treasury is taking place by outsiders."

The abbot smiled and handed Will the document he'd requested. "I can assure you, Mister Scarlett. You'll find nothing of the sort here."

Unfurling the scroll, Will looked over the ledger and found the mine's silver production for the last year. The quantity of pounds exactly matched the number he'd memorized from Adam's tax report.

The High Sheriff of Cumberland was in the clear.

Masking his disappointment, Will handed the document back to the abbot. "Everything appears to be in order, Father."

"I'm glad to hear that, Mister Scarlett," the priest said brightly. "If that's all you need today, I'll fetch a brother to show you the way back to the gate."

"That won't be necessary, Father. I can find my own way out."

"Please, Mister Scarlett," the abbot said wih a smile. "I insist on showing you this courtesy."

As Will followed the monk toward the gate, his spirits sank.

They'd failed once again. Their last chance to bring another corrupt sheriff to justice was now almost certainly gone.

* * *

"You barely touched your food, sir," the innkeeper said, clearing away Will's plates. "Was something not to your liking?"

"No," Will said with a weak smile. "Seems I've lost my appetite."

Like most soldiers, Will had learned to eat whether he was hungry or not. It was a duty to keep up your strength to fight. But after today's setback at the silver mine, the urge to fight had left him.

"Will you be staying in Carlisle another night?" the innkeeper asked.

"Yes," Will answered. He was in no hurry to leave and break the bad news to his comrades. Besides, after more than a week of hard travel, he needed a respite. "Where's the nearest bathhouse?"

Following the innkeeper's directions, Will found the bathhouse next to a baker's shop not far away.

The bathhouse owner guided him into a steamy room where a half-dozen men sat soaking in a row of large wooden tubs. Some were in pairs whilst others sat alone. After removing his clothes and folding them neatly within reach, Will slipped into his own tub. As the warm water engulfed him, Will closed his eyes.

Today's failure would anger Adam, he was sure of that. The setback might even end their relationship. But what pained Will the most was having to tell the marshal he'd failed.

His liaison with Adam, and the other lovers Will had taken since Clement's death, were dalliances driven by lust. Robert Webber was the only one who truly held his heart.

His love for Robert had begun the first day Will set eyes on him. Until then, Will had never known a man like his commander – assured, free of artifice, exuding dignity and calm. The contrast to Clement was stark. This campaign had revealed his lover to be thin-skinned, petty and craven on the field of battle.

That's why Will had stopped Clement from carrying out his threats against Robert. Killing his lover had been necessary to preserve his commander's honour. Will had no regrets about the deed – or keeping his love for Robert a secret.

Will knew his bond with Robert would never be one of the flesh. That did not matter. He found exquisite pleasure simply obeying Robert's orders.

At the sound of footsteps near his tub, Will opened his eyes.

"May I join you, sir?" a tall, well-built man wrapped in a towel asked. Will had noticed him sitting alone before.

"You're very handsome," Will said in a low voice, making sure no one else could hear, "but I prefer to be alone."

The tall man bristled. "You mistake my intentions, sir," he said tersely. "I saw you inspecting the mine today. I work there and I want to speak with you."

"I apologize for the misunderstanding. Please sit down," Will said, making room in the tub.

"My name is Cedric, sir," the man said, getting into the water. "I'm an assayer at the mine and there are things about our operation the Royal Guards should know."

Intrigued but cautious, Will said, "What kind of things?"

"The workers at the mine are being cheated by the abbot," Cedric said in a hushed tone. "We're supposed to be paid a share of the mine's production of silver each year. But the abbot, he changes the ledgers to keep the silver production numbers low."

"How do you know that?"

"There are six of us assayers. Between us, we inspect the purity of every ingot of silver produced by the mine. Although we're forbidden from doing so, each of us kept a record of how much silver we inspected last year. Then we met in secret and added up our numbers. The abbot reported the mine produced just under two-thousand pounds of silver last year. That's a lie. The mine produced over five-hundred pounds more."

"Have you shown your proof to the sheriff?"

Cedric scoffed. "The abbot and the sheriff are in league in this dirty business."

Will's eyes widened. "Would you and the other assayers be willing to testify against the abbot and the sheriff?"

Cedric nodded. "We've been waiting for that chance a very long time, sir."

Will felt his heart thumping hard in his chest. By an act of fate, they'd nabbed another pair of scoundrels.

Nones of November 1185

The chaos in Brugie was the same every autumn.

The town's only bridge over the River Parrett was choked with peasants swarming into the shire's largest port to trade the surplus of their harvests for goods imported by Brugie's merchants.

People on foot, horses and carts moved in both directions, jostling over the wooden bridge spanning about fifty paces over the river. Adding to the congestion, a bevy of roadside peddlers lined the road on both sides of the bridge, feasting on the traffic.

Wearing a monk's robe, John Little stood on the east side of the bridge near a vendor hawking chestnuts roasted on a fire pit. Shielding his eyes from the low November sun, John scanned the crowded street leading to the bridge. Their quarry was approaching.

Led by six men-at-arms on horseback, a one-mule cart with a tarp-covered load trundled down the cobbled road. Behind the cart were another six heavily armed riders. All twelve of the security escorts wore the white sash of the Order of the Cross.

Thanks to Will Scarlett's source at the Exchequer, John knew that under the cart's tarp was a locked chest. Inside the chest were the taxes collected by the Sheriff of Somersetshire from Brugie's merchants – over three-hundred pounds in sterling silver coins.

As the convoy neared the bridge, John raised the hood on his robe – his signal to Gilbert Whitehand on the west side of the span.

"The show's about to start, lads," Gilbert said under his breath to the five men beside him. The men fanned out into two groups and melted into the traffic moving toward the bridge. Out of sight under their long cloaks, each man carried a crossbow and a quiver of bolts.

"Out of the way! Clear the bridge!" the escorts of the Order of The Cross shouted at the crowd. As the throng slowly parted for the convoy, John lifted a half-burning stick from the chestnut peddler's fire and walked unhurriedly toward the mouth of the bridge. There, he casually dropped the burning stick onto several bales of hay he'd positioned earlier.

The convoy was nearly halfway across the bridge when the smouldering hay ignited into flames. As John had planned, the prevailing wind carried the smoke toward the bridge.

"Fire!" John yelled as smoke engulfed the bridge. Panicked, the crowd on the bridge scattered, leaving the convoy isolated.

Hearing John's shout, six men in hoods emerged from below the east side of the bridge. Armed with crossbows, they fired at close range into the convoy's rear guard. Four of the six riders were felled with the first volley. The surviving guards wheeled their mounts toward the attackers and charged as the archers reloaded. Each guard managed to cut down a bowman with his sword. But the other archers, their crossbows reloaded, brought down the riders. Whilst his archers dispatched the rear guard, John sprinted into the smoke toward the convoy's cart.

At the west end of the bridge, the six guards leading the convoy stopped and faced the sounds of combat behind them. With their view blocked by the smoke, the young commander of the guards gestured to one of his men and said, "Corporal, ride back there and find out what's—"

Before the commander could finish, the corporal crumpled and howled in pain as a bolt pierced his chest. A moment later, four other guards were struck by bolts launched by Gilbert and his archers from less than fifteen paces away. Watching his men fall, the commander wheeled his horse and retreated to the cart. "Get across the bridge! Now!" he yelled to the cartwright, then slapped the cart's mule on the rump.

As the mule lurched forward, John Little emerged from the smoke behind the cart. His chest heaving with exertion, John scanned the scene and quickly grasped the commander's plan.

Leaping forward, John grabbed the back rail of the cart. But before he could pull himself aboard, he stumbled and fell.

Still, John did not let go.

Dragged behind the cart, the cobblestones shredding his robe and skin, John used his powerful arms to pull himself onto the cart.

Waiting at the mouth of the bridge with his bowmen, Gilbert saw John get into the cart. "Hold your bolts!" he said to his men, fearing a stray missile might strike John. "Try to scare the mule!"

Waving their cloaks, the archers ran onto the bridge, trying to intercept the cart. But the commander, leading the way on his galloping horse and slashing with his sword, forced the men back and opened a path through their blockade.

A smile of triumph rose on the commander's face as they charged through to safety. The smile faded as he looked back and saw John.

By this time, John had scrambled across the cart and reached its driver. The big man grabbed the cartwright by the arm and tossed him over the side.

Now nearly a quarter mile from the congestion around the bridge, the driver tumbled along on the edge of the empty road.

Riding alongside the cart, the commander gripped the mule's bridle and brought the vehicle to a halt. Besting an unarmed monk, large though he was, would not be difficult.

The commander flourished his sword in the air. "I'll give you a chance to run, Friar. You don't need to die here today."

John stepped into the cart's bed and ripped a stake from the railing, creating a makeshift staff. "I'll make you the same offer," he said.

The soldier scoffed, peered into the sky and made the sign of the cross. "I gave him a chance, Lord," he said, then charged his horse toward John.

John stood calmly, staff held defensively across his chest. As the guard raised his sword to strike, John gripped his staff like a pike and thrust its point into the man's chest. The force of the blow knocked the soldier off his horse. As the guard scrambled to his feet, John vaulted out of the cart.

They now stood face to face.

"There's still time for you to leave," John said.

His confidence shaken, the young warrior ignored John's taunt. Facing only a wooden stake, the guard launched his attack, slashing repeatedly toward John's staff, hoping a rain of blows would destroy the weapon.

John retreated slowly, skilfully avoiding most of the blows aimed at his staff. As the guard continued his furious assault, John could see his opponent's arms growing weary, his movements slowing.

The time had come for John's counterstrike.

With the soldier off balance after another high slash, John ducked low and swung at the man's ankle. The fierce blow shattered bone and knocked the soldier off his feet.

As the young man writhed on the ground in pain, John retrieved the guard's sword and dispatched him with a merciful thrust. "I gave you a chance, lad," he muttered. "You should have taken it."

Exhausted and numb, John boarded the silver-laden cart and drove toward their rendezvous point.

John knew this had been a momentous day. Their war with the regent had escalated. Unlike their earlier raids, this had been a military engagement – a bloody affair fought without mercy.

The men he and Gil had recruited to battle the Order of The Cross were mostly comrades from their regiment in France, men who could be trusted to fight hard and keep their mouths shut. Like himself, they'd drifted back into civilian life without any moorings and had jumped at the chance to feel vital again.

The day had been momentous for another reason. The size of their prize in silver would be a heavy blow to Prince John's power. They were finally making headway in their resistance to the regent's rule – and in providing silver to keep innocent families on their land.

Christmastide 1185

With the snow shushing softly under their feet, Robert and his mother walked toward their family's cottage near Nottingham.

"I've neglected you, Mother," Robert said, carrying the large goose his mother had just butchered and dressed. "I should come back to Nottingham more often."

Anna Webber shook her head. "I didn't raise you to live under my skirts," she said, "I'm proud of you, Robert. I'd rather you be away doing good than nearby doing nothing. But I'm glad you and your friends are here."

"Thank you for taking them in at Christmastide. None of them have wives or families."

"They're all welcome," Anna said. "John and Gil are like kin. As for Will – he seems an odd match with that pair of rough old cobs. All the same, I can see the three of them are devoted to you."

"They're good men, Mother. I trust them with my life."

"You need good men around you right now, Robert. Prince John is a wicked man – and you've been a thorn in his side since the day the king left for the Holy Land."

"I didn't know you kept up with court intrigues, Mother," Robert said, smiling. "I've never mentioned any of that in my letters."

"We country bumpkins have our ways," she said, returning his smile. "Friar Tuck rides out here with news about you from time to time. He's proud of his young Latin pupil."

"I should ride into Nottingham and pay my respects to the friar."

"He'd like that," Anna said. "But today, we need to light the Yule Log and start roasting that bird."

Inside the cottage, Robert and Anna found Rob's companions and his grandfather gathered around the hearth.

John Little waved his hand toward the large block of seasoned wood before the fireplace. "What do you think of the new Yule Log I cut this morning?" he said to Robert and his mother.

Anna walked to the hearth and inspected the freshly cut piece of oak. "Good work, John. That should burn all twelve days," she said. "Put it in the fireplace and I'll fetch some wine and the ashes from last year's log."

Whilst Anna headed into the kitchen, John began manhandling the heavy piece of timber into the fireplace atop the smaller pieces of wood already burning.

"King John is charging the three of you with heresy," Arthur said, lowering his eyes. "He claims you wear a pagan amulet, sir. He also claims this household practices heathen rituals, charms and sorcery."

John Little shook his head. "Rob's family is no different than a thousand others in the midland shires. This new king is wasting no time in becoming a tyrant," he said in disgust.

Arthur pressed his palms together. "Please, sir. It's urgent that you leave. The king has sent royal couriers across the realm with writs for the Order of The Cross to arrest you and your family. The Order has a chapter about forty miles north of here near Sheffield. The king doesn't know where you are, sir. But you can be certain the white sashes will come here to detain your family."

"Let them come," John said, grasping the hilt of his sword. "They're expecting to find a woman and an old man. We'll give them a bloody surprise. That's for sure."

Robert raised a palm and said, "I don't want to risk a fight. We don't know how many men The Order will send. I agree with Mister Bland. It's best we leave right away."

Anna looked around the cottage, her eyes growing moist. "I can't abandon my home."

"Mother, they'll take you and Grandfather away. You'll never see this place again," Robert said, touching her shoulder. "We have no other choice. Please get ready to leave."

Anna's features tightened, her resolve rising. "I'll collect food and bedding for the journey."

"Where are we going, Rob?" Gilbert asked.

Before Robert could answer, the door opened and Simon entered. "We've got seven men riding up to the house. Most of them are wearing white sashes," he said, his face ashen.

* * *

The Sheriff of Nottingham studied the tracks in the snow leading to the Webber's cottage. The hoof prints were fresh. A lone rider had arrived not long ago.

"Seems the witch and warlock have company. Send two men ahead to scout the house. The rest of us will wait here," the sheriff said to the sergeant of his detail. As Sheriff of Nottingham, Rudolf Murdac had been ordered by King John to arrest Anna and Simon Webber for heresy. To carry out the mission, he'd been given command of six men-at-arms from the Order of the Cross.

The sheriff believed he had good cause to be wary. If Anna Webber's son Robert was their visitor, they faced a seasoned warrior with a fierce reputation. And Murdac did not like taking chances.

The Sheriff of Nottingham was not a warrior. Indeed, he was not even a lawman.

Rudolf Murdac had been recently nominated as sheriff by the shire's absentee lord, the Earl of Devon. As the earl had hoped, the indolent King John had not vetted his nominee, leaving the earl with a compliant sheriff whose previous job had been procuring his whores.

Certain that he was out of arrow range, the sheriff watched the two warriors ride their mounts at a walk to the thatch-roofed cottage. After pausing near the front door, each rider took a different side before disappearing behind the house.

After several minutes, the sheriff squirmed in his saddle. "Shouldn't our men be headed back by now?" he asked the sergeant.

"We're wasting time here, Sheriff," the sergeant said, unable to hide his disdain. "We have six warriors. Surely, that should be enough to arrest a woman, an old man and whoever else is in the house."

Murdac cleared his throat. "Perhaps you're right, sergeant. You and your men can advance. I'll wait back here and keep a lookout for anyone trying to flee."

Turning away from the sheriff, the sergeant sneered with disdain. "Follow me," he said to his men and started at a trot toward the house. As they rode away, the sheriff guided his horse behind an evergreen thicket where he could watch them from cover.

Near the front door, the four horsemen stopped and dismounted. Then, Murdac stared in shock as two sword-wielding men emerged from the door. Another two men armed with bows appeared from each side of the house. The archers launched their arrows, taking down two of his men, then drew their swords. Now, it was four against two. Within moments, his men had been hacked to the ground.

Terrified, the Sheriff of Nottingham galloped away.

* * *

A feathery snow began to fall as Robert stared at the bodies on the blood-splattered slush outside the cottage. John, Gilbert and Will gathered wordlessly around him, weapons still in hand, their chests heaving from the throes of combat.

The harsh reality of Richard's death finally struck Robert as he surveyed the carnage.

Their covert resistance to John's rule was now an open war – a war that had reached his mother and grandfather. His dreams for a barony and a marriage to Marian had died with Richard. He, along with his family and comrades, now faced a different fate.

They were in a battle just to stay alive.

"Killing this lot bought us some time," John said, jutting his chin toward the dead men.

"We only killed six of them," Will Scarlett said. "Your grandfather saw seven men riding toward the house, Rob."

"Will is right," Robert said. "If one of them survived, we still need to leave here – fast."

"Where to, Rob?" Gilbert asked.

Robert gazed into the forest for a moment. "Gil, do you remember the meadow in the woods near Angel Creek?"

"I've poached the king's game there many a time," Gilbert said, smiling. "It's a good spot... defensible... good hunting... clean water nearby."

Robert clapped Gilbert on the shoulder. "You set out for the meadow now, Gil. Make sure our path is clear of any trouble. The rest of us will follow once we've gathered some supplies."

As Gil headed toward the barn for his horse, John fell into stride beside him. "I'll collect some tools from the barn. We'll need to build shelters – wherever we go," John said.

"I'll get the horses ready to travel," Will said, joining the pair.

"We'll need a cart as well, Will," Robert called out. "We can't leave behind the chest of silver from Brugie."

Robert entered the cottage and found his mother and grandfather gathering provisions. Bland was packing the food and utensils they'd collected into bundles made of blankets held together by rope.

Robert drew his valet aside. "Mister Bland, I'm grateful that you made the journey from London with Marian's warning," he said. "But I think it's best if you part company with us now. Your association with me will put you in danger."

Arthur shook his head. "I want to stay and join your fight against King John, sir."

Robert eyed Arthur warily. "What makes you think we intend to fight King John?"

"I've known about your clandestine activities for some time now, sir," Arthur said, then smiled wryly. "It's impossible to keep secrets from a good valet."

"Even so, Mister Bland, how can a valet help? Do you think I'll need court attire whilst we're on the run?"

"I'm afraid you'll find my fashion advice for an outlaw wanting, sir.

However, I can sew, cook, ration supplies – and I'm practiced in the treatment of wounds."

"Your retainer came from Richard. With him dead, I can no longer pay you."

"Sharing your food and shelter will be enough for me, sir."

"You may regret sharing our fate as well."

"My only regret, sir, would be returning to the frivolous life I'd known before I entered your service."

Robert rubbed his chin, then sighed. "Very well, Mister Bland. I'm honoured to have you join us."

Kalends of January 1186

King John entered his chancery, sat down at the worktable and sighed. The stack of unread pipe rolls before him had grown even higher. Every day, the justiciar brought him more tax records to review – and every day he found a fresh reason to ignore them.

Today would be no different.

Becoming king was not the feast of adulation he'd expected. Instead, each day was an endless cycle of grubbing for money and ferreting out enemies. Even his brother's death, something for which he'd longed, had become a burden.

The Saracens were holding Richard's body for ransom, and haggling with them threatened to drain the treasury. The heathens knew John had no choice. The new king needed his brother's remains for the royal funeral that would precede his own coronation.

The squelching of his enemies was equally tiresome – especially his cousins in the house of Anjou. Through the justiciar's informants, John had learned that Guy and Bernard Curtmantle were again alluding to their claim as the rightful heirs to the throne in the privacy of social circles. As a result of their rumour mongering, his Anjou cousins had gained a sympathetic ear from the Earl of Norfolk – the treacherous coward who had betrayed Richard.

His cousins aside, most other challengers to his power were already in custody. That much was good. The charges of heresy and witchcraft enforced by the Order of The Cross had been a useful cudgel. But his main rival, Robert Webber, remained at large. Worse yet, John faced a quandary with Webber.

The bastard's liaison with Lady Marian was no secret. But as the daughter of the Lord Justiciar, John risked alienating his advisor's many allies if he threw Marian in the dungeon and tortured her for Webber's whereabouts. Instead, John had settled for keeping Marian under the constant eyes of his spies, hoping Webber would try to contact her.

John rose from the table and began to pace, wistfully recalling the days when he'd been a prince. Back then, his most consequential decisions had been choosing menus and bed mates.

A knock on the door brought John back to the present. "Enter," he said dejectedly.

The Lord Justiciar opened the door and bowed. "A letter from the Sheriff of Nottingham, Your Highness," he said, stepping across the room and extending the sealed document.

John sighed heavily. "These provincial sheriffs write as if I'm paying them by the word," he whined. "Read it and tell me what he says."

After unsealing the folded parchment, the Justiciar scanned the message whilst stroking his beard. Then his eyes widened. "The sheriff failed to apprehend the family of Robert Webber as you ordered, Sire."

"What? You gave the fool six warriors to arrest a woman and an old man."

"The sheriff says his detail was attacked by over two dozen armed men wearing hoods on his way to the Webber's home. According to the sheriff's account, he managed to kill three of the attackers and barely escaped with his life. All the others in his party were slain."

"That's preposterous."

"True or not, it would serve your interests to believe the sheriff, Sire."

The king raised an eyebrow. "How?"

"A coordinated attack by over two dozen masked warriors would be more than a mere band of brigands, Sire. It would suggest a rebellion's afoot in Nottinghamshire. You would be forced to deploy a large detachment of troops there to suppress the uprising – perhaps indefinitely."

John smiled. "I'm beginning to see the wisdom of your counsel," he said. "Naturally, I'd have to raise the scutage on my nobles to maintain order in the kingdom."

"And that would help solve some of the problems with royal revenues," the Justiciar said, waving his hand toward the tax scrolls on the table.

"There's only one flaw in your idea, de Beaumont. Sending my Royal Guards to Nottinghamshire will take its toll in silver. I may end up spending more than I can collect in scutage."

"Why not deploy the Order of The Cross? They're itching to root out heresy – and they work for nothing more than food. You could profit from their zealotry."

John smiled. "Send a message to the Sheriff of Nottingham. Tell him help from his king is on its way."

* * *

Marian crossed the snow-covered street hoping to evade the troupe of actors hawking their Feast of Fools performance. One performer in a demon costume was exceptionally persistent, following her across the narrow city lane.

"I implore you, m'lady. Please take a playbill," the actor called out in a thick northern accent, pressing the sheet into her hand.

Marian took the paper and tucked it into her sleeve, hoping to be rid of him. "Read both sides, Marian," the man whispered as she walked away.

Marian almost stopped as she recognized Robert's voice. But she continued down the street. The king's spies were likely watching her.

Arriving at her father's manor, Marian entered the library. Making certain she was alone, Marian unfolded the playbill and read Robert's message. After burning the note in the fireplace, she walked quickly to the butler's quarters.

"Please have a coach ready after supper, Sutton," she told the head servant. "I'll be visiting Aunt Charlotte."

"Will the justiciar be accompanying you, m'lady?" the butler asked.

"No, I'll be traveling alone."

* * *

Outside the justiciar's manor, two burly men in heavy coats stood by the curb in the evening shadows, trying to keep warm. The pair's attention became keen as the gate to the justiciar's stables opened and a one-horse carriage emerged. In the light of the coach lamps, the men spotted a familiar sight inside: the hood of Marian's blue velvet evening cloak.

"Looks like she's going somewhere," the leader of the spy team said. "Fetch the horses. I'll keep an eye on where she's headed."

"Five shillings says she's going to play cards with her aunt in Southwark. I think Webber's dead or in exile by now. Every white sash in the realm has an eye peeled for that bugger."

"Shut up and get the horses, dolt, before we lose her trail."

"Don't be so prickly, mate," his partner said, flashing a toothless grin. "This is better duty than rounding up peasants for burning Yule Logs."

As the pair of spies rode off after the carriage, they were watched by a figure in a hooded cape among the foot traffic on the street.

Once the king's spies were out of sight, Robert walked to the stable entrance of the justiciar's manor. As he expected, the door was unlocked. Stepping inside, Robert saw Marian waiting for him among the horse stalls. Instead of her usual evening gown, she wore a simple tunic and leggings like she was going hunting.

"The ruse worked," Robert said with a smile.

Marian smiled back. "My handmaid was stunned when I asked her to wear my cloak and take the coach to my aunt's house."

"Are we alone?" Robert asked, looking around.

"Yes, I gave the stable keeper the night off."

Robert walked to Marian and took her in his arms. "Thank you for sending Arthur Bland," he said. "I was visiting my mother and grandfather when he arrived. Will, John and Gilbert were there as well. His warning saved us all."

Embracing him, Marian said, "I would have gone myself but I was sure I'd be followed."

"You did the right thing, my love," he said, kissing her neck. Despite the danger, Robert felt his passion rise as Marian pressed against him.

Her breathing growing hoarse, Marian said, "The king's spies will be gone for a while." She then drew him into an empty stall, took off Robert's cloak and spread it over a pile of hay. "We've been apart too long," she said, lying down on the makeshift pallet.

Surprised by his own ardour, Robert dropped onto the cloak beside Marian, kissing her as they unfastened their clothes. In a passion swift and heated, his kisses moved from her lips, to her breasts, and then lower until she was gasping with pleasure. Marian then returned the favour, making him shudder with ecstasy.

Their passion spent, Marian wrapped the cloak around them and nestled against Robert's chest. Looking into his eyes, she said, "You seemed distracted when we were together in Windsor, Robin. But not tonight."

"That seems so long ago," Robert said, stroking her hair. "Everything's changed, Marian. I'm no longer trying to foil John's rule. I'm trying to keep everyone close to me alive."

"Yes, I know," she said, looking away. "What do you plan to do?"

"My family is hiding in Sherwood Forest for now. John, Gilbert and Will are with them – along with Arthur Bland."

"Will your mother and grandfather be safe there?"

"They're with three able warriors – and two of them know the land around Nottingham. My family is out of danger for the moment."

"I'm glad to hear that."

Robert sat up. "But I came here because there's something you must do to keep us all safe, my love."

"I'll do whatever you ask," she said, sitting up beside him.

"You need to publicly denounce me."

"I'll never do that," Marian said firmly.

Robert took her hands. "Marian, you must denounce me," he said gently. "It's the only way to keep you out of custody."

"The king wouldn't dare arrest me. My father has too many powerful friends."

"That's true for now. But John will eventually run out of patience – or feel sure enough about his standing with the nobles to lock you away."

Marian raised her chin defiantly. "If I'm in danger here in London, then I'll go into hiding with you."

"That's impossible, Marian. You'd be a burden in the wilderness. We'd have another mouth to feed and someone else to protect."

"That's not true," she protested. "I can—"

Robert gently placed a finger on her lips. "You'd be more useful here in court where you can keep us informed of John's—"

Marian pushed his hand away. "You're wrong, Robin," she said sternly. "I can use a bow as well as any man. You need every hand available to protect and feed your family. Open your eyes, my love."

"There's nothing I want more than for us to be together, Marian. But think of the danger you'd be in."

"You said it yourself. I'd be in danger staying here as well," she said, her voice softening. "I'd rather face the risks together."

Robert shook his head. "We'll never know a moment's peace. We'll be fugitives with enemies wherever we go."

"You underestimate yourself, Robin," she said, looking into his eyes. "You've earned loyalty everywhere you've gone. In time, you'll find allies. The important thing now is to survive."

Robert lowered his eyes. "I imagined marrying you as a landed lord. Instead, I'm an outlaw. You deserve better, Marian."

"I've never wanted a title or land. That's always been your dream, my love. All I've wanted is to be together – with whatever time we both have left."

Robert sighed. "You're stubborn and wilful, Marian de Beaumont – which is no doubt why I love you," he said. "How soon can you be ready to travel?"

Marian smiled. "I had my belongings packed before you arrived, my love," she said slyly, then nodded toward a pair of horses tethered outside the stalls. "We have two fresh geldings saddled as well."

Ides of April 1186

The Sheriff of Nottingham's stomach was fluttering as he rode through Sherwood Forest. Despite being accompanied by two dozen warriors from the Order of The Cross, Rudolf Murdac was terrified.

He'd been tasked by the king with suppressing a rebellion. But the revolt was Murdac's own invention. There was no danger of finding peasants up in arms.

No, what Rudolf Murdac feared was finding himself alone with the four men who had wiped out his command last winter at the Webber's cottage. They were fierce and cunning warriors who would show no mercy. Yet here he was in the wilderness, again risking an encounter with these dangerous outlaws. There were better uses for his talents.

"Muchison, make sure our men don't stray too far ahead," the sheriff said to his second in command. Their mounted patrol was approaching a shallow ford of Angel Creek and Murdac was fearful of losing sight of his protective escorts in the thick spring undergrowth.

The sergeant leaned close to the sheriff and spoke so that only Murdac could hear. "Look, Sheriff. Like I said before, shouting orders is not a good idea on patrol. We'll give ourselves away to the enemy," he said, then added, "We need to spread out the men as well. Keeping them around you all the time makes it harder for them to spot the rebels."

"I'm safekeeping the lives of these men, Muchison," the sheriff said. "I don't want to write any letters of condolence to their wives and mothers."

Lester Muchison sighed heavily, then called out to the riders at the head of their formation. "Lead squad! Stay close!"

"Aye, sergeant," the squad leader shouted back, disappointment in his voice.

Murdac took a sip from the wine pouch slung over his saddle, hoping to calm his nerves.

In hindsight, he now regretted his letter to the king about the incident at the Webber's cottage. Reporting that he'd been attacked by a superior force had made sense at the time. The exaggeration was necessary. There were some who might have interpreted his prudence as cowardice – and there was no point in that. Being reprimanded for using caution would not bring back the men who'd died.

His plan now was to get through this patrol safely and report to the king that their show of force had quelled the rebellion. The men under his command had other ideas, however.

The royal writ for Robert Webber's arrest was driving many of his troops to take this search for rebels seriously, hoping for a reward from the king. Finding Webber was the last thing Murdac wanted. The former marshal of the Royal Guards was very likely one of the four men he feared meeting again.

In truth, the Sheriff of Nottingham was searching for someone he did not want to find.

* * *

From his hiding place in the spring undergrowth, Robert kissed his amulet, nocked an arrow in his bow and glanced at his ambush team. They were ready.

Less than an hour before, Gilbert and Will had arrived at their encampment with chilling news. Whilst hunting for meat, the pair had spotted a large formation of mounted white sashes headed toward their camp near Angel Creek. Fortunately, the progress of the king's men was slow and noisy. But the direction of the roughly two dozen warriors would inevitably bring them to their hideaway.

Rather than abandon their camp, Robert had chosen to fight. They had no place else to go. Their survival now rested on his band's cunning and courage.

Choosing the site for their ambush had been simple. There was only one crossing of Angel Creek from Nottingham that led to his camp: the narrow ford where his comrades now lay in ambush.

Crouching beside him on the east side of the ford were John and Marian, each armed with a bow. In a tunic and tights, with her hair pulled under a cap, Marian looked like a young lad.

Taking cover on the ford's west side were Gilbert, Will and Arthur. All six were ready, arrows nocked into bowstrings, quivers full.

The deep clop of hooves on soft ground was followed by shouted orders. The patrol was drawing closer. Robert's heart throbbed in his chest.

The shapes of men on horseback appeared between the trees. Then the first riders emerged from the woods and entered the clearing of the ford.

The eyes of their horses were downcast, careful of their footing on the creek's rocky bed. The riders, however, scanned their surroundings warily.

Robert had ordered his team not to launch their arrows before he did. He let the intruders draw closer, hoping the nerve of his comrades would hold.

There were now nearly a dozen riders in the open ground before them. Still, Robert waited.

The first rider was less than ten paces away. The man's eyes widened with alarm as he spotted Robert crouching in the bushes. Before the warrior could call out, Robert placed an arrow in his throat.

Shouts rose from the king's men as Robert's comrades swiftly brought down four more intruders. With the first phase of their plan complete, Robert sprinted behind cover, moving toward the rear of the enemy column. John and Marian ran behind him.

The next few moments would determine whether they repelled the intruders or would die trying.

Anticipating the approach of the king's men, Robert and his team had woven long ropes through the undergrowth on both sides of the ford. Anna and Simon Webber, positioned on either side of the clearing now began tugging on the ropes, causing the shrubs to shudder. The shaking foliage gave the effect of a great many men moving along the edges of the ford.

Whilst Anna and Simon worked their ruse, Robert and his fellow archers ran along the length of the enemy column, launching arrows into the riders from several positions along both sides of the ford.

* * *

"It's an ambush! Retreat! Retreat" Murdac yelled, then wheeled his horse and rode away. Stunned and confused, the warriors under his command followed.

After the sheriff had galloped for nearly a mile, Sergeant Muchison and the rest of their patrol finally caught up with Murdac. Grasping the bridle of the sheriff's horse, the sergeant brought the exhausted animal to a stop.

"Retreat was our only option, sergeant. We had no other choice," Murdac sputtered, short of breath. "That was a vastly superior force."

The sergeant removed his helmet and lowered his chain maille hood. "Well, Sheriff. One thing's certain. We found the rebel force you reported to the king," he said, unable to hide his disdain. "But our patrol tactics led us right into their trap."

"Those cowards attacked us without warning. We were ambushed," Murdac insisted. "That could happen to any commander."

The sergeant shrugged. "You can write your report to the king however you see fit, Sheriff. But we haven't seen the last of these rebels."

As Murdac's terror subsided, it was replaced by dread. This was a nightmare come to life. The peasant uprising he'd invented had somehow materialized.

***

Robert's arrow narrowly missed the last of the king's men retreating from the ford. As the hoofbeats of the intruders faded, Robert emerged from the underbrush. Moments later, the rest of their band gathered around him.

John Little wiped his brow and sighed with relief. "That was a near squeak."

"We ran them off, didn't we?" Gilbert said, proudly tapping his bow.

"They'll be back – with more men," John answered. "We didn't take out very many of them," he said, gesturing toward the half-dozen enemy bodies strewn across the gulch.

Robert spread his gaze over the eight members of his band. "Each of us stayed calm and completed our mission – especially those not used to fighting," he said nodding toward Anna, Simon, Arthur and Marian. "That's what saved us."

Marian touched Robert's arm and looked at him admiringly. "Your plan is what saved us, Robin."

John clutched his sides and laughed. "Robin? Did you hear that, Gil?" he said, nudging Whitehand in the ribs. "The hero of Amiens now goes by the name of a little bird."

Gilbert chortled. "Well, Robin," he said. "What would you have us do now?"

Robert glanced at Marian who was blushing, then turned his eyes toward Whitehand. "We can start by burying those bodies and salvaging their weapons. Since you and John seem in such high spirits, Gil, I'd say you two earned the job."

"Joking aside, Rob," John said soberly. "We need to move our camp. The king's men will start their next search for us right here."

Will Scarlett stepped forward and spoke. "Moving our camp will not save us. No matter where we go, we'll be outnumbered," he said. "To stay alive, we need more men."

"Will is right," Gilbert said. "With more men, we can take the fight to the white sashes on ground of our own choosing. That's the best way to defend ourselves – we lead them away from our camp."

John stroked his beard. "Well, I hate to admit you're making sense, Gil. But we do have the silver to pay and feed more men," he said. "Do you think we can round up some of our mates from the raid in Brugie, Gil?"

"I don't see why not," Whitehand answered. Gilbert then smiled and said, "What do you think… Robin?"

Robert nodded. "For now, I can't think of a better way to stay alive."

Kalends of May 1186

The clatter of axes striking wood filled the village of Nottingham.
Under the eyes of warriors from the Order of The Cross, a large group of peasants was building a palisade around the village.

Where it was completed, the wall of felled trees rose higher than a man's head. Sharpened points topped each log.

Ahead of the wall's finished section, a hive of men worked in teams, some hauling in the trees, others sharpening the ends with axes whilst a third group dug trenches and erected the trunks.

The palisade had been ordained by the king to protect the people of Nottingham from the growing band of rebels roaming Sherwood Forest.

From the balcony of Talbot Hall, the Sheriff of Nottingham and Sergeant Muchison inspected the progress on the wall.

"These peasants are a lazy lot," the sheriff said, sneering. "The work is behind schedule."

The sergeant shook his head. "They're not lazy, Sheriff. These men would rather be planting their fields in the spring, not building a palisade. Come winter, their families may starve."

"All the more reason why they should work quickly."

"Will the king still expect these peasants to give up part of their harvest to the crown after all the time they'll spend building this wall?"

"Why not?" the sheriff said indignantly. "The king has generously provided the lumber from his forest to build the fortifications. It's their duty to provide the labour. This palisade is for their protection."

"Some of the peasants see this palisade more as a prison than protection, Sheriff. They think we're trying to prevent the men of the village from joining the rebellion – or providing supplies to the rebels."

Murdac raised an eyebrow. "Your comments border on treason to your sovereign, sergeant."

Lester Muchison bowed his head. "I meant no disrespect, Sheriff. I'm just telling you what I've heard. Surely, you'd want to have the best intelligence possible."

The sheriff cleared his throat. "Yes. Yes, of course," he stammered. "But keep this kind of talk from our men. It's bad for morale."

* * *

A quarter mile outside Nottingham, from the cover of a cluster of junipers, Robert and John Little watched the construction of the palisade as well.

John pointed with his chin toward the wall. "Faye was right. The sheriff is fencing in the village."

The day before, John had visited the homestead of his old flame, Faye Rolfe. He'd returned to their camp near Angel Creek with a satisfied mien – and disturbing news: King John had ordered a palisade built around Nottingham under the direction of its new sheriff, Rudolf Murdac.

Robert stroked the new growth of beard on his chin as he watched the workers. After a moment, he said, "There's only one reason the king would do this. John believes a rebellion is brewing."

"Rebellion? Where are the rebels?"

"We're the rebels," Robert answered calmly.

"That makes no sense, Rob. We're just six men and two women hiding in the woods."

"Yes, but we've managed to kill a dozen of the king's troops. The new sheriff might try to excuse his incompetence by puffing up the size of his enemy."

John nodded. "You make a fair point. Faye said this new sheriff is as crooked as a pig's pizzle. He was little more than a pimp for the Earl of Devon before the earl nominated him to the king."

"A make-believe rebellion serves the king's interests as well. It gives John an excuse to increase taxes and strengthen his military – at the expense of his rivals among the nobles."

"Building a palisade and bringing more troops to hunt us down … this doesn't sound good, Rob. What should we do?"

After a moment, Robert said, "Lead the rebellion."

"I don't understand," John said, squinting in confusion.

Robert swept his arm toward the wall. "The king is forcing the peasants around Nottingham to work on his palisade whilst their fields go unplanted. Once the wall is up, their families will be locked inside the town in miserable shelters and with very little food. By winter, we're going to find ourselves flush with new recruits – and the rebellion will be real."

* * *

Returning from the reconnaissance of Nottingham with John at his side, Robert spotted a lone rider in the distance. Approaching on the forest trail was a familiar figure: the portly frame of Friar Tuck astride his long-suffering mule.

Robert quickly guided his horse into the woods and signalled for John to follow.

Once they were both out of sight, Robert said, "It's Friar Tuck, from the abbey in Nottingham. I think it's best if he doesn't know I'm about."

"We're passing up a chance for valuable information, Rob. The priest may know how many warriors the sheriff has – and if he's expecting more," John said, then patted his own chest. "He doesn't know who I am. So, there's no harm in me asking."

Robert nodded. "I'll stay under cover."

When the priest was less than ten paces away, John stepped out into the trail, blocking his way.

"Good day to you, Friar Tuck." John said warmly. "Headed into Nottingham, are you?"

Tuck reined his mule to a stop, eyeing the big man warily. "I know all my parishioners. Yet you know my name. Who might you be, my son?"

John cringed, realizing he'd blundered. "I just want to ask a few questions, padre."

"I'll not answer questions from a stranger who won't give his name," Tuck said firmly. "Now let me pass."

John folded his arms across his chest. "Sorry to be rude, Friar. But I can't do that," he said, holding his ground.

"Then it seems I'll need to teach you a lesson in manners, my son," Tuck said, dismounting the mule.

"Stand down, Friar. I don't want to fight."

"Then you best clear the way. Or a fight is what you'll have."

"All I want is information about the warriors under the sheriff's command."

"And why would you want to know that?"

"We may have mutual friends – friends wanted by the king."

Tuck raised an eyebrow. "Anna and Simon Webber?"

John nodded. "Aye."

"Why didn't you say so?" Tuck said, a smile spreading on his face.

"I wasn't sure of your loyalties."

"I'd sooner toss my rosary in the river than side with this tyrant calling himself a king."

Robert emerged from the underbrush. "I'm glad to hear that, Friar," he called out, walking toward the priest.

Tuck stared at Robert for a moment. "Is that you under that scraggly beard, Robert Webber?"

"It is, Friar," Robert said with a grin.

Tuck rushed to his former pupil, lifting Robert off his feet with a hug. After a moment, he released Robert and looked him in the eyes. "It's good to see you, my son. I thought you were dead."

"I'm alive – and trying to keep my family and friends that way as well,

Friar," Robert said.

"Then tell me what I can do to help you."

Nones of July 1186

Gilbert Whitehand guided his horse through the stand of pines that hid their camp near Angel Creek. Following Whitehand were more than a dozen men on foot carrying an assortment of bundles. "Yo, Robin!" Gilbert called out after spotting their leader.

Robert rose from a rough-hewn stool. "That joke is getting stale, Gil," he said, putting down the arrow he'd been fletching.

Hearing their voices, the rest of Robert's band emerged from their huts and gathered around Gilbert and the new arrivals.

Gilbert dismounted. "Like Balthazar, I've come bearing gifts," he said, waving his arms toward the new men.

John Little laughed. "Well, then. If you're Balthazar, that would make Robin here our baby Jesus."

"You're a blasphemer, John Little," Gilbert said with a smile. "It's no wonder the white sashes want the likes of you dead."

Robert stepped closer to Gilbert and clapped him on the shoulder. "These men are a gift indeed," he said, then turned his gaze toward the newcomers. "I recognize most of you from the Guard. You're welcome here, lads."

The men nodded back. "Glad to be here …Robin!" one of them called out smiling. The rest broke into laughter.

"I see Gil's paltry wit has tainted the lot of you," Robert replied, rolling his eyes.

Gilbert nodded to the recruits. "Show them what we brought."

Unfolding their bundles on the ground, the newcomers laid out a cache of swords, longbows, crossbows, bolts and arrowheads.

"You've put our silver to good use," Robert said.

"I didn't forget our womenfolk," Gilbert added. "We've brought fine linen and needles, too."

"Thank you, Gilbert," Anna Webber said.

"I'm more keen on the crossbows," Marian said, walking toward the weapons. "How good is their aim?" she said, hefting one.

"They're first quality, lady," Gilbert replied as Marian inspected the weapons.

"Did you remember my cloth, Mister Whitehand?" Arthur Bland asked.

"Aye, I did," Gilbert said, nodding to one of the men who unbundled several bolts of bluish-green fabric. "The cloth in this colour you wanted cost us a pretty penny, Mister Bland. You have fancy tastes."

"What's the price of a life, Mister Whitehand?"

Gilbert cocked his head. "I don't understand your question."

"Tunics made of this Lincoln green cloth will save lives. The king's men flaunt their presence with their bright garb and white sashes. Our warriors will blend in with the forest, making us harder to see."

Robert took one of the bolts of cloth and handed it to Bland. "Then you best get to work on our combat garb, Mister Bland. The sheriff will be looking for us again – in force. We need to be ready."

Ides of August 1186

For the third time that day, Rudolf Murdac climbed the ladder to the parapet above Nottingham's gate. Shielding his eyes from the setting sun, the sheriff gazed across a pasture to the tree line a quarter mile away. There was still no sign of the patrol.

At the king's insistence, the sheriff had deployed fifty men from the Order of The Cross on their latest search for the rebels in Sherwood Forest. Feigning a leg injury from a hunting accident, Murdac had put Lester Muchison in command of the patrol. The deception was necessary, Murdac told himself. He was more valuable to the king using his wits than wielding a sword – and those wits were being tested by conditions in Nottingham.

Penned inside the palisade, the peasants had become unruly. In the three months since the stockade was completed, a day had not passed without some kind of disturbance. Stoking the tensions were hunger, idleness and the zealous suppression of pagan practices by the Order of The Cross.

But Murdac had found a welcome side to the peasants' discontent.

Maintaining law and order inside the palisade meant keeping more troops in Nottingham. The sheriff slept better knowing he was guarded by over a hundred well-armed warriors. But now, thanks to the king's orders, half of them were gone on patrol.

That's why Murdac was eager to see his troops return.

Gazing once again toward the trail out of the trees, the sheriff spotted riders in white sashes emerge into the pasture. The patrol was back at last.

But the sheriff's heart sank as he counted the number of men returning to Nottingham. Nearly half his warriors were missing.

When the patrol was finally inside the palisade, Murdac ordered four of his personal guards to escort Lester Muchison into the chancery of Talbot Hall.

"What have you done with my men, Muchison?" the sheriff said angrily as the sergeant entered the room, flanked by the guards.

"The number of rebels has grown, Sheriff," Muchison said, looking at his boots. "And they've become very cunning."

"You lost twenty-four men, idiot! What happened?"

"About a half-day's ride into the forest, we spotted six riders on the trail ahead of us." Lester said. "After seeing us, they galloped away. Before I could give an order, our lads broke after them, sure they were rebels because they'd fled."

"That's unacceptable, Muchison. It's your job to maintain discipline."

"That's true, Sheriff. But some of the men were champing at the bit. So, I tried to make the best of it."

"What do you mean, 'make the best of it'?" Murdac asked, his eyes narrowing.

"I believed the men's instincts were right. The riders probably were rebels, so I didn't try to stop them. When the rebels reached a fork in the trail, they split up. Three of the rebels went left and the others went right. To keep up our pursuit on all of them, I divided the troops and put Renault in command of half our men. Renault led his men down the left trail whilst I took mine down the trail to the right."

"That was a mistake!" Murdac yelled. "You weakened your force!"

Muchison swallowed hard. "I realize that now."

"What happened then?"

"My group chased the rebels for about another mile and we were closing on them when a tree fell across the trail between us. I knew then that we were being led into a trap, so I ordered a retreat. We made it back to the fork in the trail safely. Then I took my men down the left trail to reinforce Renault," Muchison said, his voice growing weak. "About a quarter-mile later we found Renault and his men. Their bodies were scattered on the trail. Their weapons and horses were gone. Judging by the wounds, most were killed by arrows at close range."

The sheriff stared at Muchison coldly. "I'll not take the blame for this disaster," he said, then turned toward his guards. "Lock him up. I'll decide how to deal with him later."

After the others were gone, Murdac sat down, cradling his head in his hands. How would he report this defeat to the king without incriminating himself, he wondered?

* * *

The cooking fire at the centre of the Angel Creek camp cast the shadows of nineteen men and women on the pine trees surrounding their hideaway. Gathered around the fire on logs and stools, they were a quiet lot that night, staring into the flames as they ate the rabbit and wild leeks prepared by Arthur Bland.

John Little stood and spoke. "I want to tip my cup to the men we lost today," he said, then poured some ale on the ground from his mug. "Both of them fought well and died with honour."

"Aye" the others gathered around the campfire said, tipping their own cups.

John swept his gaze over the group. "Without their sacrifice, we couldn't have sent two dozen white sashes to meet their maker today," he said. "But the day I fall in battle, I want no long faces in camp. I'll have died doing what I was born to do – and so did the men we buried," he said, then smiled. "Now let's celebrate our victory, for today we kicked the Sheriff of Nottingham in the arse hard enough to make him wish he was a pimp again!"

The wave of laughter broke the tension as murmurs became banter.

"There was no one better today with the crossbow than Lady Marian," Gilbert Whitehand said, nodding towards Marian who lowered her face, hiding the crimson in her cheeks. "She put most of our men to shame."

"Speaking for yourself, are you, Gil?" one of the new men taunted playfully.

"Says the man whose every arrow landed dry," Gilbert retorted.

Marian lifted her face and smiled. "Only a cross-eyed spindle puller could have missed at the range Robin's scheme placed us today."

Another wave of laughter swept the camp.

"Oh, Robin," John said loudly. "Did you tell the lady where your brilliant scheme came from?"

"Why don't you tell her, John?" Robert said. "You enjoy talking more than anyone I know."

John bowed theatrically, then said, "Rob's plan wasn't new. He hatched it many years ago during our first battle together in Thetford." With sweeping gestures and dramatic pauses, John told the story of the clever trap they'd set for the Baron of Thetford's men-at-arms.

"You forgot to mention I was there," Gilbert said.

"It's easy to understand why," John answered. "You mattered so little to our victory."

Gilbert scoffed. "You tell a story about as shite as your lumbering carcass rides a horse, John Little," he said, then glanced at Anna and Marian and covered his mouth. "Forgive my language, ladies."

Robert smiled with relief as the jibes continued. Like most warriors after a battle, his band was finally venting their horror and fear through laughter.

Everyone had fought well today, maintaining the discipline of seasoned troops. Their plan could not have succeeded without it.

At the cost of two men, they'd wiped out half the enemy's patrol and captured more than twenty horses along with a large haul of weapons. Still, the equation gave Robert little comfort.

Casualties in his days of commanding regular troops had not been easy. But deaths among his small band hurt deeper, like the loss of family. Most dreadful of all was the thought of losing Marian.

He'd tried to persuade her to stay out of the battle. But Marian had insisted. And, as Gil had pointed out, she was a lethal archer. Outnumbered as they were, Robert could not afford to waste her skill.

In a very real sense, she was helping them all stay alive.

* * *

Seated on the floor of an iron cage in the village blockhouse, Lester Muchison cursed the day he'd been assigned to serve under the Sheriff of Nottingham.

Murdac was a shameless coward. He'd feigned an injury to avoid facing the enemy – the same enemy Lester had fought bravely – although certainly not well. Lester realized that splitting his troops on the forest trail had been a mistake. But a real commander would have dressed him down or demoted him. Instead, he'd been locked up like a common criminal.

When the sheriff approached his cage accompanied by two guards, Lester refused to look at him.

"Stand up," the sheriff said to Muchison. As Lester slowly rose to his feet, Murdac addressed the guards. "I'll speak to him alone," he said. Once the guards were out of earshot, Murdac said, "I've decided what to do with you, Lester. Although you don't deserve it, I'm going to give you the chance to redeem yourself."

"Do what you will with me," Lester said defiantly.

The sheriff sneered. "Don't play the hero with me, Muchison. A few turns on the rack and you'll drop this petulant little show."

After Lester recalled the screams of men on the rack, their bones and sinews snapping, his anger cooled. "What do you want from me?" he said, the edge gone from his voice.

"You, my dear Lester, are going to join the rebels."

Ides of September 1186

The tweet of a woodlark sounded from a tall oak clad in autumn hues. Recognizing the signal, Gilbert Whitehand's gaze rose toward the tree. Perched atop the oak, one of his men pointed south, raised a single finger, then made walking motions with his hand.

"On your feet, lads," Gilbert said to the three men nearby. "There's a lone stranger on foot coming up the trail."

The wooded bluff where they stood offered a view to a distant clearing on the forest trail. From here, any travellers entering Sherwood Forest from Nottingham were visible from nearly a mile away. Not surprisingly, the spot had become a regular post for Gilbert and his team of lookouts.

Walking briskly to intercept the stranger, Gilbert was certain his small detachment could handle any threat from a single intruder. Had it been a larger group, he would have sent a runner back to alert their camp.

After reaching the forest trail, Gilbert and his men took cover in the undergrowth and waited.

The unarmed man Gilbert saw approaching was average in height and stout of build, his clothes that of a peasant but unusually clean. When the stranger was less than ten paces away, Gilbert nodded to his men and they stepped into the open, hands on the pommels of the swords strapped to their waists.

"Good day," Gilbert said evenly. "Who might you be?"

The man stopped and raised his palms. "If you're looking to rob me, you're wasting your time," he said soberly. "I've nothing to my name."

Gilbert shook his head. "We're not brigands," he said. "I asked for your name."

"I'm called Much."

"You don't look familiar, Much. Do you live in these parts?"

"I used to farm a plot south of Nottingham, but it's worthless now. I missed my spring planting."

"You look healthy enough. How did you miss planting your fields?" Gilbert asked, eyeing the man warily.

"Before I could get my crops in, the sheriff's soldiers put me to work raising a palisade around Nottingham. They did the same to all my neighbours. Then they locked us inside the wall we built once it was done."

"You were imprisoned, eh? How did you manage to escape?"

"A man who builds a wall knows where it's weakest," he said. "I went over the palisade from the roof of a sawmill alongside the wall."

"I'm surprised you're alone. Why did you leave your family behind?"

"My wife never bore me any children, God rest her soul. She took sick with the blue death not long after they locked us up. I buried her last week," Much said sombrely.

"No one else escaped with you?"

"There's more than three-hundred people locked up in Nottingham. I can't speak for all of them. But everyone I knew was afraid to escape. They'd rather risk starving inside the walls than face the swords of the white sashes. I don't blame the ones with families."

"But you're not afraid of the soldiers, I take it," Gilbert said with a smirk.

"No," Much said. "I'm afraid of the soldiers, all right. But I've had all I can take of this sheriff. I escaped to join the rebels."

"Rebels?" Gilbert said, cocking his head, "Who are these rebels?"

"The ones who've been killing the sheriff's men of late."

"Risking your life to join up with these rebels seems a foolish thing, Much. Why not move to another village?"

"The sheriff took all I have… I want revenge."

Gilbert recalled Rob's prediction. After feeling the pain of the sheriff's internment, the townspeople would become recruits. Apparently, the volunteers were already starting.

Taking in strangers, however, was risky. The more people who knew about their hideout, the less secure it would be. But they'd just lost two men. Adding another man would help with the defence of their camp.

"I'm sorry to hear about your wife," Gilbert said. "What's your full name, Much?"

The man looked at the ground. "They call me Much, the miller's son. They say my father was a miller, but I never met him. My mother, well… she was…" Much paused, his lips trembling.

"Say no more. I understand," Gilbert answered gently. He did not want to shame the man by having him declare he was a bastard. "Do you own a weapon?"

"Yes," Much said proudly, then reached into his boot and produced a small, dull-looking knife.

Gilbert smiled, impressed by the man's pluck. "Wait here," he said to Much, then drew one of his men aside where they could speak privately. "Return to Angel Creek and tell Rob I'll be bringing a new recruit with me this evening after our duty shift."

"Aye, Gil," the man said and walked away.

Gilbert returned to the newcomer. "Come with us, Much. I'll show you where to find the rebels."

* * *

Fists pressed against her hips, Anna Webber strode across the camp toward her son with Marian in tow.

Chopping wood for the evening meal, Robert was unaware of the storm headed his way.

After reaching her son, Anna frowned and said, "Marian just told me about the poor souls starving in Nottingham. What do you plan to do about it?"

Robert put down the axe and sighed. "I'm trying to find a way to help them, mother."

The day before, Friar Tuck had come to their camp and met privately with Robert. The priest brought disturbing news from Nottingham. The peasants penned inside the town were slowly starving. After Tuck's parting, Robert had shared the news with Marian – and now his mother knew as well.

"Did you intend to inform any of the rest of us? Anna asked loudly.

Intrigued by the confrontation, John Little, Will Scarlett and most of the others in the camp approached.

Robert glanced at the group gathered around them. "Mother, I've found it best to resolve tactical decisions in private," he answered.

"Son, this isn't one of your 'tactical decisions'. Innocent people could die."

Rubbing his face, Robert said, "We can barely feed ourselves, mother. How would we feed five times our number?"

"The sheriff allows the friar to travel. Give Tuck the silver to buy food and he can smuggle it into Nottingham."

"Most of our silver is gone," Robert said, shoulders slumping.

John stepped forward. "We've solved that problem before, Rob," he said, then smiled. "I'd say we've gotten right good at fleecing sheriffs and fat merchants."

The comment drew a ripple of laughter.

"I won't argue that, John," Robert said. "But after losing two men, we're already short-handed defending our camp. Going on raids for silver will put us all in greater danger."

"I'm one of the people in danger, son," Anna said, "and I'm willing to take the risks. We can't let innocent people die if there's a way to help."

"That goes for me as well," Marian agreed.

"I could travel to London and meet with my source at the Exchequer,"

Will said. "He might help us find some targets we can take with just a few men."

"That would be helpful, Will," Marian said. "But it might take weeks. The people in Nottingham can't wait that long."

"You're our leader, Rob," John said. "We'll do whatever you say. But you've always listened to those under your command – and I say the people in Nottingham need our help."

The impasse was broken by the arrival in camp of one of Gilbert's men. He walked to Robert and said, "I have a message from Gil. He's bringing a volunteer to camp this evening – a man who escaped from Nottingham. Gil said we should be prepared to receive him."

"Thank you," Robert said to the messenger. "Tell Gil we'll be ready."

The messenger nodded and headed back toward the lookout post.

Anna lifted her face toward the sky and made the sign of the cross. "God has heard our prayers."

"God may have sent this stranger – but we don't know who he serves," Robert said. "Gil sent word about the man's arrival as a warning. We should make the stranger feel welcome. But we need to watch what we say and not take our eyes off this man until we're clear about his motives."

"I agree," John said. "You're wanted by the king, Rob. That could bring a traitor among us."

"Then we should all call you Robin," Will said to their leader.

A peal of laughter spread among the group.

"That's not a jest," Will insisted. "If this man's a spy, it could throw him off Rob's trail."

"Being careful can't hurt," John admitted.

"If we're going to be careful, why stop with a given name?" Marian said. "We should give Robin a new surname as well."

"My mother's family name is Hodde," Anna suggested.

Robert frowned. "I'd rather not use a family name."

"How about Hood, then?" Anna offered.

"Robin Hood…" Marian said, tilting her head. "The name rings well, I think."

Will tapped his chin. "A new name is good. But the king still has the white sashes looking for Robert Webber. Is there any other way to throw spies off Rob's trail?"

The group was silent for a moment.

Then John smiled and raised a finger. "I have it!" he said. "We could spread the rumour that Robert Webber's gone into exile in France. The friar in Nottingham could help with that. What do you think, Rob?"

Robert nodded. "The next time Friar Tuck visits us, I can ask him to wag his tongue about my exile back in Nottingham," he said smiling. "My reputation may suffer – but I can live with that."

"God willing, we'll all live with that," Anna said.

***

Lester Muchison followed the rebels as they walked to a wooded bluff overlooking the trail from Nottingham.

For the next few hours, the warriors took turns in the high boughs of a tree watching for anyone entering Sherwood Forest. During that time, no other travellers appeared. The lull gave Lester a chance to study the rebels.

They all wore tunics of the same blue-green cloth and were well armed. Each man carried a sword at his waist and a crossbow along with a quiver of bolts slung across his back. They called their leader Gil.

From their manner and mien, Lester gathered the men had all once been real soldiers – not overzealous amateurs like the members of The Order. As a former soldier himself, Lester felt at ease with them – but he resisted taking part in their banter. If he failed at impersonating a serf, it would cost him his life.

For more than a week, Lester had prepared for this day, his first encounter with the rebels. He'd imagined the questions they might ask and crafted a character who would provide convincing answers.

Knowing he'd be questioned about the people of Nottingham, Lester had asked the sheriff for profiles of the town's most notable folk. Under a less fearful commander, Lester would have known this himself. But wary of betrayals by his troops in mingling with the townsfolk, the sheriff had forbidden the warriors of The Order to leave their compound when not on duty.

Even Lester's alias had been carefully wrought. Any hesitation in answering to his new name might arouse suspicion. So he'd chosen a familiar name: Much, his nickname as a lad in Sheffield.

Lester wondered how long the rebels would stay at their observation post. The answer came as the sun dipped into the trees. "Time to head home, lads," Gil called out, "Get ready to move."

Lester rose and followed the rebels deeper into the forest.

His ploy had passed the first test with the rebel sentries. But a higher barrier remained once he entered the rebel camp. There, he'd find more people asking questions – and a greater chance for a flaw in his ruse to appear.

One part of his role as Much the miller's son was true. He hated the Sheriff of Nottingham.

Rudolf Murdac had left Lester no choice but to accept this mission as a spy. The sheriff had threatened the life of his sister and her children in Sheffield if Lester did not return to Nottingham within a fortnight with the location of the rebel's camp and the names of their leaders.

Their trek through the forest brought Lester to the ford where he'd first battled the rebels. A nagging fear rose once again. Would he be recognized? Trying to remain calm, Lester reminded himself that his helmet with its nosepiece and the chainmail hood he'd worn masked his appearance.

Not far beyond the gulch, they crossed a small creek and entered a thick stand of pines. Emerging from the evergreens, Lester saw more than a dozen people around several cabins and huts circling a fire pit. A pen of rough-hewn timber held more than a score of horses – most of them steeds of the Order of The Cross.

Lester swallowed hard as he watched the eyes of everyone in the camp turn his way.

"I've brought a new recruit from Nottingham," Gil called out as they walked closer to the group. "This is Much, the miller's son," he said, sweeping his arm toward Lester.

A long silent moment followed, making Lester's stomach flutter.

A woman his mother's age approached Lester and smiled. "From what I hear of Nottingham, you must be hungry, Much," she said, then gestured toward a stool near the fire pit. "Come and sit down. We'll get you something to eat."

Grateful that the tension had faded, Lester sat down and furtively watched the people around him.

To Lester's surprise, there was another, younger woman among the rebels. Although she wore a man's hat and tunic, her beauty was unmistakeable. The rest of them varied in age and anatomy – from a stooped old man, to a giant near middle age, to a fine-featured young man with a noble bearing. Along with the same blue-green tunics, they all shared the casual banter of comrades.

Gil walked to a huddle of men near the horses, then returned a while later with a stout man with long hair and a beard, both coal black. "Much, this is Robin," Gil said. "He's our leader."

"I'm glad to be here, Robin," Lester answered.

"Welcome, Much," Robin said. "Gil told me about your wife. I'm sorry for your loss."

Lester mustered a long face. "I'll never forgive the sheriff. That's why I came to join you."

Robert nodded. "Gil tells me you helped build the palisade around Nottingham."

"Aye, that's true."

"We could use your knowledge to help us get into Nottingham."

Lester could not believe his luck. This was a chance to lure the rebels right into a trap. Now, he needed a truth to draw them in. "I can show you a spot on the palisade where we can breach the wall out of sight from the sentries. I can take you there tomorrow, if you like."

"We're not ready yet. For now, you'll patrol the forest with Gil," Robin said, then walked back to the men near the horses with Gil at his side.

Whilst Lester mulled over what he'd learned, the older woman returned holding a bowl and a spoon. "Here you are, Much," she said. "It's venison stew. Eat it slowly. Your poor stomach's probably not seen food for a while."

Lester was touched by her kindness. "Thank you, ma'am," he said, taking the bowl.

"My name is Anna," she said. "Do you still have kin in Nottingham?"

"No, ma'am," he said, lowering his eyes. "My wife died not long ago."

"How are the country folk inside the wall faring?"

Lester answered truthfully. "Whole families are living in tiny shacks between most every cottage and building... people are starving... rats and filth are everywhere... disease is spreading..."

"That's a shame," Anna said. "The Sheriff of Nottingham has blood on his hands, locking people up like that."

"Yes, ma'am. He does," Lester said, thinking of his sister and her children.

Anna gently touched his shoulder. "God bless you, Much. We need good souls like you to help us bring the sheriff to justice."

Lester lowered his eyes, suddenly ashamed.

* * *

The sentries were changing shifts for the night as most in camp prepared for bed.

Side-by-side on a rough-hewn bench, Marian and Anna were scraping deer hides for tanning by the light of the campfire. The pair had grown close since Marian's arrival at camp. Their natural affinity as women – and a mutual integrity – had quickly overcome their differences in breeding.

"Your kindness to the newcomer was most gracious," Marian said to Anna.

"A stranger should be made welcome," Anna replied.

"Having more men join us will help stop the sheriff's cruelty."

"My son was none too happy about the scolding I gave him today," Anna said, then nodded toward Robert, drinking with a small group of men standing near the horses. "He's putting some balm on his pride, but it will be sore for a while. Don't let him vent his wrath on you, Marian.

You did the right thing in telling me."

"Robin needed to hear what you said," Marian answered, then stood and gathered her tools. "All the same, I'll need to salve his wounds tonight. Sleep well, Anna."

Entering the hut she shared with Robin, Marian put away her tools, then poured a small measure of flax oil into a shallow saucer and placed it within reach of their pallet.

Not long after Marian had nestled under the blankets, the hut's door parted and Robin stepped into the small, windowless shelter lit by a small oil lamp.

Marian raised the covers, revealing her naked body. "I've kept your spot warm, my love," she said with a sultry smile.

Robin undressed in silence. His garments gone, he blew out the lamp and slipped under the covers, turning his back toward Marian. "I'm tired and ready to sleep."

Marian gently stroked his shoulders. "Robin, I know you're vexed because I spoke to your mother about Nottingham."

After a long moment, he turned to face her and said, "Being chastised in public weakens my leadership."

"That may have been a mistake, my love. But I told your mother because you seemed unwilling to do anything for the townsfolk. I thought an ally would help change your mind."

"Do you believe I want those people to starve?"

"No, Robin. You're kind and brave," she said, touching his cheek. "But I believe your urge to protect your mother and me is keeping you from doing what's right."

Robin sighed. "I couldn't bear losing you, Marian."

"Nor I you, my love," she said, embracing him.

As their bodies joined, Marian slowly rubbed the soft skin of her thighs against his loins. Before long, she felt Robin's arousal. Dipping her fingers into the oil she'd placed nearby, she encouraged his passion with her hands. Robin began to gasp with pleasure.

The covers rose and fell, slowly at first, and then faster and faster until Robin's hoarse moan brought the blankets to a stop.

After a moment, Robin repaid her pleasure, sensuously daubing the oil with his fingers until Marian reached a climax of her own.

For a long while they lay wordlessly in each other's arms, their breathing returning to normal. Then Marian broke their languor.

"Much's arrival gave me an idea, my love," Marian said, raising herself on an elbow.

"What is it?" Robin answered, his voice groggy.

"If one man can escape from Nottingham and join us, why not more?"

"More men? How would they get out – and how could we get them to join us?"

"Friar Tuck," she said.

Robin stirred, rubbing his eyes. "What are you saying?"

"Friar Tuck would know which men in Nottingham are willing to fight and are still fit enough to help us. With more men, we can defend the camp and still go on raids for silver."

Robin sat up, now fully awake. "Marian, you're a godsend," he said, then kissed her forehead and rose from the bed.

"Robin, where are you going?"

"I'm going to wake John and Gil," he said, getting dressed. "We have raids to plan."

* * *

Lester had tried to escape several times during the night. But a sentry had lingered outside the cabin where he'd been housed along with several men from Gil's patrol. Evidently, he did not yet own their trust.

After breakfast, Gil led Lester to a clearing at the edge of camp and handed him a wooden sword. "Your training as a warrior starts today, Much," he said smiling. "I don't expect you've handled a sword before?"

"Scratching enough grain from the ground to pay the lord's share and still keep from starving doesn't leave much time for learning weapons," Lester said, taking the sword.

"C'mon, then," Gilbert said, raising his own wooden sword. "I'll start by showing you how to keep your guts inside you."

As the lesson progressed over the next hour, Lester struggled to disguise his skill. His instincts were hard to curb.

"That's enough for now," Gil said, wiping his brow. "You're taking to the sword faster than a hare with a fox on his arse."

"Beginner's luck," Lester said, handing the wooden sword back to Gil.

"I'd say you've learned enough to go with us on patrol tomorrow," Gil said putting his arm around Lester's shoulder as they headed back to camp. "We can keep up your training from our lookout post on the bluff."

"I'll be glad to help however I can."

"Robin spoke with me last night," Gil said. "He thinks your knowledge of the palisade around Nottingham is going to be helpful right away."

"Are you planning a raid on the town?"

"Not exactly," Gil said. "We want to help more men escape."

Walking alongside Lester, Gil explained their plan. They'd use the new men from Nottingham to defend their camp, freeing their seasoned warriors for raids on sheriffs and merchants.

"The plan sounds clever, Gil. You'll be rich men soon, I'm sure," Lester said.

Gil stopped. "That's not why we're doing this, Much," he said, looking into Lester's eyes. "We'll use the silver from the raids to buy grain for the people trapped in Nottingham. That's why you're important, Much. You can show us how to get men out of Nottingham – and food into the town as well."

Lester was shocked. Only a fool would risk his life to steal silver and then give it away to peasants. Gil had to be lying. "That's very noble of you," he said after a moment. "When will you need me to get you inside Nottingham?"

"Friar Tuck stops by from time to time," Gil explained. "He'll recruit the men inside the town and lead them wherever you tell him."

Lester rubbed his chin. So the friar was in league with these rebels as well. Knowing that was good. But waiting for the friar to arrive might take too long to save his sister. "I could sneak back inside Nottingham tonight and bring men out to you."

Gil shook his head. "Too risky. You'd be recognized."

Lester let the matter drop. He already knew enough to save his sister from the sheriff. He'd bide his time and win their trust until the chance to escape arose.

* * *

Standing in the line of men waiting for their evening meal, Lester's mouth watered as he caught the scent of the cooking pot.

When Lester's turn came, the cook held out a bowl with his portion. "This smells good. What is it?" he asked, taking the bowl.

A tidy little man in an apron behind the cooking pot smiled and said, "It's boar and apples prepared with sage."

Lester's eyes widened. "Boar is only served to kings."

"You're Mister Much, I presume," the cook said, "the new man from Nottingham."

"Aye, I am."

"My name is Arthur Bland," he said. "You'll find we eat quite well here, Mister Much. Our men hunt for game without unjust restrictions."

Lester nodded. These rebels already scoffed at the law by attacking the sheriff and his troops. Why wouldn't they hunt the king's game with impunity? Still, he would not pass up the chance to taste boar. "Thank you, Arthur," he said. "This is a rare treat for me."

"Then I'll provide another, Mister Much," Arthur said, then took a pitcher from a table behind him, filled a cup and handed it to Lester. "I brewed the ale myself. Enjoy your meal, Mister Much," the little man said.

Lester found a stool near the fire and sat down to eat. The boar was rich and savoury, set off by the sweetness of the apples – the ale, as good as any he'd tasted.

Lester finished his meal in silence, eating alone among the men gathered in small knots around the campfire sharing stories and jokes.

Staring into the flames, Lester listened to the voices around him with a measure of envy. Their intimate murmurs, sometimes broken by a sharp laugh, were a reminder that he was still a stranger among them – despite being taken for an ally.

His own troops with The Order were not as carefree. Their conversations were guarded, their words chosen carefully. There were zealots in every unit of The Order looking to make a name by denouncing heretics in their ranks.

Hearing footsteps behind him, Lester turned to find Anna approaching with a pitcher.

"I thought you might like more ale," she said extending the pitcher.

"Thank you, ma'am," he said as she refilled his cup.

Anna pointed with her chin toward the empty stool beside Lester. "Mind if I join you?" she asked.

Lester nodded, and Anna sat down.

"Making friends will take some time around this lot," Anna said, waving her hand toward the men around them.

"I'm guessing they've known each other for a long time," Lester said. "I haven't proven myself. It's understandable."

"That makes it no less painful," Anna said. "It must be lonely, having no one to talk to – especially for a man who just lost his wife."

Lester took a deep draught of ale as he stared into the fire.

The Order claimed that women like Anna were witches – evildoers who consorted with the devil. Yet she'd shown him nothing but kindness.

Lester downed the rest of the ale and faced Anna. "Gil tells me you intend to give the peasants locked inside Nottingham free grain," he said, his words beginning to slur. "Is that true?"

"Yes," she said calmly. "It's true."

"Why should I believe you?"

Anna sighed. "Much, I can see you're no fool. Throwing in your lot with us is a risk. There's no doubt about that. But these are not brigands," she said, gesturing to the men around her. "They were all soldiers once. They won't ever betray a comrade – and that includes you. I'll tell you why I know that," she said, then turned her eyes toward Robin. "That's my son, standing there. I raised him to be a man of duty and honour. He'd risk his life for anyone in this camp – and he'll do the same for the people in Nottingham without asking for a penny."

Lester weighed her words. What she said seemed true. These men were fearsome warriors. They could be wealthy had they chosen to plunder. Yet they lived in simple huts deep in the forest, trying to help others. Could he betray these people to a cruel and cowardly sheriff whose thanks would be sparing his sister from death?

He needed time to think.

After a moment, he rose unsteadily and said, "Good night, ma'am. I should get some sleep. Tomorrow's my first day on duty with Gil."

* * *

The cooing of a morning dove announced the dawn with Lester wide awake, dossed among the men in the cabin. He'd barely slept, his mind juggling loyalties like an acrobat. His head hurt from the ale as well.

Where did his allegiance lie… to these well-meaning strangers or the Order of The Cross?

Lester had joined The Order out of necessity, not religious zeal. As a conscript of King Henry's first war in France, he'd returned to find his small freehold near Sheffield foreclosed by the baron for the taxes gone unpaid whilst he served the king.

The Order gave him shelter, regular meals and a small share of the plunder from property seized from heretics. But he'd never taken pride in his service to The Order. Far from it.

The soldiers of The Order usually showed no mercy to heretics. Men, women and even children were sometimes slaughtered by units seized with a fever of righteousness. Torture was common in obtaining confessions. Lester tolerated their cruelty, knowing it was wrong – and tried to prevent it when he could.

Turning these rebels over to the sheriff would not only save his sister – he might finally free himself from bondage to The Order. Yet, the virtue of the people in this camp held him back.

The men sleeping around Lester began to stir. Before long, they rose and began to dress. Lester joined them, still lost in thought.

Why was he even considering mercy for people he barely knew? His sister and her children would die if he failed to expose them.

One of the men opened the door, flooding the windowless cabin with light. At that moment, a thought rose in Lester's mind, filling him with clarity.

He suddenly knew how to resolve his dilemma.

Kalends of October 1186

Under a moonless sky, Robert scanned the darkened landscape around Nottingham's palisade. Convinced there were no signs of danger, he nodded to Gil and Much crouching in the bushes beside him.

The three men broke into a run

The sprint of about one-hundred yards to the wooden wall was harder for Robert and John. Each of them carried a ladder.

Much reached the wall first. "This is the spot," he whispered.

Looking around, Robert realized why Much had chosen this place to breach the wall. Nottingham's palisade had been extended like a bulge to enclose Lenton Abbey at the edge of town. Here at the bulge's tip, blocked by the abbey's steeple, was a spot not visible from the guard towers on either side.

Robert raised his ladder and carefully placed it against the wall. "Over you go," he whispered to Much.

Once Much had scrambled up the ladder and reached the top, John handed Much the second ladder they'd brought. Much then took John's ladder and quietly lowered it over the other side. Their breach of the palisade was now complete.

After nodding to Robert and John, Much disappeared over the wall.

Robert exhaled slowly. His only task for now was to wait – the most difficult job of all.

This foray had begun two days earlier with Friar Tuck's arrival at their camp.

After meeting with Robert, John and Much, the priest had eagerly agreed to their plan. Tuck would find any men inside Nottingham who were willing and able to fight, then bring the recruits to this spot behind his church at midnight of the new moon.

Robert's breath grew shorter. The length of Much's absence was becoming worrisome. Much had said the sentries patrolling inside the palisade changed shift at midnight. That left them less than a mileway to get their recruits out.

To Robert's relief, he heard the hoot of an owl, Much's signal that their recruits were coming out. When the first head appeared above the palisade, Robert began to count them.

By the time he was done, eleven men were outside the wall. But Robert had yet to see Much.

After an uneasy moment, Robert leaned close to John and said, "Get the men to our rendezvous point. I'm going to look for Much."

Climbing to the top of the palisade, Robert saw Much removing the ladder from the other side of the wall.

"What are you doing?" Robert whispered hoarsely.

"Something I should have done a long time ago." Much replied. "Godspeed to you, Robin. Now go!" he said and disappeared into the darkness, carrying the ladder.

For a moment, Robert froze, struggling to understand what Much was doing. Any thought of going after him was quickly dispelled, however.

In the distance, two sentries with torches were approaching along the palisade.

Robert climbed down the ladder and carried it away. They planned to use this spot over the wall again to bring food into the village. Leaving the ladder would alert the white sashes of a weakness in their palisade.

Once Robert reached the safety of their rendezvous point in the woods, his thoughts turned to Much. The newcomer's decision to stay inside Nottingham was puzzling. But one thing was clear.

Whatever Much intended, he planned to do alone.

* * *

After leaving Robin, Lester hid the ladder behind the abbey's shrubs and went inside the church looking for Friar Tuck. The priest was kneeling in prayer near the altar of the empty nave. Hearing footsteps behind him, Tuck turned toward the sound.

"Is something wrong, Much?" Tuck whispered, eyes darting for danger.

"No, Friar. The men are all safely over the wall," Lester answered softly, sitting down beside him. "I need you to hear my confession."

"There's no time, Much," Tuck said, rising to his feet. "The sentries will return soon and we cannot be seen together."

"Then, I'll not waste time with ritual," he said, guiding the priest to a dark alcove. "My real name is Lester Muchison," he said once they were out of sight. "I'm a sergeant in the Order of The Cross." Lester then explained the mission the sheriff had forced on him and the threat to his sister and her children for failing. "I can't betray Robin and his people, nor can I betray you," he said. "But there's only one way to save my sister and nephews. I need to kill the sheriff – tonight."

"As a man of God, I cannot help you take a life."

"I don't need your help, Friar. I only need you to tell Robin the truth and beg a favour of him," Lester said. "If I fail to kill the sheriff, ask Robin to save my sister and her children in Sheffield from Murdac's vengeance."

Tuck put his hand on Lester's shoulder. "He'll have your message tomorrow," he said.

* * *

As usual, Talbot Hall was guarded by a dozen sentries – four near the door and two at each corner of the stone-walled building. Striding fearlessly across the town square, Lester approached the torch-lit entrance. He'd decided not to hide the knife sheathed to his belt. Appearing to be unarmed might raise suspicions.

Despite his peasant clothing, the guards recognized him as he entered the cone of light around the ornate front door.

"I need to see the sheriff. It's urgent," Lester commanded as he strode toward them.

One of the guards banged the hilt of his sword against the door and called out, "Sergeant Muchison is here."

Lester held back a smile as he heard the door being unlatched. Once inside, he'd waste no time. The guards on the ground floor would let him pass to the sheriff's bedchamber on the second storey. There, he'd send Rudolf Murdac to hell without hesitation or mercy.

The door swung open and Lester stepped into the dimly lit great hall. Near the back of the large room was the stairway leading to the sheriff's bedchamber. Guarding the stairs, the corporal of the watch sat behind a small table, flanked by two warriors.

Recognizing Lester, the corporal stood and bowed. "Good evening, sergeant."

"Corporal, I have urgent news for the sheriff. I need to see him – immediately," Lester commanded.

"Inform the sheriff," the corporal said to one of the guards who hurried up the stairs.

Pacing as he waited, Lester tried to steady his nerves. He was counting on Murdac's laziness. The sheriff would not likely leave his bedchamber to receive a visitor late at night. Alone and unguarded, Murdac's indolence would seal his fate.

After an uncomfortably long time, the guard returned and gestured toward the stairs. "The sheriff said you're to go through."

Relieved, Lester bounded up the stairs and down the familiar hallway to the sheriff's bedchamber where he'd been summoned many times. At the door, he stopped, composing himself.

He would need to be swift and precise.

Drawing his knife, Lester opened the door and charged into the room.

Sitting on the bed, five paces away, Murdac turned to face him – with a wicked smile.

From each side, a pair of hands seized Lester. Caught off guard, he was dragged to the floor. Two more soldiers pinned him down and took his knife.

"Get him on his feet," the sheriff ordered.

Restrained by the guards, Lester stood before the sheriff, eyes lowered in shame.

"You're a fool, Muchison. Did you think I wouldn't see through your pathetic scheme?" Murdac said with a sneer. "I know you all too well, Lester. Men like you were born to fail," he said, acid in his voice. "You led me into an ambush. You lost half your men on a patrol. Then, after you failed to find the rebels, you decided to kill me and save your sister. Now, you've failed at that too." The sheriff then turned to his guards and said, "Lock him up. We'll execute this cur in the town square tomorrow. I want everyone to know the price for betraying me."

Lester closed his eyes, trying to hide a wave of relief. His plan to kill the sheriff had failed. But thanks to Murdac's disdain for him, his knowledge of the rebels would remain a secret – and Robin would save his sister.

Raising his eyes, Lester was ready to face his death in peace.

* * *

The people gathered in Nottingham's town square were oddly silent. Most crowds at an execution were gleeful and taunting, eager to see a notorious criminal meet his end.

But word soon spread through the village. This was no ordinary criminal. The condemned man had been a warrior of the Order of The Cross who had turned against the sheriff. Eager to see this curiosity, the square was packed. Onlookers gawked from trees and rooftops overlooking the shoulder-to-shoulder crowd.

Cutting a path through the throng, four guards from the Order of The Cross led Lester Muchison into the square. Lester walked between them, hands bound but head held high. The carpenters had begun work on the gallows only this morning and finished less than an hour ago. In the afternoon sun, the long shadow of the noose fell ominously on the six steps Lester would climb to meet his fate.

On the platform, the town crier and a black-masked executioner waited in silence. From the balcony of Talbot Hall behind the gallows, the Sheriff of Nottingham watched.

After the condemned man had climbed the steps to the platform, the crier broke the silence.

"Lester Muchison," the crier called out. "You have committed the crime of high treason. As the law dictates, you will be hanged by the neck, then disembowelled until dead." The crier paused, then said. "Do you have any last words?"

"I have something to say!" someone yelled from the rooftop of a bakery. Every face in the square turned toward the voice. "Let him go free!"

A smattering of cheers rose from the crowd.

"Arrest that man!" the sheriff shouted from the balcony, pointing toward the bakery.

The warriors in the square pushed through the crowd toward the bakery and entered the building as the man on the rooftop fled.

Standing next to the gallows and disguised beneath a floppy hat, Robert nodded to John and Gilbert who stood beside him. The big man knit his fingers, forming a step with his hands and hoisted Robert onto the scaffold. As all other eyes followed the soldiers, Robert took Lester's arm. "Come with me," he said softly, helping Lester jump to the ground. John and Gilbert steadied them as they landed.

"This way," John said, bulling his way through the crowd. Gil, Les and Rob followed closely behind him.

The crier was the first to notice. "He's getting away," he yelled, pointing toward Lester.

"After them! Now!" the sheriff shouted to his sentries at the entrance to Talbot Hall.

A half dozen warriors ran in pursuit but were slowed by the crowd.

Led by John, the four dashed between a pair of shops. After Robert freed Lester's bonds with his knife, they scrambled up the ladder Gil had placed there earlier and rose onto the ridge of the roof.

"I'm getting too old for this," John muttered, breathing heavily as he pulled the ladder onto the roof to keep the sheriff's soldiers from following.

Then all four broke into a run.

Following John, the four moved along the ridges of the thatch-covered roofs, leaping from building to building along the square.

"There – on the roof! I see them!" one of the guards below shouted.

Gilbert looked down and saw the helmets of the sheriff's men following them along the street below. "Pick up the pace, John," Gil called out. "They're gaining ground."

"Shut your yap," John said, huffing. "I'm going as fast as I can."

Knowing the layout of the town, Robert had planned an escape route that would keep them on the rooftops until they reached the sawmill on the edge of the palisade. From there, they would jump over the wall.

But Robert knew a stern test lay ahead. They were nearing a large space between the last shop on the square and an adjacent weaver's cottage. Whilst Robert watched anxiously, John launched himself across the span. The big man's body hurled through the air. To Robert's relief, John reached the ridge of the other roof – but then he stumbled, teetered for a moment and rolled down the gable, landing heavily on the ground.

"You two keep going. I'll help John," Robert said to Gilbert and Lester, then carefully slid down the gable toward the ground.

"No," Gilbert said, scrambling down the roof as well. "I'm going with you."

Lester stood on the rooftop for a moment. Escape was only a leap away. Shaking his head, he followed Robert and Gilbert to the ground.

Robert winced as he reached John. Sprawled on the stone-paved entry to the weaver's cottage, the big man was breathing but unconscious. Blood was pooling onto the paving stones where his head had struck, leaving the side of his skull flattened.

Whilst Robert crouched over John, looking for other injuries, Gilbert and Lester arrived.

"Let's get him inside," Gilbert said, pointing toward the door into the cottage.

Robert shook his head. "No, we could hurt him worse if we move him."

In the distance, someone shouted, "I don't see them on the roof anymore. Check the streets!"

"The sheriff's men are close," Lester said. "If they catch us out here, John won't fare any better."

Robert nodded. "Be careful moving him."

They carried John inside and laid him beside the loom at the centre of the room. Like most people in Nottingham, the weaver and his family were doubtless still in the square for the execution. Gilbert closed and barred the door.

Robert pointed toward the trail of John's blood leading into the cottage. "The white sashes will see that. We can't stay here long."

"We need to find another way back onto the roof," Lester said, looking around.

"What about John?" Gilbert asked.

Robert stared at his motionless comrade. "We'll have to leave him," he said soberly. "I'll get a message back to Tuck telling him where to find John."

"We can't leave him, Rob," Gil said angrily.

"Gil, we'll be caught carrying John through the streets – and we can't move him along the rooftops," Robert said.

"I say we fight our way out then," Gil replied.

Robert tapped the knife sheathed to his belt. "These are our only weapons – and they outnumber us, Gil. If we fight, we'll throw away our lives," he said. "Now go upstairs and see if you can find a way onto the roof. I'll tend to John's wound."

After hesitating for a moment, Gilbert climbed the ladder to the cottage's loft.

Robert tore a strip of cloth from a bolt by the loom and began wrapping John's head.

A few moments later, Gilbert appeared at the top of the ladder. "I've found a good spot to cut a hole through the thatch," he called out.

"Get started on that hole," Robert answered. "I'll finish tending to John."

Lester knelt beside Robert and whispered: "If John is taken alive, Murdac will find your camp."

"John won't talk."

"Have you ever seen a man put on the rack?"

"No."

"Any man will talk when his joints are slowly ripped apart," Lester said. "You're risking the lives of everyone in Angel Creek."

"I'll take the risks," Robert said, continuing the bandaging.

Lester touched Robert's shoulder. "I know it's a hard decision. Let me help you."

"What do you mean?" Robert said, facing Lester.

"His skull is cracked and he's lost a lot of blood," Lester said, gesturing toward the wound. "John's not likely to live." he said, then slowly pulled the knife on John's belt out of its sheath. "Go upstairs and join Gil. I'll make sure he doesn't suffer."

Robert rose to his feet and looked down at his comrade. He owed his life to John, many times over. But Lester was right. Leaving John here alive would risk more lives than his own. Marian, his mother and many others might die if John gave in to torture.

Robert nodded to Lester – then climbed the ladder to the loft.

The hole through the thatch was finished by the time Lester joined them in the loft.

"John is at peace," Lester said quietly before the three of them scrambled onto the roof.

Nones of October 1187

Under a violet sky flecked with stars, more than a hundred eager faces were bathed in amber by the glow of the main campfire at Angel Creek. A murmur of anticipation rose among them. Tonight, their leader would deliver a tribute to one of their fallen.

Seated on a stool at the edge of the fire, Robert scanned the crowd, collecting his thoughts. He'd never liked making speeches. But as he'd discovered at Thetford, words could be as powerful as swords and arrows.

Robert stood on the camp stool and raised his cup.

The group fell silent, turning their eyes his way.

"My friend John Little once stood on this spot and said he wanted no long faces the day he fell in battle," Robert said, casting his gaze over the crowd. "Most of you have joined our cause since then. Tonight, I ask that we tip our cups in memory of John Little, a man who gave his life fighting for justice a year ago today," he said solemnly, then emptied his cup onto the ground. Everyone across the camp did the same.

Then, Robert smiled and shouted, "Now let's celebrate in honour of John Little! Let there be no long faces tonight! Our bellies are full… the ale is plentiful… and we rule Sherwood Forest!"

A burst of cheers rose. Robert raised his fist, urging them on. When the clamour at last began to fade, Robert stepped down from the stool.

As a drinking song began nearby, a clutch of people gathered around Robert, eager for his attention. Robert accepted their praise – shaking hands, embracing them, basking in their approval.

Over the shoulders of those congratulating him, Robert saw Gilbert and Much. The pair sat in the shadows, away from the merriment, eyes downcast.

Robert's mood quickly soured.

During the past year, an unspoken pact had emerged between the three of them. Neither Robert, Gilbert nor Much ever mentioned John's last moments. Robert accepted the arrangement knowing each had his reasons for remaining silent.

"Robin! Come and listen!" Will Scarlett called out, waving Robert toward a circle formed around a man with a lute. When Robert reached Will, his young comrade said, "This is a troubadour from Sheffield with a song you'll want to hear."

Strumming on the lute, the minstrel sang.

"In Sherwood Forest dwells a man,

the leader of a daring band,
called rogues by some though they do good,
this hero's name is Robin Hood.
With wily art, the rich they lure,
to rob them and then gift the poor,
called rogues by some though they do good,
they're led by one called Robin Hood."

As the troubadour struck the last chord, the listeners broke into applause.

"I'm told this verse is being sung in all the midland shires," Will said to Robert.

Robert smiled faintly. "Let's hope the song doesn't reach King John."

After patting Will on the shoulder, Robert walked to the edge of their camp, away from the revelry. Despite the high spirits of the others, he felt empty and downcast.

Yet, they did indeed have much to celebrate.

They now outnumbered the sheriff's troops and controlled the countryside beyond the walls of Nottingham. Angel Creek, as they now called their camp, was a bastion Murdac's troops did not dare approach.

The key to their success had come from Anna and Marian. Their insistence on providing food for the peasants trapped in Nottingham had helped Robert's band survive – and thrive.

The food smuggled into Nottingham had kept the peasants from starving. Soon, more able-bodied men and women escaped, swelling the ranks of Robert's band. Some became men-at-arms who defended Angel Creek. Others provided labour for improvements to their camp. Along with more huts and cabins, Angel Creek now included an armoury, cookhouse, grain bin, stocks for a variety of animals, and several vegetable gardens – all under the watchful eye of Arthur Bland.

The king had stopped sending troops to Nottingham, a mystery Robert had yet to solve. As a result, Rudolf Murdac was hunkered down with his remaining troops behind Nottingham's palisade, unwilling to risk any sorties into the countryside.

The day-to-day lives of those at Angel Creek had flourished as well.

Whilst Robert led raids for silver with their seasoned warriors, Gil trained the new men to defend their camp and hunt for food. Going by the name of Much again, Lester oversaw the camp's defence. His sister and her children now lived in Angel Creek.

Marian taught the children in camp how to read – and their mothers and the other women how to use a crossbow. Anna had become Angel Creek's judge, resolving disputes with a stern but fair hand.

Robert walked farther from their camp. Reaching the softly burbling creek, he settled on its rocky bank.

Staring into the shadows, a vision rose in his mind – John Little lay lifeless on the floor of the weaver's home, his blood pooling slowly on the grey stones. Then John's eyes opened, wide with fear.

A hollow ache grew in Robert's chest and he began to weep.

Looking back, John's death had been a turning point. The Sheriff of Nottingham's fortunes had plummeted after the humiliation of Much's rescue.

But it was a hollow triumph – a realization Robert had not shared with the others.

By any measure, their survival had been miraculous. Yet their chances of staying alive had not grown. Eventually, the king would hear about this Robin Hood in Sherwood Forest. John would send more men-at-arms against them than ever before, commanded by someone more cunning than Rudolf Murdac.

Their camp was a fat lamb, ripe for the slaughter. Defeat and death were inevitable – and he had no answer for that fate.

The rippling of the creek was joined by the sound of footsteps behind him. Wiping the tears from his cheeks, Robert turned and found Marian approaching.

"I knew where to look when I saw you were missing," Marian said approaching him. "You only come here when you're troubled."

"Seems I have no secrets from you, woman," he said playfully, trying to mask his distress.

After reaching the bank, Marian sat down beside him. "Everyone in Angel Creek is celebrating. Yet you're out here, alone and brooding."

"Can't a man know a moment's peace?"

"Don't play coy with me, Robin. You keep worries to yourself, not wanting to burden the rest of us," she said, stroking the long locks of black hair that covered his shoulders. "But you dishonour me in thinking I'm not strong enough to know the truth."

Robert sighed. Marian was right. She'd shown the mettle to face hard facts – many times. After a moment, he spoke. "We're safe from the sheriff for the moment. But our hideout is no longer a secret. Someday soon, the king will send more soldiers, led by better men than Murdac," he said, then looked back toward the glow of the campfire. "We can't defend this place against them."

"I don't understand. Not long ago you were leading cheers. Why did you mislead the others if you know we're doomed?"

"I see no value in robbing our people of any joy with the time we have left."

Marian stared into the sky for a moment, then said, "I've never heard you talk like this, Robin."

"Since Richard's death, I've spent every waking moment trying to keep us all alive. We've bought ourselves some time now," he said, then turned to face Marian. "But we've only delayed the inevitable."

Marian shook her head. "You're wrong, my love," she said. "Did you expect to survive when you charged over the parapets at Amiens?"

"That was a choice I made for myself – in the heat of a battle."

"And the men you ordered to follow you into the fortress. Did you expect them all to live?"

"They were soldiers doing their duty. I'm among family and friends now – including women and children," he said, waving his hand toward the lights of their camp. "I can't lead them to their deaths. I've done too much of that already."

"Then what do you plan to do?"

Robert rubbed his face. "We could divide into smaller groups… evade the king's troops by moving…"

"Robin, we both know that's no less dangerous than staying together. If not, you would have split us up long ago," she said, then touched his face. "Your courage got us this far. We need more silver and more people to make us stronger. The answer is to be bold, my love. We can't turn back from this path – no matter the risks."

Kalends of December 1187

The blade of a winter wind sliced mercilessly through Robert's blue-green tunic. Perched in the high boughs of an evergreen, he gazed down a straight stretch of Sheffield Road lined with leafless trees.

Seven riders and a pack mule were slowly approaching the bridge where his men lay in wait. Although the convoy was still a half-mile away, by their bearing and deployment, Robert determined that six of the riders were personal guards. The seventh, riding with an old man's slouch, was doubtless a merchant. Their prize, Robert knew, was in the bulging saddlebags of the mule.

After waiting for hours, the right moment had finally arrived. The merchant caravans on the road earlier in the day had been either too large to take on, or too small to bother with. This group seemed perfect in size.

Pressing his fingers against his cheeks, Robert gave the call of a woodlark.

On the riverbank below, Robert's warriors began taking up their positions out of sight of the travellers – four under the near side of the bridge and four more below the far side of the thirty-pace span.

Once in place, each man cocked and nocked his crossbow, then raised a thumb toward Robert.

Staying out of sight from the riders, Robert climbed down the pine tree, took cover among its lower limbs, and prepared his own crossbow for battle.

The clopping of hoofbeats on the frozen ground announced the arrival of the slow-moving merchant party. Peering through the pine needles, Robert waited until the entire party was on the bridge.

Then he whistled loudly.

Moving as one, his men emerged from both sides of the bridge, their crossbows trained on the riders. The horsemen stopped, eyes wide with fear.

"Anyone who reaches for his sword will die," Robert called out loudly, stepping out of the evergreen.

Every face in the party turned toward the old man in the centre of their column, waiting for his orders. "Keep your weapons sheathed," the merchant said calmly.

"A wise decision," Robert said, stepping onto the bridge.

The merchant looked at Robert. "By the colour of your garb and the boldness of your manner, I can only assume you're Robin Hood."

"Think what you will," Robert said. "I'm here for the silver on that mule," he said, walking toward the animal.

As Robert began unfastening the saddlebags, the merchant said, "My business takes me on this road many times a year. If you rob us now, you'll get but one haul of silver from me. But if you let us pass and take only a share of our coin, you'll gain much more than that saddlebag holds."

Robert stopped, intrigued by the offer. "How?" he asked.

"I would pay for your protection each time I travel this road."

Robert laughed. "How can I be sure you won't travel with two dozen armed men next time?"

The old man shrugged. "I can pay for more escorts – or I can pay you. Either way, I lose the silver," he said. "I'm a man of commerce, sir. I account for the cost of security into the price of my goods. Paying you seems a smarter choice than adding more escorts."

Could he believe the merchant, Robert wondered? Examining the old man more closely, Robert noticed he wore a simple wool robe without jewels or adornments. His horse was sturdy, but its saddle and harness were plain. "What's your name, sir?" he asked.

"Jacob Cypora, I make razors in Sheffield," he said, then pointed at Robert's scraggly beard and added, "something which you could use, by the way."

Despite the tension, everyone on the bridge laughed.

"You're very shrewd, Mister Cypora," Robert said. "Yet you seem willing to trust I won't take all your silver the next time we meet."

"If what they say about you is true, I believe Robin Hood is a man who would honour his word. So tell me, can we strike a bargain?"

Robert stared at the merchant for a moment. Then patted the saddlebags and said, "I'll take twenty coins per hundred and you'll be free to go."

Jacob shook his head. "Ten per hundred."

"Fifteen," Robert countered.

The old man smiled and nodded. "We have a deal, Robin Hood."

* * *

As Jacob Cypora's party disappeared down the road, Gilbert pulled Robert aside. "Why didn't you take all his silver, Rob?" he asked, looking disparagingly at the modest sack of coins Robert held.

"The old man opened my eyes, Gil," Robert answered. "We stand to make more silver offering every merchant safe passage than seizing the booty of a handful."

"That makes no sense. Even with the sheriff's troops still squatting in Nottingham, we can't bring enough warriors this far north to control the road to Sheffield."

Robert smiled. "You're right – for the present. But think ahead, Gil," he said. "If we begin setting fees for passing through our own territory, before long we'll build enough wealth to expand our control into other areas."

"That makes sense," Gilbert conceded. "But I still don't understand why you let the old man off easy."

"I owed him that much for the lesson."

* * *

Before making his entrance into Westminster Hall, the king stopped and crooked his finger at the Lord Justiciar.

Walking across the antechamber toward the king, Robert de Beaumont tried to hide his irritation. He knew why the king was summoning him. John was lazy and refused to prepare for his royal audiences.

"Who is my first petitioner today, de Beaumont?" John asked after the justiciar reached him.

"The Baron of Sheffield, Your Highness."

"What does that clodpoll want?"

"He will ask Your Highness to deploy Royal Guards to his demesne. Apparently, there's a brigand in the midland shires called Robin Hood who is robbing merchants."

John pursed his lips. "That's out of the question."

Without asking, the justiciar knew why. John's cousins in the house of Anjou had recently won a key ally for their claim as legitimate heirs to the crown: the Archbishop of York. After being disgraced by John whilst he was regent, the archbishop had eagerly recognized the legitimacy of the Curtmantle brothers in the royal line of succession. As a result, John was now keeping his fortresses across the realm heavily garrisoned to quickly suppress any military moves by his cousins.

The justiciar nodded. "I understand, Sire."

"Speaking of the midland shires, what word do you have of Webber?"

"He's believed to have gone into exile, Sire."

John brushed some lint from his sleeve. "With your daughter's help, no doubt," he said, distractedly.

"Sire, we have no proof of that."

"Well, you must admit the timing of her disappearance is suspicious."

The justiciar bristled, then leaned close to John and spoke softly.

"Your Highness, if you think Marian's actions have put my loyalty to you in question, you need only request my resignation."

John clapped his justiciar on the shoulder. "Come, come, de Beaumont. Unruffle your feathers," he said, smiling slyly. "We've all had family members with questionable motives, have we not?"

Nones of April 1189

Robert sat astride his horse at the foot of the wooden bridge. A warm breeze stirred the trees nearby, casting their dappled shadows on the same bridge where Robert had encountered Jacob Cypora sixteen months earlier.

Back then, Robert had bartered with the old man for passage along this stretch of the Sheffield road. Now, his toll squads controlled key chokepoints in the area, extracting a fee from every merchant along the road.

They owed that dominance to constant inspections and drills. And today, Robert was testing the readiness of the most distant toll squad in the territory under his control.

The need for inspections among his troops was never ending – with good reason.

Most of the men under Robert's command were peasants who had abandoned their ploughs to join Robin Hood. Spread among these farmhands unfamiliar with weapons and military discipline were Robert's former Royal Guards – the glue that held his army together.

That cadre of experienced field officers had come courtesy of the king. John's fear of Royal Guard officers loyal to their former marshal had led him to purge its upper ranks.

Despite its shortcomings, through sheer size alone, Robin Hood's green-clad troops were an unrivalled force in the midland shires.

Moreover, Robin Hood's strength was growing each day whilst the strength of the midland lords was withering. Each defection of a peasant from a lord's estate weakened that lord's wealth – and his means to pay for warriors.

His inspection of the toll squad complete, Robert called its commanders aside. "What news do you hear from the merchants on this road, sergeant?" he asked.

"There's talk that the lords of the midlands will petition the king for troops to take back the roads from us," the sergeant said.

"I've heard the same rumour," the corporal added. "But I doubt it's true, sir. I'd say the merchants just want to scare us off."

"There's something else, sir," the sergeant said. "We've got more recruits wanting to join us. But a pair in this lot is different. Two warriors serving the Baron of Sheffield turned their swords over to us yesterday. We've got them tied up over there," he said, pointing toward a small copse of trees.

Robert stroked his beard for a moment. "I want to speak to them," he finally said.

Reaching the defectors, Robert found the two men bound to trees. "Release them," he said to the sergeant.

Once they were unbound, the men dropped to a knee before Robert and bowed their heads. "Thank you, Mister Hood," the older of the defectors said. "We've come to serve you."

"Why have you left the Baron of Sheffield?" Robert asked.

"We haven't seen a penny of our pay for near on to three months," the older man said.

"The baron's stopped feeding us, too," the younger man added. "He told us to forage in the countryside for food."

"How long have you served as a warrior?" Robert asked the older man.

"Fourteen years, sir."

"And you?" Robert asked the other.

"Five years, sir," he said.

Robert turned to the sergeant. "See that these men are fed and ready to travel. I'll be taking them south with me."

* * *

"Silence!" King John screamed, rising to his feet, jowls quivering.

The eight men in the royal parlour stopped squabbling and bowed their heads. But the tight-lipped faces of the lords of the midland shires gathered around the king's table revealed anger, not submission.

"For the last time," the king said. "I will accept no response to Robin Hood's mischief that includes removing a single Royal Guard from any of my palaces."

Sitting at the other end of the table from King John, the Lord Justiciar fought the urge to speak. John's obsession with keeping his palaces fully garrisoned was clouding the king's judgment. These nobles had fair grievances –and ignoring them would only make matters worse.

From his informants, de Beaumont had learned the Archbishop of York had launched a whisper campaign against the king. The rumours accusing John of being a debauched sodomite were having a devastating impact.

Believing that John was depraved and unholy, defections had spread among warriors of the Order of The Cross in service to the king. Through their alliance with the archbishop, John's cousins had weakened his military power.

Compounding this setback, John's petulance was now risking a rebellion with the lords of the midlands. This was clearly a blunder. But de Beaumont held his tongue. He knew his dissent before these lords would only feed John's rage.

After the king sat down, the Earl of Devon said, "Your Highness, with all respect, calling Robin Hood's actions mischief is like calling a hungry lion a kitten. That brigand has wreaked havoc in Nottinghamshire."

"I agree with the earl," said the Baron of Sheffield. "Robin Hood controls most of the trade routes through our shires. Scarcely a merchant travels through his territory without paying his highwaymen for so-called protection."

The Baron of Ashby turned his gaze toward the king. "Every day, Robin Hood grows stronger – and the nobles of the midlands grow weaker," he said. "Our serfs are leaving their fields to join the brigand. He lures them away with promises of plunder. Sire, Robin Hood has created an army right under our noses."

"Your Highness," the Earl of Lincoln said, his face taut. "I'm losing my serfs to Robin Hood as well. Yet you've raised our taxes and scutage again. How can you expect us to meet these obligations without serfs to work the land?"

The Earl of Devon spoke again. "Sire, most of the warriors from the Order of The Cross you sent to suppress the rebellion in Nottingham have abandoned the sheriff there. I've had to send men-at-arms from Devonshire to keep Nottingham from falling into rebel hands. My military resources are stretched to their limits."

"We've lost the support of The Order in my demesne as well," the Baron of Ashby added. "We need your help in these matters, Sire. If you cannot offer us troops, at least give us some relief on our obligations to the crown."

A chorus of assent rose from the other lords.

John slammed his hand on the table. "Enough!" he shouted angrily.

A stony silence followed.

John swept his gaze over the faces around him. "I've sat and listened to your snivelling and I'm disgusted by your weakness. Each of you has men-at-arms. Yet you come to me begging for troops and dispensation from your obligations to the crown because you lack the wiles and the courage to bring a common criminal to justice," he said, then flicked his wrist toward them. "Begone, the lot of you, I have more important matters to attend."

Ides of April 1189

Gilbert Whitehand looked over the men standing before him. They were a ragged lot, still in the rough-hewn peasant clothes they'd worn into camp. Their only semblance of a uniform was a strip of Lincoln green cloth tied around their hats – or the foreheads of those without them.

"Scouts, I'll be training your group today," Gilbert called out to the men. "Pikes and Swords, you'll report to Arthur Bland for kitchen duty. Archers and Cavalry, you'll help Much Millerson with defence construction. Any questions?"

"When will we be getting horses and saddles, sir?" one of the men in the Cavalry team called out. "Training on logs all day is putting splinters in my arse."

A chortle rose from the men. Glaring at the recruit, Gilbert said, "Jenkins, you'll find my boot in your arse if you ever waste my time at morning assembly again." Whitehand watched their smiles fade. "Dismissed," he said.

The men grumbled as they walked away – and Gilbert understood their frustration. Their military training was often busy work. But there was little he could do about that.

As the camp's only trainer, Gilbert had to divide his time among raw recruits who arrived at random intervals and in varying numbers. Gilbert's solution had been to sort the men into five stages of training and divide his time among the teams.

Over the last week more than a dozen new men had arrived in camp, swelling the ranks of the Scouts team, the place Whitehand started his rawest recruits. The next four groups reflected escalating levels of martial skill: Pikes, Swords, Archers and Cavalry. The most promising men in each group quickly graduated to the next level of training. Those who Gilbert deemed ready, were given a green tunic and deployed to active duty.

Gilbert was leading his Scouts team toward their training ground when he spotted Robert crossing a meadow toward him with two men Whitehand did not recognize. "Wait here," he said to the platoon.

Meeting Robert and the strangers in the meadow, Gilbert smiled and said, "It's a rare day when Robin Hood himself brings me new recruits."

"These aren't ordinary volunteers," Robert said, nodding toward the pair. "They were men-at-arms for the Baron of Sheffield."

Gilbert's eyes widened. After a moment, he said, "We need to speak alone."

"Wait for us by the creek," Robert said to the men, nodding toward a stream about fifty paces away.

Once they were alone, Gilbert said, "Did you shite your brains with breakfast, Rob? These men could be spies."

"That's true for any of the men who've joined us, Gil. Besides, I think the last thing a spy would do is tell us they'd soldiered for a baron."

Gilbert rubbed his face. "I don't like it, Rob. Those men may have the blood of our own people on their hands. I say we hang them."

"If we hang defectors, our enemies will only fight harder. They'll never surrender."

"Then put them on our most dangerous duty up north. Let these sods take the risks. Don't bring them back here where it's safe."

"Think that through, Gil. Up north, they may face men they know. Forcing someone to fight against his old comrades is too much to ask. If we do that, we'll risk losing their loyalty."

"Loyalty?" Gil scoffed. "These curs have none."

"They have something we lack… military experience. The older one has been a soldier fourteen years. The younger one for five."

"What good will that do if we can't use them on the battlefield?"

Robert exhaled slowly. "The lords of the midland shires are running short on silver. They're struggling to pay their men-at-arms. These won't be the last defectors we'll see, Gil," he said. "We've been given a gift. Let's not squander it."

"Why bring these men to me, then? If they're already warriors, they don't need my training."

"No, they don't need you, Gil," Robert said. "You need them."

As Robert's words dawned on Gilbert, a smile spread across his face. "I think the older one can take over the training of my Swords team right away."

Nones of September 1189

"**P**lease wait here, Sheriff. The justiciar is expected presently," the butler said before leaving the room and closing the door behind him.

Rudolf Murdac cast his eyes around the parlour. The large room was meant to impress visitors with Robert de Beaumont's wealth and power. The effect was not lost on Murdac.

The wood-panelled walls had ornate sconces and fine tapestries of forest scenes. Plush curtains framed the tall windows. Over the fireplace was the de Beaumontheraldic coat: a white cinquefoil with black ermine markings on a red shield. Murdac took a seat in a corner of the room amid an array of carved chairs placed around several tables.

The impact of the lavish room made Murdac question the wisdom of his visit. He was entering a world of status and power far beyond his own. Was he ready for this?

His move into this high-stakes game had started a fortnight ago after being summoned to Exeter by the Earl of Devon. There, the absentee lord of Nottingham had given him a directive that left the sheriff paralysed with fear. The earl ordered Murdac not to pay the king's taxes and scutage due at Michaelmas. The other lords of the midland shires had agreed to do the same, the earl explained. Their goal was to force the king to send an army north to subdue Robin Hood. Masking his terror, Murdac had agreed.

After leaving Exeter, however, Murdac's nerve began to falter.

Would it be worse to defy the Earl of Devon or defy King John? After considering the king's reputation for cruelty, Murdac headed for London instead of returning to Nottingham.

Still, there was risk in revealing the earl's plan to the justiciar. Before he could ponder his misgivings any further, the door opened.

Murdac rose to his feet as the justiciar entered the room.

"Please state your business, Sheriff," de Beaumont said brusquely, his disdain unmistakeable. Murdac could see the justiciar had not forgiven his unlucky mishaps.

The sheriff raised his chin, screwing up his courage. "The Earl of Devon has ordered me to withhold payments of the king's taxes and scutage. Every baron in the midlands will do the same come Michaelmas. I thought you should know that, m'lord."

The justiciar's eyes widened. Then his face warmed into a smile. "You did the right thing coming here, Sheriff."

"I thought telling you of this treachery was my duty to the crown, m'lord."

"You'll return to Nottingham and say nothing about this to anyone. When you learn of anything new about this alliance – especially any military plans – you'll send word to me immediately. Do you understand?"

Murdac nodded eagerly. "Yes, m'lord."

"Wait here," the justiciar said and left the room. De Beaumont returned a few moments later carrying a fat leather purse. "Your loyalty to the crown will continue to be rewarded," he said, handing Murdac the pouch. "I'll see to that personally."

* * *

De Beaumont approached the king's bedchamber rehearsing what he was about to say. He'd carefully chosen the time and place for this conversation with the king. The justiciar had learned that catching John in a good mood was the best time to give him difficult news.

Following his noonday meal, the king was usually pleasured in his bedchambers, often by a lass, at other times a lad, sometimes by both. After dismissing his bed mates, John took a nap and usually awoke in placid spirits.

The justiciar knocked gently on the door.

"Enter," John said from inside the bedchamber.

Stepping into the room, the justiciar found the king on a four-poster bed, propped up by pillows, his large belly rising like a mound of snow under rumpled white sheets. Despite the open windows letting in a mild fall breeze, the room smelled of sex.

"I hope Your Highness enjoyed his nap," de Beaumont said with a courteous bow.

The king yawned. "What brings you here?" he said, reaching for a goblet of wine from a table beside the bed.

De Beaumont cleared his throat. "Several lords of the midland shires are trying to make a statement – and they've chosen a rather unfortunate way to do it, Your Highness."

"What kind of statement?" John asked, his eyes narrowing.

"They're showing their displeasure about your lack of assistance in capturing the brigand Robin Hood, Sire."

John took a sip of wine. "I've made myself clear on this, have I not? Why should I change my mind?"

"They're applying considerable leverage, Sire," de Beaumont said. "I've learned from a reliable source that these lords will publicly refuse to pay their obligations to the crown unless Your Highness sends an army to rid the midlands of Robin Hood."

"The impudent pismires!" John screamed, throwing his goblet across the room.

The justiciar silently thanked his stars John's reaction had not been worse.

His rage spent, John's shoulders sank. "What am I going to do, de Beaumont?" he whimpered, eyes welling. "Those pious bigots of The Order have betrayed me. If I send my Guards north to put down this bandit, my cousins will close on me like wolves."

"There's a way out of this dilemma, Sire," the justiciar said. He then walked closer to the bed. "They want to send you a message. You can send one in return."

John wiped his eyes and nodded for the justiciar to continue.

"We know what they plan to do, Sire. You can seize that advantage and turn it against them," the justiciar explained. "Before they reveal their ploy, announce you'll send a powerful army north in the spring to destroy Robin Hood – and do it with great fanfare. Make a proclamation. Send out heralds. Convince everyone in the realm that you'll have Robin Hood's head on a spike by Easter."

"How will that keep my cousins from exploiting the absence of my troops?"

The justiciar smiled. "You're sending a message, Your Highness. Not an army," he said.

"I still don't understand."

"Once the midland lords hear the Royal Guards are coming their way, they'll pay their taxes and scutage. They won't dare do otherwise. After all, you can turn that army against any one of them who defies you." De Beaumont paused and tapped his fingertips. "When the silver they owe is in your hands... well... circumstances may arise that keep you from mobilising the army. Say, a small rebellion near London for example."

"The lords will be furious when they realize they've been tricked," John said warily. "They might form a military alliance against me."

"I have a spy inside their circle, Sire. If they take up arms, we'll know their every move."

A sparkle rose in John's eyes. "Defeating them in war would put more land under my control."

"Yes, Your Highness. That would be a happy consequence."

John took the justiciar's palm and placed it between his hands. "You're a faithful servant of your king, de Beaumont. Draft the proclamation announcing my army's march against the brigand."

Ides of October 1189

The crunch of breaking wood made the young buck lift his head, ears perked for danger.

Forty paces away, Robert grimaced as he looked down and saw the snapped twig under his boot. The chance to get any closer to his quarry was gone. There was still time to launch an arrow – but at this range a kill wasn't likely.

As Robert drew back his longbow, the whoosh of a projectile passed his ear.

The buck stumbled to his knees, a bolt half-buried in his hip.

"Launch, Robin!" Marian said, reloading her crossbow, two steps behind him. "Take him down!"

Squinting at his target, Robert let his arrow fly.

"Shite!" he yelled as his arrow missed.

The wounded deer staggered to his feet and limped into the under-brush.

Robert hurled his bow to the ground. "We'll never catch him," he said bitterly. "He's wolf meat now."

Marian sighed. After a moment, she smiled and said, "We've been on many hunts, my love. But I've never seen you sulk. There's something troubling you."

"The white sashes say women who read minds are witches," he said, a smile spreading on his face. "I fear they may be right."

"Out with it, then. What are you holding back?"

Robert's smile faded. There was no point in hiding the news from Marian. Everyone in camp would know soon enough. "We're planning an assault on Nottingham."

"Why, Robin?" she asked, brows furrowed. "The sheriff isn't a threat to us."

"You're right. Murdac is not a threat at all," Robert said, picking up the bow. "The real threat is the king."

"The king?"

"John's heralds are spreading the word in all the northern shires. He's sending an army of Royal Guards against us in the spring. Friar Tuck brought me the news yesterday."

"Then why assault Nottingham?"

"We have an army of farmhands, Marian. If we face the Royal Guards in open battle, they'll slaughter our men like sheep. We'll stand a better chance against them inside the palisade."

"Fighting two battles seems risky, Robin," she said. "The Earl of Devon's men guarding Nottingham are fewer, but they're also better soldiers."

"I've taken fortresses far stronger than Nottingham."

"That's true. But you had well-trained troops – and John Little to build siege towers."

"I met with Will, Much and Gilbert last night. We all agree," he said with an air of finality. "Storming Nottingham is the best chance we have."

Marian folded her arms, giving him a hard look. "You didn't think I had a place at your council last night?"

"Well… I didn't think you'd be interested," Robert said, tugging at his collar.

"If you'd bothered to include me, Robert Webber, you might have heard a different way to capture Nottingham – a way that puts fewer men at risk."

"I'm listening now," he said contritely.

"The first mistake you're making is thinking like a soldier."

"How else should I think?"

"Like a lord," she said firmly.

As the pair walked back to camp, Robert listened in awe.

Nones of November 1189

Rudolf Murdac took a draught of wine, then scowled in disgust. "This wine has turned," he said, tossing the remains of his chalice to the floor. "Have the steward open another cask," he said to the soldier stationed near the door.

The soldier bowed and left the dining chamber of Talbot Hall.

The Sheriff of Nottingham continued his noonday meal, annoyed but still bolstered by the recent turn of events. Over a hundred peasants had voluntarily returned to Nottingham – a fact he would soon report to the justiciar with glee.

Apparently, this Robin Hood character was no longer willing or able to feed the peasants who had flocked to him. The brigand's rations must have been meagre indeed. The peasants returning to Nottingham knew the most they'd get inside the walls was a pottle of grain per head each month.

Most likely Robin Hood had tired of giving away the silver he stole – if he'd ever given it away at all. Minstrels were such liars.

A white-faced soldier rushed into the dining hall.

"Where's my wine?" Murdac demanded.

"Wine? I know nothing about that, Sheriff," he said breathlessly. "The corporal of the guard sent me. He needs you at the main gate – it's urgent."

Murdac rose from the chair. "This better be important," he said angrily. The men the Earl of Devon had sent to replace the defectors from The Order were a haughty lot.

Arriving at the main gate, the sheriff climbed the ladder to the parapet above the fortified entrance. The corporal of the guard and a dozen other warriors stood waiting for him, swords and bows in hand.

"They arrived just moments ago," the corporal said, nodding his head toward the meadow outside the wall.

Murdac swallowed hard. Before him were more than a hundred men-at-arms on horseback in helmets and full chain maille. Their shields bore a crest he did not recognize: two white swans on a field of green. Their steadiness and calm unnerved Murdac. These were clearly hardened warriors – and their number was equal to the men under his command.

"What's your purpose here?" the sheriff called out, his voice unsteady.

One of them removed his helmet. The man was clean-shaven with closely cropped hair. He said, "I'm Sir Robert Webber, the rightful Baron of Nottingham and heir of Talbot Hall. You'll open the gate and let us enter."

Murdac shuddered at the sound of Webber's name. Evidently, the bastard had returned from exile. Before the sheriff could decide his next move, the church bell began to peal. As Murdac turned toward the sound, his eyes widened with horror.

Peasants were emerging from every hovel inside the palisade armed with pitchforks, hoes, and knives. Wordlessly, over a hundred of them converged on the parapet, their eyes boring into Murdac's own, their menace toward him unmistakable.

"It's time you set us free, Sheriff!" one of the peasants yelled. Shouts of approval rose from the throng.

"What's your answer, Mister Murdac?" Webber called out from his steed.

Murdac looked into the angry faces on one side of the parapet and the hardened warriors on the other. "Open the gate," he said, his voice hoarse with dread.

A cheer rose from the crowd as the door swung open and Robert Webber's contingent rode inside the palisade.

Murdac scrambled down the ladder and dropped to his knees beside Webber's horse. "Spare me, Sir Robert," he said, eyes downcast. "I was only following the orders of a wicked king."

Turning to one of the men in his contingent, Robert said, "He's all yours, Much."

Murdac's mouth gaped in terror as he recognized his former underling. Much dismounted, grabbed the sheriff by the collar, and led him toward the village blockhouse.

Robert then addressed the sheriff's soldiers on the parapet. "You're all free to leave Nottingham in peace. But your weapons will stay."

Sneering at the cowardice of their commander, the men-at-arms unbuckled their sword belts, dropped their bows and quivers, and climbed down from the wall.

Most of Nottingham was gathered around the gate by now. As the sheriff's men left the village, they were jeered by the crowd.

A rider beside Robert doffed his helmet and chain maille, revealing a cascade of golden hair. Whilst the onlookers gasped at the sight of a woman in armour, Marian drew her sword and thrust it in the air. "The rightful Baron of Nottingham has returned to his people! Justice and honour will rule here again!" she shouted.

The roar of approval that followed was thunderous.

When Robert and his contingent began riding toward Talbot Hall, the crowd followed, eager to touch him, showering him with praise. Robert saw familiar faces… Faye Rolfe and her family… the bullies who had taunted him, now grown men… Friar Tuck waving from the steps of Lenton Abbey.

Riding among the villagers, Robert could feel their pride. He was one of them. Although he would now live in the manor, his heart would always be with the common folk. Robert took deep breaths, holding back tears.

The triumphant procession moved slowly through Nottingham until they reached Talbot Hall on the town square. There, they dismounted. Robert's men dispersed among the crowd who gleefully embraced them as heroes. Meanwhile, Robert stepped through the front door of the manor with Marian beside him.

He fought an urge to gawk as they walked through the great hall with its high ceiling, family portraits and tapestry-covered walls. This was Robert's first time inside his father's manor.

Near the centre of the room stood the manor's steward. "I've heard the news of your arrival, m'lord. Welcome to Talbot Hall," he said with a bow.

Robert stared for a moment, uncertain what to say.

"The baron would like a tour of the manor," Marian said to the steward.

"Of course, m'lady," the steward said. "Please follow me."

Over the next half-hour, Robert and Marian were guided through the grounds of Talbot Hall. The manor house was modest by royal standards. He and Marian had seen the opulence of a king's palace as Richard's guests. Still, Robert could not help but swell with pride.

"We'll have eight for the evening meal," Marian said to the steward after the tour ended in the master bedchamber on the second storey.

"Very well, m'lady. I'll inform the staff," the steward said, then bowed and left them alone.

Marian walked closer to Robert and stroked his smooth-shaven cheek. "I've missed this face against my skin."

Looking into Robert's eyes, Marian slowly removed the warrior's garb and let it drop to the floor. Shedding the last of her garments, she lay back across the bed. "Since the first day we met, I've known you wanted a barony. Shall we inaugurate your first day in the manor, your lordship?" she murmured.

* * *

A jubilant din filled the dining chamber at Talbot Hall.

Seated at the head of a long table lit by two candelabras, Robert savoured the moment.

The people closest to him were gathered here tonight... his mother and grandfather, Marian, Friar Tuck, Will, Gilbert and Arthur Bland. Their faces were exuberant as they feasted on a bounty of food and drink.

The steward appeared with another pitcher of wine and began filling goblets.

With his cup full, Robert stood and raised it in a toast. The others fell silent and he said, "I want to recognize the person most responsible for bringing us here tonight." He nodded toward Marian, then said, "Marian argued that duping Murdac into a surrender would be wiser than taking Nottingham by storm... and she was right."

A chorus of assent and cheers rose from those around the table.

Gilbert downed a gulp of ale, wiped his lips on his sleeve and said, "Rob, did you see Murdac's face after the friar rang the bell?"

Much answered instead. "I thought he'd piss himself," he said, sparking a peal of laughter.

Robert tipped his cup toward the priest. "Our dear Friar Tuck was very timely with his bell chorus – and in arming our friends who turned themselves in to the sheriff. We wouldn't be sitting here without you as well, Friar."

The priest smiled and lifted his cup. "Nottingham once again has its rightful lord."

"And let's not forget Mister Bland," Robert added, raising his cup toward Arthur. "How you managed to dress up our scruffy lot to look like noble men-at-arms was a feat of magic."

Arthur covered his mouth as he laughed. "I'm glad you kept your distance from the sheriff or he'd have noticed the paint was still wet on the shields."

"Why two swans as your crest?" Friar Tuck asked Robert.

"That was inspired by Marian – a long time ago," Robert said, looking toward her.

Marian smiled slyly. "I'll say no more about that to this churlish lot."

A roar of laughter followed.

Anna stood and raised a silver goblet. "Almost three years ago, Arthur brought us the news that King Richard was dead. Who among us then could have dreamed that God's will would bring us to this place?" she said, sweeping her hand around the opulent room. "As we celebrate our good fortune, let's also honour a man who gave his life to bring us here... to John Little," she said, then raised her goblet toward the others.

"To John Little," they responded, raising their cups.

Robert noticed that Gilbert and Much looked away during the toast, a sign their unease over John's death still lingered. His own memories of the big man still haunted Robert as well. Burying the thought, Robert rose and spoke.

"I stand before you tonight as the Baron of Nottingham, a title that justice demanded be mine. Yet justice could not have been served without the sacrifice and support of everyone here," he said, sweeping his eyes over the group. "Therefore, as your baron, I pledge to always rule with fairness and honour, for the well-being of my people."

Even the servants cheered their righteous new lord.

Later that night, whilst Robert lay beside Marian, the bliss of the wine and revelry began to fade. In its place came a sober reminder.

Come spring, they would face John's army behind the palisade of Nottingham. If they failed, his days as the Baron of Nottingham would be very short lived.

* * *

Robert entered the parlour at Talbot Hall rubbing his temples. Last night's wine had become this morning's pain.

Scanning the room, he found an array of meat and fruit the steward had laid out for breakfast – but was surprised to find no sign of Marian. He'd awakened to an empty bed and expected she'd be here.

Gilbert, Much and Will were missing as well.

At last night's feast, the five of them had agreed to meet at the prime hour this morning to begin preparations for the defence of Nottingham. Now, the time of that agreement seemed like a folly wrought by wine.

Ignoring breakfast, Robert dropped into a padded chair away from the windows. The glare of the morning sun pierced his eyes like daggers.

When Marian arrived smiling brightly, Robert barely opened his eyes. "Where have you been?"

"I didn't want to wake you when I went for a ride, my love," she said cheerfully, putting pear slices and dried venison on a plate. "You seemed to need the rest."

Whilst Marian took a seat beside Robert, Will Scarlett and Gilbert Whitehand entered the room. Both looked as bedraggled as Robert.

"Have either of you seen Much?" Robert asked as the two men sat down.

"He was headed for the blockhouse when I left the officers' quarters," Gilbert answered.

Marian put down her plate and looked at Robert. "Do we need to wait for Much?"

"Any plans we make for Nottingham's defence should include Much's military experience," Robert said.

Waving a pear slice at Robert, Marian said, "That assumes we'll need to defend Nottingham with warriors."

"Perhaps the lady proposes we scold the king in a letter," Gilbert said sourly.

Rising to her feet, Marian said, "When the king sends his army north in the spring, we can fight the Royal Guards from inside the palisade – or we can live here in peace without any bloodshed at all."

Gilbert scoffed. "How could we get the king to leave us in peace? John's made it known he aims to destroy Robin Hood."

"Yes, Gilbert," Marian answered. "The king is sending his army to subdue Robin Hood. But Robin Hood does not rule Nottingham. Sir Robert Webber does."

Will's eyes brightened. "Yes, I understand. That's very clever, m'lady," he said. "So far as the king knows, Robin Hood remains at large."

"No, this is foolish," Gilbert grumbled. "Even if the king believes it's Rob who rules Nottingham and not Robin Hood, what's to stop John from using the Guards to oust a rebel baron?"

"We start by paying John the taxes and scutage on this demesne – with an extra half-share more than the Earl of Devon to sweeten the bargain," Marian answered.

Will nodded. "John is greedy and battles are costly," he said. "The king will take the silver and avoid the fight."

"Where will we get all this silver? We've spent most of what we had," Gilbert said. "If Rob's a baron, he can't very well sack the rich around us, can he? That would create enemies of the nobles in these parts."

Marian smiled slyly. "The Baron of Nottingham can't sack rich merchants. But Robin Hood still can."

The three men stared at Marian, stunned into silence.

"The solution is simple," Marian explained, "Robin Hood can continue to liberate silver from the merchants," she said, then put her hand on Robert's shoulder. "Meanwhile, the Baron of Nottingham will rule peacefully over his demesne – with enough wealth to pay the king and still build up our defences."

Gilbert shook his head. "Rob can't be in two places at once."

"We can use impersonators," Marian countered. "Not many people know what Robin Hood looks like. They just know he wears a green tunic, has long hair and a beard."

"There's still a flaw in that scheme," Gilbert said. "Over a hundred people in Angel Creek who know Robert Webber is Robin Hood. How will we keep that a secret?"

"That's a risk, it's true," Marian said. "But in Angel Creek, we trusted those same people not to betray Robin because he gave them food, shelter and protection. Why should that be any different now?"

"Even if a loose tongue lets the secret out, it will still be a rumour without proof," Will offered.

Gilbert stared hard at Robert, gripping the arms of his chair. "I can't believe you'd grovel before this crooked king and pay his taxes," he said bitterly. "This turns my stomach, Rob."

Marian's eyes flashed angrily. "My stomach turns every time you call the Baron of Nottingham by his given name," she said to Gilbert. "It's time you showed some respect."

Eager to defuse the confrontation, Robert said, "I called us together to gain from your counsel. I value each—"

Before Robert could finish, Much entered the room holding Rudolf Murdac by the collar. The sheriff's face was bruised and bloodied. "Tell them," Much said to Murdac.

His eyes on the floor, Murdac said, "The Earl of Devon and the other lords of the midlands made a secret pact. They agreed to stop paying the king's taxes until he rids the midland shires of Robin Hood."

Much shoved the sheriff. "Tell them all of it."

"I travelled to London and told the justiciar about the lords' agreement."

Robert rose to his feet, his gaze intense. "When did you tell the justiciar?" he asked Murdac. "Was it before the king announced he was sending an army north?"

"Yes, m'lord," Murdac answered. "The royal proclamation came not long afterward."

"Guards!" Robert called out. Moments later, four soldiers entered the room. "Take this man back to the blockhouse."

When Murdac was gone, Robert turned to the others and said, "John is bluffing. He won't be sending an army north in the spring."

Ides of May 1190

Standing at the altar, Friar Tuck raised his palms in benediction. The priest's voice echoed through the near empty chapel as the wedding mass drew to a close. "May God bless your union and look upon you with grace so that you may both live together in this world and be joined in life everlasting. Amen," he said, making the sign of the cross over the couple kneeling before him.

Robert and Marian rose and kissed tenderly.

The newlyweds then walked arm in arm from the altar.

In the first row of Talbot Hall's chapel were the wedding's only guests… Anna, Simon, Will, Arthur, Gilbert and Much. They watched the couple leave the church before following them outside.

A light spring rain fell as the wedding party gathered under a canopy where food and drink awaited them. After the customary congratulations, the guests soon divided by class or kinship, leaving Gilbert and Much apart from the others.

Nodding toward the newlyweds, Gilbert leaned close to Much and said, "There won't be any blood on their bed linens tonight. The wine in that cask was tapped long ago."

"That's a harsh thing to say, Gil."

"You're right," Gilbert said, sneering. "Those two won't waste any time humping. They'll spend the whole night scheming up yet another way to stroke the king's staff."

Much shook his head. "The wedding is a shrewd move, Gil. Marrying the justiciar's daughter gives Rob more standing among the gentry – and that's good for all of us."

"Maybe," Gilbert said reluctantly. "But I can't abide sending our silver to that pig on the throne. Did you see Will when he returned from London? He crowed like we'd won a battle after giving John the money our men bled to get."

"Rob is trying to lull the king to sleep," Much said to his comrade. "Meantime, he's sending couriers to all the lords in these parts, trying to build alliances. Rob is thinking ahead, Gil. Wars are won with guile, not just spilling guts."

"I'll say this… Rob was right about the king's bluff. John's army never came."

Much laughed. "The king's excuse about a rebellion in Kent was thinner than a goat penned in a stone quarry."

"But John still got what he wanted, didn't he?" Gilbert said bitterly. "Rob and the other lords paid their taxes."

"Aye, but John's trick will only work once. Rob will make sure of that."

* * *

Robert was surprised to see Marian wince the first time he entered her. The long, sensuous start to their lovemaking had left her thighs glistening. He had not expected her pain – until he saw the blood.

"Don't stop, Robin," she said hoarsely. "We've waited too long."

Slowly, sinuously, their bodies melded in the rhythm of passion until Marian moaned and arched her back in ecstasy.

Her climax heightened Robert's excitement and he groaned as his own pleasure peaked.

After a time, Robert gently lowered himself alongside her. "I didn't know you were a maid, Marian," he whispered, stroking her hair.

A smile warmed her face. "I understand why you're surprised," she said, then laughed softly. "Being a widow with my reputation, you expected someone more worn than a brood mare. Admit it."

"Your past never mattered to me," he said, shaking his head.

Marian sighed. "There's something I've never told you," she whispered. "The French nanny who raised me after my mother died had been my father's mistress when she was young. Her name was Julie. When I came of age, she taught me how to pleasure men without bearing a child. Julie insisted that privilege should only be my husband's. Clement never claimed that privilege."

"The night we met, you taunted me for believing in honour," he said, gently pinching her chin. "Yet you were secretly keeping a vow of your own."

"My promise to Julie made me feel stodgy and provincial in those days. Now I realize the value of her wisdom. Julie led me to a man like you, my love," she said softly, then laid her head on his chest.

Before long, they were making love again.

* * *

A grey dawn seeped between the bedchamber curtains as Robert awoke. Nestled under his arm, Marian was still asleep. Looking at her face, he sighed.

His dreams had been granted. He was a baron and Marian was his wife. But dreams were tenants of the night. The day shed its light on harsh truths.

His marriage was only one step on the path to safety for those he loved. So long as John was king, they were all still in danger.

Yes, John had been pacified. The bloated tax payments Will had delivered to the king were a thinly veiled bribe John had gladly accepted. In time, however, the king's hatred would overtake his greed. John was too petty to forgive a long-time rival. The day the king really sent an army against him, all would be lost. Robert had no doubt of that.

Nottingham's wooden battlements were no match for the king's might. The only fortress that could withstand John's forces was an alliance with other lords. That kind of stronghold would take time to build.

He'd already sent messengers to the earls and barons near him with invitations to talk of trade and mutual defence. The foundation of his fortress was being laid.

The next phase of this bastion was underway as well.

With Will's help, he was drafting a mandate to the king demanding rights for nobles and commoners. He'd named it the Charter of Honour.

Beside him, Marian stirred but did not wake. He breathed in the scent of her hair, relishing their first dawn as husband and wife.

He'd expected the day he wed Marian would begin a life of bliss. Instead, their battle to survive had shifted to a new front.

Kalends of September 1190

Rising from a steep earthen motte, Lincoln Castle's stone towers loomed ahead of the merchant caravan.

The 14-man convoy approaching the fortress drew little attention from the serfs reaping the fall fields near the road. Traders visiting the castle were a common sight, and this caravan was like all the others. At the centre of the column, a pair of men in fine clothes rode side-by-side with the pack mules, accompanied by a dozen heavily armed escorts.

This, however, was not a merchant caravan.

The Baron of Nottingham had chosen to travel undercover instead of brandishing the heraldic banners and shields of his demesne. Robert Webber had good reason.

He had come to Lincoln Castle for a clandestine gathering of the lords of the midlands. Their aim was to defy King John's rule – a dangerous endeavour.

Although Marian rode beside Robert dressed as a man, the pair remained silent. Robert's thoughts were on the negotiations that awaited him. Nearly a year of diplomacy had led to this moment.

The lords of the midlands had been eager for revenge against the king. John's false promise to send an army north against Robin Hood had foiled their tax revolt. Adding to the lords' resentment was the spread of the rogue's highwaymen. Mimicking Robin Hood's well-known beard and flowing hair, Robert's impersonators were fleecing more merchants than ever.

With hostility toward the king mounting among the lords, Robert had proposed this secret assembly. His invitation to the nobles had included a tantalizing promise. With his military skills, Robert could rid the midland shires of Robin Hood.

Now, that clandestine gathering was finally taking place.

In all, nineteen earls and barons of the midland shires had pledged to attend Robert's gathering hosted by the Earl of Lincoln, Sir William d'Aubigny.

At the entrance to Lincoln Castle, Robert noticed a half-dozen tents pitched outside the walls with heavily armed men around them. This was clearly a security detachment. That meant at least one other lord was already here.

"Gilbert," Robert said to his security chief riding just ahead. "Set up the men's camp near those tents and then join us inside." As they'd agreed beforehand, each lord would be allowed one personal bodyguard inside the castle.

Gilbert nodded and called out the order to his men, then followed Robert and Marian into the castle.

As they passed through the gate, Marian guided her mount closer to Robert. Leaning toward him, she whispered, "Stay alert, my love. The Earl of Devon may have hired assassins. A humiliated man can be dangerous."

"Diplomacy is as risky as war," Robert answered softly. "I'll be careful. But what worries me more is the coalition the earl will try to build against me among the lords."

Arriving at the castle's guest quarters, an aging servant bowed to Robert, Marian and Gilbert. "Welcome to Lincoln Castle, Sir Robert. I'm Hughes, Sir William's valet," he said. "I'll show you to your quarters."

Robert nodded and said, "Thank you, Mister Hughes."

With a shuffling gate, the valet led them down a corridor to a heavy door with a wooden bench beside it. "Your guard can sleep here, m'lord," he said to Robert, gesturing toward the bench.

Gilbert gave Robert a sidelong glance, then sat down and sighed. "I'll make myself comfortable."

After Hughes opened the door, Robert and Marian followed him into a large, richly decorated suite. "The earl hopes you and the baroness will join him in the parlour for supper this evening," the valet said.

"Please thank the earl for his invitation, Mister Hughes," Robert said, then added, "Which delegation is already here?"

"The Earl of Devon was the first to arrive, m'lord. He and his wife will be dining with you as well," Hughes said, then meekly backed out of the room and closed the door behind him.

Marian put a palm on her cheek, her eyes wide. "Your main adversary and your sister?"

"The battle is starting early," Robert said, taking off his travel cloak.

* * *

Robert and Marian followed Hughes into the large, stone-walled parlour. Seated at both ends of a table set for six, the Earl of Lincoln and his wife rose to their feet.

"Sir Robert… Lady Marian…" the earl said, nodding courteously. "I'm glad you could join us," he said gesturing to the chairs on his left.

Robert dipped his chin. "Thank you, Sir William."

Walking toward their seats, Robert took in the room. What could have been a cold, dungeon-like space was warmed by the glow of a twelve-candle chandelier suspended from the domed ceiling.

As Robert and Marian reached their chairs, the valet led the other guests into the parlour.

The first thing Robert noticed about the Earl of Devon was his height. Baldwin de Redvers was unusually short. Yet the earl still tried to look down his nose at Robert, an affectation that gave him the air of a banty rooster about to crow. Following at a distance behind the earl was his wife, Juliet Talbot de Redvers.

After formal introductions, the three couples took their seats.

Despite the importance of his conversation with de Redvers, Robert could not resist observing his sister. Until their introductions, Robert and Juliet had never spoken.

His sister was no longer the spindly lass Robert had last seen at his father's funeral. Juliet was now a stout woman near middle age with a plain face and a serious mien. Given the earl's reputation for womanizing, Robert was certain de Redvers had seen their marriage as an opportunity to expand his fiefdom.

After a long silence, the Earl of Lincoln finally spoke. "How was your journey, Sir Baldwin?" he asked de Redvers.

"Uneventful," the earl answered, glaring at Robert.

"And your journey, Sir Robert?" the Earl of Lincoln asked.

"Long," Robert answered evenly, staring back at de Redvers.

The tense silence continued as Hughes and a footman served the first course of their meal: leek soup. The only sound heard in the parlour was the slurping of the diners.

Once the servants had cleared away the bowls, the Earl of Lincoln turned his gaze from de Redvers to Robert and said, "Sir Baldwin… Sir Robert… I realize this is a difficult moment. But I believe it serves our mutual interests for the two of you to resolve your differences."

"Sir William," de Redvers said stiffly. "Only my respect for you allows me to sit at the same table as someone who has illegally seized my property."

"I respect you as well, Sir Baldwin," the Earl of Lincoln answered. "Your family is one of the oldest in the kingdom, a dynasty esteemed for generations. Yet, I also respect the contribution Sir Robert has made in service to our realm. As a soldier he risked his life many times in our defence and was knighted by a king for his valour. It's time we recognized that, save a wedding vow by his father, Sir Robert is the heir to a barony."

The Earl of Devon stood and thrust his chin in the air. "Sir William. You impugn the integrity of my wife and her family."

After a moment, Juliet spoke. "Sit down, Baldwin," she said sternly. "My family has not been insulted. I take pride in my brother's deeds.

Now listen to Sir William."

Robert held back a smile as the stunned de Redvers sat down.

The Earl of Lincoln offered de Redvers a comforting smile. "Sir Baldwin, we all face a common enemy in Robin Hood," he said. "Sir Robert says he can rid us of this outlaw if we join him in an alliance and I have good reason to believe him. His skills as a warrior are unmatched in the kingdom," the earl explained. "But we face a bigger challenge… What can we do about a king who behaves like an outlaw?"

Robert looked at de Redvers and said, "John has raised taxes and scutage more than any other king. Lords across the kingdom face ruin and peasants risk starvation. This king has used zealots to persecute traditional practices among his subjects as heresy and seize their property. John has abused his power to feed his avarice for wealth. That's why we must join together and press the king to sign the Charter of Honour. It demands John respect the rights of all his subjects."

"What is this 'Charter of Honour'?" de Redvers asked his fellow earl, ignoring Robert.

"As I'm sure you recall, we considered sending John an unspoken message – and the king betrayed us," d'Aubigny said, then paused to let the meaning of his words sink in. "The time has come for us to speak out in public. The Charter of Honour prescribes the rights of all the king's subjects, rights he cannot violate. Each of the lords who is meeting here will have the chance to read and revise the charter before it's sent to the king," he said, then tilted his head toward de Redvers. "As one of our wealthiest lords, you'll hold great sway among the others. I urge you not to let your anger toward Sir Robert prevent you from joining our alliance in resisting this tyrant."

"You speak of honour," de Redvers said. "But it's my honour that's been sullied. How can I stand before my fellow lords without shame when they can see I've chosen to ignore being robbed?"

"Sir Baldwin, I'm prepared to compensate you for the land," Robert said. "You'll receive five hundred pounds in silver each year."

"That's a very generous bargain, Sir Baldwin," the Earl of Lincoln added.

Before de Redvers could answer, Juliet spoke. "I've been silent about this long enough, Baldwin," she said to her husband. "You entrusted my family's demesne to an incompetent fool. My brother has offered you compensation that's more than fair for land that should rightfully be his. That gesture should be more than enough to establish your honour."

"Your wife speaks wisely, Sir Baldwin," d'Aubigny said.

The Earl of Devon sat upright in his chair. "Considering the importance of this alliance, I'll accept the compensation," he said magnanimously.

* * *

Gilbert Whitehand strode through the tent village outside Lincoln Castle. The encampment of the security escorts was alive with talk and laughter.

During their four-day bivouac, each lord's contingent had kept to themselves, maintaining a silent truce. But now, as they prepared for the evening meal, the men were chin wagging with their peers like peasants at a carnival.

Gilbert, however, did not share their mood.

Arriving at his campsite, Gilbert found Much forming their men into a meal line and signalled for his second-in-command to join him in Much's tent.

Once both were inside, Gilbert closed the flap and said, "We're breaking camp after supper. Rob wants us out of here before the other contingents."

"Why so glum, Gil? Everyone's saying the charter's been signed."

"The lords changed the charter so that it only guarantees the rights of nobles. The Earl of Devon threw out the rights for peasants that Rob put in the charter."

"Did Rob get his army?"

"Aye," Gilbert said flatly. "All nineteen lords agreed to put a hundred men under Rob's command to march on London if the king doesn't sign the charter by spring."

"What's the problem, then? That's what we came here to get."

"Rob's shutting down our toll squads," Gilbert said bitterly. "He plans to parade with a brigade of swan shields through each shire. After he arrives, he'll disband the toll squads. It's all a sham to make him look like the hero who's defeating Robin Hood. That's what Rob promised the lords if they signed the charter."

Much's mouth gaped for a moment. Then he said, "If we stop sacking merchants, how will Rob raise silver?"

Gilbert spat on the ground. "Just like any other blood sucker with a family crest. He'll squeeze the peasants who farm his land."

Ides of February 1191

Anna Webber rose from the table. "Good night, lads. You've been a comfort," she said in a faltering voice to the four men around her. "May God bless you."

Robert, Much, Gilbert and Will stood in respect. Taking Anna's hand, Robert kissed it. "Rest well, Mother," he said. "Grandfather would not have wanted you to fall ill as well."

"Good night, ma'am," the other men said.

Once Anna was gone, the men slumped back into their chairs. The table before them in the parlour of Talbot Hall was littered with goblets and pitchers of ale and wine.

Robert took another draught of claret and wiped his eyes.

They'd buried his grandfather today. Over a half-dozen cups of wine had brought him little solace.

Simon Webber had started coughing just after the new year. Within a fortnight, sweating and chills began and the old man took to bed. Before long, Simon was too short of breath to speak above a whisper.

Robert sent for the best physicians he could find. The bloodletting they administered only seemed to weaken the frail 68-year-old.

Less than two months after Simon Webber's cough began, he drew a last laboured breath with his daughter and grandson at his side.

Robert had borne his grief without Marian. She'd left for Sussex to seek alliances with other lords in the south – an idea Marian herself had proposed.

Their need for more allies was growing dire.

For nearly six months, King John had obstinately refused to meet on the Charter of Honour. Reluctantly, the rebel lords had agreed to make good on their threat. The Army of Honour would be formed at Cotgrave under Robert's command. If John did not meet with them on the charter, the army would march south toward London.

Downing the rest of the wine, Robert poured himself another cup. Despite the men's hard drinking, they'd been unusually quiet that night, their old banter quelled by the growing chasm between them.

"This winter is hanging around like an in-law with a whiff of pie from the oven," Much said, trying to make conversation.

Gilbert took a gulp of ale, then pointed his goblet toward Robert. "Much is right. The ice has got so thick, it's brought down the roof on one of our barracks," he slurred. "We need to fix that before the spring rains."

"We can't spare any silver," Robert said, staring into the bottom of his cup.

"Our lads from the old regiment live there, Rob," Gilbert said, his face growing red. "We had us a right fancy burial today. The pall alone could have bought them a new roof."

Will Scarlett slammed his cup on the table. "You're out of line, Gil," he growled.

Gilbert glared at Will. "I've seen what our toll squads put into the coffers with my own eyes. The last haul we brought in before shutting everything down was over five hundred pounds."

"You're talking through your arse, Gil," Will said tersely. "That silver's going to be used for—"

"You've said enough, Will," Robert interrupted.

Gilbert's eyes flashed angrily. "Used for what?" he said to Robert. "We've already paid this fat, blood-sucking tick of a king his taxes and scutage. What are you hiding, Rob?"

Robert looked up from his cup. "I'm buying this demesne from the Earl of Devon," he said evenly. "That will use up most of our silver."

Gilbert's mouth gaped for a moment. He then said, "You already hold this land, Rob. Why would you throw away silver to buy it?"

Robert exhaled slowly. "Gil, you don't understand these matters."

"No, I understand just fine," Gilbert said, rising unsteadily from his chair. "Now that you've gotten a taste of life as a noble, you're ready to toss the rest of us aside. You're going to bleed the common folk who put you in power just like all the other parasites in finery," he said bitterly. "Well, don't forget, m'lord. There are some of us here who knew the Baron of Nottingham when he wore Lincoln green," he said, then staggered out of the parlour.

The three men remaining at the table sat wordlessly for a time, each mulling Gilbert's threat. Much finally broke the silence.

"That was the ale talking. Gil probably won't remember any of this tomorrow," Much said.

Robert nodded. "You're right, Much. Gil needs to sleep this off."

"I should get some rest myself," Much said, rising from the table. "Sleep well," he said before leaving the parlour.

For a time, Robert and Will stared into their goblets, saying nothing.

"Gil's fit of temper is ill timed," Robert said finally, his voice nearly a whisper. "I'll be leaving for Cotgrave to form our army in two days. If Gil betrays me, it will cost us the chance to bring this tyrant to justice."

Will nodded. "I understand," he said, then walked out of the room.

The following day, the body of Gilbert Whitehand was found in the rain-swollen open sewer that ran along the east side of Nottingham. Village rumours soon spread. They said Gilbert had been drunk and stopped to empty his bladder. He then fell, struck his head on the culvert, and drowned in the cold, putrid water.

When the news reached Talbot Hall, the Baron of Nottingham decreed the day of Gilbert Whitehand's death would become a permanent holiday of remembrance in the village.

* * *

The two pikemen guarding the door to the king's parlour stared stone-faced at the justiciar. For the last half hour, Robert de Beaumont had been waiting in the anteroom, his mind racing with the news he was bringing the king.

When the door was finally opened by a footman inside the hall, soft music, laughter, and moans of pleasure spilled into the anteroom. Looking through the doorway, the justiciar saw King John approaching, his fleshy frame draped in a linen robe. Behind the king, in the dim candlelight, the justiciar caught glimpses of naked bodies sprawled on couches.

The Royal Guards stepped aside smartly as the king entered the antechamber.

"What's so important that you interrupted my feast?" the king said, his voice slurred by wine. "Has your daughter married a Saracen prince this time?"

The justiciar ignored the gibe and bowed. "I bring good news, Your Highness."

"And this news could not wait until morning?"

"I think it's best if you respond promptly, Sire."

John sighed and closed the top of his robe. "Very well. What is it?"

"The Earl of Norfolk has pledged his military support if the lords of the midlands carry out their promise to bring an army against you."

"Why would he do that?" the king asked, swaying slightly. "Hugh Bigod has been in league with my cousins since the day Richard became king."

"The earl's messenger did not explain why Sir Hugh made this pledge, Sire. But I suspect the earl hates Robert Webber enough to see his plans thwarted," de Beaumont said. "If Your Highness will recall, the animosity between Sir Hugh and Webber goes back to Richard's rebellion as a prince."

John nodded. "Yes, I remember. Sir Hugh has always detested Webber's insolence."

"This alliance with the earl offers a diplomatic opportunity, Sire," the justiciar said, opening his palms in a request to continue.

The king flicked his fingers. "Go on," he said impatiently.

"A public announcement of Sir Hugh's alliance will dampen the mood for war among the lords of the midlands. The earl's troops will nearly double the size of your —"

"That's obvious, de Beaumont," the king interrupted. "Stop wasting my time and draft the announcement. I'll sign it in the morning," he said, then turned back toward the hall.

"A moment more, Your Highness," the justiciar called out. "I have something else for your consideration."

John sighed and turned to face the justiciar. "What is it now?"

"If the lords of the midlands carry out their threat to fight, Robert Webber's leadership on the battlefield will give them an advantage. But you can take that advantage away, Sire," the justiciar said. "Tell them you'll meet to consider their charter on one condition… Robert Webber must be excluded from any talks."

The king's face reddened. "Haven't I made myself clear?" he shouted. "I will never meet with anyone about this treasonous charter! It goes against the will of God and the Church!"

"You don't need to meet with them, Sire," the justiciar said soothingly. "Your demand to exclude Webber from the talks will drive a wedge in their alliance. Some will take Webber's side, others will not. From what we know of Webber's arrogance, he'll likely turn against his allies. In the end, you'll shatter their unity and weaken their military strength."

John wiped the spittle from his chin. "Perhaps this could be useful," he said, his voice returning to normal.

"Sire, may I have your permission to draft a message announcing your alliance with Sir Hugh – and your willingness to hold talks about the charter if they exclude Robert Webber?"

"Yes, yes. Get on with it," John said distractedly before returning to his feast.

Kalends of March 1191

From the saddle of his horse, Robert scanned the valley below Mill Hill near Cotgrave. The unplanted farmland was dusted with a light snow – solid footing that would make good ground for military exercises by the Army of Honour.

God knew, they would need the training.

Forming a cohesive force from the nineteen separate regiments sent by the lords of the midlands would be a slow and painful task.

Each lord had agreed to provision his regiment for a three-month campaign. Some lords, however, had sent their men with orders to forage for food. As a result, these men would be away from camp instead of training for large parts of each day. Worse still, they would be ransacking the local peasants, creating ill will for the Army of Honour.

To prevent this catastrophe, Robert commandeered the provisions of all the regiments. Under Arthur Bland's control, the food was rationed to keep every man fed and available for training. Dispatches were sent to the negligent lords. But if his demands were ignored, the Army of Honour would run out of food in less than two months.

A clear chain of command was the next hurdle. The regiments' officers were chosen by each lord. Some were competent. But most held their rank thanks to nepotism or political patronage.

Robert's solution was to "promote" these officers to his general staff and replace them with his own men. But the need for reorganization went even deeper.

Each lord's regiment included a mix of infantry, cavalry and archers. To create a cohesive force, these soldiers had to be regrouped according to their tactical specialty.

By their third day in camp, Robert had managed to create the structure of an army. But turning this motley collection into a true military unit would require long hours of training on the frozen fields below.

Wheeling his horse, Robert rode toward the crest of Mill Hill, the site of their encampment. Passing through the rows of tents, he reached the abandoned barn at the centre of their bivouac he'd chosen as their headquarters. Entering the ramshackle building, Robert found Will and Much trying to organize his new general staff. The officers sent by the lords were angry and unruly, all feeling slighted by the loss of command.

To salve their damaged pride – and perhaps improve their chances of victory – Robert formed them into intelligence teams and tasked them with strategic objectives.

Some would scout locations for the battle site with the king's troops. Others would gather intelligence on the size of John's forces. Yet another group would seek ways to interdict the king's supply routes to the battle site.

With that done, Robert left the barn accompanied by Will and Much and walked to the mess area where Arthur Bland was supervising the cooks serving the evening meal. The men standing in line ceded the first spot to their commander and his adjutants. Instead, Robert joined the back of the mess line, drawing approving looks and murmurs.

Carrying their bowls of venison stew, Robert and his comrades found a private spot near the campfire, then sat on the ground like the other soldiers.

Will sipped from his bowl and smiled. "As usual, Arthur has worked his magic. I doubt any of these men has ever eaten this well in camp."

"They're a quiet lot," Much noted, gesturing toward the men.

"They're among strangers, for the most part," Robert said. "They'll form bonds during their training."

"See how they look at you, Marshal?" Will said, glancing at the men around them. "They're forming bonds with their leader. That bodes well for our army."

"Our first day of field training tomorrow will tell," Robert replied.

* * *

On the hill overlooking their training ground, Much sat astride his horse with Robert and Will on their own steeds beside him. Scanning the formations of warriors scattered in the unplanted fields below, Much sighed in disgust. "This is worse than I expected," he said to Rob and Will, "In a pitched battle, the Royal Guards will have this lot for breakfast."

The disparity of the soldiers' uniforms matched the disorder in their ranks. Ignoring the commands of their officers, the men wandered in confusion, colliding with each other as they tried to form an attack formation.

Will shook his head. "The only soldiering most of these lads have seen is bullying unarmed peasants."

"We've won battles with worse. These men lack motivation," Robert said. "When Richard was a prince, he taught me a lesson. Men who fight for money need more of a reason than duty to risk their lives," he said. "Tonight, we'll announce that each man will share in the plunder of the king's wealth if we defeat John in battle. That will sharpen their resolve."

Much tried to hide his surprise. Perhaps Gilbert had been right. The man he'd first met in Sherwood Forest had changed. Gone was any talk of honour or duty. Robert Webber was becoming a ruthless schemer, no better than the lords he was in league with.

Since the morning Gil's body was found, Much had suspected his comrade's death had been no accident. Yes, Rob had honoured Gil's memory and praised him as a friend at his funeral. Yet, Gil's death ended a threat to the Baron of Nottingham. Hearing Rob's callous words today only strengthened his suspicions.

All the same, in just three days Robert Webber had already inspired loyalty in his men. Much could not deny that.

In contrast to the officers who normally led them, Rob often ate among the men. His tent was larger than those of his troops but not opulent like the other lords in camp. Rob sought the counsel of his men and gave orders in a respectful tone. These traits, combined with a reputation for fearlessness in battle, had already made him revered among the troops.

Rob's voice broke Much's thoughts.

"We've wasted enough time with group manoeuvres today," their commander said. "Much, you take the infantry units aside and show them how to form pike squares. Will, I want you to teach the cavalry how to stay in formation as they charge. I'll work with the archers. By tomorrow, maybe some of them will know how to nock an arrow without putting out an eye on the man beside him."

Guiding his horse down Mill Hill, Much grudgingly admitted to himself that whatever else Robert Webber might be, he was a military leader like no other.

Nones of March 1191

Urging his horse to a gallop, Robert crested Mill Hill. On the plateau before him, the Army of Honour's tents came into view. Most of the encampment was deserted – the army's warriors were in the valley below, practicing battle manoeuvres.

Riding between the vacant tents, Robert brought his horse to a stop and dismounted outside the barn serving as his headquarters. Walking into the draughty building, a dozen faces turned his way, several of them scowling.

In the barn were twelve of the nineteen lords of the midlands, the finery and colour of their clothes contrasting the grey, weathered walls. These were the nobles who had chosen to accompany their men-at-arms in the Army of Honour. Among the missing lords were those too old for a military campaign and one who had suddenly taken ill – the Earl of Devon.

"Why was I summoned?" Robert asked sternly. "Our troops need to train together – and we don't have a moment to waste."

"The king has taken the upper hand!" the Baron of Sheffield said, his voice tight with anger. "We were fools to believe in you, Webber."

A few of the other barons murmured in agreement.

"John outfoxed you," the Baron of Ashby added. "He has the Earl of Norfolk on his side now. That makes defeating John in battle impossible."

"That's not all," the Baron of Sheffield added. "The king is now willing to hold talks about the Charter of Honour. But he has one condition… you cannot be a part of it, Webber."

"You say you were fools to believe in me," Robert said to the Baron of Sheffield. "Yet you're willing to take the word of a king who has already betrayed you. Is that any less foolish?" he said. "The only way we'll get John to the bargaining table is to defeat his troops in battle."

The Earl of Lincoln stepped forward and said, "Sir Robert is right. John promised he'd send an army to rid our shires of Robin Hood. But Sir Robert is the man who kept that promise. The king did nothing – except keep our silver."

"The stakes are higher now," the Baron of Ashby argued. "If we can't defeat the king in battle, we stand to lose our lands – and our lives."

"I agree," the Baron of Sheffield said. "We finally have the king coming to the bargaining table. Let's resolve our differences without bloodshed."

"My friends," the Earl of Lincoln said warmly. "You're being deceived by the king. He has no intention—"

Robert raised his palm, cutting off the earl. "Save your breath, Sir William. I've known men like these before. They'll fold in battle. We don't need them – or their troops," he said, then swept his eyes across the nobles gathered around him. "Any of you who believes the king will bargain with you in good faith can leave."

After a moment of hesitation, the Barons of Ashby and Sheffield walked silently out of the barn.

Robert waited until they were gone. "Unless any of you have further business, I'll return to the training of our troops," he said, then strode out of the barn.

Whilst Robert prepared to mount his horse, the Earl of Lincoln approached him. "The barons of Ashby and Sheffield are close allies of the Curtmantles. They're leaving with over three-hundred men. Yet you still seem certain of victory. I trust this isn't bluster," he said softly.

"Sir William," Robert answered. "Leaders certain of victory have been defeated many times. But no leader who doubted himself has ever tasted glory."

Kalends of May 1191

Marching along the road to Barking, the king's army stretched for more than a mile. As the soldiers reached the bridge at the River Lea, their sprawling formation narrowed to a line just four men wide to cross the granite span.

Near the centre of the column rode the king and the justiciar, surrounded by the monarch's personal escorts, the Household Knights.

"It's happening again," John said, covering his mouth, trying to hold back the contents of his stomach.

Unceremoniously, the king of England vomited on the neck of his war horse.

"His Highness needs to rest for a moment," the justiciar said from his own steed to the captain of the Household Knights.

The young officer pointed toward a lone oak just off the road and called out to his men. "Form a perimeter around that tree."

Clad in gleaming helmets with red plumes, the fifty-man cavalry detachment swiftly created a circle around the oak as their sovereign was led by the justiciar under its branches.

John dismounted from his horse, his face the colour of celery. "I'm too sick. I can't go on," he said, staggering under the weight of the chain maille covering his corpulent frame. Tossing his helmet aside, the king dropped to his knees and retched again.

The scene drew curious glances from the long line of soldiers marching past them along the road.

The justiciar dismounted and stood close to the king. "Sire, you need to compose yourself," he said softly. "The men are watching."

In over twenty years as Lord Justiciar, Robert de Beaumont had never accompanied a king on a military campaign. The idea of advising Henry or Richard on a battlefield would have been preposterous. But John was another matter. The king's mercurial nature and lack of military experience made de Beaumont's steadying influence necessary.

"This is all your fault, de Beaumont," John said panting. "You said they wouldn't fight if I insisted they shun Webber."

"That demand weakened Webber's forces, Sire. With the Earl of Norfolk's troops, you'll still prevail today."

Wiping his mouth, John rose unsteadily to his feet. "I still think this battle on open ground is a fool's game. I have the strongest fortresses in the realm."

"This is not the time for a change of heart, Sire," de Beaumont said patiently. "We cannot let Webber hold the ground he's taken."

For nearly a fortnight, the justiciar had repeatedly explained to the king that the so-called Army of Honour camped outside Barking had to be defeated. Webber's position, a day's march from London, threatened supply lines to the capital from the north and east whilst also choking off access to the city along the Thames River.

In truth, had the king engaged the Army of Honour sooner, they could have chosen to fight on better ground. But thanks to John's indecision, Webber had forced their hand. Worse still, fearing an attack from the Anjou cousins, John had refused to commit any Royal Guards to the battle.

"Your reasoning has yet to convince my guts," John said, arms folded over his bloated belly.

The justiciar turned away from the king and looked back along the road. "Sir Hugh and his men are approaching," he said after spotting the shields of warriors bearing the Earl of Norfolk's coat of arms.

Gathering himself, John mounted his horse and headed back toward the road. "If anything goes wrong today, de Beaumont, this will be on your head."

* * *

Looking west, Robert scanned the prairie in spring bloom sloping upward toward his army. Before the day was out, this pristine field near Barking would be a quagmire littered with bleeding bodies.

Robert sighed. He took no pleasure in the carnage of battle. But war was as necessary for power as a plough was for farming.

Knowing the king would be compelled to attack, Robert had chosen this high ground to favour his weakness in numbers. His men were deployed on a rise with their backs to the River Roding. Their line was anchored by a bend in the Roding to the south and a dense woodland to the north. Their position revealed Robert's confidence and courage.

There was no line of retreat. They would prevail today – or perish.

In the far distance, Robert spotted a lone rider galloping across the prairie toward his troops, waving his sword in the air – one of their scouts.

Robert mounted his horse. "They're coming," he said to Will and Much standing by their own steeds nearby. "Make your men ready."

Today, Will would command the Army of Honour's cavalry. Much would lead the infantry and archers.

Robert's decision to place his long-time comrades in high command had raised eyebrows among some of the lords who had coveted the posts.

These nobles were here now and keeping a sharp eye on their rivals.

After mounting his horse, Much called out to Robert. "I still don't like that gap at the end of our line, Rob," he said pointing to the woods north of them. "We're just begging to get flanked."

Robert locked his officer in a hard stare, annoyed by Much's casual manner. In an icy voice, he said, "You have your orders."

Much bowed his head. "Yes, m'lord," he said with a shade too much deference.

* * *

The justiciar's first sight of the Army of Honour came as their column emerged from the East Ham forest. In the far distance of a wide prairie rising before them, the neat rows of Webber's regiments bristled across the crest of the hills.

The justiciar's heart began to pound, his mouth grew dry. Studying the men around him, he saw the same expression: lips tightly drawn, eyes saucer-wide.

As the junior officers shouted orders, the troops broke their narrow road-march column and began to spread across the prairie. Soon, their men were moving forward on a wide front parallel to the enemy line.

Riding beside de Beaumont inside the human walls of the Household Knights were the king and the Earl of Norfolk. The three of them had been silent over the last few miles, each lost in his own thoughts. Just behind the Household Knights, a half-dozen generals trailed them, bickering over tactics.

As they rode closer to their foe, de Beaumont's aging eyes could see Webber's force more clearly. Huddled behind an assortment of baronial shields, Webber's infantry formed the army's front line. Behind the foot-men, the justiciar saw companies of archers and regiments on horseback, waiting to counter their assault.

The Earl of Norfolk broke their silence. "Your Highness, I see an op-portunity here," he said, then pointed to the north side of Webber's reg-iments. "The end of their line doesn't reach those trees."

Although not a soldier, the justiciar had prepared for this battle by reading military texts. Based on that knowledge, the earl's observation made sense. The king did not seem as certain, however.

"You assured me we outnumber them." John said anxiously. "Won't that be enough?"

Sir Hugh sat up straight in his saddle and said, "Exploiting Webber's blunder gives us a chance to destroy him completely, Sire. His troops have their backs to a river. If we break Webber's line, they'll have no place to retreat."

"How would we do this?" John asked, suddenly more confident.

"As our army advances, my regiments can charge toward the gap at the end of their line and attack from the flank. I'll lead the men myself," Sir Hugh said. "With the rest of our troops engaging their line on a wide front, my men will roll up their flank and crush them."

"But if all our troops are engaged, won't that leave us without any reserves?" de Beaumont asked. "According to what I've read, that would be—"

"Stop clucking like a hen, Justiciar," the earl interrupted. "I've led men into battle many times. There's little risk here."

"I'll ask my generals for their thoughts," John said, swivelling toward the covey of officers behind them.

"There's no time, Your Highness," Sir Hugh insisted. "That gaggle of geese will waste the rest of the day arguing. If Webber notices his mistake, our chance for an easy victory could vanish."

The king squirmed in his saddle. "What are the risks to your plan?"

"With our advantage in numbers, there are none, Sire," Sir Hugh answered. "I believe we'll win either way. But what I propose will bring us victory faster, with fewer losses. Do I have your permission to proceed?"

John blinked several times, then nodded his assent.

"A wise choice, Your Highness. I'll notify the generals," Sir Hugh said, then rode off toward the officers trailing them.

* * *

The king's regiments marching toward Robert's lines were still out of arrow range. But he could already distinguish John's troops by their uniforms.

The distinctive red helmet plumes of the Household Knights told Robert the king was near the centre of their formation, far behind the front lines. More importantly, he spotted troops with the Earl of Norfolk's red and blue coat of arms on their shields moving laterally, toward the north side of his line.

Urging his horse to a trot, Robert rode just behind their line until he reached Will Scarlett. "I need a word," Robert said to the commander of his cavalry and led Will aside where they could speak in private.

After a few moments, Will rode back to his mounted troops.

Whilst Robert watched, Will called out an order. "First and Second companies… Prepare to move!"

* * *

Nearly a quarter mile behind the front line of their advancing army, the justiciar and the king rode at a walk, surrounded by the Household Knights. Sir Hugh and the generals had left the pair behind after taking command of troops closer to the front.

Ahead of them, de Beaumont saw their infantry drawing closer to Webber's line.

"Halt," the captain of the Household Knights called out to his men.

"Why have we stopped?" the justiciar asked the officer.

"We need to stay outside the range of their archers, m'lord," the soldier replied.

"A wise precaution," the king said, reining his steed to a stop.

When the front lines finally came within arrow range, the justiciar witnessed warfare for the first time.

Safe from the enemy archers, de Beaumont saw streams of arrows cross paths in the air as each side launched their weapons. The infantrymen of both armies raised their shields, trying to ward off the deadly rain. Men advancing in the royal ranks ahead of them fell in shrieks of pain as arrows found their way between the bucklers. The other soldiers closed ranks around the fallen and continued moving forward, leaving the wounded writhing in their wake.

Relentlessly, the king's men pressed ahead.

When the infantry lines finally clashed, the battle became pure mayhem.

Although the justiciar was over a quarter mile behind the front lines, the troops' hoarse bellowing blotted out all other sounds. Shields pressed against shields whilst pikes and swords jabbed and slashed from above. The wounded staggered away from the fray, one man blinded, another disembowelled, others with severed limbs.

The king vomited again. The carnage made de Beaumont queasy as well – but what he saw next, left him stunned.

Instead of attacking Webber's open left flank as they'd planned, the Earl of Norfolk's troops were leaving the battlefield and heading into the woodlands to the north. The left flank of their own army was now undefended.

Then, as the justiciar watched in horror, Webber's cavalry swept in and charged the unprotected edge of their infantry. Without a line of shields and pikes to deter them, the horsemen ploughed into the men on foot, cutting down the king's troops with their swords.

Panicked, a number of the king's soldiers began to flee.

The justiciar pointed toward the faltering line. "We've been betrayed by Sir Hugh," he said, grasping the earl's motive. "Captain," he called out to the commander of the Household Knights. "Reinforce the line!"

"Sorry, m'lord. I only take orders from the king," the officer answered.

"Sire," the justiciar pleaded. "Order the captain to repel Webber's cavalry."

John's eyes pivoted from side to side. "Don't we have other troops?"

"Look, Sire!" de Beaumont said, waving his hand along the length of their line. "Our men are tied down by the enemy in front of them. Your knights are the only troops left."

Trembling and pale, the king stared at the combat.

More men on their left flank were falling back, trying to save themselves as Webber's cavalry pressed their attack. Behind the horsemen, the justiciar saw Webber's infantry rushing into the breach in their formation.

"Your Highness, our line is about to collapse! Give the order!" de Beaumont yelled.

Webber's archers had drawn closer as well, a few of their arrows landing less than twenty paces before them.

John turned to face the commander of his Knights. "Your king is in danger!" he said, voice hoarse with fear. "Back to London!"

"Your Highness," de Beaumont pleaded. "If you leave the field, you'll demoralize our men."

The king ignored the justiciar and spoke to the leader of his Knights. "Do your duty, Captain."

The officer nodded stiffly. "Yes, Sire," he said, then addressed his men. "Column formation! Follow me!" he called out. Wheeling his mount, the officer then led the king and his Knights away from the battle.

The justiciar watched in shock as they abandoned the field.

The king's troops fleeing the fight were now reaching de Beaumont. The aging court official drew his sword and thrust it in the air. "Stand and fight!" he yelled at the men from his horse. "Stand and fight!"

A stream of terrified men ran past him. "Tell that to the king!" one of them shouted.

The lone figure on horseback caught the eyes of Webber's archers. Moments later, a volley of arrows killed Robert de Beaumont, the Lord Justiciar of England.

* * *

Riding toward the north end of their lines, Robert allowed himself a smile.

The rout of King John's army was nearly complete.

The Earl of Norfolk had kept his bargain – not a certainty considering Hugh Bigod's history of treachery.

Marian's secret alliance with the earl had been more significant to their victory than the number of troops Robert brought to the battle. That closely-guarded secret had been the source of his confidence all along – something that Robert had kept even from Will and Much. But the price for Sir Hugh's allegiance had been high.

The Earl of Norfolk would be Prolocutor of the Charter of Honour – a bargain that meant Robert's former enemy would lead the assembly to determine John's fate as king. Moreover, by insisting on a withdrawal from the field, Sir Hugh would emerge from this battle with his regiments intact. But those consequences were too far away to contemplate for now.

Robert had a victory to complete.

Arriving at the north end of their line, Robert rode to the cavalry unit he'd deployed here before the start of the battle. Drawing his sword, he pointed toward the red-plumed helmets of the Household Knights retreating in the distance. "Follow me!" he called out to his men. "We're going to capture the king!" he said, then spurred his steed.

Over a hundred horsemen broke into hot pursuit behind him.

* * *

The king wavered between sobs and curses as he rode away from the battle, surrounded by his escorts.

Why had he trusted Bigod? That had been de Beaumont's fault, he told himself. The justiciar had reminded him that the Earl of Norfolk had betrayed his brother, of course. But de Beaumont should have been more adamant. And now the fool had gotten himself killed, leaving his king without counsel when he needed it most.

Their hurried retreat took them across the prairie and through the East Ham forest. As they emerged from the woodland road into a meadow, the captain of the Knights brought his horse alongside John's steed and pointed behind them. "The enemy is in pursuit," he called out over the pounding hooves.

A chill passed through John as he saw a detachment of cavalry larger than their own charging toward them in the distance. "Do something!" he shrieked.

"We'll make a stand at the bridge," the captain yelled, nodding toward the narrow stone span over the River Lea about a half mile ahead.

His hands on the reins trembling with terror, John begged God to save him. The gelding under him drew ragged breaths, his neck working up a lather as he strained with the burden of the corpulent king.

After finally crossing the bridge, the captain stopped their detachment and spoke to his men. "You six will accompany the king back to

London," he said to the last half dozen knights to cross the span. "The rest of us will make a stand here."

The terrified king rode away with his escorts, oblivious to the men giving their lives to save him.

* * *

Robert's heart sank as he rode within sight of the stone bridge on the Lea.

The Household Knights had formed a defensive line at the river crossing. One row of men blocked the narrow span with their shields. Behind them, another row stood with their crossbows cocked and ready. In the distance beyond the soldiers, seven riders galloped away. Robert was certain the king was among them.

Although Robert's cavalry outnumbered the Household Knights, forcing the knights off the bridge would take time – enough time for John to reach safety in London. A detour to the nearest river crossing would delay them as well.

There was only one way left to capture the king.

"Halt!" Robert called out to his horsemen before they entered arrow range. "Perhaps I can talk some sense into these soldiers," he said to the sergeant of his cavalry unit.

Taking off his helmet, Robert rode alone toward the bridge.

At thirty paces from the river, Robert stopped and dismounted. "A word with your commander," he called out.

A tall man in his twenties emerged from their ranks and approached Robert. Taking off his own helmet, the officer stood before him wordlessly, his gaze steady.

"Enough men have died today," Robert said. "You and your men don't need to join them."

"Today's body count doesn't matter. A Household Knight is always ready to die serving his king."

"Even if the king is without honour?"

"It's not my place to judge the king. My duty is to protect him."

Robert nodded approvingly. "I admire your courage and loyalty," he said warmly. "I'm Robert Webber, Baron of Nottingham. What's your name, soldier?"

"Everett Blake, m'lord," the officer said. "My older brother served with your regiments in France."

"Sir Everett, we both know your stand here will end with all your men dead. I have twice as many troops. All your deaths will buy is more time to keep a despot in power. The king's army has been defeated.

Sooner or later, John will face justice before the demands of the Charter of Honour."

"Perhaps," Blake said calmly. "But not whilst I command this unit."

Robert sighed. "This king doesn't deserve a man like you, Sir Everett," he said, then opened his palms. "Tell me. How much time would your lives buy the king if I chose to attack?"

Blake shifted his weight and gazed into the fast-sinking sun. "Until sunset, I suppose."

"Then let's reach an accord between warriors. After sunset, you withdraw and let us pass. Do we have a truce?"

"No, m'lord," the young officer said. "Doing that would betray my honour."

Robert folded his arms. "I'm willing to concede the time your lives would have bought," he said, his voice suddenly stern. "Isn't that enough?"

"Bargaining for your life with an enemy is not an act of honour."

"Stop being a child," Robert said, his lips curling into a sneer. "You're choosing a senseless death – for yourself and your men."

"Accepting a compromise like the one you offer is how honourable men become corrupt."

Robert glared at Blake for a moment. "Very well," he said, then donned his helmet and mounted his horse. From the saddle he called out, "If only death can preserve your precious honour, then it's honour you'll have."

After returning to his cavalry company, Robert spoke to the sergeant. "Divide the men into three groups. We'll attack from the flanks and centre."

"M'lord, this assault will take time," the sergeant said softly. "We can cross the river at a ford less than five miles from here and avoid any bloodshed."

Robert stared straight ahead, his eyes fixed on the bridge. "I know that, sergeant. My orders stand."

Just after sunset, Robert's cavalry continued their pursuit of the king.

Around the blood-smeared bridge behind them were the bodies of sixty-three dead.

* * *

An orange glow above the buildings was all that remained of the sun as John and his escorts reached the outskirts of London. The king was relieved to find the streets quiet. After a day of hard riding, he'd managed to beat the news of his defeat to the city.

"To Westminster Palace," John said to the sergeant commanding his six remaining Knights.

Entering the palace's main hall, the king was swarmed by a score of anxious ministers calling out to him. "What's the news from the front, Sire? Have you defeated the upstarts? Where is the justiciar?"

"Not now," John said, waving them away as he hurried toward his apartments. "I don't have time."

The murmurs that began in his wake were not reassuring.

The palace steward intercepted John in the hall. "Your Highness," he said with a bow. "Let's get you out of that maille and into a hot bath."

"Leave me!" John shouted. "I need time to think."

Alone in his parlour, John paced the room, rubbing his face. During the hard ride back to London, his mind had been occupied with a single thought: to reach the safety of his palace. But now that he was here, a new worry emerged. How would he announce their defeat without stirring a panic?

Should he explain this disaster wasn't his fault? After all, the justiciar was behind the whole debacle, pressing him for decisions he wasn't ready to make, encouraging an alliance with Hugh Bigod. And yet…

John felt empty without the old man. What would de Beaumont advise right now, he asked himself?

Following a knock on the door, the steward entered the parlour. "I'm sorry to interrupt, Your Highness. But I think it's important you know," he said, eyes downcast. "Many of the ministers and courtiers are fleeing the palace. There are rumours your army was defeated. The Royal Guards have shed their uniforms and are deserting their posts as well. I fear for your safety, Sire."

John began to tremble. The secret was out – and the message was unmistakable. His monarchy was over. He was no longer safe in England.

There was no time to lose now, he told himself.

He needed to reach Southampton.

* * *

The slow progress of his cavalry in the moonless night infuriated Robert. Every delay increased John's chances of reaching the protection of his palace. But after injuring several horses whilst galloping in the dark, he'd slowed their unit to a walk.

When they at last came within sight of London, Robert saw a string of torches tracing every road out of the city. Drawing closer, he noticed finely dressed people on horseback, accompanying carts loaded with their possessions. Clearly, word of the king's defeat had reached London.

Like rats abandoning a sinking ship, the king's allies were streaming out of the city in every direction.

There was an opportunity here, Robert suddenly realized. "Send a courier to Much Millerson and Will Scarlett," he said to his unit's sergeant. "Tell them to bring our troops to London with all haste. The plunder we promised the men for victory is theirs for the taking on these roads," he said. As the sergeant turned away, Robert stopped him and added, "Our men are free to seize any possessions. But no one is to be killed nor any woman violated. Understood?"

"Yes, m'lord," the sergeant said.

Robert turned his gaze toward the torchlit road. The stream of exiles offered another opportunity. Their torches lit the way to London, giving him a last chance to catch the king outside his palace.

Spurring his horse into a gallop, Robert charged down the road, his men following closely. "Clear a path or be cut down!" he shouted to the courtiers leaving the city.

Two miles later, the hooves of their horses were clattering on London's cobblestone streets.

When Robert and his horsemen arrived at Westminster Palace, they found its large doors open and unguarded. Townsfolk carrying furniture, drapes, tapestries and other household goods were scurrying out of the mansion.

"Post guards around the palace to stop the looting," Robert said to his sergeant as he dismounted and walked inside.

The pillagers fled from him like starlings as Robert strode through the palace. Every room had been ransacked. In the kitchen, he found a scullery maid cowering in a corner, clutching an injured leg and unable to move. "Where's the steward?" he asked, helping the young woman to her feet.

"All the servants are gone, m'lord," she said, eyes turned toward the floor. "There was talk of the king deserting the palace and everyone left."

"And the Royal Guards?"

"They're gone too, m'lord," she said. "They say the Guards were the first to leave."

A slow smile spread on Robert's face.

John had evaded him. But the king's escape had given Robert a gift.

Westminster Palace was now under his control – and his entire army would be in London within the day.

* * *

From the deck of the sloop, John gazed back toward shore. Would this be the last time he'd see England? In the gold light of dawn, the distant coastline of the Isle of Wight was a thin smudge on the horizon.

John sighed. The shock of his downfall was gone, replaced by a stark reality. Yesterday he'd been king of the realm. Today, he was an exile sailing to the safety of his mother's home in Aquitaine.

A litany of regrets still haunted him, each with a different culprit. Yet his reveries of remorse always ended with a measure of revenge against his enemies.

In the hold of John's ship were the crown jewels of England and all the silver from the treasury he could lay his hands on.

Nones of May 1191

The royal bedchamber at Westminster Palace echoed with the soft rustle of linen and moans of passion.

Drenched in sweat, Robert uttered a final groan of pleasure then rolled onto his back in the bed beside Marian. After catching his breath, he said, "You seemed distracted, my love. Our reunions usually shake the rafters."

Turning to face him, Marian stroked his cheek. "I'll be fine, Robin," she said with a smile. "My thoughts wander when we have so much to celebrate."

"Without the pact you made with Sir Hugh, there would be nothing to celebrate," he said then laughed dryly. "In any case, whoever becomes king will inherit an empty treasury and a mountain of debt."

"There's still hope for justice. You'll be a kingmaker soon."

In three days, the Council of Honour would convene as planned – but with a different purpose. Instead of meeting to make demands of King John, the council would likely choose a new monarch. Robert's popularity could tip the scales between the most likely contenders: the Earl of Norfolk and Guy Curtmantle of the Anjou line.

"I have doubts about my influence," Robert said, then kissed her hand. "But I don't think it was good news that distracted you, my love."

After a long moment, Marian said, "My father's death? Is that what you mean?"

"You've refused to mourn him, Marian."

Marian turned away, closing her eyes. "I hated my father for using people – even his own daughter. But the way he died made me proud of him. He showed courage."

"And you find that troubling?"

"My father was ruthless. But his death revealed something I'd never considered. Everything he did was for country and king. My father never manipulated others for his own gain."

"Politics is war without weapons, my love. Your father was defending what he believed. Some men are willing to sacrifice their sons in time of war. Perhaps your father felt the same about his daughter."

Marian sat up in the bed. For a long time, she stared at the floor, her eyes welling with tears. "I felt better hating him," she said, then covered her face and wept.

Robert put his arms around her shoulders. "Stay with me in the palace today. Your journey to Lancaster can wait."

Wiping her cheeks, Marian said, "No, what I need to do cannot wait. I'll see the Curtmantle brothers as we planned. My father would have done the same."

* * *

Much followed the sergeant of the sentries down the long, narrow passageway to the royal chancery. He had no doubt why Rob had summoned him.

He'd disobeyed Rob's order and refused to let his troops plunder the exiles leaving London. Taking advantage of those frightened wretches was wrong and Much had no regrets. Given the same circumstances, he'd disobey Rob again.

He'd seen Rob change – and not for the better.

Rob's selfless courage had once inspired Much to reject the cruelty and pretence of The Order. Rob had fed and protected strangers, even saved his sister. But from the day he became a lord, Rob had turned ruthless and cold.

As a front-line soldier, Much had never been close to powerful men. Perhaps that was the way of the world. Men traded their integrity for power.

The sergeant led Much through the open door into the chancery. "Much Millerson is here, m'lord," the sentry said, then left. Rob sat behind a large table covered with documents. After a moment, he looked up.

"You no longer command my infantry, Much. Tomorrow, you'll go back to training the troops," Rob said evenly. "I wanted to tell you face-to-face. Your courage and loyalty in the past have earned you that."

"What you ordered me to do was wrong… m'lord."

"It's not your place to decide that, Much. As a soldier, your duty is to follow orders."

"I refused to do my duty when we first met. You had no objections then, did you?" Much said bitterly.

Robert stood. "Much, if you were any other soldier, I'd have you in chains for that remark," he said. "A commander can't afford the luxury of friendship – and you presume too much of ours," he said, then sat down and returned his gaze to the documents. "You're dismissed," he said, without looking up.

Ides of May 1191

Even from a great distance, an observer would have noticed the difference in the two men strolling the walled garden of Saint Albans monastery. Although both men wore opulent tunics befitting their status as earls, one was large and burly, the other short and frail.

Their differences went beyond physique, however. Whilst the Earl of Norfolk was brash and loud, the Earl of Devon was sly and subdued.

Yet, a common purpose had brought this odd couple together two days before the council for the Charter of Honour. Both men were determined to control the gathering of over one-hundred lords.

The pair also loathed Robert Webber.

"With John in exile, this council presents a new opportunity," the Earl of Norfolk said. "We're no longer gathering to chastise a king. This council could determine who rules England."

"But will the rest of the lords accept our judgment?" the Earl of Devon asked.

"Less than half the nobles in the realm are coming. Most feared angering John and stayed away."

"Then the timid will lose their say in choosing the next king."

"If this council is to select a king, it will need to be a unanimous decision," de Redvers said. "With the Curtmantle brothers coming, I do not think that's likely."

"I'll not mince words," Bigod said, thrusting his chin. "My wealth and lineage make me the obvious choice as monarch. My great uncle was a king."

"The Curtmantle brothers will surely differ," de Redvers said, smiling wryly. "They're the nephews of King Henry and were named in his line of succession."

Bigod sneered. "The Curtmantles lack the spine to rule."

"How will you convince the other nobles of that?"

"When I learned John had looted the treasury and stolen the crown jewels, I asked Guy and Bernard to join me in a raid to Aquitaine to recover them. The cowards refused."

"Most nobles want peace, Hugh. An invasion of Aquitaine will not be widely favoured."

Bigod's face reddened. "The Charter of Honour was created to bring John to justice. Should we now let him escape with his greatest crime of all?"

"You don't know the minor barons like I do, Hugh," de Redvers said. "Some have had enough of powerful kings. They want a monarch who can't oppress the nobles."

"But how will we protect the realm from foreign invaders without a powerful king?"

The Earl of Devon smirked. "You've just defined the impasse that will mire this assembly."

"All these arguments are rubbish," Bigod said angrily. "I'm the Prolocutor of the council. My actions on the battlefield led to the victory that drove King John from power. I've earned the honour of being king."

Tapping his chin with a finger, de Redvers said, "Do you fail to see the irony of an 'Army of Honour' that gained its victory through treachery?"

Bigod's eyes narrowed as he grabbed the hilt of his sword. "I'll not tolerate that insult from any man."

"Stay your sword, Hugh," de Redvers said calmly. "I meant no offense. I'm simply pointing out the flaws of your reasoning. Others will whisper what I've just said aloud and you'll be branded as a hypocrite. You should be grateful for my candour."

"I'd be more grateful for your support. We have a common enemy – and as king I'll behead Robert Webber. You can count on that."

"Then, tell me," de Redvers said, his tone turning sharp. "Why did you form a secret alliance with that arrogant bastard?"

"From the day I laid eyes on him, I've detested the preening peasant. My alliance with Webber was the means to an end. His pretty little strumpet convinced me of that. Making me Prolocutor of the assembly only sweetened the bargain," Bigod said, then added, "Rest assured, Baldwin. When I'm king, Webber will pay for his arrogance – and the demesne he stole from you will be returned. But I'll need your support to make that possible."

The Earl of Devon nodded. "Your assurance of justice is what I've been waiting to hear. You'll have my support, Hugh," de Redvers said. "But I should warn you. If you make your intentions toward Webber known to the barons, you'll never take the throne."

Bigod's eyebrows furrowed. "Do you want your lands back or not?"

"As I said, Hugh. I know the barons. Most of them admire Webber. His opinion will influence many of the lesser nobles – especially now that he has an army behind him and controls the royal palace," de Redvers said. "Webber can never be king, of course. But seeking his support during the council will help your cause."

Bigod sighed heavily. "That's a foul cure to swallow," he said. "But you may be right."

"Cheer up, Hugh," de Redvers said grinning. "The vengeance will be sweet when Webber learns he backed the king who sent him to the gallows."

* * *

The afternoon sun cleaved the courtyard of Saint Albans monastery into pools of light and shade. More than a hundred lords within the cloister milled about in groups that randomly formed and dissolved. The drone of their voices was accompanied by a swirling sea of gestures… raised fingers, open palms, shaking fists, folded arms, hard stares, scowls and obsequious smiles.

From a corner of the courtyard, the Earl of Norfolk and the Earl of Devon studied the assembly, keeping their voices low.

"Four days of bickering and these bleating sheep are no closer to a decision," said Hugh Bigod

"We're deadlocked – as I predicted," Baldwin de Redvers said smugly. "Your coalition is solid, Hugh. But Guy Curtmantle's supporters will not abide you as king."

Bigod shook his head in disgust. "This is a congress of fools," he said. "They want a king too weak to tax them yet somehow strong enough to defend them from foreigners."

"This looks intriguing," de Redvers said, nodding toward the Curtmantle brothers working their way toward them through the crowd.

Bigod held back a smile. "Perhaps these jackasses are finally ready to concede."

Once the Curtmantles reached them, the elder brother, Guy, nodded politely. "Good day, gentlemen. May we have a word in private?"

After retreating to a vacant vestibule, Bigod looked at Guy and said, "I trust you've come to your senses."

"I have," Guy replied.

"A wise decision," Bigod said, thrusting his chin in triumph. "You have my word that as your king, you and your brother will have roles as counsellors in my court."

Guy inclined his head. "You mistake my intentions, Hugh. I'm here to reach a compromise, not make you king."

"Compromise?" Bigod said, suddenly flushed.

"This assembly is stalled," Guy said calmly. "The nobles gathered here will be forced to return to their fiefs soon. Neither of us will leave here as king. The factions are too hard set."

Bigod rubbed his chin. "You speak of compromise," he said. "I'm willing to make a concession that could end this stalemate."

"Go on," Guy answered.

"Suppose I promise not to invade Aquitaine," Bigod said. "Will that win the support of the weak-kneed lords who back you?"

"I fear not, Hugh," Guy said.

"Why?" Bigod growled.

"They don't trust your word," Guy said without flinching.

Bigod's cheeks trembled in anger. "You'll pay for that insult in blood!" he said, grasping the hilt of his sword.

Touching Bigod's arm, de Redvers said, "Hear him out, Hugh."

"I'm not here to offend you, Hugh," Guy said. "We need to speak plainly if we're to reach an agreement. You're not trusted by the barons. Ask de Redvers if I speak the truth."

Bigod turned his gaze toward the Earl of Devon. "Well?"

Casting his eyes toward the ground, de Redvers said, "It's true, Hugh. Many of the barons have noticed your… changes of loyalty."

"Our realm faces a crisis," Guy said, looking into Bigod's eyes. "King Philip is already laying French claims to Flanders. If he succeeds, it won't be long before he casts an eye for conquest across the channel. To deter Philip, we need someone who can marshal our forces in defence of the realm – without delay."

"Who?" Bigod asked

Guy opened his palms. "The finest warrior in the land – and a man who already leads a standing army."

"Webber?" Bigod sputtered. "That low-born bastard? Never!"

"Sir Robert would not be king," Guy explained. "He would be given the temporary title of Protector of the Realm. That would give us time to convene a parliament from all the lords across the kingdom. This assembly was never intended to select a king."

"Why do I suspect Webber's whore had something to do with this?"

"Yes, Lady Marian approached us with this idea," Bernard admitted.

Bigod scoffed. "What kind of men allow a woman to think for them?" he said, glaring at the brothers.

"What does sex matter when someone speaks sense?" Guy answered.

Bigod glared at Guy for a moment then said, "You claim the barons don't trust me. But what's to stop Webber from seizing power permanently?"

"My cousin Richard made Webber the Marshal of the Royal Guards," Guy replied. "Richard knew his own brother was corrupt and Sir Robert could be trusted to control John's worst impulses. Only Richard's death kept Sir Robert from that mission."

"Then tell me, Guy," Bigod said. "Where was Webber's integrity when he stole the lands of the Earl of Devon?" he said, waving his hand toward de Redvers.

"Sir Robert reclaimed his birthright through honourable force of arms," Guy answered. "Since then, he's brought law and order to the region – something other lords had failed to do before him. He's also compensated the earl for his loss, has he not?" he said, looking toward de Redvers.

"Well… Yes, I suppose…" de Redvers stammered.

Guy turned his gaze back to Bigod. "Hugh, we need to put aside our rivalry and consider the defence of the realm. We face a threat from France. What my brother and I propose is a way to protect the kingdom until we resolve our impasse. Will you agree to this compromise?"

Before Bigod could answer, de Redvers said, "Hugh, I think we should discuss this matter in private before you make a decision."

Bigod nodded his consent.

After de Redvers guided them out of earshot, he leaned close to Bigod. "I've come into some information on Webber you should know about," de Redvers said softly. "One of Webber's commanders was demoted for refusing orders to loot John's courtiers leaving the city."

Bigod shrugged. "So? Every victor seizes the spoils of battle."

"True," de Redvers agreed. "But this soldier revealed a secret that can destroy the bastard. He said Webber was the bandit known as Robin Hood."

Bigod's mouth gaped for a moment. Then he scowled and said, "Why didn't you tell me this before?"

"I've been waiting for the right moment."

"You're a snake, de Redvers," Bigod said in disgust. "But at least you're my snake," he added. "We need to tell these jackasses the secret about their choir boy," he said, then turned toward the Curtmantle brothers.

Tugging at his arm, de Redvers said, "Wait. This isn't the time to use this weapon."

"Why?"

Smiling slyly, de Redvers said, "Let them make the bastard Protector of the Realm. Once Webber is in power, you can destroy him with this secret – and take the throne as the champion of justice."

Bigod's eyes brightened. "That's the advice of a man who deserves to be Lord Justiciar once I'm king," he said, clapping de Redvers on the shoulder.

By nightfall, with the cloister lit by torches, the grand council of the Charter of Honour finally reached an agreement.

For the first time in England's history, a parliament of lords from every corner of the realm would convene at Westminster Hall in the fall to select a king. The Earl of Norfolk would serve as Prolocutor. Until then, Sir Robert Webber would act as Protector of the Realm at the head of their forces.

Nones of June 1191

From the balcony of the three-storey keep, the Protector of the Realm surveyed the walled compound below him. Sprawling over more than six acres was the heart of England's monarchy: the Palace of Westminster, Westminster Hall and St. Peter's Abbey.

During his days as Marshal of the Royal Guards, Robert had stood on this spot many times. The view was no different. But his viewpoint had changed. Everything in sight was now his to command.

The thought was more sobering than thrilling.

Within the bailey below him, what had once been the royal gardens was now a teeming campground for the Army of Honour. The tent city was an overflow measure. Numbering more than two thousand, his soldiers had filled the Royal Guards' garrison and taken up all the palace's guest quarters as well.

From the corner of his eye, Robert saw Arthur Bland emerge onto the balcony.

"You asked to see me, Your Excellency?" Bland said, using Robert's new honorific.

"Mister Bland, I want to commend you for the way you've put our men to work restoring the palace and repairing our defences after the looting."

Bland bowed courteously. "Thank you, Sire," he said, then smiled. "However, I suspect your kind words are the sugar for some bitter medicine."

Robert returned his smile for a moment. Then his features hardened. "We need to start rationing meals for the men, Mister Bland. I'm expected to keep this army together until fall. But the supplies from the nobles who funded this army will run out long before that."

"Won't the lords who chose you as Protector provide the means to supply our army, Sire?"

"Marian is with the Curtmantle brothers now, trying to arrange more support. But I'm not counting on it. They promise much and deliver little," Robert said, turning his gaze toward the campground. "If our food supplies run out, it will be impossible to keep these troops together."

"May I offer a suggestion, Sire?"

"Of course."

"During times of war, monarchs have issued royal certificates of warranty for essential supplies. The debts incurred to the merchants were later repaid. I would think as Protector of the Realm you can assume the same authority, Sire."

Robert rubbed his chin. "How would these certificates work?"

"The royal scribes can draw up the certificates specifying whatever supplies we need. With your signature as Protector, merchants will be required to accept them as payment."

"And if they don't?"

"You command an army, Sire. Will the merchants have any choice?"

Robert laughed softly. "Have the scribes prepare the certificates for whatever you need, Mister Bland. They'll have my signature."

"There's one other thing, Sire."

"What's that?"

"The men are satisfied with the plunder from the king's cronies – for now. But without regular pay, we may see defections. I suggest the royal scribes prepare a certificate of warranty for each soldier equal to one month's pay."

"One month's pay for each man is a steep expense, Mister Bland."

"That's true, Sire. But without pay, some men may desert – and desertions can become contagious."

After a moment, Robert said, "Your logic is sound. Prepare the pay certificates as well."

"Very good, Sire," Bland said. "With your permission, I'll take my leave and see the scribes."

"Before you go, there's another matter that needs your discreet attention," Robert said, nodding toward the palace's private quarters. "Throughout the royal bedchambers are a series of secret passages. I want you to find a half-dozen men you can trust to seal them. I'll show you where they are once you've selected the workers."

Bland nodded. "Of course, Sire," he answered, then walked away.

As Robert pondered how this credit scheme would be received by the nobles, he saw a sentry sprinting toward him along the balcony.

"Your Excellency!" the man called out. "Grave news!"

"What is it?" Robert asked, his stomach tightening.

Gasping for breath, the soldier reached Robert. "It's your mother, m'lord," he said, chest heaving. "There's been an accident."

* * *

As the sound of the hoofbeats drew nearer, Friar Tuck felt the wooden floor tremble under his feet. The portly priest walked to the single window in the cramped room and looked down the road to London. Robert Webber was galloping toward Bisheye's only inn with over a dozen mounted soldiers.

"He's here," the priest said soothingly to Anna Webber, who lay on a tottery bed.

Anna barely opened her eyes, her gaze unfocused. The left side of her face and neck were purple with bruises – her left arm and torso bandaged with the inn's tattered bedding. "Thank you for sending for my son, Friar," she said feebly.

"I'm going to leave for a moment and bring him to you, Anna."

Tuck reached the main room of the inn as Robert burst through the door.

"What's my mother doing here?" Robert asked the friar, his face drawn. Judging by the sweat and dust on his tunic, Tuck guessed Robert had galloped the nearly thirty miles from London.

"Catch your breath, Robert," Tuck said gently.

"I'm sorry, Friar," Robert answered. "Thank you for getting a message to me. But why isn't my mother in Nottingham?"

"Anna insisted she needed to see you – but she wouldn't tell me why. So I came with her to visit you in London. Last night, as I rode my mule alongside her coach, the driver lost control of his horse and they went into a ravine. She's been badly hurt, Robert."

"I've sent for physicians from London. They should be here soon."

Tuck put his arm around Robert's shoulders and led him toward Anna's room. "She may not have much time. There's bleeding inside, I fear."

Anna opened her eyes when the men entered the room.

"I'll leave you two alone," Tuck said, backing toward the door.

"Please stay, Friar," Anna said, "You're like family to us."

Robert took his mother's hand. "The best physicians in the realm will be here soon, mother. You're going to be well again."

"That's not important, Robert," she said hoarsely. "After I heard you'd been made Protector of the Realm, a vision came to me." She tried to sit up, but her face knotted in pain.

"Be still, mother. Please," Robert said, stroking her forehead. "We can talk after the physicians have seen you."

Anna shook her head. "This cannot wait, Robert. Listen to me," she said, taking his hand. "Your destiny has arrived, my son. God has given you the chance to finally deliver justice for the common folk of the realm. You must find a way to stay in power and rule with honour and fairness for everyone."

"Mother, we can talk about this later. You need to rest now."

"No!" she said sternly, squeezing his hand. "A chance like this may never come again. I beg you, Robert. Promise me you'll take the throne and change the heartless way we've been ruled."

Robert sighed softly. "Yes, mother. I promise. Now, save your strength."

Anna lay back and closed her eyes, lips forming the wisp of a smile. "I'll rest now," she said softly.

They would be her last words.

***

An old man dressed in rags limped to Anna Webber's body at the altar of St. Peter's Abbey and made the sign of the cross. He was the last in a long procession of mourners who had come to pay their respects to the mother of the Protector of the Realm.

Seated in the first pew, Robert watched the old man leave, his uneven footsteps echoing in the empty church. Hundreds of London's common folk had filed past his mother's body today. But not a single member of the gentry had deigned to attend her viewing.

Robert had dwelled on the snub for hours, deliberately stoking his anger. Hatred was easier to bear than grief. He'd discovered this after learning the coachman who'd caused his mother's accident had been drunk. Robert ordered the man hanged on the spot.

Watching the coachman suffer had given him respite from his mother's loss. Now, the realm's nobility had replaced the coachman as the focus of his wrath.

His mother's life had been his lodestar of dignity and grace. She'd kept her vow of silence to his father and had never spoken an ill word against him. Indeed, she'd never impugned anyone – regardless of their rank. Yet London's smug aristocrats considered this righteous woman beneath them, someone unworthy of a simple courtesy.

The patter of footsteps in the silent abbey drew his attention. Turning toward the sound, he saw Marian.

Robert rose and walked toward her. Near the western transept, they met and embraced.

"I came the moment word reached me," Marian said clinging to him, eyes welling with tears. "I loved her like a mother."

"She loved you as well," Robert said, guiding her to Anna's body at the altar.

Whilst Robert stood behind her, Marian knelt before her mother-in-law. Following a silent prayer, Marian made the sign of the cross and rose.

Putting his arm around her, Robert led Marian out of the church.

The afternoon light was fading as they emerged into the large courtyard between the abbey and the palace. For a long time, they walked arm in arm in silence, taking comfort from each other's touch.

Near the entrance to the palace, Marian stopped and looked into his eyes. "You seem distant, my love. Don't be afraid to grieve."

"I'm not hurt. I'm angry," he said, a chilling calm in his voice. "Not a single noble paid their respects to my mother today – not even my cousins from Chatham Manor."

Marian turned her eyes toward the ground. "I'm ashamed for the people of my class. Their prejudices blind them to the virtues of someone like your mother. She was a kind and generous soul. But hate won't bring her back. It will only poison you, my love."

Robert's eyes turned toward the sky above the palace. After a moment, he said, "That anger may help keep my promise to her."

"What did you promise?"

"My mother travelled to London with a purpose," he said softly. "She asked me to use my power as Protector to defend the rights of England's common folk." Robert stopped walking and took Marian's hand. "Her dying wish was for me to stay in power and rule with justice."

"And you agreed?" Marian asked, cocking her head.

"At that moment, I was only trying to console her. It was an oath I never meant to keep," he said. Then his eyes narrowed. "But she spoke the truth, Marian. England's common folk give their sweat and blood to serve a gentry that accepts their sacrifices as a birthright. All these titled parasites offer in return is contempt and arrogance. I saw that for myself once again today."

"Your mother's instincts were shrewd, Robin. No English monarch has ever sought the support of commoners to rule. By becoming a champion of the people, you could gain the power to take the throne."

Robert shook his head. "My mother's dream is just that… a dream. As matters stand, there's nothing I can do about our realm's injustice. I'll be lucky just to keep my army intact until the parliament," he said. "Tell me about your visit with the Curtmantles. Did they offer any help?"

"Guy and Bernard may have favoured you as Protector at the council, but their faction won't back you with any silver to keep the army together. All they offered was vague promises."

"Arthur Bland may have bought us some time," Robert said, then explained Bland's scheme for creating certificates of warranty.

"That man is worth his weight in silver, Robin."

"We're fortunate to have him," Robert agreed.

"Now that we have the funds, you should bring back the Royal Guards, my love," Marian said, as they neared the palace entrance. "Those red tunics around you will increase your prestige."

"I'll speak with Mister Bland. I'm sure he can recover the tunics left by the deserters and produce new ones as well."

As the pair arrived at the royal suite, the steward met them at the door. "A letter from Lady de Redvers, Your Excellency," he said, handing Robert a sealed sheet of parchment.

Robert dismissed the steward and read the letter.

Marian waited until his eyes rose from the parchment. "What does your sister say?" she asked.

"Juliet may have given me a way to keep the promise I made my mother," he said, a faint smile warming his face.

Kalends of September 1191

The stone walls of Westminster Hall throbbed with the voices of over four-hundred nobles from across the realm. England's first parliament to select a king was at hand.

The nobles sat in rows of benches divided by a centre aisle. On the dais before them, two stately figures faced the crowd in the cavernous room.

To the left sat the parliament's Prolocutor, Sir Hugh Bigod, Earl of Norfolk. To the right, the Protector of the Realm, Sir Robert Webber, Baron of Nottingham. Between the throne-like chairs were a clutch of black-robed clergy.

The entrances into the hall on either side of the dais were manned by a pair of Royal Guards at each door, their stern faces contrasting the animated talk among the nobles.

Westminster Hall's Sergeant-At-Arms banged his pike against the stone floor three times, bringing the gathering to silence. "This parliament is now in session!" he shouted.

The Earl of Norfolk stood and addressed the assembly.

"We have convened this parliament to carry out the solemn duty of selecting a king. But before we embark on this highest of missions, it is my duty as Prolocutor to attend to a matter of justice," Bigod said. "Evidence has been brought to this bench of criminal behaviour by a member of this gathering and it must be addressed before this body can proceed." Bigod paused and glanced toward the entrance to the dais closest to him.

A dozen soldiers overpowered the two Royal Guards at the doorway and rushed onto the podium, their swords drawn. Clad in tunics bearing the Earl of Norfolk's red and blue coat of arms, the warriors formed around Bigod.

The unarmed lords in the hall stared in shock.

"M'lords," Bigod called out to the assembly. "I have first-hand testimony that a member of this parliament is the notorious criminal known as Robin Hood!" Then, with a theatrical sweep, Bigod pointed across the dais. "Detain Robert Webber!" he ordered his warriors.

As the earl's men moved toward Robert, a larger group of warriors clad in the red uniforms of the Royal Guards charged onto the dais from the opposite entrance.

Whilst the priests fled in fear, the troops met in a furious melee near the centre of the podium. In the crush of bodies, the ring of clashing swords merged with grunts, curses and screams of agony.

Another detachment of red-clad warriors ran up the centre aisle, attacking the flank of the Earl of Norfolk's men.

Outnumbered and outfoxed, the earl's men still standing surrendered.

Having disarmed Bigod's men, the Royal Guards seized the Earl of Norfolk.

With his troops now in control, Robert walked to the centre of the dais.

"M'lords, I knew about the Earl of Norfolk's treachery against me today," Robert said to the nobles. "But I wanted you to witness his treason for yourselves. As he has done before," he said pointing toward the earl, "Hugh Bigod has spun a web of lies and betrayed an ally. This is the last time this blackguard will be allowed to deceive us."

"I have the testimony of one of your officers!" Bigod screamed, trying to free himself from the soldiers holding him.

"We've heard enough of your lies, Bigod," Robert said. "Take him away," he ordered his men.

"You're lying, Webber! You're Robin Hood! You're Robin Hood!…" Bigod's screams faded in the distance as he was dragged out of the hall.

Robert stared at the nobles gathered before him, his eyes narrowing. "M'lords, Hugh Bigod was not alone in his plot of treason," he said sternly. "His accomplices will be hunted down and prosecuted!"

Heads swivelled among the lords as each warily assessed the men around him.

After a moment, Robert continued. "As Protector of the Realm, it's my duty to maintain law and order. We will postpone this parliament until all the collaborators of this treasonous plot are in custody."

A murmur of dissent rose from the crowd.

At Robert's signal, the Royal Guards on the dais divided into two lines and sprinted along the walls of the hall, surrounding the unarmed nobles. Then, at the command of their sergeant, the soldiers drew their swords in unison. The deployment brought the lords to a stunned silence.

"Clear the hall!" Robert yelled, pointing toward the main door. "This parliament is concluded. Anyone who protests will be detained."

Exchanging furtive glances, the earls and barons of England grudgingly filed out of Westminster Hall.

* * *

The Crown Inn was a stone's throw from the entrance to Westminster Hall. In a cramped room on the guesthouse's second floor, Lester Muchison waited anxiously.

Walking to the window, Much looked outside again.

Not long before, he'd seen a dozen of the earl's warriors rush into Westminster Hall. That was all according to the plan. But they should have sent for him by now.

The earl's men had brought him to this room at The Crown and told him to wait until he was summoned to testify before the parliament.

Trembling with anticipation, Much sat down on the bed, the room's only furnishing.

Part of him still regretted betraying Rob. Webber had saved his sister and made him a commander. Thanks to Rob, he'd lived far better than his wildest dreams. Still, the price Rob asked for his loyalty was too high.

Hearing footsteps in the hallway, Much rose to his feet.

Suddenly, the door burst open, flying off its flimsy hinges.

Much's jaw dropped as he saw Will Scarlett in the doorway. Behind him were several Royal Guards, their swords drawn.

In a cold voice, Will gave the soldiers an order. "Seize this traitor."

Ides of September 1191

The crowd at the Elms-at-Smithfield cheered as Robert's entourage arrived. "God bless you, Your Excellency!" several of them called out. Astride his horse among two dozen red-clad Royal Guards, the Protector of the Realm smiled and waved to the townsfolk gathered to watch today's executions.

Riding alongside her husband, Marian said, "The people are pleased to see you, Robin. Word of your reforms is spreading."

"Justice is long overdue for the humble folk of our realm. But there's still more to be done," Robert answered.

Shortly after cancelling the parliament a month earlier, Robert had decreed that peasants performing military service would be exempt from rent to their lords. In addition, their families would be allowed to stay on the land the men had worked whilst they served as soldiers. The reforms had delighted commoners – and sparked a surge in the ranks of Robert's army.

The lords of the realm, on the other hand, detested the decree. But Robert's search for traitors among the nobles had muted their dissent. They feared finding themselves among those with their necks on the block today.

On the scaffolding six feet above Smithfield's grassy meadow, the men who'd conspired against Robert at Westminster Hall awaited execution. Their eyes downcast, the Earl of Norfolk, the Earl of Devon, and Lester Muchison awaited their fate. Each condemned man was restrained by a soldier, his hands and feet chained.

The prisoners had been quickly tried and sentenced by a military tribunal. The arrests of other collaborators were expected.

Dismounting from their horses, Robert and Marian climbed the steps to the podium built for them to witness the executions. As the couple settled into ornate chairs, the Royal Guards formed a protective screen around the dais.

Marian nodded toward the condemned men on the scaffold. "I have no pity for these wretches," she whispered to her husband. "If not for your sister's loyalty, we would have never known about their plot against you."

"I'm not surprised Juliet was willing to tell us about de Redvers' scheme with Much," Robert answered. "My sister was humiliated by her husband's whoring every single day."

"Yes, I suspect Juliet had been waiting for a chance at revenge."

Robert scanned the crowd. The throng's excitement rose as the masked executioner climbed the stairs to the platform, axe in hand. "After today, there will be no turning back," Robert whispered.

"What do you mean?" Marian asked, leaning close to him.

"I'll need to be ruthless to honour my mother's wish. The nobles will not accept justice easily," Robert said. "There are only two ways this ends now. Either I become king, or one day, I'll find my own neck on the block."

Moments later, the crowd cheered lustily as the first head rolled.

Kalends of April 1192

The Earl of Lincoln entered the campaign tent and turned his back toward his valet, waiting for the servant to remove his cloak. "The Baron of Sheffield will be joining me shortly," he said over his shoulder. "We'll need refreshments, Bennett."

"The captain of your escorts said you were expecting a guest, m'lord. I took the liberty of preparing some food and drink," the valet said, taking the earl's cape.

Glancing toward the back of the tent, William d'Aubigny smiled. On a small table between two chairs was a tray with an assortment of cheeses, fruit and two goblets beside a pitcher of wine. "I must thank the Earl of Dorset again for parting with you, Bennett. In less than two months of service, you seem to know what I need before I ask."

Bennett bowed his head. "Thank you, m'lord. My predecessor set a high standard."

"Yes, Hughes served me well for many years, God rest his soul," the earl said, then added, "Why can't more commoners comport themselves like you and Hughes – people who know their place?"

A sentry parted the opening to the tent. "The Baron of Sheffield is here, m'lord," the soldier announced.

"Show him in," the earl replied.

After exchanging greetings, the earl and baron sat down as the valet filled their goblets. The pair each downed a cup of wine as they ate.

Wiping his lips after a belch, the earl asked, "I take it the Protector summoned you without any explanation as well?"

"I have no idea why Webber sent for me. But this tribunal is an ugly business."

The Protector of the Realm had summoned both lords to the town of Ashby for a disturbing event: The Baron of Ashby was facing a charge of treason before a military tribunal. Now, both lords were camped outside the town, awaiting tomorrow's trial.

"I noticed you brought a large retinue," d'Aubigny said, taking a draught of wine.

The baron's lips formed into a bitter smile. "I brought fifty warriors to assure the 'Protector of the Realm' will act honourably. I wanted to bring more men but I've had to reduce the size of my troops."

The earl nodded. "Yes, Webber's damnable decrees have depleted the ranks of every lord."

"In the meantime, Webber's forces are growing at our expense," the baron said. "Each day more of my serfs stop farming and join his so-called Army of Honour," he said in disgust, then downed another draft of wine. "The lazy scoundrels know I can't throw their families off the land whilst they're in military service."

"It's a double blow to every lord," the earl agreed. "Every acre that goes unplanted depletes our silver to pay for warriors."

"Webber's a clever bastard. I'll give him that," the baron said grudgingly. "His certificates of warranty are forcing merchants to extend him credit and provide food and weapons for his army."

"His forces are growing, without a doubt," d'Aubigny said. "Webber brought five hundred men with him to detain the Baron of Ashby. With barely a hundred warriors left under his command, the baron had no choice but to surrender."

"His surrender is no surprise. Most nobles and their warriors fear Webber and his Royal Guards. They think he's invincible," the baron said. "No lord will dare test Webber's strength alone."

The earl sighed. "Webber once seemed to be a man of honour. King Richard trusted him to control his brother as regent. That's why I vouched for Webber with the Earl of Devon at my castle last year. Now, de Redvers is dead," he said, lowering his eyes and draining his cup. "I feel responsible for his death."

"That must be a heavy burden," the baron said softly.

The earl held out his goblet and the valet dutifully filled it. "Webber's haughtiness is galling," he said, scowling. "Nearly six months have passed since Bigod tried to seize him at Westminster and he's yet to schedule a new parliament. Webber has used this failed plot against him as a cudgel to keep every lord under his thumb."

"Exactly," the baron agreed. "This tribunal against the Baron of Ashby reeks of tyranny."

"Not many lords will dare challenge that tyranny now that Philip's troops are threatening Flanders. Some lords still believe we need Webber's army to deter the French."

"An invasion from France is speculation. But there's no doubt of Webber's tyranny," the baron said, draining his cup.

Swirling the wine in his goblet, d'Aubigny said, "Looking back, your decision to break with Webber at Cotgrave now seems prophetic."

"I'm not a sage," the baron replied. "More than anything, it was Webber's arrogance that led me to withdraw my troops."

The earl took a long draught of wine. "In times past, noble families have formed alliances to resist a tyrant," he said, then rubbed his lips.

"Perhaps that time has come again."

"If you're considering an alliance against Webber, you can count on me," the baron said, extending his palm.

"I detest intrigue. But Webber has forced this conspiracy upon us," the Earl of Lincoln answered, taking the baron's hand.

* * *

Riding at the head of three-dozen warriors, the Earl of Lincoln approached the site of the Baron of Ashby's tribunal, his head throbbing from last night's excess of wine.

In a forest clearing outside the town, a perimeter of five-hundred red-clad Royal Guards formed the walls of an outdoor courtroom.

At a passage through the human barrier marked by regimental banners, the earl dismounted and followed the bailiff into the tribunal area, leaving his escorts behind. The space inside had been laid out to resemble an indoor courtroom, d'Aubigny observed.

Under an awning in the centre of the square were the judges: three Royal Guard officers seated at a long table. Behind the magistrates, the Protector of the Realm sat on a low platform.

Seated to the left of the judges was the accused, the Baron of Ashby.

The bailiff led the Earl of Lincoln to the right of the judges where the Baron of Sheffield sat next to an empty chair. The earl sat down beside the baron, then glanced behind him.

A gallery of scruffy townsfolk and peasants stood behind a line of soldiers.

"The prisoner will now stand," the head judge announced.

The Baron of Ashby rose unsteadily as the bailiff read the charges of treason against him. The judge then called the first witness: the baron's butler.

Emerging from the gallery, the servant faced the judges, hat held over his chest. After stating his name and occupation, the butler turned a hard eye toward the Baron of Ashby. "I heard the baron tell the Earl of Norfolk that he would support Sir Hugh if he tried to remove the Protector."

"Do you deny this, baron?" the judge asked the prisoner.

The baron shook his head. "I – I – didn't offer the Earl of Norfolk military support," he stammered. "I simply said that I would not oppose the earl's attempt to remove the Protector."

"Nonetheless, your intent was clear. Both word and deed are considered treason before the law," the judge said.

Shouts rose from the gallery. "Put him on the block! Off with his head!"

"This witness is dismissed. The court now calls Conrad Bennett," the judge said loudly.

The Earl of Lincoln swallowed hard as he saw his valet remove the hood of his cloak and walk out of the gallery. Once Bennett was before the magistrates, the judge said, "State your name and occupation."

"My name is Conrad Bennett, sir. I'm the valet of the Earl of Lincoln."

"Do you have any testimony pertinent to these proceedings, Mister Bennett?" the head judge asked.

"I do, sir," Bennett said calmly. "While serving the Earl of Lincoln, I heard him discuss a plot to overthrow the Protector of the Realm."

As a gasp rose from the gallery, d'Aubigny looked toward the regimental banners where he'd entered the perimeter of the Royal Guards. The gap was closed – and the Royal Guards were overpowering his men and those of the Baron of Sheffield. This was a trap.

"Who did the Earl of Lincoln conspire with in this plot, Mister Bennet?" the head judge asked.

"The Baron of Sheffield, sir," Bennett said, pointing toward the lord.

Shouts rang out from the common folk. "Traitors! Traitors!"

The judge waited for the clamour to subside then addressed d'Aubigny. "Do you deny this testimony about you and the Baron of Sheffield?"

The Earl of Lincoln stood, thrusting out his chin. "It's time for the rot of this tyranny to finally be exposed," he said defiantly, then levelled a finger toward Robert Webber. "This man is abusing his power as Protector of the Realm! He's removing his rivals through these preposterous tribunals and obstructing the parliament to select a legitimate king!"

A chorus of heckling and jeers rose from the crowd.

"You have just confessed to treason, d'Aubigny!" the head judge shouted. He then addressed the soldiers standing behind the earl and baron. "Guards! Detain them!".

Four of the Royal Guards holding back the gallery stepped forward and seized both men.

All three of the accused men were shoved by the guards until they stood before the judges.

"This tribunal will now confer on its decision," the head judge announced.

With heads inclined toward each other, the three judges spoke privately. The earl felt streams of sweat under his tunic despite a raw spring wind. Finally, the three officers nodded in assent.

The head judge stood. "After weighing the testimony given here today, it is the judgment of this court that the Baron of Ashby, the Baron of Sheffield and the Earl of Lincoln are guilty of treason. By law, the punishment for this crime is death," he said above the cheers from the gallery.

Ides of April 1192

Pale green sprouts were awakening on the oaks as Robert led his mounted entourage through Sherwood Forest. Not more than a mile ahead was the stone cottage where he'd been born.

Returning from the tribunal at Ashby and bound for Nottingham, an inexplicable urge had driven Robert to divert his column toward his childhood home.

Robert's pulse rose as each tree and boulder became familiar, bringing back the memory of his last days here – and of his mother.

Her dying wish had inspired him to seek the throne. But the toll on his conscience had been high.

He felt no satisfaction in punishing the nobles who had conspired against him. Indeed, sending these men to the block troubled him deeply at times.

In those moments, Robert reminded himself that the executions were carried out for an honourable cause… justice for the realm's commoners.

That's what he told himself.

And yet, there was a dark allure to the executions – something he was loath to admit. They had propelled him on a path he'd never imagined.

He was now on the brink of becoming king.

Emerging from the dense forest, Robert stopped his escorts as his homestead came into view. Not much had changed. Then, something unexpected drew his attention: a wisp of smoke rising from the cottage's chimney.

A wave of rage coursed through him. Someone was squatting on the property, desecrating his mother's memory. Urging his mount into a gallop, Robert rode toward the house, his troops in tow, the hooves of their horses shuddering the ground.

As he reached the cottage, the front door opened and a woman stepped outside, a small boy clinging to her legs. She wore a crudely sewn woollen dress and a defiant expression.

"What are you doing here?" Robert asked from his horse.

"My husband serves in Nottingham's garrison," she answered, eyes meeting his without fear. "The Protector says the likes of you can't run us off anymore."

A burst of laughter rose from Robert's men.

Their amusement faded when they saw their leader's face. "The law says a wife can stay on the land whilst her husband is in the army. But you don't belong here. You're nothing more than a squatter," Robert said sternly. "Now, clear off."

"The place was deserted," the woman said, head held high. "I have no husband. My child and I have nowhere to go. If the Protector's law was meant to create justice for common folk, it should apply to me as well."

Staring at the woman, Robert remembered his mother on that same threshold, standing before Richard's men at arms. "What's your name?" he asked, the edge gone from his voice.

"Sarah Payne."

"Your son has a brave mother, Sarah Payne. He deserves a place to grow into a man. You can stay," he said before turning his horse toward Nottingham.

*　*　*

"Open the gate for the Protector of the Realm!" one of Robert's men called out as his mounted column approached the entrance to Nottingham's palisade.

Under a full moon, Robert could see the faces of four guards peering over the wooden wall. Moments later, a pair of sleepy soldiers opened the gate.

He'd chosen to arrive near midnight to avoid the throng that would have received him in daylight. The attention and fawning made him uncomfortable.

Arriving at Talbot Hall, Robert was met by the steward. "Welcome back, Your Excellency," the servant said, his nightshirt showing below a partially buttoned tunic.

"I'll see Lady Marian and Will Scarlett in the parlour," Robert said.

The steward's drowsy eyes widened. "Now, Sire?"

"Yes – and bring food and drink as well."

Robert was filling three goblets with wine when Marian entered the parlour, her hair loose above a fur stole covering her nightgown.

"Why didn't you come to our bed, Robin?" she asked frowning.

"I felt no need to sleep."

Marian walked to him and stroked his chest sensuously. "We needn't have slept."

"There are urgent matters to attend with you and Will."

Marian untied her nightgown, letting it fall open. "There are urgent matters to attend with your wife," she said in a husky voice, pulling him against her. "The moon is full, my love – the time a woman is most fertile."

His pulse rising, Robert said, "Perhaps our discussion can wait."

"Go to our bedchamber and wash away the travel dust, my love. I'll tell the steward we'll meet Will for breakfast."

* * *

Walking arm in arm, Robert and Marian entered the parlour at Talbot Hall.

"I'm not very hungry this morning," Marian said, glancing toward the breakfast set out by the steward on a table along the wall. "My appetite is satisfied," she said with a sly smile, squeezing his arm.

Robert returned her smile, then filled a goblet with ale from a pitcher on the table. "Well, a husband's duty is thirsty work, my love," he said before taking a long drink.

"You wanted to tell me about the tribunal at Ashby last night… before I lured you upstairs."

Robert kissed her hand. "I'm grateful for the distraction."

"By your manner, I gather all went well."

Robert nodded. "Will's connections helped us uncover three more traitors."

"These men Will consorts with…" Marian said, rubbing the back of her hand. "Can we trust them, Robin?"

Robert took another drink of ale. "The men Will recruits have been keeping a secret all their lives. They know how to be discreet."

"You never told me how Will managed to place one of his informants as d'Aubigny's valet."

"When the earl's valet died of a fever, Will had his uncle recommend a man from his own household – a man in Will's network."

"The death of d'Aubigny's valet came at an opportune time," Marian said, averting her eyes.

Robert nodded and looked away. "Yes, it was," he said as they lapsed into a long silence.

The sound of footfalls rose from the hallway.

Wrapped in a heavy robe, Will Scarlett entered the parlour, face drawn. "I pray the news from Ashby is good," he said anxiously.

"There's no cause for concern, Will," Robert said, handing him a cup of ale. "Thanks to you, the tribunal put us in a stronger position at the new parliament."

"Do you think we have the votes?" Will asked.

"Guy and Bernard lost three of their allies at Ashby," Robert said. "Support for the Curtmantles is growing weaker – especially now that Philip is massing an army near the border of Flanders. The other lords know our realm needs a proven warrior with a large army."

"Yes, but how can we make sure you win at the parliament?" Marian asked.

"We can discuss that later," Robert said, pacing the room. "At the moment, we need to appoint a successor for me here. I can't be the king and Baron of Nottingham."

Marian spread her palm toward Scarlett. "What about Will?"

Will's eyes rose expectantly from his cup.

As Robert shook his head, Will's chin dropped. "I have more important work for Will."

"Who, then?" Marian asked.

Robert took a sip of ale. "Rudolf Murdac," he said evenly.

"Are you joking?" Marian asked, eyes wide with surprise.

Robert spread his palms. "Murdac knows the shire better than anyone. Yes, he's treacherous, but he's also a coward. If he's watched closely, we'll keep him honest enough to do his job," he said, then faced Scarlett. "Will, I'm counting on you to do that. Can you find someone to keep our eyes on him?"

Will nodded. "I'm sure I can."

"Good," Robert said.

"I still think Murdac is dangerous," Marian said. "But I'd rather resolve how you'll hold sway at the parliament, Robin. We have less than three months to win over the nobles."

"I think my uncle may be helpful," Will said. "Let me explain."

For the next hour, Robert and Marian listened raptly.

Kalends of August 1192

*C*arrying packages covered with finely wrought cloth, three royal footmen entered the king's dining chamber at Westminster Palace. With decorous grace, the servants approached the table where the Protector of the Realm sat with his wife and two guests, then bowed.

Robert faced the man in long grey locks seated to his right. "Sir Arnold… Lady Marian and I thank you for gracing us with your presence. And as a token of our esteem, we would like to present you with a gift."

As Robert waved his hand toward the servants, they removed the fabric draped over their bundles.

"Magnificent! Simply magnificent!" the Earl of Dorset said as he saw three sleek falcons inside cages. "I assume these lovely creatures were John's?"

"Yes," Robert answered. "Your nephew told me you were fond of falconry," he said, nodding toward Will Scarlett.

The Earl of Dorset smiled. "Say what you will about that fat reprobate, John had an eye for fine things," Sir Arnold said, then nodded graciously toward his hosts. "I'm honoured to be invited to the palace, Your Excellency. Your hospitality is matched only by the loveliness of your wife," he said, beaming toward Marian.

"Uncle, I shall have to tell Aunt Evelyn about your shameless flirting," Will said, laughing.

"Beauty is owed its due, Will," the earl countered with a grin.

Will tilted his cup toward the earl. "And you, dear uncle, never forego the opportunity," he said with a wink.

The banter sparked a round of laughter.

"Speaking of opportunities, Sir Arnold," Marian said, touching the earl's sleeve. "With the parliament not long away, there are opportunities of mutual benefit to be had there. I hope we'll have a chance to speak of them during your stay with us."

"That would be most agreeable, Lady Marian," the earl replied. "I don't often travel to London but—"

A sentry hurrying into the chamber, interrupted the earl. "Your Excellency," he said to Robert. "Friar Tuck is here and says it's urgent that he speaks with you."

"Show him in," Robert said.

The corpulent priest rushed into the room, robe swishing in his wake. "Philip has captured Flanders!" he called out, approaching the table. "He's assembling a fleet in the harbour of Calais!"

"Can you trust the source of this news?" Robert asked the friar.

Tuck nodded. "The bishop of Calais sent a messenger to our diocese."

"Rumours of this will spread quickly, Robin," Marian said, her voice tight. "Philip is only twenty miles off our shores. This can't go unchallenged."

"I fear Lady Marian is right," the earl said to Robert. "The Curtmantles will say naming you Protector has not deterred Philip. Without some kind of action, you'll risk losing the support of many nobles."

Will rose from the table. "We should move the army to Dover immediately and strengthen the castle's garrison."

"I agree, Will," Robert said. "Let's make a show of it. We'll march out of London flying the regimental colours and playing the war drums."

"That will alert Philip's spies that you'll be waiting for him in Dover, Robin," Marian said. "But there are Englishmen here who may try to take advantage of your army's absence for their own gain."

"That's a risk I'll have to take," Robert said. "I'd rather be deposed defending our island than cower here in fear of my rivals."

Will stepped back from the table. "With your permission, I'll alert our commanders to make their men ready to travel."

"Thank you, Will," Robert said. "I want to be ready to march by morning."

"I should excuse myself as well," the earl said rising to his feet. "You have important matters to attend."

The priest looked at Robert. "Would you like me to stay, Rob? You may want to pray on this."

"Thank you, Father," Robert answered. "That won't be necessary."

Marian and Robert watched the men leave the chamber. Then Marian embraced him. Looking into his eyes, she said, "Promise me you'll come back, my love. I've felt the quickening for days now. You're going to be a father."

Ides of August 1192

The channel was at low tide when the rowboats made landfall on the beach.

Stepping ashore, Robert looked east down the coastline. More than a mile away, the fortifications at the mouth of Calais harbour were barely visible, black pillars against the deep blue of the moonless sky.

They had about four hours until sunrise. If their raid was not over by then, they would almost certainly be dead.

Ahead of him, Robert eyed the steep bluffs beyond the beach. His group of forty-eight men in six small boats would have to portage their vessels over these cliffs. On the other side of the narrow peninsula, they would put into the waters of Calais harbour where their target waited:

King Philip's fleet.

As the men hoisted the boats onto their shoulders, Robert set out ahead, guiding their way.

At the summit of the bluffs, Robert caught sight of Calais harbour, a narrow crescent curving away from him, its waters gleaming in the starlight. Near the centre of the crescent was a countless mass of ships, their masts piercing the sky, night lamps twinkling.

Their descent toward the harbour was as exhausting as the climb.

When they reached the water's edge, Robert ordered his men to rest. They had rowed nearly a mile from their mother ship in the channel, then carried their boats filled with weapons over another half-mile of hills. Robert had hand-picked the boat crews, hardened warriors whose courage, battle skills and stamina he'd seen first-hand.

As Robert sat on the ground beside his men, he could only hope Will Scarlett's part of their operation had been successful. For the last few days, Will's men had been ambushing Philip's troops in the countryside disguised as peasants. If Philip took the bait, the French king would have weakened his forces around the harbour to put down an apparent rebellion against his occupation of Flanders.

"Let's move," Robert said when the men were breathing normally again.

As six of the men in each boat rowed, the other two prepared their weapons. Longbows were strung… quivers of resin-soaked arrows were unpacked… unlit torches were distributed… finally, shields were mounted along the strakes for protection.

The six boats rowed along the deserted side of the harbour until

Philip's fleet was just a quarter mile away across the bay. After muffling their oarlocks, all eyes turned toward Robert.

His heart throbbing, Robert kissed his amulet, drew his sword and pointed toward Philip's fleet.

There were sentries on every ship ahead of them. Once the guards spotted Robert's men, the full crew of each vessel would rise to man their weapons. Robert hoped to have the advantage before that.

When Robert's boats were near arrow range of their targets, the crew of each boat changed roles. Two men rowed whilst the other six took up their bows. The boats then dispersed.

Robert's craft would attack the ships in the centre, the others would take the flanks. From here on, every boat would act on its own.

Longbow in hand, Robert scanned the deck of a knarr ahead, looking for the sentry. He found the man leaning on the main mast, barely awake.

An arrow from his longbow took the sentry down.

Moving on to a cog, Robert repeated the attack, leaving another ship unguarded. He hoped his men in the other five boats were sharing his luck. A voice rising in the distance told him they were not.

"Nous sommes attaqués!" a French crewman yelled.

"Light the fire arrows and launch at will," Robert said calmly to his crew. After torches were lit with fire starters, the bowmen in Robert's boat began a volley of flaming arrows onto the French ships. Their targets were the furled sails and pitch-soaked rigging, the most combustible parts of the vessels.

By now, the crews of the French ships were awake and rushing into action. Some tried to douse the fires whilst others launched arrows toward Robert's boat.

Taking cover behind their shields, Robert's archers continued their attack. Some of their fire arrows struck the crewmen. But even the misses were deadly as the arrows spread the flames.

As the burning missiles from Robert's boats found their targets, the sky above the French ships filled with smoke and embers. As Robert had hoped, the night-time breeze blowing toward shore was spreading the blaze to the ships closer to the docks.

Fed by the cascade of their arrows, the fires grew, sowing chaos through Philip's fleet. Ships collided and ran aground as their crews scrambled to weigh anchor, put out fires and defend themselves from the intruders.

The arrows in his boat depleted, Robert's chest swelled as he watched the mayhem. Before long many of the ship's in Philip's fleet would be in flames. Their raid had succeeded. The time to leave had come.

His moment of pride was short lived.

A French skiff was heading toward them, launching arrows as they drew nearer. "Shield wall astern," he said to the two men supplying arrows to the archers. "The rest of you, take up oars. Get us back across the bay."

Scanning a battle scene now lit by the fires, Robert saw his other boats retreat out of arrow range from the burning ships. That much was according to his plan. But instead of five boats, he saw only three. As always, war brought more regret than glory.

An arrow splashed into the water near Robert. Looking back toward the French skiff, he saw the gap between them closing. The enemy craft was lighter, the men rowing her fresher. Another arrow flew over them. The French archers were shoddy. But given enough time, they would decimate his crew if they remained exposed.

"Take cover behind your shields and draw your swords," Robert said to his men as they reached the middle of the bay. "We're going to hold here and fight," he said, unsheathing his blade.

As the skiff closed, Robert could see that just one of the eight Frenchmen in the small boat was now launching arrows whilst the other seven rowed. Even when the French archer's missiles found their mark, they struck harmlessly on English shields.

"Wish we'd held back a few arrows. We'd give these pastry eaters what for," one of Robert's men said, crouching behind his shield.

"Stop your carping, Bailey," another soldier said. "These bastards couldn't hit a bull in the arse with a long oar."

Robert did not relish fighting in a small boat on open water. Neither he nor his men could swim. But, without arrows, their only advantage would come at close quarters.

Moving to the front of the boat, Rob handed Bailey a rope and said, "Throw this over their stempost and pull our boats together when we're close."

As the French craft drew nearer, its crew began shouting, ginning up their courage.

Robert and his men waited silently until the French were less than a man's height away. "Now, Bailey," Robert called out.

The rope caught the skiff's stempost, pulling the boats bow-to-bow. With the two craft joined at their narrowest point, Robert stood and stepped onto the bow behind his shield, sword thrusting ahead of him. A French sailor with a sword and heavy shield stood to confront him.

Robert's assault was risky but cunning. The French archers could not launch without hitting their own man in the back.

The sailor and Robert traded sword blows over the bow, each careful to keep his balance. Robert feinted a slash to his opponent's knee, making the Frenchman lean away. With the sailor off balance, Robert kicked the Frenchman's shield. The man screamed in terror, flailing his arms as he splashed into the water.

"Follow me," Robert called out to the men behind him as he stepped onto the enemy skiff.

Another French sailor with sword and shield moved toward him in the narrow boat.

Robert thrust the edge of his shield into the left side of his opponent's buckler. When the sailor's shield twisted, Robert jabbed his sword into the man's exposed torso. As the sailor screamed and crumpled, Robert shoved him overboard.

The Frenchman who now faced Robert wore an ornate hat and cloak. He was likely their commander. "Je me rends," the man said, dropping his sword and putting up his hands.

Shouts of victory rose from Robert's men.

After throwing the Frenchmen's weapons and oars overboard, Robert's crew cast the sailors adrift.

Once aboard their own boat and rowing toward their rendezvous point, Robert looked behind him. The flames of the burning ships rose high into the night.

Philip's fleet was all but gone.

Nones of November 1192

Entering the large doors of Westminster Hall, Guy Curtmantle was struck by the change in mood of the realm's second parliament. The animated talk among the nobles at the last assembly was gone. In its place was an ominous silence.

The size of the gathering had withered as well. Entire rows of benches were empty in a hall that had once been full. The nobles here today were huddled in small clusters, casting wary glances around them.

Scanning the hall, Guy saw his brother on a bench near the back and sat next to Bernard.

"Almost half the realm's lords have avoided this parliament," Guy whispered.

"With good reason, brother. Webber's tribunals have made the gentry afraid to be near him. Who knows when some servant will suddenly appear and denounce you?"

"It's appalling," Guy said, shaking his head. "The mobs cheer him on every time Webber executes a lord – and now that he's stopped Philip's invasion, even some of the nobles are singing his praises."

Bernard sighed. "I thought the clergy might speak out against him," he said bitterly. "The church has always preached against the pollution of noble blood."

"You were wrong, brother," Guy said. "Once he gave the church full rights to the Carlisle silver mine, they rolled over for him like lap dogs."

"Still, I can't believe the bishops agreed to let Webber name a friar from Nottingham as the Archbishop of Canterbury."

"They're whores in vestments, the lot of them," Guy said bitterly. "What about the merchants? Has their guild allied against him?

Bernard shook his head. "Any merchant who complains too loudly about those worthless certificates finds his shop has caught fire in the night."

Guy sighed. "Who would have thought we'd come to this?" he said bitterly. "We were fools to trust Webber, brother."

"He's not the same man Richard trusted to keep his brother in check."

"Would you take John back now?"

Bernard rubbed his beard. Before he could answer, a roar of cheers rose outside the hall. The bellowing surged as the doors of the hall opened. A flourish of trumpets rose from the balcony.

Preceded by two-dozen Royal Guards, the Protector of the Realm strode into the hall accompanied by his wife. In a gross display of impropriety, Lady Marian was in public heavy with child.

Whilst Webber and his wife walked toward the ornate chair at the centre of the dais, a larger detail of Royal Guards entered the building.

Moving in lock step, the red-clad soldiers marched until they'd lined every wall inside the hall, surrounding the nobles on the benches. Then, in unison, they turned to face the unarmed lords.

Guy's eyes lowered under the Guards' hard stares.

The Sergeant-At-Arms near the dais banged his pike three times on the stone floor. "This parliament is now in session!" he called out.

The Protector of the Realm slowly cast his gaze over the lords gathered before him. He then stood and spoke, his voice echoing through the hall. "M'lords, our realm is under siege. The king of France covets our island. A conspiracy of traitors haunts our realm. These dangers call for a strong monarch, a king who can protect his people from threats beyond and within our kingdom," Webber said, then paused. "The Archbishop of Canterbury will now bless the selection of our new king."

The archbishop rose from a seat near the edge of the dais. In an opulent robe bulging at the seams, Tuck walked to the centre of the platform and made the sign of the cross. The nobles in the hall stood and echoed his gesture. "Lord, may you grant this assembly Your infinite wisdom. The man chosen today will rule with God's blessings for the honour of our realm. Amen." The archbishop then lowered his palms, directing the lords to sit.

As the prelate returned to his seat, the Protector spoke again. "We will now open the assembly for nominations."

From a bench near the front of the hall, Sir Arnold Osmund, the Earl of Dorset rose. Turning to address his fellow lords, he said, "I nominate a man who has already shown the courage, wisdom and integrity to rule wisely." The earl then gestured grandly toward the dais, his long grey locks swirling. "I nominate His Excellency, Sir Robert Webber, the hero of Amiens, victor at Calais and Protector of the Realm."

Guy felt his bile rise. The Earl of Dorset was the uncle of Webber's chief adjutant.

"This is most unusual, Sir Arnold," Webber replied, tenting his fingers. "I'm here to lead the selection of our new king. I cannot be considered a candidate."

"Can anyone here name a candidate more qualified than the man who defeated an invasion of our island before it began?" the Earl of Dorset asked loudly, sweeping his eyes over the assembly.

Guy looked around him. Surely someone would show the courage to resist this travesty. For a moment, he thought of nominating himself. But it would be unseemly if either he or his brother dared break with tradition.

From the rear of the assembly, Sir Edward Blake, the Baron of Thetford rose. "I second the Earl of Dorset's nomination."

Bernard leaned close to Guy and whispered, "Sir Edward fought a battle against Webber once and later struck a truce with him. There's no doubt a prize for him in this charade."

The Earl of Dorset spoke again. "Are there any other candidates?"

Heads swivelled expectantly throughout the hall. The silence remained unbroken.

Guy covered his mouth, lowering his gaze, silently cursing his own cowardice.

"Then I say we put this to a vote!" the Earl of Dorset called out. "All those in favour of making the Protector of the Realm our new king say 'aye.'"

A thin chorus of "ayes" rang through the hall.

"All opposed say 'nay!'" the earl said loudly.

Guy shrank as a dreadful silence followed.

"The selection is unchallenged! We shall have a resolute and just monarch to lead us from this day forward!" the earl said, smiling broadly. "Long live the king!"

The smattering of cheers that followed were drowned out by the sudden pealing of St. Peter's bells and another flourish of trumpets from the gallery. Amid the din, Guy met his brother's eyes.

They were brimming with tears.

Kalends of January 1193

The fair-haired infant squinted as King Robert carried her into the sunlight. Swaddled in an ermine mantle, the princess began to cry, frightened by the sudden roar of cheers. The king stroked her cheek, trying to calm the babe as he led a parade of dignitaries out of St. Peter's Abbey.

Despite the bitter cold, thousands of London's common folk had gathered outside the church, eager for a glimpse of the newly baptised princess. "Long live the king! Long live the princess!" they shouted, their voices merging into a jubilant bedlam.

Robert raised the infant above his head, slowly sweeping her before the crowd, basking in their adulation.

His coronation had been a long, tedious affair that Robert tolerated without much pleasure. But this moment before the people was a thrill that made his pulse surge.

He wished Marian could be here with him to savour the celebration. But as custom dictated, she would remain in confinement for several more weeks.

Although her labour had been difficult, Marian had assured him this would not be his last heir. That pleased Robert. Nonetheless, he was smitten by the infant whose colouring and features favoured his wife.

Named after Robert's mother, Princess Anna Mary Charlotte Webber carried the blood of lords and common folk. As Marian had predicted, this trait had immediately endeared the princess to the realm's masses – further strengthening Robert's bond with the people.

Thanks to his decrees establishing greater rights for peasants, King Robert had already become a name spoken with reverence in the houses of the humble.

The estates of the privileged were another matter.

Among the realm's nobility, bitterness seethed toward the king. But that anger was tempered by fear. Every lord spoke cautiously about the king – especially before any servants. The royal tribunals still roamed the countryside.

Robert looked into the crowd. Their joyous faces were a testament to the promise he'd made his mother.

The dark times of executing his enemies were behind him. From this day forward, he would rule in peace, with justice for all.

Nones of January 1193

"This is disgraceful," The Earl of Dorset muttered to his nephew as the pair entered the anteroom to the palace's privy chamber. The floor was tracked with muddy snow and littered with dead leaves blown inside during the fall.

Will Scarlett shrugged. "His Highness has more urgent matters than the upkeep of the palace."

"Every monarch faces distractions, nephew," Sir Arnold said sourly. "This neglect does not reflect well on the king."

In the two months since King Robert had appointed him Lord Justiciar, Arnold Osmund had begun to question the character of their new sovereign. The man had always shown a certain lack of breeding and refinement. But worse than that, he seemed to harbour a deep contempt for the realm's nobility.

The king had not held a single feast or ball since his coronation. His court lacked people of wit or charm – save his wife. This dreary state of affairs was doing little to win the hearts of the gentry. In fact, the king's only sensible action had been naming him justiciar – a reward he was amply due for his support at the parliament.

Sharing these views with his nephew, however, would not be wise. Will was now Chief Constable and fiercely loyal to the king. Indeed, given his nephew's proclivities, Osmund often wondered about the nature of his bond with Robert Webber.

Entering the privy chamber, the justiciar saw the king, the queen, the chancellor of the exchequer, and the archbishop of Canterbury seated around an unadorned table.

The chancellor arched an eyebrow. "Ah, Sir Arnold. We've been awaiting your sage counsel," Arthur Bland said with a mirthless smile.

The justiciar bowed to the king and queen, then cast a sneer toward Bland before sitting down. Naming his former valet as chancellor of the exchequer was another of Webber's ghastly decisions.

"I'm pleased you could join us as well, Will," the king said, nodding toward his chief constable. "Please sit down."

"I'm honoured to be invited, Sire," Will said, taking a chair.

Osmund was surprised when the queen spoke first.

"His Highness wants to better the lives of the most humble in our realm," she said. "Today we'll discuss a new royal decree toward that end."

The justiciar spread his palms. "Your Highness, I think the king's decrees have been exceedingly generous," he said to the queen. "The families of peasants in the military cannot be removed from the land. What more can we do for these people?"

The chancellor answered instead. "The realm's richest lords have so much land, most would lose their way through their estates without a warden," Arthur Bland said. "I've proposed that His Highness annex part of those lands and give them to the neediest peasants within each lord's demesne."

The justiciar's mouth gaped. "Are you mad?" he asked the chancellor. "Every peer of the realm would resist such a preposterous scheme."

"Will, you're a peer of the realm," the queen said to the new chief constable. "Does this scheme seem preposterous to you?"

Scarlett's eyes shifted between his uncle and the queen. After a moment, Will said, "Your Highness, every lord is a subject of the king. If our sovereign issues a decree, it's every noble's duty to obey."

The justiciar addressed the chancellor, avoiding a confrontation with the queen. "Our kingdom is ordained by God, Mister Bland. To take land from noble families would be blasphemy."

"When Danes and Normans came to England, they took the lands of many Saxon lords. Was that blasphemy as well?" the chancellor countered.

Raising his index finger, the justiciar said, "Those lands were won through the right of conquest."

The chancellor laughed bitterly. "I see," Bland said tartly. "When foreigners take land from our lords at the point of a sword, it's God's will. But if our king issues a decree giving land to the poor, it's blasphemy."

"You twist my words, Bland!" the justiciar said angrily, rising to his feet, tresses awry.

"Please sit down, Sir Arnold," the king said calmly. "Your objections to the chancellor's proposal have merit."

Relieved, Osmund smoothed his hair and sat down. "Thank you, Sire. I'm pleased to know you agree."

"I did not say I agree," the king replied, lifting his palm. "You're correct that some lords may raise religious objections to the crown annexing lands for the poor. However, I'm certain our new Archbishop of Canterbury will assure them otherwise."

All eyes in the room turned to the prelate. "The Lord's word on this is clear," Tuck said. "Proverbs tells us, 'He who oppresses the poor shows contempt for their Maker. But he who is kind to the needy honours God.'"

The justiciar wagged a finger at Bland. "Your reforms will hurt the very people you want to help. Can't you see that?" he said, his voice rising. "Without the bargaining power of a lord, each peasant will be swindled by the merchants when he sells his crops for the silver to pay his taxes."

"The peasants will not pay taxes at all," the chancellor answered.

The justiciar's face reddened. "You'll bankrupt the crown," he said, veins in his neck bulging.

"The scribes at the Exchequer assure me the crown can absorb the loss of revenue," Bland answered calmly. "Our previous monarch was wasteful and greedy."

"Sire, this is a grave mistake," Osmund said, facing the king.

"Sir Arnold, I trust the judgment of my chancellor of the exchequer," the king said, his voice turning cold. "Can I trust you as my justiciar to carry out my decrees? If not, then I'll ask for your resignation today."

Osmund swallowed hard. Would he give up the prestige of his new office to protest this foolish decree? Even if he did, wouldn't another less-principled noble take his place and completely bend to the king's will? "I will make it my duty to enact your decree, Sire," the justiciar finally said.

Kalends of December 1193

Rudolph Murdac moved warily through the woodlands, staying in the shadows of a waning moon. Arriving at a lone cottage in the middle of a clearing, he pressed his ear against the door.

Behind the wooden portal, the Sheriff of Nottingham heard the unmistakable moans and grunts of sex. This would not take much longer, he told himself, then walked to an ancient oak and hid behind its trunk.

As he waited, Murdac mused on the changes of his fate. Just over a year ago, he'd been in prison, hopeless and alone. Webber had set him free and even restored his former office.

But that was no reason to be grateful.

His reinstatement as sheriff served the bastard's purposes as much as his own. Indeed, Murdac knew that Webber's spies watched him constantly. That's why he made these visits here late at night and alone.

The cottage door opened and a burly young peasant stepped outside hugging the collar of his coat against the cold December night.

Murdac waited until the man was gone, then entered the cottage without knocking. "I see trade is brisk," he said as he stepped into the one-room house and moved close to the fireplace, rubbing the chill from his arms.

A woman in her late twenties was tidying the covers of a bed in the corner, her hair and clothes askew. "Seems the colder it gets, the more these yokels get hot for humping," she said wearily.

"If this keeps up, you'll soon be richer than I am, Eva," Murdac said, sneering. "I may need to raise your house fee."

"My garden can't take much more ploughing each week, Murdac," Eva said, pulling up her bodice to retrieve an errant breast. "If you're looking to get richer, you'll need to add another whore."

Settling onto a bench near the fire, Murdac stroked his beard. Eva's idea made sense. God knew, he needed more sources of coin. Each day, there were fewer – thanks to the idiot on the throne.

The king's decree had taken large tracts of land away from the lords. As a result, the size of Murdac's kickbacks for reducing their taxes had plummeted. Collecting bribes from the peasants was out of the question. There were far too many serfs with small parcels of land – and one of the dimwits would inevitably give away the game to Webber's spies.

As Murdac's prospects had diminished, those of the peasants had improved.

The fall harvest had been plentiful this year. For the first time in their lives, many peasants had a surplus of crops which they could sell for coin. Although most were hoodwinked by sharp-dealing merchants, many of the new landowners managed to buy livestock and improved their farms. But temptation got the better of many others.

By the start of winter, taverns across the shire were packed with peasant men swigging ale as they gambled at cards and dice. Their squandering was an inspiration to Murdac.

From the prostitutes he'd once procured for the Earl of Devon, Murdac sent for one of de Redvers' favourites. He set up Eva Brewer in a one-room cottage that had fallen into his lap after the death of a widow without kin. A month later, Eva was busy day and night. The arrangement brought Eva a tuppence per customer and fetched Murdac a shilling each week as a house fee. Adding another whore would double his take.

Although a far cry from the bribes he'd once raked in, for now, there was no other way to augment his paltry stipend as sheriff.

Murdac rose, rubbing his hands. "You're a clever one," he said, pointing a finger at Eva. "I'll send for Maggie Ames from Devonshire and have another bed brought in."

Eva rolled her eyes. "You can't have two women working in one room, Murdac. These men aren't lords who fancy orgies. They want their business done in private. Most of them worry about a mate catching sight of the size of his willy – or they ask for something they'd rather keep secret."

"I don't have another house," Murdac said as he stared into the fire.

Reaching under the bed, Eva produced a leather pouch. After counting out twenty coins, she tossed them onto the bed and said, "Then you'll have to settle for a shilling a week until you do."

Nones of April 1194

The justiciar covered his nose as he entered the privy chamber. Although it was mid-morning, the rancid smell of the tallow candles burned the previous night still lingered. A fitting stench for the topics they were about to discuss, Osmund mused, before taking the last empty chair at the council table.

Gathered in the room were the king and members of his privy council, ten of the monarch's most trusted advisors. In a break with tradition, the queen was part of the group and was the first to speak.

"Please forgive the odour," Lady Marian said to the men around her. "We're trying to reduce costs in the royal household."

The justiciar looked away, trying to hide his disgust. Every noble he'd known used beeswax candles as a courtesy to his guests, regardless of the circumstances. After composing himself, Osmund turned his eyes back to the queen and said, "Whilst this austerity is admirable, Your Highness, I fear it will not resolve our fiscal dilemma."

"We've done more than lower the cost of candles, Sir Arnold," The chancellor of the exchequer answered. "We've reduced the palace staff, lowered the stipend for ministers, and done away with feasts and balls."

The justiciar stared hard at the little man. "Mister Bland, you assured us that giving peasants land without imposing property taxes was sensible. A year later, the royal treasury has been depleted by half. If this continues, the monarchy will be bankrupt," he said, pursing his lips. "Using inferior candles until doomsday and all the rest of your paltry measures will not correct the extent of your blunder."

"We're not seeking a scapegoat, Sir Arnold," the king said. "Let's turn our minds to solving the problem of our debt."

"The solution is clear, Your Highness," the justiciar said with a shrug. "The peasants must be taxed."

"That would betray the king's mission of justice for common folk," said the queen.

The justiciar lowered his chin in deference. "Your Highness, no one here wants to thwart the king's good works. All the same, given our current path, we risk making things worse," he said soothingly. "For example, the unpaid certificates of warranty issued by the crown have caused many merchants and tradesmen to close their shops. Shortages of goods are being reported across the realm. These shortages create hardships for the poor and the gentry alike."

Bland leaned toward the king, placing his palms on the table. "Your Highness, instead of taxing the peasants, I propose we raise the taxes of the lords for the land they have left."

Osmund rolled his eyes and sighed.

Noticing the justiciar's reaction, the king said, "You disagree, Sir Arnold?"

"Sire, if we press the lords for more silver, they'll take the same austerity measures as the royal household," Osmund said. "Cooks, maids, butlers, gardeners and grooms will find themselves out of work all over the kingdom. Without employment, the families of these workers will suffer."

"The idle men can join the king's army," one of the ministers said.

The justiciar glared at him. "Adding more soldiers is folly. Our barracks are already full – and the pieces of paper we use to pay the troops are bankrupting our merchants. Our only recourse is to tax the new landowners."

Bland shook his head. "If we tax the peasants, they'll feel betrayed and cheated. Many of them may turn against the king."

"Mister Bland," the justiciar said. "This is not a choice between good and bad. It's a choice between bad and worse." Osmund then faced the king. "Your Highness, this is a difficult decision, but the situation leaves no other recourse. We made a mistake that must be corrected. The monarchy cannot operate without revenue from nearly a third of its land. These taxes must be collected."

The king stood, meeting the eyes of all in the room. "I erred in the cause of justice," he said soberly. "Following the harvest season this year, taxes on all land in the realm will be paid to the crown – without exception."

Ides of September 1194

A shaft of afternoon light fell on the dais from the large arched window at the rear of Westminster Hall.

Seated on the throne, King Robert squirmed.

He was growing accustomed to receiving petitioners. But he had not grown fond of the ritual. Being eyed by hundreds of courtiers, clergymen and gentry as he dispensed his decisions was more daunting than facing enemies in battle.

The contrivance of wearing a crown and ermine robe stiffened his speech and gestures, making him feel pompous. Worse still, was the flowery fawning by his petitioners.

For the last three hours, a procession of nobles had streamed before him, begging indulgences that were inevitably self-serving… requests for knighthoods… disputes over boundaries… decisions on inheritances…

The pettiness of these claims belied the grave threat before his monarchy.

Nearly six months had passed since he'd ordered the new peasant landholders to pay taxes on their farms. With the fall harvest upon them, those taxes would soon be due.

The need for that silver was dire. Without it, the exchequer would be bankrupted – and he would almost certainly be deposed.

Turning left, he glanced at Marian. The queen sat upright, showing no signs of the threat they faced. To his right, the justiciar was equally circumspect. They both knew the risks of making their financial strains public.

Facing the petitioners again, Robert saw the Archbishop of Canterbury approaching the dais in the line of supplicants. Beside Tuck was a woman in a plain, undyed wool dress.

After bowing to his sovereign, the archbishop said, "Your Highness, I bring before you a petition from one of your subjects unaccustomed to the ways of the court. She sought me out with her plea, and I bring her before you now. Her name is Emma Bentley from the village of Wickford." Tuck then faced the woman and said, "Please tell your king what you told me."

"Your Highness," Emma said, "My children may not live through the winter. Our harvest was poor this year on account of the drought. If my husband has to sell a third of our crop to pay the crown's taxes, we won't have enough food to last the five of us until spring. Please, Sire. Don't let my children starve. Have mercy on us."

Robert exhaled slowly, trying to control his anger. Turning to Sir Arnold he said, "Justiciar, did the archbishop register this petition with you?"

"He did not, Your Highness," Osmond answered.

Robert shifted his gaze back to Tuck. "Archbishop, this petition is highly irregular and was presented outside of the protocols of our court. For that reason, I will not render a decision. You're dismissed."

His face crimson, the archbishop bowed, took Emma's hand, and began backing away.

"Wait!" the queen called out. "Surely we can make an exception to the rules of court for this woman, Sire," Marian said to the king. "Her family's needs are dire."

Robert gripped the arms of the throne and faced his wife. "I will remind the queen that chaos will rule if we do not abide by the protocols of the court. There can be no exceptions." He then waved his hand toward Tuck. "You may leave, archbishop," he said coldly.

* * *

Seated by the bedchamber's fireplace, Robert stared into the flames and downed another draught of wine.

When Marian entered the room, his gaze never strayed from the burning logs.

Walking to the bed, Marian turned back the covers and began to undress.

A strained silence grew between them.

After slipping on her nightgown, Marian finally spoke. "You scarcely said a word during supper."

"I had nothing to say," Robert answered, still staring into the fire.

"I won't accept that," Marian said tersely. "If you're still angry, tell me why."

Robert exhaled slowly, then stood and faced her. "How could I not be angry when you openly defy me at court? I'm the king. Your disrespect demeans my authority."

"The archbishop risked your wrath to bring Emma Bentley before you," Marian said, eyes flashing. "He showed the courage to stand up for the poor."

Robert scoffed. "Tuck's motives aren't all lofty. He fears losing the poor's tithes to the church if they're forced to pay taxes to the crown."

"What's happened to you?" she asked, striding across the room toward him, nightgown clinging to her bare legs. "That woman and her family may starve this winter. But you hid behind the rules of the court and turned her away."

"I don't need you to tell me that," Robert said, his face flushing. "I know they may die. But how can I make an exception for just one family?"

Stepping close to him, Marian stared hard into his eyes and said, "Then we should help other families as well."

"How many, Marian?" he growled, voice rising. "Five? Ten? A dozen? A thousand?"

"As many as we can," she said defiantly.

Robert hurled his cup across the room. "We cannot save them all, Marian!" he shouted. "We'll bankrupt the monarchy! We'll be deposed and beheaded! Is that what you want?"

Marian was close now, her breath hot upon his face. "I can't believe what I'm hearing!" she yelled, her nightgown opening, exposing her breasts and netherhair. "Have you become so obsessed with power that you'll let innocent people die to stay on the throne?"

Pulse throbbing and short of breath, Robert found his gaze drawn to her bare skin and was suddenly aroused.

Panting, Marian stared back at him, her lips parted.

Robert drew Marian to him and kissed her.

To his surprise, Marian returned the kiss and pressed against him, her hands caressing his loins.

Lifting her into his arms, Robert carried Marian to the bed, surprised by the intensity of his ardour as he lowered her onto the mattress. Lifting her nightgown, Marian wrapped her legs around him, receiving him eagerly.

For a long time, they made love with fiery abandon.

The next morning, they both awoke from a sleep more sound than either had known in weeks.

With the glow of sunlight seeping between the bedchamber curtains, Robert stroked Marian's hair. "You're my conscience," he said softly. "I'm grateful for that, my love."

"You mean well, Robin. I know that," she whispered, resting her cheek on his chest. "But I feel helpless seeing people suffer."

"Giving that land to the peasants was a mistake, no matter how well intentioned. But if we want what's best for the realm's poor, I must remain their king. Another monarch will not be their champion. Those taxes must be paid if I'm to stay on the throne, my love."

Marian sighed and began to weep. "I dread how much I've become like my father."

Christmastide 1194

With a slashing backhand of his oaken staff, the Scotsman struck his opponent's temple. The man collapsed in a heap, his helmet dented by the blow.

A roar rose from the hundreds of troops gathered to watch the quarterstaff contests in the barracks mess hall at Westminster Palace.

"The Scotsman is unbeaten, Your Highness," a soldier next to Robert said with a grin, then extended his palm. "I'm afraid you owe me again, Sire."

From the purse in his tunic, Robert counted out two coins and dropped them into the soldier's hand. He smiled and said, "Best me again, sergeant, and you'll see nothing but latrine duty."

"Is there any other man here who challenges me?" the Scotsman called out defiantly, removing his helmet, revealing a wild mane of red hair.

"I will," Robert answered loudly.

An uncomfortable silence fell over the troops as they recognized the challenger.

The Scotsman stared in shock as Robert walked toward him through the crowd of soldiers. "Your Highness," the redhead said, bowing. "I cannot strike my sovereign."

"You will," Robert said firmly. "And if you hold back, I'll have you flogged," he said, taking a helmet and quarterstaff from one of the previous challengers.

The Scotsman saluted, donned his helmet, and gripped his staff for battle.

Entering the circle of soldiers, Robert nodded to his opponent, then took up his own stance. The troops responded with a chorus of cheers.

Robert had watched the Scotsman for several bouts. The redhead had a flaw in his attacks – a weakness Robert was surprised the Scotsman's challengers had failed to notice.

Circling to his right, Robert studied the Scotsman's movements. The redhead was a counter striker who relied on superior quickness to turn the tables on an attacker. But his repertoire of parries was predictable.

Shifting his grip to one end of the staff, Robert levelled the rod and thrust directly toward the Scotsman's head. As Robert expected, the redhead blocked his thrust with a cross parry, then jabbed quickly with a thrust of his own to Robert's head.

Ducking in anticipation, Robert lowered his staff, stepped forward and shoved the tip of the rod toward the man's head.

"My eye!" the Scotsman screamed in pain as he covered his face and staggered to the ground. Watching the blood ooze between the man's fingers, Robert's surge of triumph changed to remorse.

"Make sure this man still gets the winner's prize," the king said to one of his officers before walking away.

Behind him, the troops were silent.

Robert left the mess hall fists clenched in anger. These weekly games had become a welcome distraction from the bleak news of the realm.

His land decrees were failing. The harvest had been poor and the winter already harsh. By spring, many would be dead.

Immersed in the mess hall competitions, for a time, he could forget his failures. Now, his vanity had destroyed the respite the games had given him. He'd failed at that as well.

In a cloister ahead, the king saw Arthur Bland.

"Your Highness, the queen asks to see you in the royal parlour," Arthur said as he bowed. "The queen has some Christmastide gifts for you."

"I haven't seen Marian since breakfast. Where has she been?"

"Giving food to the hungry, Sire."

"Every day, the number of hungry people grows across the kingdom, Mister Bland," Robert said bitterly. "The royal coffers cannot match the queen's feelings of guilt."

"She looks for families with babes, Sire."

Chastened, Robert said, "Thank you for delivering her message, Mister Bland."

Entering the royal parlour Robert found Marian knitting by the fireplace whilst Anna toddled on the floor nearby. "I'm told you have some Christmastide gifts for me," he said, his voice dry.

Marian rose from her chair. "Look, my love," she said, pointing toward the fireplace. "Arthur told me it's a tradition of the Midlands."

Waiting to be placed into the fire was a Yule Log.

Staring at the square-sided block of oak, Robert's eyes welled. Memories of his childhood washed over him, a remembrance that brought joy and longing in equal measure. At the core of these recollections was his mother. She would have doted on her namesake now playing near the log.

He would tell Anna of her grandmother one day, make her understand the legacy of honour she'd inherited. But for now, he was content with the treasure of Anna's innocence.

"I can't think of a better gift, my love," he said, taking Marian in his arms. "Thank you."

"I have another gift for you," she said, then took his hand and placed it on her belly. "You're going to be a father again."

Nones of May 1195

Traveling on foot along the woodland trail, the Sheriff of Nottingham heard a noise behind him and stopped, scanning the starlit landscape. One of the king's spies perhaps? Seeing nothing, he decided to move on. His nerves were frayed – and with good reason.

The dolt on the throne had driven the kingdom to chaos and ruined another of his ventures in the bargain.

The peasants had been delirious two years before when Webber had annexed lands from the lords in every shire and given it to the lazy louts without collecting any taxes. Then, with the royal coffers nearly empty, the king had revised his decree. The new peasant landowners would be taxed during the following harvest.

Most of the former serfs were unprepared for the shortfall, having squandered their profits from the year before.

Murdac had been gleeful at first. He'd relished the shock on the faces of the bumpkins as his soldiers hauled away a third of the harvest from those who could not pay in coin. Better still, the sheriff had gained a new source of wealth.

Although the peasants were too poor to bribe him, Murdac was able to confiscate several farmsteads for unpaid taxes. But his gains had come with a price.

Many peasants died of hunger over the winter. Not long after that, the unrest began – along with the sheriff's regrets.

In early spring, an angry mob gathered outside Talbot Hall, demanding an end to the taxes. The peasants hurled dung on the manor walls and desecrated tombs in the Talbot family chapel whilst calling for Murdac's head. Fearing for his life, the sheriff ordered his troops to disperse the peasants. Over a dozen were killed before the horde retreated.

To the sheriff's dismay, the retribution brought more turmoil.

By summer, Murdac's troops patrolling the countryside were being ambushed. Traveling merchants were waylaid by brigands. Sherwood Forest was once again a haven for bandits.

The town of Nottingham had fared no better. Shops and homes were being robbed. Bands of boys roamed the streets, extorting bribes from the weak.

Although it gave Murdac little consolation, Nottingham's troubles were not unique. Few towns across the realm had been spared the same upheavals.

Leaving the forest trail, Murdac walked into the clearing where his whorehouse stood. The farmstead he'd confiscated from spinster Faye Rolfe was ideal for his purposes. The house had a small parlour where customers could wait. Adjoining the parlour were two bedchambers where Eva and Maggie could ply their craft in private.

Seizing the property had been easy. He'd ordered his soldiers to scare away the hired hands who worked the harelip's inherited land. Without their labour, the spinster was unable to bring in a crop and pay the land tax, allowing Murdac to confiscate a property he'd coveted for some time.

But his satisfaction was short lived. Not long after acquiring Faye Rolfe's farmstead, Eva and Maggie's business had plummeted.

Entering the house, the sheriff found the main room empty. "Eva! Maggie!" he called out. "Get your worthless hides out here. The rent is due!"

Maggie Ames emerged from the doorway of a dark inner room. Her face was dirty. The crude woollen dress she wore was stained and torn.

"Eva is gone, m'lord" she said, staring at the dirt floor.

Murdac scowled. "Where did she go?"

"I don't know. She took all her things with her yesterday.

"Did Eva leave the rent she owes me?"

"There isn't no more silver, m'lord. All the men stopped coming. We haven't seen one here for days. That's why Eva left."

"Damn that ungrateful whore!" he screamed, kicking over a bench near the fireplace. He then stepped toward Maggie, eyes blazing.

Trembling, the woman dropped to her knees and folded her hands. "Please, Sheriff. Don't thrash me again. I stayed."

Murdac exhaled slowly. There was nothing to gain from beating her. She was his last whore. Being bruised and bloodied might cost him a customer – should one somehow appear. "Get up," the sheriff said. "From now on, you'll give me all you earn, understand? I'll have spies watching to make sure you don't cheat me," he lied.

"Yes, m'lord," the woman said, cowering in fear as he left.

Taking the narrow forest trail back to Talbot Hall, Murdac tried to cheer himself. Perhaps Webber would come to his senses and return the land to the lords. That would be best for everyone. Giving property to these ignorant brutes had been madness from the start.

The rustle of leaves from the undergrowth broke his thoughts.

Turning his gaze, Murdac saw Faye Rolfe step into the trail.

In an icy voice, she said, "I've been waiting for you, Sheriff."

The dagger that flashed in her hand would be Rudolf Murdac's last sight on earth.

Kalends of June 1195

Stepping into the last pew of the empty chapel, Robert kneeled and made the sign of the cross. During his years as a soldier, he'd never prayed for his life before a battle. Trusting the luck of his amulet had seemed more fitting. But today, Robert was asking God to protect a life.

Marian was in labour with their second child.

Would God listen? Not if he was judged as a king. That bitter realization came with the latest reports from sheriffs across the kingdom. Angry peasants were lashing out at any symbol of his authority – even in Nottingham where Rudolf Murdac had been killed.

Hearing footsteps behind him, Robert stood as he saw the Archbishop of Canterbury waddling toward him.

Putting a hand on Robert's shoulder, Tuck said, "The midwife has asked to see you."

"Do I have a son or a daughter?" Robert asked anxiously.

"The midwife said I should fetch you, nothing more, Sire."

* * *

At the birthing chamber, Tuck watched Robert approach the midwife who was waiting by the door. "She was very brave, Your Highness," the midwife said to the king, wringing her hands. "We did everything we could, Sire," she said, then lowered her eyes. "The child was lost as well."

Robert walked past the midwife and entered the darkened chamber. Following the king inside, Tuck squinted into the gloom. The windows were shuttered. A familiar smell sent a chill through him. Blood.

"Open the shutters," the king commanded.

In the sudden rush of light, Tuck saw Marian's lifeless body on the bed, surrounded by her ladies in waiting. Walking closer, he gasped as he caught sight of the baby in her arms. The child's face was ashen and blotched, eyes closed, tiny mouth agape and breathless. Stillborn.

Tears began to well in Robert's eyes. "Please leave us, ladies," he said, a catch in his voice.

With the women gone, the king kneeled by the bed. "I'm here, my love. I'm here," he whispered, cradling Marian in his arms, pressing his face against hers. Turning his gaze toward the baby, Robert stroked its forehead.

He then bowed his head and wept, chest wracked with sobs.

After a time, his tears spent, Robert stood and faced the priest. "This is a sign from God, Tuck. He's punishing me for my arrogance. I'm not fit to be king."

Tuck placed a hand on Robert's shoulder. "That's your grief speaking, my son. No one knows God's will – or his judgment."

"I don't know what I'll do without her," Robert said, staring at the floor. "Marian helped me rule. I had good intentions, father. But all I did was bring misery to our people. My days as a king are over. Let the Curtmantles have this burden."

"You lost a wife and a son today. That's a blow that would level any man," Tuck said gently. Then his voice turned firm. "But you still have a daughter, Robert. You need to protect her. And for that, you need to remain on the throne."

"I can protect Anna without being king."

"You're wrong, Robert. Whoever follows you as king will forever see Anna as a threat to his rule. She'll be in danger for the rest of her life – and you'll no longer have the power of a king to keep her from harm," Tuck said. "You chose to be king. But Anna didn't ask to be a princess. You cannot shirk your duty as a father," he said. "Now pray with me for the souls of your wife and son – then walk out of that door as the ruler of the realm."

Nones of June 1195

The sunshine felt like a taunt from God as Robert stepped outside the palace chapel.

For the last hour, he'd stood numb as the bodies of his wife and son were placed in their tombs after a long spectacle of pomp and prayer. The Archbishop of Canterbury's final homily had given him little solace. Tuck's words in praise of God's wisdom were like the incense his acolytes had spread in the chapel – clouds of smoke to mask the stench of death.

But Tuck's counsel at Marian's bedside still rang true. For Anna's sake, he needed to put aside his grief. There were hard deeds to be done if he was to remain a king.

After leaving the chapel, Robert walked across the cobblestone plaza to the palace. Arriving at his chancery, he found Will Scarlett already there.

The chief constable rose from his chair as Robert entered the chamber. "My deepest condolences for your loss, Your Highness," he said soberly, placing a palm on his chest.

"Thank you, Will," Robert answered evenly. "Please sit down. We have much to discuss," he said. "I want the uprisings and turmoil across the realm brought to an end."

"Shouldn't you consult with the justiciar on this matter as well, Sire?"

"No. Your uncle does not have the stomach for what needs to be done, Will. You'll leave for Nottingham tomorrow."

Ides of May 1215

From a vast blackness, a hazy light began to form... undulating... quivering...

Then came a sound, a repeating rhythm... thump-thump-thump... thump-thump-thump...

A voice, faint and far away, gradually brought him back from oblivion.

"Your Highness..."

The voice was familiar and comforting.

"Your Highness..."

As he recognized the voice of Arthur Bland, reality fell into place.

The peasant revolt had reached his chancery and nearly succeeded.

Robert lifted his head from the table, his eyes regaining their focus on the candle before him. He had fainted.

Looking down, he saw the cause. A large pool of blood was spreading on the floor beneath the table from the spear wound on his thigh. There was not much time left, Robert realized. He'd never known a man to lose that much blood and live.

His reaction surprised him. The thought of death held no fear. Perhaps this was God's justice – that he'd been killed by the peasants he'd once vowed to protect.

The knocking on the door returned. "Your Highness. May I come in?" Arthur said again.

"Enter," Robert called out, wiping the blood from his hands on the lap of his night shirt.

The Chancellor of the Exchequer hobbled into the room on a cane. "I heard about the attack, Sire," Arthur Bland said, a long robe draped over his bony frame.

As if seeing him afresh, Robert studied his former valet. Time had not been kind to him. In the twenty-three years since Robert had made him a minister, Arthur had grown stooped and crippled.

He thought of telling Arthur about the wound to his leg but dismissed it. There was no point in alarming him. What could the old man do but worry?

"Everything is fine, Mister Bland," Robert assured him.

"You've been wounded, Sire," Arthur said, pointing to the bandage on his forehead.

"It's nothing serious," Robert said. "Go back to sleep."

"I was already awake, Sire. These old bones of mine complain when

I move. But they grumble even more when I lie still in bed," Bland said with a weary smile. "I'll fetch us something to drink. Would you care for wine or ale?"

"Neither," Robert said, shaking his head. "If you must stay, Mister Bland, then please make yourself comfortable," he said, gesturing to one of the chairs before his worktable. He did not want Arthur to see the blood pooling at his feet.

Once Bland was seated, Robert closed his eyes, returning to his reverie of the past. After a moment, he opened his eyes and said, "Do you remember Anna's baptism?"

"I remember it well, Sire. That was a grand day," Bland said, then added, "It's hard to believe the years have passed so quickly."

"That may have been my last happy day as king," Robert said, gazing into a distance far beyond the walls of the chancery. "I thought all the ugly deeds I'd done to rule were behind me."

"You've done nothing beyond those things necessary for a king, Sire."

"I wish I could believe you," Robert said softly. "The people of Nottingham would not agree."

"The atrocities in Nottingham after the death of the queen were Will Scarlett's doing, not yours, Sire. Everyone knows that."

Robert cradled his head in his hands, shielding his eyes. That widely held myth had haunted him every day since he'd conceived it. The time had come to speak the truth.

"No, old friend. When Will died of side sickness not long thereafter, he took a secret with him to the grave... I sent him to Nottingham. The executions and massacres were carried out on my orders."

Arthur leaned forward in his chair, eyes widening. "Why, Sire?"

"I told Will to make an example of Nottingham," Robert said, staring at the tabletop. "I wanted to put fear into the serfs rebelling in other parts of the realm – and any nobles who tried to exploit the unrest. If the uprisings in the king's own shire were ruthlessly put down, the rebels in the rest of the kingdom could expect much worse," he said in a cold voice.

"Perhaps you spared more lives than you took, Sire. The other uprisings ended soon after the carnage in Nottingham. Defeating them all would have caused much more bloodshed."

"You have a generous soul, Mister Bland," Robert said. "But my purpose was not farsighted or noble. I chose Nottingham because crushing the revolt there would be easier. Will knew the people and the land. Finding the ringleaders didn't take long."

Left unsaid was something Robert had learned from Will. Two of the agitators had been women he knew: Faye Rolfe and Sarah Payne. Along with five other rebel leaders, they were hanged in the town square.

"But the ringleaders could not have been more than a handful, Sire. Why did Will kill so many others?"

His eyes turning dull, Robert said, "There were over a hundred people with us at Angel Creek. Almost every one of them knew I was Robin Hood. That secret could not escape."

Bland covered his mouth. "My God," he whispered.

"You never had children, have you, Mister Bland?"

Arthur looked puzzled. "No, Sire. My life has been devoted to my work."

"If you'd been a father, you might understand," Robert said. "Yes, I ordered the deaths of people who trusted me and warriors who fought at my side," the king said, then sighed. "I regretted their suffering every single day. But I believed those monstrous deeds were necessary to protect my child from a new monarch who would see her as a rival."

The two men sat in silence for a time. Then Arthur finally spoke. "In any case, that was long ago, Sire. No one will ever know. They'll say your rule prevented a French invasion and kept order in the kingdom. That will be your legacy."

"I find no solace in that, Mister Bland," Robert said bitterly. "On her deathbed, my mother made me swear to become a just king… I failed her. That's my true legacy."

"You may have failed in that cause, Sire. But Anna might succeed."

Robert was stunned for a moment. Then a slight smile warmed his face. "Help me bandage this leg, Mister Bland," he said, waving him closer. He now had a reason to stay alive.

* * *

When Princess Anna entered the room, King Robert was propped up in bed, barely conscious and surrounded by physicians, ministers and clergymen.

She had never seen her father like this. His face was ashen and seemed to have aged a decade since she'd left to visit her aunt in Devonshire.

"The infection in his wound is making him delirious, Your Highness," one of the doctors whispered as she approached the bed. "We've bled him several times. But the evil humours refuse to leave his body."

Ignoring the physician, Anna walked toward the bed. Seeing her approach, the king extended his hand and tried to sit up.

"You're going to be well again, Father," Anna said, taking his hand. "Lay back and rest now."

"There's something I must tell you, Anna," the king said, grimacing as he leaned toward her.

"Whatever it is can wait. You need to recover your strength."

"No," he said, shaking his head. "There may not be another chance."

Anna stroked his forehead and leaned close to him. "I'll listen," she said gently. "But then you'll rest quietly. Agreed?"

The king nodded, then said, "You'll soon follow me as monarch, Anna. Be the ruler I should have been."

"You're not going to die, Father. Please stop talking like this."

"No, my child. I became too blinded by pride. I realize that now," he said, then laboriously removed his amulet and pressed it into her hands. "You know the story behind this pendant."

"Yes, Father. You've told me many times," Anna said patiently.

"It's yours now, Anna. Keep the vow I made to your grandmother. Promise me you'll make this a fair and just land for all the people in our realm."

"Yes, Father. I promise," Anna said soothingly, placing the amulet around her neck. "Now rest. Please."

The king lay back and closed his eyes.

Not long thereafter, Robert Webber drew a last, ragged breath.

All those in the room rose to their feet, then solemnly kneeled before Queen Anna of England.

* * *

The queen's initial act in a reign that lasted thirty-four years was to convene the realm's first annual parliament, ending the absolute rule of England's monarchs.

Anna's decree placed the kingdom on an arduous path. Many lifetimes later, the island nation would come to be governed by the consent of its people.

ABOUT THE AUTHOR

R. A. Moss earned his keep as a writer long before penning *King Robin*, a journey into a new genre. Under his birth name, Moss has authored four previous novels in other genres that earned accolades from Library Journal, Publishers Weekly, and USA Today. As a commercial writer who has garnered over 200 national and international creative awards, Moss' clients have included Bell & Howell, Penton Publishing, McGraw Hill, NCR, Sun Microsystems, Lexis-Nexis, Teradata, Standard Register, and Cintas.

Learn more at the King Robin website:
www.king-robin-novel.com

9 780099 445709